PRAISE FOR
SUE MARGOLIS'S NOVELS

A CATERED AFFAIR

"Wickedly funny. . . . I laughed until I hurt while reading *A Catered Affair*. It's a delightful romp with a theme lots of women can empathize with, but it's got a lovely message too."
—Pop Corn Reads

"A guilty pleasure . . . bawdy and fun."
—The Romance Reader

"British chick lit at its finest. Sharp-witted humor with warm, breathing characters . . . [a] unique love story."
—*RT Book Reviews*

PERFECT BLEND

"Frothy, perky . . . titillating fun."
—*Publishers Weekly*

"A fun story full of an eccentric cast of characters. . . . Amy is an endearing heroine."
—*News and Sentinel* (Parkersburg, WV)

"Laugh-out-loud funny, passionate, sexy, mysterious, and truly unexpected, Sue Margolis has created the *Perfect Blend* of characters, romance, and mystery. Read it!"
—Romance Junkies

"A fun, sassy read. . . . The romance blooms and the sex sizzles. This is a hilarious and engaging tale. Sue Margolis has whipped up a winner."
—Romance Reviews Today

FORGET ME KNOT

"A perfect beach read, with a warm heroine."
—*News and Sentinel* (Parkersburg, WV)

"A wonderful glimpse into British life with humor and a unique sense of style. . . . If you're looking for a lighthearted romance with original characters and lots of fun, look no further. . . . This is one British author that I'm glad made it across the pond, and I will definitely be looking for more of her books."
—Night Owl Romance

continued . . .

"Quick in pace and often very funny."   —*Kirkus Reviews*

"Margolis combines lighthearted suspense with sharp English wit . . . [an] entertaining read."   —*Booklist*

"A joyously funny British comedy . . . just the ticket for those of us who like the rambunctious, witty humor this comedy provides."
                              —Romance Reviews Today

"[An] irreverent, sharp-witted look at love and dating."   —*Houston Chronicle*

SPIN CYCLE

"This delightful novel is filled with more than a few big laughs."   —*Booklist*

"A funny, sexy British romp. . . . Margolis is able to keep the witty one-liners spraying like bullets."   —*Library Journal*

"Warmhearted relationship farce . . . a nourishing delight." —*Publishers Weekly*

"Satisfying . . . a wonderful diversion on an airplane, poolside, or beach."
                              —Baton Rouge Magazine

NEUROTICA

"[A] screamingly funny sex comedy . . . the perfect novel to take on holiday."
                              —*USA Today*

"Cheeky comic novel—a kind of *Bridget Jones's Diary* for the matrimonial set . . . wickedly funny."   —*People* (Beach Book of the Week)

"Scenes that literally will make your chin drop with shock before you erupt with laughter . . . a fast and furiously funny read."   —*The Cleveland Plain Dealer*

"Splashy romp . . . giggles guaranteed."   —*New York Daily News*

"A good book to take to the beach, *Neurotica* is fast-paced and at times hilarious."   —*Boston's Weekly Digest Magazine*

Coming Clean

Sue Margolis

NEW AMERICAN LIBRARY

New American Library
Published by the Penguin Group
Penguin Group (USA) Inc., 375 Hudson Street,
New York, New York 10014, USA

USA l Canada l UK l Ireland l Australia l New Zealand l India l South Africa l China

Penguin Books Ltd., Registered Offices: 80 Strand, London WC2R 0RL, England
For more information about the Penguin Group visit penguin.com.

First published by New American Library,
a division of Penguin Group (USA) Inc.

First Printing, September 2013

 REGISTERED TRADEMARK—MARCA REGISTRADA

LIBRARY OF CONGRESS CATALOGING-IN-PUBLICATION DATA:
Margolis, Sue.
Coming clean/Sue Margolis.
pages cm
ISBN 978-0-451-23699-9
1. Married people—Fiction. 2. Marital conflict—Fiction. I. Title.
PR6063.A635C66 2013
823'.914—dc23   2012038750

Printed in the United States of America
10 9 8 7 6 5 4 3 2 1

Set in Spectrum MT STD
Designed by Alissa Amell

PUBLISHER'S NOTE

This is a work of fiction. Names, characters, places, and incidents either are the product of the author's imagination or are used fictitiously, and any resemblance to actual persons, living or dead, business establishments,
events, or locales is entirely coincidental.

The publisher does not have any control over and does not assume any responsibility for author or third-
party Web sites or their content.

Coming Clean

"**S**o," Greg says, getting even more irritable as he tries and fails to front into the parking space. "You're determined to tell this therapist woman about the tank and make me look like a complete nob." Our fender makes contact with the one in front. "Shit."

"It's all right," I say. "You only tapped it." But I can't resist the scolding add-on, "I told you the space was tight. You should have reversed in."

"Thank you. I don't need your advice." Realizing he needs to back up a couple of feet before he can pull out, he rams the gearshift into reverse. Only it isn't reverse. He revs the engine. The car doesn't move. I point out that he's in neutral.

"Yes, I know I'm in effing neutral."

Two gear changes later, he edges out of the parking space and draws parallel to the car whose fender we just bumped.

"Do you get a kick out of trying to belittle me?" he says, twisting around and looking over his shoulder as he prepares to reverse the car back into the space.

"What, you're so insecure these days that I can't even point out you're in neutral instead of reverse?"

"I don't mean that."

I realize that we're back to the subject of the tank and my decision to "rat on him" to our therapist. Her name is Virginia Pruitt. Apparently she offers sex therapy as well as couples' counseling, which is good because neither of us is entirely sure which service we require—probably both. I found her through my best friend, Annie, who has a friend who knows a couple who saw her last year and said she's brilliant. We're about to have our first session—if we ever get parked.

"Greg, I am not trying to belittle you. The way I see it, you buying the tank was totally out of order and there's no doubt that it's put even more strain on our relationship. Surely that makes it a legitimate subject to bring up with our therapist. Before the tank our sex life was pretty dismal; now it's nonexistent. I can barely remember the last time we did it."

"That's right—blame it all on the tank. Like you always do. Can't you accept that you're at least partly to blame for our sexual decline?"

He's not wrong. Of course I have a role in all this—that's one of the reasons we're here, to examine my contribution—but right now we're discussing him and sodding Tanky and I'm determined to stay on topic.

"Greg, most men make do with a den or a garden shed."

"I'm too young for a shed. A tank's cool."

Meet my husband, the forty-year-old adolescent.

I should point out that the tank isn't the sort you fill with guppies and rainbow fish. Greg didn't go out and buy an aquarium. (I wish. The kids would have loved it.) No, we are talking military vehicle here: thirty tons of Second World War military vehicle. Three months ago—having promised he was going to Tanks for the Memory merely to window-shop—Greg became the proud owner of a genuine Sherman tank. He tried to sell it to me on the grounds that he'd got it cheap (being a rusty, clapped-out fixer-upper, it had "only cost three grand"). "Plus," he said, "the Sherman possesses the first ever seventy-five-millimeter gun, mounted on a fully traversing turret."

Even though Tanky—my mocking, less than affectionate pet name for the killing machine—does up to thirty miles per hour (or will do when Greg has got it going), he was forced to agree with me that it didn't make the ideal inner-city runabout, so presently he has it "stabled" on his mate Pete's five-hundred-acre farm in Sussex. The kids and I have met Tanky once, when the whole family called in at Pete's one day on the way to Brighton. Ben immediately started clambering over it, making loud machine gun noises. He asked if it had killed real Nazis. (The child is eight and he knows what Nazis are. I still haven't forgiven my dad for letting him watch *The Great Escape*.) His sister, Amy, who is two years older and more of a Hello Kitty tote bag with rhinestones kinda gal, took one look at the rust heap in front of her and curled her lip. After which she put her iPod buds back in her ears and carried on listening to her Miley-Justin Radio Disney music. I prefer to call it muse-ache.

I think I might have said something noncommittal re the tank, like: "Oh my God, Greg. I cannot believe you spent three grand on this pile of crap."

"**B**ut why is it out of order?" Greg is saying now. "I still can't see what's meant to be so wrong with buying a tank. I could understand if I was into war games or I'd become a survivalist with a mullet and a bunker full of AK-47s and I'd started indoctrinating the kids about the New World Order. But I'm a pacifist who just happens to think it's a bit of a lark to ride around the countryside in a tank. And it's not like we couldn't afford it."

Despite my original outburst about the cost of the tank, lately I've come to see his point. Last year, just before Christmas, Greg's gran died. She left him twenty thousand pounds in her will. Once it's restored, the tank will end up costing around four and a half grand, maybe five. Not cheap, but I guess everybody deserves to indulge themselves occasionally. "Plus," he said, "it will be something to remember my gran by." I told him that I could think of no better memorial to this sweet, gray-haired old lady who always smelled of Estée Lauder Youth-Dew.

Greg insisted I had a few treats, too, so I splashed out on a couple of new outfits and a posh handbag. The rest of his inheritance was put into a savings account, which we'd opened a few years ago to help with the kids' secondary school fees.

Had our marriage been jogging along OK, I don't think I would have begrudged him his ridiculously over-the-top übergadget. I would have laughed and taken pride in my husband's eccentricity. "God," I'd have said to my girlfriends, "you'll never *guess* what Greg's been out and bought." I might even have found it sexy.

But because our marriage wasn't "jogging along," his buying the tank seemed—and still seems—like the ultimate selfish indulgence.

"I'll tell you what's wrong with you buying a tank," I say, stabbing the air with my index finger. "It lives fifty bloody miles away and you insist on visiting it practically every weekend. During the week you're working all hours. Now you spend all day Saturday tinkering with your Tanky. The kids really miss you. What's more, you're absenting yourself from our marriage and you know it."

"That's such bollocks."

"It isn't bollocks."

"And stop calling it Tanky. Why do you always have to take the piss?"

"Because I'm angry."

"You're always bloody angry."

Even though I'm still determined to raise the subject of the tank with Virginia Pruitt, I can see how under attack Greg feels and decide to offer a compromise. "Look," I say. "Instead of me mentioning it, why don't you bring it up. That way you get to put your side of the story first and you won't feel belittled."

My generosity is met with a grunt. "She's bound to side with you. Women always gang up against blokes over stuff like that."

Finally, Greg pulls down hard on the steering wheel and eases his foot off the brake. In one perfect maneuver, we're parked. I decide against saying "well done" as I'm not sure how he'll take it.

"Oh, and another thing," Greg says, once we're out of the car. "If this Virginia person gets onto the subject of sex and starts asking us to give our genitals 'safe, nonsexual names,' I'm out of there." Clunk of the electronic door locks.

He's never forgotten that cringe-making episode of *Sex and the City*, which he half watched with me one night while he was waiting for some soccer game to appear on Sky Sports, in which Charlotte and Trey go for sex therapy and the therapist suggests they each name their bits. Charlotte decides to call her vagina "Rebecca" and Trey starts referring to his penis as "Schooner."

"OK," I say, "I'm with you on that." I feel myself grinning. "But if you absolutely had to name your penis—I mean, purely hypothetically speaking—what would it be?"

Greg grimaces. "I really don't want to talk about this."

"No, come on . . . what would it be?" I don't know why I'm pushing him—trying to lighten the atmosphere, I suppose.

"I dunno."

"You must have some idea."

"OK . . . Doric, as in column."

"Ooh, very phallic, I'm sure."

"Well, you did ask."

He doesn't ask me what I would call my vagina, so I tell him that I'm considering Miss Moneypenny . . . because Bond-wise she never saw any below-the-waist action. I think it's pretty clever of me to come up with something so witty on the spot, but he barely responds beyond another grunt.

I can't believe that Greg and I are about to start couples' therapy. When we first got together, eleven years ago, we were crazy about each other. We laughed at the same things, shared the same worldview. We both insisted on extra olives and anchovies on our pizza. It was the perfect match. It wasn't long before we were mapping out our future together. If I'm honest, we were pretty smug and we probably annoyed the crap out of our friends with our plan to get pregnant as soon as we were married, take sabbaticals from our jobs and schlep our infants around India and Nepal.

Back then, I fancied Greg like mad. He was tall, good looking with thick chestnut hair that skimmed his shirt collar, but most of all he had a great sense of humor. I remember the night we met—at my friend Kat's birthday party. He got me a beer, and as we stood chatting he confessed that he suffered from serious paranoia. I was planning my exit route when he said, face deadpan: "Yeah, when soccer players go into a huddle before the game, I'm convinced they're talking about me."

I always said that Greg laughed me into bed. He did brilliant impressions—still does. You should hear his Dr. Zoidberg from *Futurama*. There was a time when he only had to say, "The president is gagging on my gas bladder. What an honor," and I was his. Occasionally he would try to excite me by playing *The Flintstones* theme tune on his head. He could also play "God Save the Queen" on his teeth.

Greg was always goofing around, but in a cool, sexy way that I found irresistible.

After our first date—the Comedy Store, followed by pizza—we walked to Leicester Square tube. Outside the station, a busker in full evening dress was playing *The Blue Danube* on his violin.

"May I have the pleasure of this dance?" Greg said, bowing before me. Before I could tell him to behave and that there was no way I was about to waltz with him down Charing Cross Road with dozens of people watching, he had pulled me into his arms and we were dancing. He wasn't half bad—far better than me. We twirled and laughed and people stood and clapped. It was like being in a forties musical. I fell in love that night.

Greg said he fell for me because I was the first woman who had ever laughed at his jokes, plus I had great tits and looked like a young Barbra Streisand. I asked if the Streisand remark was his way of telling me I needed a nose job. He said no, it was his way of telling me I looked like a Jewish matriarch. "So now you're saying I look like my dead bubbe, Yetta?" I seem to remember he got over his embarrassment by taking me in his arms and snogging me thoroughly.

We couldn't keep our hands off each other. We would meet at his place or mine and within seconds we'd be tearing off each other's clothes. We used to have these weekend-long shagathons—breaking off only to order curry or Chinese. Before falling asleep we would lie in bed watching comedy videos. I loved watching *Fawlty Towers* reruns. Greg was into people like Eddie Izzard, Chris Rock, and Jerry Seinfeld. When we went out, it was usually to a comedy club.

Twelve years, a couple of kids, two full-time jobs and a Second World War Sherman tank later, sex has become like Belgium: always there, but we never go.

"Nice house," Greg says, pushing open Virginia Pruitt's wooden garden gate and letting me through first. "Great restoration job. Must have cost a fortune." This is a most un-Greg comment, since he rarely notices people's homes, how they're done up or whether they're clean or chaotic inside. He rarely notices ours in particular. Or if he does notice, he doesn't care.

The only thing domestic about my husband is that he was born in this country. He leaves wet towels on the bathroom floor, ditto dirty socks and underwear. Then there are the milk cartons, pots of yogurt and jars of pickles and jam that he refuses to put back in the fridge after use. When he does put jars away, they are always minus their lids, but plus a spoon, fork or knife sticking out of the top.

Before we were married—i.e., when we still had our own flats and were living together only part-time—I found it hard to get worked up about his slobbish behavior. After all, I was in love and everything else about our relationship felt so right. That's not to say that I ran around picking up after him. I was no surrendered girlfriend. This relationship wasn't going to start with my sinking into his arms and end up with my arms in his sink.

My plan was to reform Greg and I was determined to succeed. I wasn't about to turn into my mother, who spent decades nagging, pleading and yelling at my father because he refused to help around the house, only to eventually give up.

I didn't feel daunted. That's because nearly all the women I knew were dating "projects" of one kind or another. Compared with my old university friend Beth, who was planning to marry a guy who wore fat white trainers and cropped pants, I thought I'd done rather well. Mum's experience had taught me that nagging wasn't the answer. I decided to teach Greg by example. I was always scrupulous about cleaning and tidying up after myself and hoped that he would follow suit. He didn't.

Six months after having Amy, I went back to work full-time. I did the same after Ben. To give Greg his due, if he got home before me, he would always start dinner. Much as I appreciated the gesture, I soon put a stop to it. The food wasn't bad, but he turned even the simplest meal into a production number and the chaos was too much. He would leave the kitchen floor awash with vegetable peelings, garlic skins and stray knobs of butter. Then there were the cupboard doors he'd leave open, on which I would inevitably bash my head. If that wasn't enough, the counters were always covered in umpteen used bowls, dishes and frying pans—not to mention saucepans—full of hard, dried-up food that he hadn't had the sense to put to soak. It felt like my husband had turned into some kind of utensil fetishist.

As a young Fleet Street journalist, Greg could spend weeks on the road working on a story. It wasn't unusual for him to fly home from one trip, shower and change, only to head straight back to the airport. In a few years, he rose from reporter to political editor.

Meanwhile I was made senior producer on *Coffee Break*, a daily radio show aimed at women. Going back to work after Amy and Ben were born wasn't easy, but we had a huge London mortgage and we needed my salary. Plus full-time motherhood wasn't for me. Much as I adored my children, I needed the stimulation my job provided. That's not to say I waltzed out of the house every morning without a thought for what I was doing. When I went back to work after having Amy, the guilt was overwhelming. What sort of mother abandons her precious six-month-old baby? Greg was quick to remind me that I wasn't abandoning her—any more than he was—and that we were leaving her in the care of a kind, loving, highly trained, highly vetted middle-aged nanny with children of her own who, by the way, was costing a fortune.

We were lucky. Amy adored Joyce and so did Ben. She held them, soothed them and sang to them and loved them as if they were her own. She ended up staying with us until both children started school. We all cried when she left—even Greg. The kids and I made her a going-away cake, which Amy and Ben covered in sprinkles and wobbly pink icing. Joyce still sends the kids birthday cards and a couple of times a year they go and stay with her at her bungalow on the coast. I've lost count of the times that Greg and I have lain in bed in a self-congratulatory mood, telling each other what excellent judges of character we are and how we got it spot-on with Joyce. That may be true, but I'm never quite sure how I feel when Amy and Ben tell me now that, when they were little, it felt like they had two mummies.

Working on a daily live show isn't without its stresses. I'm in at eight each morning; the junior producers arrive an hour earlier. The program goes out at eleven and lasts an hour. Afterwards there's always a postmortem in the editor's office. It's not until that's over that we start to come down from the adrenaline and caffeine.

Strictly speaking, the buck stops with the program editor, but in reality I'm responsible for program content, commissioning prerecorded features and making sure they run strictly to time. If a guest is going to be late for an interview because they're stuck in traffic or, worst of all, they've dropped out for some reason, it's down to me to rejig the program. This has been known to happen minutes before we're due on air.

As a political editor on a daily newspaper, Greg also has some hefty responsibilities. Not only is he expected to beat his rivals to the best political stories, it's up to him to ensure that the *Vanguard*'s political pages are filled with intelligent, thought-provoking analysis. He's also in the prediction game. His job involves sniffing the parliamentary wind, having a sense of how a Commons vote will go, knowing how the government is going to tackle an issue before even it knows. He knows that his job isn't guaranteed, that there is always some young, thrusting Oxbridge graduate, with a brain the size of a small continent and an even larger contacts book, ready to usurp him.

We didn't pay too much attention when frazzled and exhausted married friends who were trying to run careers, homes and babies told us how hard it was. We told ourselves we would be more organized, that parents who had babies who refused to sleep at night were clearly getting something wrong. Not only were we naive and romantic (remember it was Greg and I who wanted to schlep our babies around India and Nepal), we were also supremely arrogant.

When the strain got too much and our marriage started to suffer, we should have got professional help. Instead we spent years being permanently irritable with each other.

We still compete about who's had the worst day. My thirty seconds of dead air is nothing compared to the flak Greg has just taken from the justice minister because one of his reporters ever so slightly misquoted him. If I have two reporters off sick, he has four.

When I developed thrush, which the doctor said was probably stress induced, I knew that Greg couldn't compete. Gotcha. What was he going to say? That he had an entire flock of the things nesting inside his vagina? But compete he did. He managed to catch mumps from the kids. His balls swelled to the size of oranges, and for a week he had a fever of a hundred and two. Whereas I had been suffering from a mild yeast infection, he was close to death—although maybe he could force down some pre-termination eggs (lightly boiled), a slice of toast (whole wheat, buttered) and a cup of jasmine tea (the posh loose stuff, not the bags that came free with the Chinese takeout).

We both spent a lot of time ruminating about work issues, but I don't think I retreated into myself the way Greg did. To his credit, he usually managed to pull it out of the bag for the kids, but when we were alone in the evenings his mind was always on work. We would sit in the same room and I'd kid myself that we were "together," but we weren't. I would try to make conversation, but he would either ignore me or grunt. Then one evening he sent me an e-mail that was meant for a female colleague. There was nothing remotely flirty or sexual about it—and when I pointed out what he'd done, he didn't give off anything that suggested embarrassment or guilt—but the e-mail was witty and funny, and I realized that he was more intimate with his workmates than he was with me.

Greg's slobbish tendencies increased in direct correlation to his workload. To that end he would leave little "presents" lying about the house. Picture it. After my own hectic, adrenaline-filled day at work, the kids are finally in bed and I'm relaxing in the bathtub. I've added oils that promise to soothe the soul. I've lit a Jo Malone lime, basil and mandarin candle. Eyes closed, I reach out for the soap. But instead of happening upon the satiny, subtly scented handcrafted bar, my fingers discover a pile of Greg's toenail clippings, which have been left on the side of the bath. Other gifts—often left on my dressing table—could be anything from a sticky, booger-filled handkerchief to a couple of Q-tips covered in orange ear gunk.

His best and most frequent gift was, and still is, a blocked toilet. Having produced a turd of gargantuan proportions, he avails himself of half a toilet roll. The waste pipe can't cope and he comes running to me. "Soph, the toilet's blocked again." Note the lack of personal responsibility.

"So get the plunger and unblock it."

"But the smell of shit makes me gag."

"Yeah. Me, too."

Over time, the irritation I've always felt about his slovenliness turned to real resentment and I started yelling at him. Greg is much better than me at controlling his temper in front of the kids, so he rarely yells back. As far as the kids are concerned, it's Mummy who's the baddy.

It goes without saying that it wasn't long before our sex life was on the skids. Most nights we would turn our backs on each other. Or we would engage in a whispered (so as not to wake the kids) fight. Our fights were always identical. Greg would accuse me of being self-centered. "You're not remotely interested in any of my worries or struggles."

"Er, hello—since when did you acknowledge mine? On top of that, you think you have the right to treat me like some skivvy."

By the time Tanky rolled in, our sex life was already severely wounded. Tanky merely delivered the fatal shell.

The thing that hurts most about Greg's slovenliness is that he claims to be a feminist. Gender equality, free child care, a woman's right not to shave—he's into it all. I've often asked him how he reconciles this with behaving like an idle git at home. His defense is two-pronged. First he insists that he does his best and that any lapses are down to his being exhausted and preoccupied with work. Then he accuses me of being hung up and obsessed about untidiness and hygiene. According to Greg, my so-called neurosis is typically petit bourgeois and born out of the need of the middle classes to ape the grand, well-ordered homes of the aristocracy. Whenever he comes out with this, I tell him he's talking arrogant claptrap and make the point that his background was just as petit bourgeois as mine. He refutes this on the grounds that his mother was—and is still—prone to dropping her cigarette ash into the Bolognese sauce and keeps a grease-spattered notice on the kitchen wall asking people not to feed the dust bunnies.

Being tarred with the neurotic woman epithet really pisses me off. For a start—as I keep telling my husband the feminist—it's male chauvinist piggery at its worst. Second, it makes me sound like I've turned into some kind of mad, pacing Lady Macbeth constantly fretting about the spots she can't seem to get out of her granite countertops.

Let me be clear. I do not want to raise our kids in one of those perfectly coordinated, sterile homes you find in interiors magazines, where the mum is the type who uses vaginal deodorant, irons the family's underpants and adds talcum powder to the kitty litter to make it smell more fragrant. Nor do I want to be like my grandma Yetta, who was rarely to be seen without a sponge in her hand. "You have to use the toilet now?" she would moan to my granddad. "When I've just cleaned it?" To which he would reply, "No problem. I'll tie a knot in my penis and wait until you tell me I can go."

All I want is to live in a house that doesn't look like we just had burglars in. I'm fed up with our domestic chaos: the whole of the downstairs is strewn with books, comics, game and puzzle parts. Even the breadboard isn't fit for its purpose, since it's covered in screws, pliers, a couple of iPod Shuffles that haven't worked for months, not to mention a pickled cucumber jar full of sea monkeys.

I'd like to stop thinking it's normal to find a can of tick repellent in the pasta saucepan or screw plugs in the sugar bowl. I'd like to come into the kitchen and find the counters clear of loose change, junk mail, CDs and a giant lattice of drinking straws, Ping-Pong balls and cereal packets, which turns out to be Ben's latest school science project. I'd like to stop finding shoes in the middle of the living room, coats on the backs of chairs, Greg's beard shavings in the sink, his tarry turds mixed with loo roll blocking the toilet. But none of this will happen while my husband carries on being a slob and teaching our kids to be slobs.

He says that my mind should be more like his, focused on life's "big issues" instead of a bit of grease and rank underpants. Just because Greg reads the *Economist* and knows what the Large Hadron Collider is (does it also come in medium and small?), he thinks he exists on a higher intellectual plane than the rest of us and should be excused housework detail.

For Greg, life's big issues include soccer. Therein lies another of his exit strategies. If I ask him to help with some chore or other—often while he is sprawled on the sofa, scratching his balls and watching soccer on TV—his response is: "OK, give me a couple of minutes. The game's just gone into extra time." I'm happy to give him a couple of minutes. It's when he hasn't shifted his backside off the sofa after an hour that I get pissed off.

By the time he appears, the task I wanted him to perform has been completed—by me. "Why couldn't you have waited five minutes?" he protests. "I would have done it. But you can't resist making a martyr of yourself. You're not right in the head. You do know that, don't you?"

When I go upstairs, I discover the toilet is blocked. I shout at him to get the hell up here and deal with it, only to be told he has a sudden work emergency and needs to make a load of calls.

From time to time, I force myself to hold out until he's done in the loo. Then I hand him the pile of laundry—or whatever—that needs putting away. On these occasions, he starts out looking enthusiastic, but it's clearly a pose. I know he's thinking, "How do I sabotage this so that she won't ask me to do it again?" And sabotage it he does—by running downstairs every five minutes, demanding to know, "Whose sock is this?" or "Is this underwear yours or Amy's?" Yeah, Greg, like I'm really into briefs with pink ballet shoes appliquéd to the crotch.

Virginia Pruitt's is indeed a "nice" house. It's a large, imposing Edwardian villa: red brick, original porch and lead pane glass. It's been freshly painted white. The old wood-paneled front door is an understated subfusc gray.

"They call that color lamp room gray," I announce to Greg, nodding towards the front door.

"And you know that how?"

"Annie. She's got it on one of the walls in her living room. The rest is Wimborne white."

"Riveting." That's the reaction I recognize.

We continue up the garden path. It's early evening, but the sun is warm on my neck and bare arms. I can't help getting cross as I watch Greg taking in the terra-cotta tubs full of lavender, the sweet peas on their canes, the honeysuckle climbing Virginia Pruitt's red brick. He's clearly appreciating the pretty cottage garden, but whenever I suggest we clear ours of the weeds and rocks, the rusting garden furniture, the kids' ancient toy tricycles and tractors, the red plastic faded from the sun, he says it's fine as it is. He takes the view that there's no point tarting up the garden while the kids are young and still using it for soccer, trampolining and camping purposes.

I want Virginia Pruitt to be plump and mothering, with a huge bosom. Most of all, I want her to make it better.

"What I hate about therapists," Greg says, "is all the psychobabble." He thinks he's an expert on shrinks because of the handful of sessions he had with one during his second term at university. He'd been experiencing a listlessness and lassitude, which—by his own later admission—was nothing more than a touch of freshman-year miseries. "I'll never forget that Tina woman I saw on campus," he says now. Cue his famous Tina impression. "Greg," he says, adopting the familiar overly soothing, empathetic voice, "thank you for unpacking your pain and laying it on the table. It seems to me that your depression is a result of your father failing to validate you while you were growing up and that now your inner child is in desperate need of hugs from Daddy."

I can't help smiling.

"Tina based her entire theory," he is saying now, "on the fact that when I was a kid my dad never let me win at Connect Four."

"Well, that is a pretty mean, childish thing for a parent to do. Maybe it did affect you."

"Crap. I was feeling down because I was anxious and shy and spending too much time alone in my room jerking off. Once I'd moved out of Palmdale and got laid, I was fine."

We've reached Virginia Pruitt's front door. Greg looks at his watch. It's seven o'clock. (Although we both left work early, I can't believe we made it home to Putney and then to Muswell Hill in less than a couple of hours.) "Right on time," he says. "She'll either see that as proof of our commitment to therapy or she'll decide we're people pleasers, neurotically obsessed with timekeeping."

A woman I assume to be Virginia Pruitt opens the door. I feel my face fall. Virginia Pruitt is tall, reedy and—off the top of my head— a 32B. This isn't the plump, bosomy mummy I ordered. My inner child already wants to start acting out. The only thing that puts Virginia Pruitt into the mummy category is her age. She is maybe sixty. I take in the gray hair, which has been cut into a sensible bob. She's wearing a calf-length skirt in beige linen. Her short-sleeved blouse—cream—has one button open at the neck to reveal a single row of pearls. How a sex therapist can look so prim beats me. I decide the name Pruitt suits her.

"Ah, you must be the Lawsons." Plummy voice. I picked this up when I called to make our appointment. "I'm Virginia. Do come in." I fear she is used to organizing garden fetes and gymkhanas and is going to be bossy and strict, but she offers us a warm, welcoming smile. As we shake hands I start to relax.

Virginia Pruitt's entrance hall is large and a bit grand. I take in the parquet flooring and antique Indian silk rug. She leads the way down a wood-paneled passage, towards the back of the house. Greg makes small talk about it being a beautiful evening and how it looks like summer has finally arrived. Virginia is friendly enough, turning to offer him another smile, but keeps her reply brief. "We can only hope," she says. Greg has warned me that shrinks don't do chitchat and that they tend to keep their facial expressions pretty deadpan.

Apparently, revealing their thoughts and emotions gets in the way of the therapeutic process.

While Greg prattles on about the warm weather and the possibility of another drought, I'm taking in the watercolors on the walls— landscapes, mostly. We pass a mahogany table. I'm guessing Victorian. Sitting on it is that Indian god, the one with a man's body and an elephant's head. I'm damned if I can remember his name.

"Beautiful statue," Greg says. "It's Ganesh, isn't it? Did you get it in India?"

Virginia Pruitt turns around again. "Yes. My husband and I bought it in Mumbai last year."

OK, I know what's going on. Before we've sat down, before I've even had a chance to mention the tank, Greg is trying to suck up to Virginia Pruitt and get her on his side.

She shows us into her counseling room. It's small and cozy with French doors at one end. These open onto a pretty paved garden and more plant-filled pots. A breeze has started and the long net curtains are billowing gently. As Virginia Pruitt pulls the doors closed, I notice the framed botanical prints on the walls, the pretty cast-iron fireplace with its original blue and white tiles. For some reason, I start to imagine Virginia's kitchen. I'm thinking cream Shaker units with pine doorknobs to match the long farmhouse table and antique dresser. In the middle of the table there's a Victorian crackle-glaze jug full of sweet peas. The kitchen is, of course, spotless. It's impossible to imagine Virginia Pruitt having used tea bags blocking her drain or cobwebs hanging from under her sink waste pipe.

What little I've seen of Virginia Pruitt's house exudes quiet calm and order. It's a proper grown-up home, and even though her style is a bit too English country house for my taste, I'm jealous.

She directs us to a sofa covered in poppy and daisy Liberty print linen. Greg and I sit down, putting a "meaningful" distance between us. I wonder whether Virginia Pruitt has noticed and will remark on this. I find myself running my fingernail along the sofa arm and thinking how clean it is. A few months ago, Greg and I made the mistake of buying a white sofa from Ikea. In a couple of weeks it was covered in chocolate, dried-up cereal and general kid-crud.

Virginia Pruitt lowers herself into a black leather armchair. Between her and us is a low coffee table. On this sits a small clock. It's positioned in such a way that all three of us can see the time. Next to it is a box of apricot-colored tissues.

Greg is looking towards Virginia's bookcase. "Ah, I see you have Simon Schama's *A History of Britain*. Excellent book. Really well written and informative, I thought."

Oh God. He's still sucking up to her. I'm relieved when Virginia Pruitt doesn't respond beyond a polite nod. She is *so* on to him.

She crosses her legs and adjusts her skirt hem, signaling she's ready to start. "So, Greg and Sophie, what brings you to therapy?"

"My tank," Greg blurts, clearly deciding to get his retaliation in first after all. "That's to say, it didn't physically bring us here. I mean, it's twenty feet long. It would have taken up God knows how many parking spaces."

Virginia Pruitt looks puzzled.

"Greg, when you say 'tank' . . ."

"I mean a Second World War Sherman tank."

She's nodding in a manner that can only mean she thinks my husband is a total weirdo. Round one to moi, methinks.

Greg continues: "I keep it at my mate Pete's farm in Sussex. I'm not into war games or anything. It's just a toy. I'm in the middle of restoring it."

"And when that's done?"

"I'll ride around the countryside in it."

Virginia Pruitt's face breaks into a smile. I assume it's one of pity.

"Huh . . . I can see that might be fun." Her voice is measured, but approving. "So it will be a chance for a bit of frivolity and pleasure. A bit of *you* time."

"Absolutely. You've got it." Greg is blinking, clearly taken aback by her approval. He is also beaming.

I can't believe that Virginia Pruitt is siding with Greg without bothering to ask me how I feel about the bloody tank. She's a woman, for crying out loud. She's meant to get it. She's supposed to be on my side. Earlier, when Greg and I were in the car discussing the tank, even he was convinced she'd take my side.

I've barely finished this thought when Virginia Pruitt turns to me. "So, Sophie, how do you feel about the tank?"

I feel myself warming to her again. "Well, to quote Princess Diana, 'There are three of us in this marriage, so it's a bit crowded.'"

"And the third person—if you will—is the tank, and you're having to compete with it for Greg's affection."

OK, finally she's getting it.

"That's right." I explain that Greg works long hours during the week and now most Saturdays are taken up with the tank.

She asks Greg what he does for a living.

"I'm a journalist. I'm the political editor of the *Vanguard*."

Virginia Pruitt acknowledges his professional status with a slow, approving nod. I'd put money on her being a *Vanguard* reader. She has all the credentials: middle class, educated and a shrink, she's bound to be to the left politically.

She's looking at me again. "So, Sophie, you must feel quite abandoned on the weekends."

Hang on. Why hasn't she asked me what *I* do for a living? Is she thinking I'm some pathetic, bored housewife who is so in need of her husband's attention that she can't be left to cope alone on the weekend?

I'm still working out how to respond when she adds a postscript. "I mean, during the week you're working full-time in a very demanding job and on the weekends you're lumbered with the children."

How does she know I work? . . . OK, got it. I told her on the phone. I'm impressed that she's remembered. It's dawning on me that Greg isn't the class pet. I'm beginning to trust her.

"That's exactly how it is," I say.

"You seem angry," she says, spotting that I've turned away from Greg.

"I am. You see, this isn't just about the tank."

Virginia Pruitt is smiling in a way that tells me she isn't remotely surprised. "I find the words 'straw' and 'camel's back' coming to mind," she says.

I nod. Greg tuts. I ask him why he's tutting and he says it's because I'm about to go on the attack re his domestic shortcomings.

"Too right I am." I can feel myself getting really cross now. I turn to face Virginia Pruitt. "The thing is, Greg refuses to do his share of the housework or clean up after himself. He's like a big kid. He expects me to tidy up after him. I'm at the end of my tether. I just can't cope any longer."

"Wrong. I do not expect you to tidy up after me. You *choose* to tidy up after me because you're so neurotic about keeping the house tidy."

"I don't *choose* to unblock the loo after you've filled it with half a toilet roll. You simply refuse to do it."

I'm finding it hard to keep my cool. "I don't think it's neurotic to want a toilet that will flush and a bathroom free of toenail clippings, do you?"

Greg unfolds his arms and grudgingly concedes the point. "Look, I don't do it on purpose. I have stuff on my mind. Sometimes, I just forget to clear up or I don't realize how much toilet paper I'm using."

"*Sometimes?* Greg, you *always* forget."

Greg is looking straight at Virginia Pruitt now. "My wife is a clean freak and a martyr. What can I say?"

"Sophie, how do you feel when Greg calls you a martyr?"

"I feel angry and worthless. It's his way of telling me that the things I regard as important don't count."

"That is such bullshit."

Virginia Pruitt doesn't bat an eyelid at Greg's expletive. "And it's bullshit because?"

"She's saying I don't respect her and that's not true."

"But it seems to me that Sophie is telling you that she wants to live in a clean, comfortable home, and instead of helping her create an adult space for the two of you, you're sabotaging her efforts. Is that showing her respect?"

This shuts him up.

"It's got to the point," I say, "where I can't do my job and run the home on my own."

"But we have help," Greg butts in. "Mrs. Fredericks comes in once a week."

"Yes, but she can't reach the actual dirt because there's so much crap in the way. She's always moaning about how all the surfaces are covered with junk."

Virginia Pruitt asks me to describe a typical working day. It's clearly occurred to her that Greg needs reminding. I'm starting to really like Virginia Pruitt.

My husband snorts.

I tell her that I'm up at six to prepare the kids' lunch boxes and maybe put a casserole in the slow cooker so that it'll be ready when I get home. "Then I take a shower, blow-dry my hair and put on some makeup. By now it's seven and Klaudia, our Polish nanny, has arrived. She's great—kind and totally unflappable. The kids love her and I'd be lost without her. I'm always running late, so I end up half walking, half jogging to the tube."

"So you're wrung out before you even get to work."

I nod. She is so getting this.

"An hour later, I reach the office." I remind her that I'm the senior producer on *Coffee Break*. "The moment I walk in, I'm accosted by Nancy, the presenter who's inevitably having some kind of hissy fit. I deal with her humongous ego and tantrums, watch the show go out, make notes and attend the daily postmortem with the other program producers and the editor. After the meeting, I deal with admin, respond to a stack of e-mails and eat a limp canteen sandwich at my desk. I usually manage to get away by six. I pick up any urgent shopping on my way to the tube. If there are no problems with the trains, I'm home by seven. I supervise homework and attempt some bonding time with the kids. I might read to them or they come onto my bed and we have cuddles. If Greg's coming home at a reasonable time, I'll have dinner with him. I'm usually in bed by nine thirty."

"It sounds exhausting," Virginia Pruitt says.

"That's it, side with her," Greg blurts, clearly furious.

If Virginia Pruitt is irritated or ruffled by his comment, she gives no hint. "Greg, I'm wondering why my sympathizing with Sophie makes you think I'm siding with her. Did you assume I wasn't interested in hearing about your workday and wouldn't bother asking you about it?"

"I dunno. Maybe. It's just that I'm fed up with being cast as the bad guy in all this."

Virginia Pruitt nods. "Go on."

Greg turns to me. "Have you any idea how stressful and exhausting my job can be? During the last election, I was doing fifteen-hour days. Then there was the MPs' expenses scandal . . . WikiLeaks. And almost every evening there's some tedious political do I'm expected to attend. I'm convinced you just think I sit on my arse all day."

"That's ridiculous. Of course I don't think that. I know how hard you work."

"So," Virginia Pruitt cuts in, "it's not easy for either of you." She looks truly concerned. She asks us when we last went out on our own. I tell her it was for the kids' parent-teacher evening a few weeks ago.

"OK, but when did you last go to the movies or out to dinner?"

We admit that we can't remember. "I have so many evening commitments," Greg says. "On the nights I'm free, I just want to come home and sink a few beers in front of the TV."

"And even if we did go out," I say, "we'd only sit in silence or fight."

Virginia Pruitt asks us what we'd fight about.

I tell her that I'm so angry with Greg that everything about him seems to irritate me these days—what he's wearing, his hair, how he holds his knife and fork, expressions he uses.

"Yeah—the other day she told me I was breathing too loudly."

He's not wrong. I feel myself blushing.

She asks us to think back to when we first started dating. "How did you get along?"

"Finding Sophie was like coming home," Greg says.

I can't help feeling touched.

"It was the same for me." I tell her how I fell in love with him waltzing down Charing Cross Road.

We tell her that the sex was pretty hot and regale her with tales of our acrobatic, clothes-ripping, three-day shagathons.

"When we weren't having sex," I say, "we would sit up till all hours putting the world to rights and planning our future."

I tell her about our dotty plan to give up work and schlep our kids around India and Nepal. "We only gave up on this idea after Amy was born. What with the sleep deprivation, the hemorrhoids and the cracked nipples, I could barely wheel her up the road to the supermarket."

Greg starts talking about our first holiday together. "We went to Spain. We'd only been going out a few weeks."

"And on about day three or four," I butt in, "Greg took me to this new beach he'd discovered. Of course, he failed to tell me it was a nudist beach. We sat there in hysterics while we watched naked men barbecuing. You should have seen them. Their dangly bits were all over the chicken drumsticks. Then Greg says maybe we should join in—not with the barbecuing, just the naked bit. Anyway, eventually he persuaded me and we ended up making love in the dunes."

He's laughing. "Yeah, only we had a bit of a sand issue . . . and things got slightly abrasive."

Virginia Pruitt is wincing and smiling at the same time.

"So you have some really good memories from your early days. There was clearly a real intimacy between you, both physically and emotionally. I think you need to recapture some of that."

"That won't be easy," I say. "How do you start to rekindle your love life when your husband has turned into a sofa that farts?"

She doesn't have a chance to reply because Greg is straight in there.

"Oh, and I suppose you think you really turn me on by coming to bed in your PICKLE MAKERS DO IT WITH RELISH T-shirt?"

Virginia Pruitt raises her hand to stop us bickering and says she would like to change the subject.

"So, Greg, if you're not having sex with Sophie, do you masturbate?"

Greg looks taken aback, but my guess is it's only partly due to embarrassment. I know what he's thinking, because I'm thinking it, too: Virginia Pruitt with her sensible skirt and string of pearls just said "masturbate." A look passes between us. Any moment I'm going to start laughing. I turn away from Greg and bite my bottom lip. Finally he admits to Virginia Pruitt that he does masturbate.

"And you're able to come?"

Come? Women like Virginia Pruitt don't say "come." They talk about having "arrived." I refuse to look at Greg and cough to stifle my giggles.

Greg says yes, he is able to come.

"He masturbates when he thinks I'm asleep," I manage to blurt, "but I'm always catching him at it."

"And how does that make you feel?"

"I'm past caring," I say.

"Really? You don't feel rejected?"

I shrug. "A bit maybe. I mean, OK, we're not having sex with each other, but I guess it still hurts."

Greg throws up his hands. "Do you mind telling me what I'm supposed to do?"

"I'm just saying, that's all."

"So, Sophie, are you having solo sex?"

"You have to be kidding." I manage a bitter laugh and inform her that being tired most of the time and living with a lazy slob isn't great for the libido. She responds with an understanding nod.

"In my opinion, the lack of physical intimacy between you is merely a symptom of what's wrong with your relationship. It's not the cause. I think you both know that."

I guess we do.

"While the pair of you are at loggerheads, you can't expect to fancy each other. If, on the other hand, you are prepared to work through your issues, things in the bedroom should improve automatically."

"So you don't think we need sex therapy?"

"No. Our focus needs to be on getting the two of you to reconnect at an emotional level."

"I have no objection to reconnecting," I say, "once my husband has started pulling his weight around the house." I am aware that my arms are folded in front of me.

"I'll pull my weight, but in my time frame and to my standards, not yours."

I turn to Virginia Pruitt. "You see. That's how he wheedles his way out of taking responsibility."

Virginia Pruitt doesn't respond. Instead she tells us that our time is up. "But before you go, I am going to give you some homework." She pauses and purses her lips, as if she's not sure she's doing the right thing. "I would like you to go on a date."

"You mean with each other?" Greg pipes up, and he isn't entirely joking.

Couples' Therapy—Session 2

Hey, Annie—OMG, China trip sounds amazing. Cannot believe you ate chicken stomach and fish lips. Fish have lips? Who knew?

Loved pix of you and Rob at the Great Wall. What a fabulous way to spend your anniversary. Can't believe you guys have been married ten years.

Looked again at photo of Rob in trilby and have to say I think you're wrong. Even with the paunch—barely noticeable, I might add—he doesn't look remotely like some shady bloke selling knocked-off Rolexes off a market stall.

Did as you asked and have been over to your place a couple of times to check how your mum and dad are coping with the kids. (Loving the new garden decking btw!) Your dad was frolicking with them in paddling pool while your mum made lunch (fish pie from scratch!! Now I know where you get the cooking gene from). And before you start panicking—yes, both kids were smothered in factor fifty. Not many people their age could cope with looking after a four- and six-year-old for a fortnight, but they've got so much energy and seem to be taking it in their stride. So please stop worrying and relax.

Oh, have to tell you . . . was at local pool with Ben yesterday and bumped into Rosie from that book club we used to go to. You remember her—mahoosive mammaries, ginger twins. Haven't seen her in ages. Anyway, turns out she's almost ready to pop with baby number three. Ben takes one look at her bump and says, "So will you have to go on *Maury* to find out who your baby's dad is?" I could have throttled him!!!! Klaudia clearly letting Amy and Ben watch daytime TV when they get in from school. Will have to have a word with her, but don't want to lose her 'cos she's so brill with them and they adore her.

OK . . . you wanted to know how our first sex therapy session went. Virginia Pruitt very plummy. Greg and I haven't laughed together in God knows how long, but we practically cracked up whenever she said "come" and "masturbate." (More of the latter when you get home. No, that came out wrong. I don't mean you will be masturbating more when you get home. I mean I will explain more.)

We discussed Greg's lack of domestic finger lifting, but he's adamant that I'm the one with the problem. End of story. Virginia Pruitt seems to understand that I need him to change but, as ever, he's digging in his heels. Women joke about their husbands being slobs—years ago, I used to—but this has gone way beyond a joke. Greg's behavior is really threatening our marriage. I'm so angry with him for the way he's treated me over the years.

Pretty heavy session, so we didn't talk much on way home, other than to admit that we both like VP. Think we were scared that she would have a favorite, but she really listens to both of us. Have decided to carry on seeing her.

Our homework was to go on a date. VP thinks we need to reconnect. We decided to meet for dinner at Chez Fred. I thought we could try to talk a bit more about what's going wrong with us. Always easier in a public place 'cos you can't shout. I think that may have been VP's thinking.

Long story short, I left work early, dashed home, had a long soak in tub, shaved my legs, took ages over my hair and makeup. I used this article I'd cut out from *Cosmo* to help me do smoky eyes. Amy took one look at me and said I looked like Lord Voldemort, which seemed a bit harsh. She's been really moody lately. God, hope she's not about to start her period. Apparently, it's not unknown for girls to start at ten. :—(((

Decided to wear that green wrap dress I bought for your birthday do last year. Greg kept saying how much he liked it. Killer heels practically killed me, though, just walking to car. Had to wear Nikes to drive. Imagined myself being in accident and having to explain my look to gay male nurses.

Arrived Chez Fred right on time and ordered a kir royal to get in the mood. A bowl of olives and three slices of walnut-raisin bread later and Greg's still not turned up. Assume he's got held up in some meeting at work. Finally I text him and he texts back to say I've got the day wrong and we'd agreed we were having dinner the following night. But I booked the table, so I know I've got the right day. He accuses me of not communicating. I accuse him of sabotaging our date on purpose. Was so angry with him that I ordered a fifty-quid bottle of wine, lobster and crème brûlée. Ended up getting drunk and flirting with waiters. Then threw up when I got home.

Me and Greg still barely speaking, but hey, what's new? Beyond practical, day-to-day issues we've got nothing much to say to each other. Last Sunday was classic. We read Sunday papers in bed in silence—other than when Greg started swearing because the *Observer* had dug up some new dirt on that Home Office hooker story that the *Vanguard* had missed. At some stage I asked if he wanted some tea and toast. I think he may have grunted in the affirmative. Eventually we got up. Greg took Ben to soccer practice. I took Amy to get her hair cut. We ate lunch out with our respective child. In my case with Amy moaning that her haircut made her look like Prince Valiant and she had no intention of going to school the next day.

In the afternoon, Greg napped. I popped round to see Mum and Dad. Part of me still can't believe they're actually going through with this move to Florida. They both turned eighty this year. I know it's for the best. Who wouldn't want to live out their final years away from the cold and damp, with their son the doctor to keep an eye on them. The thing is—and I know I'm just feeling sorry for myself—I can't help feeling abandoned. It wouldn't be so bad if my marriage weren't in the toilet.

I can't remember the last time Greg and I discussed a movie or had a conversation about current affairs. It's like it's all been said and now we're just going through the motions until we die. (Miserable? Moi?)

Anyhow, got home from Mum and Dad's and cooked dinner while Greg disappeared to his study to catch up with his e-mails.

Later, the kids ate in front of *Britain's Got Talent* and Greg told them he was thinking of auditioning. At this point he started playing "God Save the Queen" on his teeth. Kids in stitches. To give him his due, when he's around he does make a real effort with Amy and Ben.

Thing is, until Chez Fred debacle, I really thought our marriage stood a chance and that with the help of counseling we could patch things up, but occurs to me we've left it all far too late. Greg's made it clear re domestic stuff that he isn't going to change. He says he wants to work on our relationship, but I don't think his heart's in it and to tell you the truth I'm not sure that mine is. Could it be that subconsciously we're actually looking to VP to help us end our marriage instead of heal it? Are we talking endgame here? All feels pretty bloody heavy.

OK, gotta go. Just heard Greg come in. We're off to our second session. Wonder if VP will give us detention for not doing our homework.

Sorry for long miserablist missive. Enjoy Terra-Cotta Army. Tell Rob I say hi and that hat v cool.

Love and hugs,

S XXX

PS: Still convinced I can hear mice under floorboards in kitchen.

I press "send" and look up to see my son trotting into the bedroom.

"Mum, what's happened to my room? It's all floor."

"Yeah, I know," I say, wiping away the tear that has started rolling down my cheek. "I just picked up a whole load of your clothes. Ben, we have a laundry basket. Why do you refuse to use it? Do you actually enjoy sleeping in a sea of stinky socks and underpants?"

"I just forget, that's all." Where have I heard this before? He climbs onto the bed beside me. Since it's only six in the evening, I'm "on" it rather than "in" it. Earlier, I'd been tempted to get under the duvet, but I knew I'd only fall asleep. So I decided to e-mail Annie instead.

I transfer the laptop to the nightstand and Ben snuggles in for a cuddle. He smells of school—a mixture of paint, crayons and school dining room. I can tell he's tired because he's got his blanky.

"You know how Arthur is coming to stay on Saturday?" he says. Arthur is his best friend from school. "Well, would it be OK if we built a time machine in my bedroom?"

"I don't see why not."

"Cool."

"Any thoughts about where you might go?"

"Well . . . Arthur wants to go back to the Stone Age."

"But you're not so sure?"

Ben wrinkles his nose. "I'd like to go, but what if we got attacked by a mammoth? Or a pterosaur? They had a wingspan of sixty feet."

"Huh. That's pretty scary. Maybe you could suggest going somewhere different."

"If it was just me on my own I'd like to go back to when you and Dad were my age and we could play and be friends."

"Aw . . . that's so sweet." I give him a squeeze.

"You won't tell Arthur I'm scared of mammoths and pterosaurs, will you? He'll laugh and make fun of me."

"What? As if."

"So where are you and Dad going tonight?"

"Oh, just out to eat." Neither of the kids has the remotest idea that Greg and I are in therapy.

"I like it when you and Dad go out together."

"You do?"

Ben nods.

"It means you're friends again. And maybe you'll stop yelling at Dad."

I'm suddenly overcome with guilt. I guess I've been in denial about how much our fighting is upsetting the kids. "Do I shout a lot?"

"Yep. And you shout at me and Amy, too . . . but not as much as you shout at Dad."

"I'm sorry, hon. It's just that I'm always tired when I get home from work and I get irritable—particularly when you lot don't tidy up after yourselves. I know I shouldn't yell. Tell you what—from now on I'll try really hard not to."

"Good. The reason you yell is because you kvetch too much."

I laugh. He's been picking up Yiddish words from my parents.

"Granddad says that you kvetch a bit, but not as much as Grandma Esther. She kvetches the most."

"Tell me about it."

"What about when she came to look after us last Halloween and I had that skeleton costume with the luminous bones. It was the most amazingest costume ever and when we went trick-or-treating she made me put on my coat."

Could I ever forget? He went on about it for weeks. Since then it's become a bit of a family joke, but I'm not sure that my mother will ever be truly forgiven by her grandson.

"Grandma didn't want you to catch cold."

"But it was my bestest-ever costume."

"Well, maybe this year we'll find you another one that's just as good." I give Ben another squeeze and a kiss and start disentangling myself from him. "Look, I gotta get going. I just heard your dad come in. Why don't you jump in the bath now and afterwards you and Amy can watch a movie with Klaudia."

" 'K," he says, amenable for once. He climbs off the bed and heads towards the bathroom.

"And don't forget the cabbages," I call out after him. It's a joke I've had with the kids since they were tiny. I always used to tell them that if they didn't wash behind their ears, cabbages would start to grow in the dirt. Ben doesn't reply. These days, the joke has worn a bit thin.

I'm slipping on my shoes when an e-mail pings. I open my laptop. It's from Annie. I look at the bedside clock and do a quick calculation. It must be one in the morning in Beijing.

Hey, hon, just a quickie 'cos about to fall into bed. Boozy night with nice-but-dull Swedes we met at Great Wall. He in timber . . . owns horizontal boring mill. Or should that be a boring horizontal mill? Anyway, just to say I read your e-mail and that am thinking of you. I know everything feels hopeless right now—especially with your mum and dad moving to the other side of the world, but please, please hang in there. And don't give up on you and Greg. I will not have my two favorite people in the world splitting up. Counseling definitely the way forward. It'll take hard work from both of you, but you will get through

this. Glad you like VP. Back in a few days. Talk then. Love you, A
XXX

PS: Hope you don't mind, but probably won't mention to Rob
that you like hat, as will only encourage him.

PPS: Sorry about mice.

This was typical Annie, coming home tired and trashed at one in
the morning and still finding the wherewithal to let you know she's
there for you.

I hit "reply."

Love you too. Thanks for the pep talk. Who knows—maybe
you're right and we will get through this . . . although right now
I'm really not sure. Doing my best to hang in. Sleep tight and
sweet dreams.

X

As I cross the landing, I pick up a pair of Ben's sneakers, remove
the potato chip packet that's been shoved into one of them and toss
them into his room. Then I head downstairs.

As usual I just avoid tripping over the pile of stuff at the bottom.
The pile is like some giant single-celled organism that is forever
morphing and changing shape but never disappears. No sooner
have I cleared away a mass of clothes, books and CDs than it will
take on a new form consisting of shoes, comics and a jumbo pack of
Tampax.

I can hear laughter coming from the kitchen. Amy is shrieking
with delight. She and Greg have gotten into playing Connect Four. I

assume that, as usual, he's letting her win. Unlike his own father, Greg actually gets a kick out of being a noncompetitive parent.

I walk into the kitchen and it hits me again—the poo smell that's been hanging around for days. No matter how much I complain, Greg refuses to keep his Gorgonzola in the fridge. Apparently the guy in the posh cheese shop told him it ruins the taste.

The game appears to be over. Amy is laughing, fit to burst because Greg is doing a perfect impersonation of the kids' ever so jolly and ever so Scottish school principal, Mrs. McKay. Like most of the state school principals in our oh so boho part of West London, Mrs. M is well known for her gentle, uncompetitive, unpushy approach to education. The not-quite-so-boho prefer to call it second rate.

"You're in a good mood," I remark to Greg, putting the potato chip packet in the trash can, which is already overflowing.

"Och, aye," Greg responds, staying in character. "That is because ay am so proud of the wee ones here at Parkhall School. They are so incensed by the government cuts in education spending that they have just sent the minister for education an angry collage."

"That's not fair," Amy says, indignant, but still giggling. "We may be at public school, but we can all read and write."

"If you say so," Greg snorts.

I tell Amy that he's only teasing. By now I'm gathering up dirty plates from the kids' dinner, which are lying on the table. A couple of Connect Four counters have found their way into a bowl of half-eaten ice cream, which has since melted. Bearing in mind the promise I just made to Ben, I try not to snap at Greg. Instead I just moan. "Greg, would it have been too much for you to put the dirty plates in the dishwasher?"

Greg says that, typically, I've walked into the room just as he was about to do it.

"Yeah, right."

I carry on clearing the table, huffing and puffing as I go.

"There you go again. Making a martyr of yourself."

I don't want to start a fight, so I just glare at him. He picks up an end of baguette and starts chewing. I turn on him and tell him off for eating so loudly.

"Jesus was a martyr," Amy announces, clearly trying to deflect the impending conflict. "Because he died on the cross for all our sins. It says so on that great big notice they've got outside Saint Michael's."

"Actually, not everybody believes those stories," Greg says. He's doing his best to be diplomatic, but as an atheist he finds it hard. "I mean, we don't really know if Jesus ever lived."

"You mean, like the Loch Ness monster?" Ben has just appeared, still in his school uniform, still holding his blanky. So much for his going willingly to the bathtub.

"Not exactly," Greg says. We're both doing our best not to laugh.

At this point, Greg disappears upstairs to change out of his work clothes and I turn my attention to the trash can. As I tug on the black plastic liner I start muttering to myself, begging it not to burst.

"Anyway, I like Mrs. McKay," Amy continues, getting back to the subject of her head teacher. "After Chloe Peterson started telling everybody she hated her fat thighs, Mrs. McKay gave all the girls in our class a talk on body image. She says we should be proud of our bodies and that it's OK for girls to be any shape they want."

"What, even an oblate spheroid?" Ben pipes up.

"And what," I ask, "might an oblate spheroid be when it's at home?" Yay, the liner has come out intact. I gather up the top and start knotting it.

"It's a round shape, but it's squished at the top and bottom. The Earth's an oblate spheroid. We did it in science class."

It occurs to me that maybe Greg and I, along with the other "concerned" (i.e., pushy) Parkhall parents, don't give the school the credit it deserves.

Ben turns to Amy. "You'd look really weird that shape."

"Oh, shuddup, Ben. You smell."

"Schlemiel!"

Fighting back the laughter, I just about manage to pull off a stern: "Ben, don't use that word. It's not nice." I take the plastic liner over to the back door. Greg can take it out when we get back.

"Granddad says it."

"I don't care what Granddad says. I don't want you saying it."

"Mum doesn't want you using it," Amy chips in, "because it means penis."

"What's wrong with penis?"

Just then the front door opens. Klaudia is back from her English class.

"What's taking your dad so long?" I mutter. "We need to get going in case there's traffic."

"But will somebody please explain what's supposed to be wrong with penis?"

I tell Ben that there's nothing wrong with penis per se, but people tend not to respond well to being called one.

I kiss the kids good night and remind them about having baths and washing their hair. "And for the last time," I say, "will the pair of you please stop trying to convince Klaudia that Starbursts are part of your five veggies a day."

Just then Greg reappears wearing a pair of crumpled chino shorts that he's clearly just pulled out of the dirty-laundry basket. Over the top he's wearing a white T-shirt. This is clean at least, and unless you're standing inches from his chest, you can barely read the DUNDER MIFFLIN PAPER COMPANY logo.

"So," I say, looking him up and down. "You're going out in those shorts, are you?"

"I couldn't find a clean pair. If you're too embarrassed to be seen with me, don't come. But it's eighty degrees outside and there's no way I'm wearing jeans."

I'm about to say that I suppose I should be grateful he's not wearing socks with his sandals, when I notice that he is staring at Amy. "Amy, are you wearing eye shadow?"

"Yeah, great, isn't it?" She flutters her eyelids to show off the wobbly turquoise eye frosting. "It was Klaudia's, but she didn't want it anymore. And she gave me nail polish, too."

Amy presents her newly painted fingernails. It's her very first effort and she's got pink glittery polish all over her fingers. I think she looks so cute—not that I'd allow her out in the eye shadow. I'm reminded that my first baby is growing up and that a few years from now she'll be wearing makeup and nail polish for real. Part of me wants her to be ten forever, but at the same time I can't wait for us to start bonding at the MAC counter.

Amy takes one look at her father's expression. "What's wrong with it?"

"You're ten. That's what's wrong with it."

"At least I'm not going out with Mum in dirty, crumpled old shorts. And anyway, all the girls in my class practice putting on makeup and painting their nails."

"That doesn't mean you have to."

I tug Greg's T-shirt and remind him that time's getting on. He gives his daughter a look as if to say, "This discussion isn't over," and then heads into the hall. Before following him, I whisper to Amy that she looks fab and that she should leave her father to me.

"He's such a schlemiel," she mutters.

"Mum, Amy said 'schlemiel.' "

"Shut up, Ben," Amy says.

I tell my son to be quiet, pick up my handbag along with my large canvas tote and decide to leave the situation.

Klaudia comes flip-flopping down the hall in her yellow Havaianas. Her blond hair is swept back into a giant claw clip. A few wenchlike wisps hang around her face.

Klaudia is twenty and for a moment I want to be her—sexy, confident, sun-kissed Klaudia, her life barely begun, her head full of plans and possibilities.

She says hi to both of us and apologizes for being late. "Zey cut bus," she announces. Despite nine months of English lessons, her Polish accent is as pronounced as ever.

I tell her it's not a problem, adding that the kids have eaten and require baths and hair washes.

"We should be back by half ten."

"No prob-lyem." Klaudia smiles. "You take time."

No sooner has Klaudia closed the front door behind us than I can hear Amy and Ben shrieking for her to come quick. Apparently a mouse is scratching its way out of the trash can liner.

I look at Greg. "I told you we had mice. You wouldn't listen."

"Great, so it's my fault as usual."

"I think we should go back."

"Klaudia will be fine. She was raised on a farm. A mouse isn't going to faze her."

We keep walking and I make a mental note to call in a pest control company.

"Do you fancy Klaudia?" I blurt.

"What? Where did that come from? She's practically a child."

"She's twenty."

"Whatever. I can barely tell her apart from Amy's friends. And anyway, she's got a boyfriend back in Warsaw."

"So what? That wouldn't stop you feeling tempted."

"Oh, please." He looks genuinely appalled.

"And these Saturdays, when you go to Sussex . . . you are spending them with the tank, aren't you?" It strikes me that these are odd questions, bearing in mind that I've just told Annie I'm not sure my marriage has a future. Surely I shouldn't care if Greg's having an affair—or if he fancies Klaudia. But part of me clearly does.

My suspicions seem to amuse Greg. He starts laughing. "Sophie, do you honestly think I've got the energy for extracurricular sex? I mean, for starters, having an affair takes a great deal of organization, not to mention expense. There are the secret rendezvous to book, cool trendy adultery clothes to buy."

"Of course, because you wouldn't want her to see you in dirty, creased shorts. Whereas I don't matter."

"Absolutely. And I'd have to start working out. Then there's the stress of making sure you didn't find out. The moment I booked a hotel room I'd be worrying about you finding my credit card statement. On top of that, I'd need constant alibis, a secret cell phone and e-mail address. Then there's all the guilt. That alone would be enough to ensure I couldn't get it up. I swear that all I do on a Saturday is go to Pete's. We work on the tank, have a pub lunch and then I come home. Ask him . . . ask the pub landlord."

"OK, I get it. I just wanted to be sure, that's all. Bearing in mind everything we're going through, nobody would think it strange if one of us had an affair."

We head towards the car, which is parked a few yards down the street. Greg says he'll drive. What is it about men—even supposed feminists like Greg—insisting on driving when they're out with their wives and girlfriends? Would their testicles fall off if they let a woman get behind the wheel?

"OK, so what about you?" he says as we climb in.

"What about me?"

"You could be having an affair just as easily as me."

"Greg, I go to work. I come home. I eat, attempt to have something resembling quality time with the kids and go to bed. The last time I went away overnight, Gordon Brown was prime minister."

Greg turns the key in the ignition and we pull away. "So I take it we're speaking again," he says.

I shrug. "I guess. Look, I'm sorry if I didn't communicate properly, but I was sure I told you the right day."

"Maybe you did and I got confused. Can we just agree that our wires got crossed? I absolutely did not set out to sabotage our date."

"OK, whatever. Let's just forget it."

"Good."

We drive in silence for a minute or so.

"It was nice," I say eventually, "watching you and Amy laughing together."

He nods. "It's funny how kids drive you mad most of the time and then you have these moments when you're so overcome with love for them that it brings tears to your eyes."

"I know." I tell him about Ben wanting to go back in time so that he can be friends with us when we were children.

He gives a slow shake of his head, clearly touched. "God . . . sometimes you just don't want them to grow up."

"Particularly Amy?"

"Look, I know she's on the verge of puberty, but she's ten. I can't bear the way young girls are sexualized these days."

"Oh, come on. It's a bit of eye shadow and sparkly nail polish. She's having fun experimenting. I did the same when I was her age. You make it sound like she was cavorting in a Wonderbra and suspenders."

Greg grimaces. "I just want her to carry on being my little girl."

"Same here, but the reality is that a few years from now she'll be a teenager. If you're always on her case, she'll pull away and your relationship with her will really suffer."

"I know," he says with a sigh. "You're right. I need to back off."

I'm aware that Greg and I are having a rare "moment." We're actually connecting. I wonder if he's feeling it, too. This has to be a positive sign. Maybe this isn't the endgame after all. I can't wait to tell Virginia Pruitt.

And then I go and spoil it all by saying something stupid: "The kids love you so much. I wish you'd spend more time with them."

"I don't believe this. Sophie, you've just lectured me about not getting on Amy's case, but you're on mine the entire time. Do you realize that you never, ever stop nagging? I can't take it anymore. I do my best with the kids, like I do with stuff around the house. Now just back the fuck off."

"Actually, you know what? I'm not going to back the fuck off. If you want our marriage to work, then you need to start upping your game."

"And if *you* want our marriage to work, you have to stop telling me what it is I *need* to do."

Our "moment" is well and truly over.

It's only when we pull up outside Virginia Pruitt's house that I realize we haven't come up with an excuse for not doing our homework. Since it wasn't a written assignment, we can hardly say the dog ate it. While I'm trying to work out what to say, Greg is still irritable and interrogating me as to why I'm carrying the canvas tote as well as my handbag. I tell him there are things in the tote that I might need.

"In our therapy session."

I shrug. He doesn't push it.

Of course our homework is the first thing Virginia Pruitt mentions.

"So, how did the date go?" Her expression is wide-eyed and hopeful.

"It didn't. There was a mix-up. We got the days confused."

Virginia Pruitt seems disappointed, but not surprised. My mind goes back to last week. I remember sensing that she had qualms about giving us this homework. I think she half expected it to go tits up.

"I see, so you both chose to sabotage it?" she says.

I'm taken aback. It never occurred to me that I might have had a hand—albeit a subconscious one—in our "mix-up."

"So you've had no Greg and Sophie time this week?"

We shrug like a pair of naughty kids up before the school principal. But she lets it go. There's no telling off. No punishment. Her lack of a rebuke makes me feel guilty. I feel like we've let her down.

She says she wants to spend the session asking about our childhoods. I describe mine as your average angsty Jewish upbringing, from which I emerged unscathed, apart from a fear of raw egg products (cause salmonella, possible death), squeezing zits (causes blood poisoning, possible death), silk (flammable, catches fire, possible death), motorcycles (no explanation required, certain death). Virginia Pruitt actually laughs.

"And now my parents are moving to Florida—to live with my brother, Phil, and his wife and their two teenage boys. They're getting on and we all thought the climate would do them good. Plus Phil's a doctor and his wife's a nurse, so they're going to be well looked after."

"And how do you feel about them going?"

I find myself admitting to my feelings of abandonment. "I think I'd be coping better if Greg and I were OK."

"Do your parents know how things are between you?"

I shake my head. "Like I said, they're elderly. They've got enough to worry about with the move. It would be too much for them to cope with."

"That must be a strain—keeping it bottled up."

"I guess."

Greg looks at me. "So, go on . . . say it."

"Say what?"

"That since you found out your parents were moving, I haven't exactly been the supportive husband."

"Well, you haven't. When your dad died, I was so there for you."

"You were and I was very grateful, but he *died*. Your parents are still alive."

"I know, but they won't be in my life the way they used to be and I'm really going to miss them. I know we can visit, but I find myself wondering how many times I'll get to see them before they die. The kids keep telling me they're going to miss them, too, but it hasn't even occurred to you to ask them how they're feeling."

"Great. Something else to blame me for. OK, I'm sorry I haven't been very sympathetic towards you and I will speak to the kids. How's that?"

"Don't knock yourself out."

Virginia Pruitt says that this issue is something we can pick up in our next session, but for now she wants to stay focused on our childhoods. She wants to find out more about Greg's early years. Greg often talks about his upbringing, so I know that he's not about to tell Virginia Pruitt anything that he hasn't told me.

He begins by explaining that he isn't Jewish. "So significantly less emoting and fretting went on in our house compared to Sophie's.

For example, my mum and dad tended not to call the dermatologist if somebody had a paper cut."

I'm straight back at him. "On the other hand, your father did die of heartburn."

Virginia Pruitt looks puzzled. Greg explains that his workaholic father ignored his symptoms for years on the grounds that a) he didn't have time to get them checked out and b) nobody ever died of heartburn. "When he finally saw a doctor, it was too late. Stomach acid had eroded his esophagus and it had become cancerous. He's been gone two years."

I wonder if he's going to tell Virginia Pruitt the Connect Four story, but he doesn't. "When she was young, my mother was a legal secretary, but she stopped working to raise my younger brother and me. I guess she fussed over us rather a lot." Virginia Pruitt presses him for details. Before he has a chance to say anything, I hear myself butt in.

"Val thinks all human beings in possession of a penis are totally helpless. Even now, she cuts the crusts of his bread."

"OK," Greg says, red with embarrassment. "I admit that I was pretty cosseted and that I still have a few bad habits."

"A few? That's a laugh."

Greg glares at me.

Virginia Pruitt suggests that Val babied her two sons in order to prevent them from growing up.

"Possibly," Greg says with a shrug. "But what I know for certain is that my mother taught me and my brother about the things that really matter in life. Mum might have spoiled my brother and me, but she had another side to her personality. She did charity work. She thought about the world. She went back to school and got a degree. Most of all, she never got het up about the house being a bit grubby or untidy. She certainly didn't nag and yell because there were a few dirty dishes in the sink."

"And you wish that Sophie would stop nagging and be a bit more like your mother?"

"Yes, I do."

I turn on him. "I can't believe you just said that. How dare you set your mother up as some kind of gold standard. This is the woman who takes a drooling greyhound to bed with her and lets it sleep under the duvet. This is the woman who goes on holiday leaving a stack of filthy dishes in the sink and comes back to a kitchen full of maggots. Every time we visit with the kids, I think they're going to come back with salmonella. But worse than any of that, this is the woman who would still bloody breast-feed you if she could."

Greg is grimacing. "Thank you for that last image."

"You're welcome. The thing is, all you ever do is sing your mother's praises. Meanwhile, here I am trying to run a career, two kids and a home and what thanks do I get?"

"What do you mean, what thanks do you get? I'm always thanking you."

"In your dreams. OK, when was the last time you thanked me for unblocking the toilet or digging hair out of the drain?"

"I dunno. You want actual dates?"

"Yes."

"Don't be so bloody ridiculous. I thank you all the time, but, being a martyr, you choose not to hear it. And anyway, what about me? What about the career I'm trying to run? The people I've got on my back? The worries I have? The exhaustion I feel? Do you thank me for taking all that on my shoulders?"

"Actually, yes, I do. Frequently."

"Bollocks. You take me completely for granted. This whole thing has only ever been about you and your neurotic obsession with the state of the house. It has to stop."

I'm practically weeping with frustration. He's called me neurotic once too often. I want to ask him if it's neurotic to yearn for a clean, tidy adult space where, after the kids have gone to bed, we can sit and have a glass of wine, read a book or listen to music . . . and practice "connecting" again. But I can't get the words out. I'm way too angry.

That's when that I do it. I wasn't intending to put my plan into action so soon into our therapy. It was meant as a last resort—when I felt that talking had failed. I hoped the moment would never come, but it has. I open my large canvas tote, pull out a plastic carrier bag and tip the contents into Greg's lap.

Greg sits blinking. "What the fuck?"

"That, Greg, is a week's worth of your smelly, crusty underpants and socks. All of which I have picked up off the bedroom floor." I'm not done. I produce a small freezer bag and dangle it in front of his face. It contains a load of toe and fingernail clippings. There are also several earbuds thick with orange earwax. I tip the lot onto the pants and socks. Then comes the coup de grâce. "And in here," I say, waving a second freezer bag, "is a load of your pubic hair." I open the bag and shake the contents onto the rest of the pile.

He recoils in disgust. "Oh, for crying out loud!"

"And do you know where I found the pubes?" I'm looking at Virginia Pruitt, who for once is giving the impression of being ever so slightly ill at ease. "On top of a frozen chicken casserole."

Greg tells me I'm being ridiculous. How could pubic hairs have got onto a casserole?

"I'll tell you how. Last night, you were in the upstairs bathroom trimming your pubes, right?"

"I dunno. I may have been."

"And may you also have thrown them out the window?"

He's coloring up again. "Possibly."

"Well, the wind blew them in through the kitchen window and onto the counter where I had left a chicken casserole out to thaw."

"Oh, come on. That's an act of God. It's not like I did it on purpose."

"Stop making excuses." I'm yelling now. "For once in your life, just take some bloody responsibility."

"But it wasn't my fault." He is staring down at the mess of pants, pubes and nail clippings, clearly not knowing what to do.

I want to hear him say he's sorry, that he didn't realize how much he's hurt me over the years, that I could be right when I accuse him of being a spoiled overgrown kid. But all he says is: "You're mad— you know that."

"Fine. If this is madness, then so be it. I don't care."

I have made my point. There is nothing left to say other than that, as far as I am concerned, this session is over. I get up to go.

"Please stay," Virginia Pruitt says. "Believe it or not, I think this has been very positive. Sophie, you have communicated something very powerful here today."

"Yeah, that she's totally insane," Greg says. His tone is bitter and weary. He waves his hand. "Let her go. I've had enough."

Virginia Pruitt is still pleading with me to come back, but I'm already heading down the hall.

I open the front door and step onto Virginia Pruitt's immaculately restored porch. It's raining pitchforks. I can hear thunder in the distance. I haven't got a jacket or an umbrella and Greg has the car keys.

of: "OK, what is it now? Talk to me." Then I'd adjust the air-conditioning or whatever and the whole thing would be over. But today was different. Until now, she'd confined her behavior to her office. I'd never known her to lock herself in the loo or risk the program not going out.

"Nancy, I'm not going away. Whatever has happened, we need to discuss it."

I could hear her sobbing. This was a first. Her tantrums never included actual tears. It occurred to me that for once something serious was going on.

"Come on, what is it?"

"I hate my Volvo," Nancy wailed.

"Why? What's wrong with it?"

"Nothing as far as I know."

"So trade it in for a new one."

"What? I didn't say Volvo. I hate my *vulva*."

"Ah. Oh . . . kay."

"I have this friend who's a shrink and she says I'm suffering from a poor genital self-image."

I took a deep breath. "I see. So why do you think that might be? I mean, has your vulva changed in any way? I was reading this article in one of the women's magazines about how the lips sag as we age."

Bad move. Nancy had just turned forty-five and hated being reminded of it. She was also a mother. Not that this fact was relevant to her plight, since she had refused to give birth vaginally.

"Omigod. You're suggesting that I've got saggy labia?"

"No, of course I'm not. I shouldn't have said that. I don't know what I was thinking. So why do you think you have a poor genital self-image?"

Chapter 1

Six months later

I knocked on the cubicle door a second time. "Nancy, what's going on? Please talk to me. Why won't you come out?"

"Go away."

It was ten minutes to airtime and Nancy Faraday, the presenter of *Coffee Break*, had locked herself in the ladies' and was refusing to come out. Nancy was your regular program presenter nightmare. I'd worked with many like her in my time. These people were the "talent." They had fans, hair and clothes budgets and they let it go to their heads. Hence the tantrums and hissy fits. With Nancy, these tended to be about nothing much: the air-conditioning in the studio was too low, too high; she'd been given a cappuccino when she'd ordered a flat white; the new intern stood too close and invaded her personal space.

It was always me who was called upon to calm her down. Apparently I was the only one who knew how to handle her. Coming from a home where emotions and opinions were expressed freely and at volume, I wasn't frightened by her outbursts. I would give Nancy this careworn look along with a sigh add-on and say something along the lines

"When Brian and I have sex, he never remarks on it." Brian was her chap. They'd been together a year or so and he'd just moved in with Nancy and her children. "It's not fair. I'm always telling him how powerful and hard his penis is—even when it isn't because he's forgotten to take his Viagra." Brian was over sixty. Nancy had a penchant for stylish silver foxes even if, like Brian, they sometimes struggled to rise to the occasion.

"Well, I admit the situation does seem a bit one-sided."

"I've told him that he should return the compliment by telling me how beautiful my vulva is, but he says he can't think of anything to say. He says it's embarrassing. How can he find my vulva embarrassing?"

"Nancy, he doesn't find your vulva embarrassing per se. It's just that he has difficulty talking dirty. Men of his age can be a bit conservative. You need to encourage him."

"How?"

How? Why wasn't her friend the shrink telling her how? "OK, let me think . . . Well, you could suggest the odd phrase, like, 'Your pussy's so hot and wet. I can't wait to come inside you.' That kind of thing."

"That could work. I'm not sure where he stands on 'pussy,' though. He'd probably prefer 'love tunnel.'"

" 'Love tunnel' is fine. Now, then, why don't you come out of the loo? We can do the program and then afterwards we could go for a coffee and talk about this some more."

"OK, I'd like that." Sniff. She slid the bolt across, opened the door and stood in front of me puffy eyed, her face streaked with mascara. She was otherwise immaculate in a size six navy blue wrap dress, patent slingbacks and shoulder-length auburn curls. Style-wise, Nancy was embracing "the new prim" as championed by Catherine, Duchess of Cambridge. I reached for some loo roll and dabbed at her implausibly well-defined cheekbones. Nancy was perfectly open about her Botox habit.

"Come on," I said. "Let's go down to the studio. I've sent somebody to fetch you a cup of tea from the canteen."

"Oh God—not canteen tea. The stuff tastes like cigarette ash in water." Nancy preferred her favorite orange pekoe from the specialist tea shop across the road. Her face performed a half grimace. The Botox wouldn't allow her muscles to complete the full contortion.

"Thanks for the advice, Sophie," she said as we stepped into the lift. "I really appreciate it. I couldn't bear Brian dumping me for another woman the way Greg dumped you."

"Excuse me? Greg didn't dump me for Roz. When we split up he didn't even know her."

"Well, that's not what I heard. You know what the gossip's like in this place."

No, I knew what Nancy was like.

As the lift began its descent towards the basement, I explained that Roz had been living in the States for ten years and had only just returned to London when she and Greg met.

"Really? I had no idea." I waited for Nancy to apologize for her original comment, but she didn't. Instead, as we stepped out of the lift, she gave me one of her looks. Nancy did this a lot—stared at normal-sized women and tried to figure out why they hadn't committed suicide.

———

Phil, the studio manager, looked up from his copy of *Official Xbox Magazine*. "Blimey, you're cutting it a bit fine," he said by way of greeting.

I said something vague about us getting held up and took a seat next to him at the control panel. Meanwhile, Nancy went through to the studio. She put on her headphones. Phil did a quick sound check. Nancy's voice—honed during her years at the BBC—was authoritative but smooth and easy on the ear. Male listeners found it exceedingly sexy and wrote in to the program asking for signed photographs. A few dared to admit that her voice, combined with her intelligence and stern interviewing technique (particularly with scoundrels and politicians), triggered dominatrix fantasies. I imagined these saddos jerking off in seedy bedsits as they listed to the program, crying out: "Beat me, Nancy, beat me."

A moment later the green light on Nancy's desk started to flash and she was welcoming listeners to another edition of *Coffee Break*—her poor genital self-image forgotten, for the time being at least.

Today the program lineup included a report on female craft cooperatives in Uganda, a live debate on whether the law on payments to surrogates should be updated and a ten-minute feature on the English hedgerow in winter. *Coffee Break* had been going for forty years and the stuffy-but-worthy formula had barely changed.

Until recently there seemed no need to change it. Middle-aged, middle-class women in middle England adored the program and appreciative letters and e-mails flooded in daily. Several newspapers had even reported that the Queen was a fan. Since most mornings the monarch was too busy reigning to catch the program, she would instruct a footman to record it and would listen in later with a cup of tea and a slice of Dundee cake.

The problem was that, after four decades, the program's fiercely loyal fan base was dwindling. The audience was aging and even dying off. As a result, listening figures were falling at an alarming rate. Everybody who worked on *Coffee Break* agreed that the program required a revamp and that we needed to attract younger listeners. There were far too many features of the English-hedgerow-in-winter variety. Liz Crawford, the program editor, who had worked on the show for over twenty years and was its fiercest and most outspoken champion, wasn't against modernization in principle, but she knew it would have to be done with much thought and care, so as not to take the program down-market.

Dated as the program was, *Coffee Break*—not to mention Nancy Faraday—was "intelligent." There wasn't a daytime show on radio or TV that came close to offering such a high standard of debate on issues that concerned women. We regularly discussed topics like rape, female circumcision, incest and domestic violence. Recently, after an item on postmastectomy breast reconstruction, a newspaper critic described our coverage of women's health issues as "second to none." The program was also well known for its campaigns. For years we'd fought to increase the number of state-run nurseries and preschools. A few months ago we launched a campaign to improve care for the elderly. As a result, writers and commentators as well as politicians— mainly male—who rather enjoyed sparring with Nancy, flocked to appear on the show. "Lose that intelligence, that *gravitas*," Liz insisted, "and the program as we know it will be dead in the water."

Everybody knew that she was making a valid point. We were all worried about what the future held, but most of us were convinced that Greater London Broadcasting, the company that made *Coffee Break* and syndicated it to radio stations all over the country, would be crazy to destroy a national institution.

After forty-five minutes we were approaching the final item: the serial. This was always a novel, suitably abridged, invariably literary. Today was the first installment of Saki's *The Unbearable Bassington*. It had all been prerecorded and approved, so unless something went drastically wrong technically, my attention was free to wander—at least a little.

These days, when nothing else was pressing (and sometimes even when it was), my thoughts turned to Amy and Ben and how they were coping with Greg and me splitting up. I worried about the kids all the time. When I wasn't worrying, I was feeling guilty about how we'd let them down.

Looking back, maybe we didn't try hard enough to stay together. Maybe Annie was right when she said that we'd ended therapy too soon and hadn't given Virginia Pruitt a chance.

After the fiasco of that second session, Greg and I had a huge fight. It happened in the car. Greg found me walking along Virginia Pruitt's street, heading towards the bus stop, in what had turned into a summer hailstorm. He pulled up, opened the passenger door and barked at me to get in. Under any other circumstances, I would have refused, but I was wearing a cotton dress with nothing on top and was quite literally soaked through.

His gallantry was in no sense a peace offering. Before I'd even shut the car door he was yelling at me: "How could you humiliate me like that?... In front of our *therapist*? After you left, all the hair and nails and earbuds fell onto the floor. I was on my knees for ten minutes clearing it up."

"Ten minutes! Ten effing minutes! Have you any idea how long I spend tidying up after you? And I don't care if I humiliated you. You humiliate me in front of the children every day. You tell them I'm neurotic . . . that I'm a martyr."

"Only because I get so frustrated and angry."

"You're angry! What about me? How do you think I feel after years of you treating me like the hired help?"

Greg pulled over and yanked on the handbrake and said that if I wanted a divorce it was fine by him.

"It's fine by me, too."

"OK, I guess we're both fine with it."

There was nothing left so say. We drove home in silence.

That night he slept in the spare room. The next morning he came into our bedroom to get dressed. By then, we'd both calmed down and were feeling a bit sheepish. Greg said that he was still angry, but had been having second thoughts about getting divorced. I let him know that he wasn't the only one who was still angry, but I agreed that we'd made a decision in the heat of the moment and that more discussion was required. We decided to carry on with therapy.

We had four more sessions with Virginia Pruitt, but it felt as though we were simply going through the motions. There was still the odd moment when we found ourselves connecting, but deep down we knew our marriage was over. We'd known it that night in the car. The problem was that neither of us was strong enough to come out and say it. Deciding to divorce when you're both high on vitriol and adrenaline is easy. People did it all the time and then took it back, the way we had. But it's not so easy in the calm of a new morning. And as for ending it all in the home you've made together, surrounded by wedding photographs, goofy snaps of the kids, your babies' plaster of paris hand- and footprints hanging on the kitchen wall . . . It brought tears to my eyes just thinking about it.

Neither of us had the courage to draw a line under eleven years of marriage. We couldn't say good-bye to a relationship that had begun with so much love and hope. Then there was the question of the children. Other kids coped with divorce, but Amy and Ben weren't other kids. How would they manage? Would they ever forgive us? The pain was too excruciating, so we held off saying what needed to be said.

Virginia Pruitt, on the other hand, seemed desperate to "save" us. So much so that she decided to throw all her psychotherapeutic recourses at our problem. This involved her performing a complete U-turn regarding our need for sex therapy. She informed us that it would be of help after all and started setting us all sorts of "sexy" homework.

There was the nude picnic, which required us to take food and champagne to bed. Spillages that landed on our bodies had to be licked off by the other person. This failed to have the required effect since neither of us found being covered in tuna mayo and saliva very sexy. The naked Ping-Pong ball fights—in which we had to pelt each other with Ping-Pong balls—were sort of fun, but we kept losing the balls under the bed or behind the wardrobe. Retrieving the things took forever and in the end the game became a chore.

The end came quietly, late one night. We were lying in bed, both aware that we should be doing our sex homework. That week we were required to stroke each other's naked bodies with a feather duster, but neither of us could be bothered. As I lay staring at the ceiling, I was overcome by a feeling of utter leaden defeat. Nothing was changing between us. For me at least, the cycle of arguments and silences had finally got to be too much. "Greg, I can't go on like this," I heard myself say.

My husband turned to face me. His voice was gentle. I detected a hint of fear. "Me, neither," he said.

"We've done our best. We've given therapy another go, but it's time to stop kidding ourselves. Neither of us has the energy to make this marriage work."

We talked into the small hours without exchanging a single cross word. A strange calm had descended. Looking back, I think it was relief. It was only when we started discussing what splitting up would do to the kids that we shed a tear.

Finally, when there was nothing left to say, Greg took himself off to the spare room. That night and for many nights to come, I cried myself to sleep.

We had a final "courtesy" session with Virginia Pruitt in which we told her that we'd decided to divorce. She tried to persuade us to give therapy a bit more time, but we insisted that we were done.

"Well, if you need me," she said, "my door is always open." Before we left, she hugged us both and wished us all the best.

It took us several days to find the courage to tell Ben and Amy. We did it with all of us sitting on the big sofa in the living room. I put Ben on my lap. Greg had his arm around Amy. As gently as we could,

Greg and I tried to explain that our love for each other had changed, but we still loved them to bits. We promised that we would always be there for them and that our splitting up wasn't their fault. Of course, they cried and begged us to stay together. As the days went by they even tried to bribe us with promises of good behavior from now until they died. When that didn't work, Amy started throwing tantrums. She said how much she hated us and didn't want us for parents. At one point she called us bloody bastards and said she was moving to Florida with Grandma and Granddad.

Ben didn't lose his temper. Instead, he became sad and withdrawn. He would climb onto Greg's lap and tell him how much he was going to miss him. Greg would try to cheer him up with talk of outings and day trips, but Ben said it wouldn't be the same as hanging out at home. Greg and I would exchange anguished glances. All our hearts were breaking.

It took him a couple of weeks, but eventually Greg found a studio flat a few streets away. He left on a Saturday. We agreed that Ben and Amy would find it too distressing to watch him go—even if it wasn't very far—so I arranged for them to be invited to friends' houses.

I felt guilty as Greg loaded up his newly acquired fourthhand hatchback, but with two kids and their assorted friends needing to be ferried to and from school, birthday parties and after-school activities, it made sense for me-slash-Klaudia to keep the station wagon.

I didn't offer to help him move his stuff. The sadness would have been impossible to bear. Instead I sat outside on the kitchen step while he shifted suitcases and books, his collection of CDs and ancient vinyl.

It was a perfect, cloud-free summer day. Picnic weather. Right now Richmond Park would be full of mums and dads frolicking with kids and dogs. I suddenly felt guilty that we'd never gotten Amy and Ben a dog. They adored Bernard, the drooling greyhound who shared a bed with their grandmother and were always nagging about getting a puppy, but I knew that, with Greg out most evenings, I would get stuck with walking him on dark winter nights. I would be the one who'd have to clean up his accidents. More mess. More stress. I'd told them no. How mean and selfish was that? I took a sip of lukewarm coffee from the TOP MUM mug the kids got me for Mother's Day. I thought about flinging my arms around Greg and telling him we were making a huge mistake and that we should give it another go—for Amy and Ben—if not for us.

"Right, I guess this is it," Greg said, making me jump. I put my coffee down on the step and pulled myself up. I turned to face him. My arms were at my side. I'd decided against any last-minute flinging.

"You got everything?" I said.

"I think so."

"Well, you can always pop back if there's something you've forgotten. You've got a key."

"Sure. And it's not like I'm going far. So . . ."

"Right, then."

"I'll call you," he said. "I'll have the kids on Sunday."

"Great."

"And I suppose we should think about getting lawyers."

"Absolutely. I'll let you know when I've found somebody."

"Ditto."

He gave me a chaste kiss on the cheek and told me to take care.

"You, too."

I went upstairs to pee. The toilet was blocked.

The dozen or so *Coffee Break* producers and reporters—plus Nancy and me—piled into the conference room for the program postmortem. Nancy was in a more upbeat mood. She and I had spent the half hour between the end of the show and the postmort in her office, I listening while she continued to vent about Brian's failing to pay sufficient attention to her vulva. When I suggested that the two of them have a few sessions with Virginia Pruitt, she leapt at the idea. (Her therapist friend didn't "do" couples.) This didn't surprise me, since Nancy loved any opportunity to talk about herself. She thought Brian might take some persuading, but she was sure she could get around him.

Liz had already taken her place at the head of the long table. She was a youthful sixty, but today she looked gray and pinched—completely done in. As everybody sat down, she offered me a tight-lipped smile.

"What?" I said, putting a hand on her shoulder.

She squeezed my hand and I knew.

Liz waited for everybody to settle down and for Nancy to stop moaning about how freezing it was in the room. How quickly the woman's moods changed. In the end she sent one of the interns to fetch her pashmina.

"OK," Liz began. "Before we discuss today's program, I need to let you know that the latest audience figures are in and they're down again." She explained that she'd just come out of a meeting with James Harding, the chairman of Greater London Broadcasting. "Bottom line . . . he feels that we've dithered long enough about making changes on *Coffee Break*. He's insisting on a complete face-lift and a program relaunch."

"So will he be letting people go?" Nancy asked, voicing what we were all thinking.

"Absolutely not. There are to be no redundancies. Jim's assured me on that score."

"That's well and good," one of the reporters broke in, "but precisely what kind of changes is Harding planning?"

"He won't say. He's playing this thing very close to his chest, but you all know my thoughts on this. All he would tell me is that he's taking on a media change consultant—whatever that might be— and that he will be guided by this person's recommendations."

Eyes rolled, including mine.

"I think we can all guess what sort of changes he'll have in mind," Liz said. "During our meeting, Jim made it clear that he thought the program needed to be made more accessible."

"In other words, dumbed down," I said.

"I suspect so. To be honest, this isn't looking good. You all need to make up your minds about what you will do."

"Have you made up yours?" I said to Liz, knowing full well what was coming.

She took off her specs. "I have. I suggested to Jim that since I am only a few years off retirement, this might be a good time for me to stand down as program editor. He didn't raise any objections."

Chapter 2

Annie opened the oven door, peered in and said that the scones would be ready in a few minutes.

She'd phoned at lunchtime to invite me and the kids over. She said she felt like having some company because Rob had arranged to spend the afternoon at his tennis club, trying out one of the newly built indoor courts.

"But he usually takes the boys swimming on Saturdays," I said.

"I know, but he's had a really stressful week at work and he's off to Tokyo tonight, so I thought he deserved some downtime."

She'd seemed unusually delighted when I said we weren't doing anything and would love to come. By the time we arrived, Annie's house was full of glorious baking smell.

She returned to the table. "So, getting back to Liz," she said, reaching for the teapot (vintage Royal Albert, decorated with rosebuds and forget-me-nots). "She'll get a decent payout, plus a pension. I suspect she'll do rather nicely . . . Top up?"

"Please." I slid my mug (Cath Kidston) across the refectory table (antique pine, painted and "distressed" by Annie). "That's the point.

She *is* quids in, and if I'm honest, we're all a bit envious. Nobody be-grudges her the money. *Coffee Break* has been Liz's baby for twenty years and she's worked her socks off. The point is that she's in a posi-tion to walk away over a matter of principle and nobody else is. Un-like Liz, we'd have to find new jobs, but with all the cuts and redundancies we wouldn't stand a hope. Everybody's petrified about what this media change consultant is going to do to the program. I'm still trying to convince them that the program won't go *that* down-market, but if I'm honest, I'm pretty sure it will."

"If you ask me," Annie said, handing me the milk jug, "only an idiot would take it down-market. *Coffee Break* is an institution. You don't tamper with institutions. There would be an outcry."

"That's what I thought until now, but these days there's such an appetite for trash."

"That doesn't mean there aren't thousands of people crying out for good-quality, intelligent programs. I bet this media whatnot per-son gives *Coffee Break* a few painless tweaks and that'll be it. Liz could even end up regretting her decision to go."

"God, you're so . . . so *Elmo*," I said.

Annie laughed. "Well, it's better than going around like Dr. House all the time." She stopped herself. "I'm sorry. I shouldn't have said that. You've been through a really rough time these past few months. You have every right to be cynical."

"I do my best not to be. And I thought I'd really cheered up lately."

"You have. God, if I think back to how you were . . ."

———

I hadn't expected to feel on top of the world after Greg left, but the depth of the sadness that came over me caught me off guard. After all, it wasn't as if I'd had to deal with the trauma of discovering he'd been cheating on me. Our marriage had simply run out of steam. Nor was it as if he'd left suddenly, without warning. I'd been prepared and was ready for him to go. Or so I thought.

In those early days, it was as much as I could do to get out of bed. All I wanted to do was sleep—which was ironic, because at night I couldn't get to sleep.

I couldn't eat, either. And my body felt like a ten-ton weight. I kept going because I knew that Amy and Ben were depending on me to be strong and because I needed to earn a living.

I soon realized that I was in shock. Part of me couldn't believe that my marriage was over.

It didn't help that Mum and Dad had left for Florida a month or so after Greg and I split up.

When I told them that Greg and I were getting a divorce, they were heartbroken, but not in quite the way I'd expected. In the days after I'd broken the news to them, Mum would call and weep down the phone: "I can't believe this is happening. It's all too much. I've started waking up in the night with palpitations and your dad's acid reflux has gotten so bad the doctor has upped the dose of his proton-pump inhibitor."

It wasn't that they didn't care about how the kids and I were doing—or about Greg, come to that—it was simply that, these days, they found emotional upheaval hard to deal with. Mum and Dad were eighty. They had their aches and pains, but they were by no means frail, either mentally or physically. That said, over the last couple of years Phil, my sister, Gail, and I had noticed that their ability to cope with life relied heavily on certainty, routine and an absence of emotional turmoil. When their equilibrium was disturbed, it threw them. Heaven forbid the washer broke down, a delivery was late or they were invited out to dinner, which meant them having to eat at seven rather than six.

Whereas Mum seemed to take the aging process in stride—"Look at me, I'm falling apart, but what can you do?"—Dad found it harder to accept. He got frustrated with the stiffness in his bones, his lack of puff, his occasional forgetfulness.

It didn't help that he wasn't really cut out for old age. "It's so demeaning. Now I'm the first person they're going to let off the plane during a hijack," he said.

Until he was seventy, Dad had run his own printing business. Mum and us kids aside, the business had been his life. It defined him. Now it was gone. He admitted that without work he found it hard to fill his days. This particular struggle did, of course, drive my mother crazy. He hated not being the boss, not having a staff to run, that nobody (apart from Mum) was relying on him. He often said that he regretted letting the business go when he did, forgetting that he'd spent the years leading up to his retirement complaining that he didn't have the energy to keep working.

Even though Mum found it easier to accept that her body was slowing down, there were some frustrations she shared with Dad. Both of them hated it when younger, often well-meaning people—doctors or nurses—patronized them with their fake jolliness and insistence on addressing them by their first names. Their generation liked to be called "mister" and "missus"—it was a mark of respect.

Being patronized was bad enough, but the worst crime a person could commit was to ignore them. It drove them crazy. "Excuse me, young lady, but do you mind telling me why you've been busy serving all these people when we were here first?" Mum and Dad believed that once a person hit seventy or so the world pretty much stopped noticing them. They became invisible.

The move to Florida had been Phil's idea. He hadn't seen much of Mum and Dad since moving to the United States more than two decades ago—a couple of trips back home a year, if that—and now he wanted to make it up to them. It also seemed to make particular sense, since he and Betsy, whose work as a nurse at the local hospital often took her to the geriatric wards, had a big house with a pool and a granny annex.

At first, Mum and Dad wouldn't even consider the idea, which of course came as no surprise. A move to the next street would have been enough to send their anxiety levels soaring, let alone a move to "the other side of the world." They couldn't bear the idea of uprooting themselves from their home and the neighborhood where they'd lived for fifty years, of leaving Gail, me and the grandchildren, the few friends they had left who hadn't departed this life.

Gail and I said we'd miss them, but we promised to visit with the kids and did our best to persuade them that, at their time of life, lazing beside a pool in the Florida sun was infinitely preferable to struggling in the cold and damp. It was like talking to a brick wall.

Phil refused to give up, though, and spent months working on them. He even came over to pitch the idea in person. Gradually they came around. They could see that it made sense for them to be living in a warmer, healthier climate where, when they became frail, they could be looked after by their son the doctor and his wife the nurse.

We promised them that the move would be as stress-free as possible. To that end Gail's husband, Murray, handled the sale of their house and Gail and I helped them clear out all their junk—not that it was easy, particularly where Mum was concerned: "Don't throw out all those plastic carriers. There are some nice strong bags there! . . . I'll make room in my suitcase for the sachets of sugar and Sweet'N Low."

Mum and Dad might have been old, self-absorbed and ill-equipped to offer me their shoulders to cry on, but it didn't stop me from pining for them. It reminded me of how I pined for them as a child when they went away for the occasional weekend, leaving me with Grandma Yetta, who sat in the armchair all day, watching the wrestling and sucking on chalky indigestion tablets that turned her lips white.

They had a computer and the Internet now, so we were able to Skype, but only when Phil was around to show them what to do. Because Mum and Dad weren't at ease with being "on camera," it was all a bit stiff and overformal.

I missed the intimacy we'd once shared: our mutual "pop-ins," Mum calling to say she needed a pound of Jersey Royals and some Ex-Lax and could I pick them up the next time I was in the supermarket? Part of me was even missing the way she walked into my kitchen, ran her finger over the cooker hood and grimaced. "Darling, why don't you let me and your dad pay to have the kitchen deep-cleaned by one of those companies—you know, the ones who specialize in cleaning up at messy crime scenes? It could be your birthday present." Cheers, Mum.

In the days and weeks after Greg left, I felt unbearably, excruciatingly lonely. Night after night, I found myself lying in bed, thinking back to when we were first married. I remembered the laughter, the sex, his warm body lying next to me, his affectionate touches, the arms that would wrap me up when I was feeling down. I remembered the daft late-night discussions we'd have. Why isn't "palindrome" spelled the same way backwards? What's another word for "thesaurus"? What do you talk to a coma victim about if they don't like sports?

All I could remember were the good times. I had to keep on reminding myself why my marriage fell apart.

Annie was the person who came over with wine and pizza and held me while I cried.

"And on top of everything, we've still got mice in the kitchen," I wailed. It was Annie who made the call to the pest control people.

When I told her that I couldn't forgive myself for failing Amy and Ben, she assured me that kids were resilient and that so long as Greg and I carried on loving them and remained united as parents, they would be fine.

But they weren't fine—at least not in the beginning. Amy started coming into my bed in the middle of the night, saying she was scared that I was going to die. Ben wanted to know if parents could divorce their children.

I knew they were also missing their grandparents. Mum and Dad's house was as familiar to them as their own, and now that was gone, too. Another great chunk of their security chipped away. They spent a lot of time reminiscing about Grandma and Granddad. I enjoyed hearing them share their memories, but at the same time it made me sad. I couldn't help thinking that it was almost as if Mum and Dad had died. Ben said he remembered my dad teaching him how to swim underwater and about Nazis. Amy said there were two things she remembered most about my mum. "She taught me to say 'mother' instead of 'muvver' and how to blow my nose."

I saw Greg only when he came to collect Amy and Ben or drop them home, or if there was a school function. I never got any sense that he was struggling with the breakup, which—since I was taking it so badly—sort of pissed me off. On the other hand, I had no idea what he was feeling, alone at night in some soulless flat. (I'd never seen it, but the kids seemed to like it. They loved the idea of having a queen bed in the same room as the microwave and TV.)

Then, one Sunday night after he'd brought the children home—we were a couple of months into the separation—Greg asked me if we could speak in private. It occurred to me that he was going to say he'd had second thoughts about the separation and wanted to come home. Back then, feeling the way I did, I might have said yes.

We went into the kitchen. I closed the door. It turned out that I couldn't have been more wrong .

"I thought I ought to let you know," he said, "that I'm seeing somebody."

Call me naive, but this was the last thing I'd been expecting.

"Wow! Really? Well . . . hey . . . good for you." I did my best to give the impression I was totally cool with Greg's new "dating" status, but discovering that he had a girlfriend—with our marriage barely cold in its grave—felt like being punched. For a start, it made our separation seem even more real. And don't ask me why, but for some absurd reason I felt instantly and overwhelmingly jealous. I didn't want Greg, but at the same time I didn't want anybody else to have him. At least not yet. Plus I had wanted to be first to find somebody new. It felt somehow ungallant for Greg to start dating before me.

The new woman in his life turned out to be Roz Duffy, the feminist academic, author and newly appointed professor of English at King's College. They had met at the launch of her latest book, *The Fanciful Vagina: Women as Mythology.*

I couldn't help myself. "I always thought Roz Duffy was a lesbian," I said by way of congratulations.

When I told Annie about feeling jealous, she said that part of me would always have feelings for Greg. After all, he had been my first true love and he was the father of my children. I suspected she might be right.

Eventually, the melancholy lifted. Life settled into a new routine, which I was starting to enjoy. On the weekends when Greg had the kids (in the beginning we agreed that this should be sans Roz), I would go shopping, see people for dinner, take in a movie or just lie on the sofa reading the papers or watching TV. I began to look forward to those days on my own. I hadn't realized how much stress I'd been under living with Greg. It was such a relief now that he and it were gone.

The house was still pretty chaotic. It wasn't as if the kids had left, too. On the upside, it had been ages since I'd had to unblock the loo. And the mice were long gone.

I was doing my best to stay on top of things housework-wise, but the truth was, even with Mrs. Fredericks coming in twice a week, I'd lost control years ago. It occurred to me that if I hired a cleaning company and enlisted friends to give me a hand clearing out all the junk and clutter, I could have the place sorted in a week. Then I could think about redecorating. It would be fun choosing paint and wallpaper—Annie would help. But I kept putting it off. My job and running the kids took up all my time. I would get around to it, though. Eventually.

Greg had been seeing Roz for three months or so when he asked me if I thought it would be OK for the children to meet her. I played for time by telling him that I would think about it. When he pressed me for a decision, I made excuses. I said that Amy and Ben weren't ready and that I wasn't sure how they'd cope. It might have looked like I was trying to protect my children, but in fact I was trying to protect myself. I was terrified that the already gifted Roz Duffy would turn out to be some kind of child whisperer. She would cast a spell on my children and make them fall in love with her. She would steal them from me— emotionally, if not physically.

On the other hand, I knew that if Greg and I were to remain on civil terms, I had to agree to her becoming part of the children's lives. It wasn't easy, but I gave in.

The first time they met—at her place, for Sunday lunch—I held my own lunch party. I was determined not to spend the day alone, getting maudlin. Annie was there, along with some of the mums I'd known since prenatal classes, when I was pregnant with Amy. I cooked a huge shepherd's pie and for dessert I made baguette and butter pudding. Before they left, the kids saw I was preparing their favorite dessert and were really cross. (Could I possibly have done it on purpose to make them feel bad about what they were missing?) I promised to save them some.

Over a boozy lunch, we women talked about the usual girlie stuff: clothes, diets, house extensions, but mainly we talked about our kids. Debbie, my neighbor from down the road, mother to Ella and Jack, who were the same ages as Amy and Ben, said she was thinking about having a third. Somebody recalled how she'd been in labor for seventeen hours with her last baby. "There I was lying there, screaming for an epidural, and you know what my husband says? 'Come on, just relax and enjoy the moment.'"

I suggested that maybe Victoria Beckham had got it right, having four cesareans.

"Typical of a Spice Girl, though," Annie said. "Always miming."

Everybody knew that I was fretting about the kids meeting Roz. They kept trying and failing to cheer me up.

"I mean, she's got a brain the size of a planet," I said, draining my third glass of wine. "She's published umpteen books. What's the betting she's kind and funny and brilliant with kids? Oh, and she's bound to be gorgeous."

Annie frowned. "You mean you've never seen her on TV? She's never been a guest on *Coffee Break*?"

"Don't think so."

"And you haven't Googled her?"

I said that I hadn't, on the grounds that I already knew enough about her to feel intellectually inadequate. I had no intention of torturing myself further by discovering she looked like Angelina Jolie.

Annie noticed my laptop lying on the sofa. She got up and brought it back to the table.

"Please, Annie," I pleaded. "If you're my friend, don't do this."

"Believe me, I am *so* your friend." She started hitting the keys.

Soon everybody was gathered around the computer, except me.

"So go on, tell me," I said, necking more wine. "She looks like a goddess, doesn't she?"

Everybody was laughing. "Come on," Annie said. "Take a look."

I got up and looked. Roz Duffy would have been rather attractive if it hadn't been for the mass of comedy hair.

"Omigod," I heard myself say. "Look at that frizz. It's Art Garfunkel."

I carried on peering at the picture. What was she wearing? It looked like some earthy chic patchwork jacket—the sort of thing one might team with thick woolen tights and clogs. "OK, I have to admit that I'm relieved my soon-to-be ex-husband's girlfriend is somewhat lacking in the babe stakes, but could somebody please tell me what he sees in her?"

"Big brains," Debbie-from-down-the-road said.

"Oh, and check this out," Annie was saying. "Is that a mustache?"

In the end, we decided it was a trick of the light. Debbie-from-down-the-road said it was disappointing, but you couldn't have everything.

"So what's Roz like?" I asked Amy and Ben after they'd gotten back from their visit. I knew it was wrong to pump my children for information in order to assuage my insecurities, but only a saint could have held back.

"Nice," Ben said. "She's got a dog."

Of course she did. She probably went out and adopted it especially in order to win the children's affection.

"And she's got two sons. They're called Dan and Tom. They're big. They go to university and they sleep a lot."

The fact that her kids sounded pretty normal only made me dislike her more.

Ben helped himself to a bag of salt-and-vinegar potato chips and disappeared into the living room to watch TV.

"The dog's this really old Irish setter," Amy explained. "She's called Dworkin. She came to the park with us."

Dworkin? You couldn't have made it up.

"She's named after this really famous dead woman who said it's wrong for men to look at pictures of naked women. Roz and I had this long talk about pornography."

What? Frizzy-Haired Feminist had been discussing porn with my ten-year-old daughter. How dare she? I was Amy's mother and conversations like that were my province.

"Really? What did you talk about exactly?"

"Roz said that when men look at pictures of naked women, it turns them into sex objects. What's a sex object?"

"OK . . . well . . . it's complicated, but what she's trying to say is that men shouldn't simply see women as attractive items or things. Because that way, they're ignoring their intelligence and their personalities . . . and it's those things that make women who they are."

"OK . . . so is it wrong that I like Justin Bieber just 'cos he's good looking?"

"It's a bit different with men, but I guess it is, yes."

Just then, Ben reappeared and took an apple from the fruit bowl. "Mum, why can't we get a dog?"

"Oh, hon, I've told you. I'm at work all day. Klaudia has classes. Who would walk it and talk to it? The poor animal would be so lonely."

He bit into his apple. "Roz says there are people who look after dogs during the day."

"Did she also tell you that these people cost money?"

"Uh-uh."

"So what did Roz make for lunch?"

"Lasagna," Amy said.

"Nice?"

"Great."

Crap.

"It was vegetarian. Roz doesn't believe in killing animals for food."

Of course she didn't.

The moment the kids were asleep, I was on the phone to Greg.

"Can you explain to me why Roz thought it was OK to talk about porn with our ten-year-old daughter?"

"What are you on about? It was nothing. Amy asked her why the dog was called Dworkin, that's all."

"No, that isn't all. Our little girl has just asked me what a sex object is. My God, Greg, you're the one always going on about preserving the innocence of childhood."

"Look, Amy's nearly eleven. She's an intelligent kid and it's not like she doesn't know about sex. She asked questions and Roz answered her honestly. Does she seem disturbed to you?"

"No, but that's not the point. Roz crossed a boundary. I'm Amy's mother and it's me, not Roz, who gets to talk to her about this kind of stuff, when I decide the time is right."

"OK, I'll speak to her."

"You do that."

"Oh, by the way, I have some news. Roz and I have decided to take our relationship to the next level."

"Meaning?" I came back, aware of the sharpness still in my voice.

"She suggested I move in with her and I've said yes."

It took me a moment to take in what he'd said. "Wow . . . So you're in love with her?"

"Yes. Very much."

Back in Annie's kitchen, the oven timer pinged. She slipped her hands into an oven mitt and removed a tray of scones. Golden cushions of perfectness.

As she hunted for a cooling rack, she carried on moaning about having to go to her aged in-laws for Christmas, which was only a couple of weeks away. "Their place is so big, they refuse to heat it during the day. And Rob's mum always refuses to let me help with lunch, so we end up with overcooked veg and half-raw turkey. It's going to be a nightmare. Before they invited us, I was planning to ask you and the kids to come here."

I explained that it wasn't a problem, as Greg and I would be putting on a show of parental togetherness over the festive season and that as far as Amy and Ben were concerned it was Christmas as usual. Roz and her boys were going to Wales to stay with her mother.

"So how are you feeling about Greg moving in with Frizzy-Haired Feminist?" By now Annie had found a cooling rack and was laying out the scones.

"Maybe this will give you some idea," I said, reaching into my bag and pulling out a Christmas card. Amy and Ben had given it to me the other day after they got back from staying with Greg and Roz. I'd been bursting to show it to Annie.

"Take a look," I said.

Annie wiped her hands on a tea towel and came back to the table. She took the card from me, peered at it and gasped.

"Apparently, just as the kids were leaving her place after a visit, Roz's cards arrived from the printers. She said they could bring one home to show me."

"Good God. I don't believe it. Just look at that photograph. It's appalling."

"The kids love it. They haven't stopped telling me how much fun they had doing it."

Annie carried on staring at the picture. It showed Greg, Roz, her kids and mine, plus Dworkin, arranged in front of a blazing log fire. Stockings hung from the mantelpiece. All of them, including the dog, were wearing Santa hats and beards. Ben was pulling a cracker with one of Roz's sons. Roz and Greg were clinking champagne glasses.

"This is one big bowl of wrong," Annie said. "The swine. You've been separated for six months. You're not even divorced yet. How dare Greg play happy families like this."

"I know. Not only is he in a new relationship, but he feels the need to rub my nose in it. It's so mean."

"Bloody cruel is what it is. What are you going to do? You have to say something."

"No, I don't. I'm damned if I'm going to give either of them the satisfaction of letting them know they've upset me."

"Great if you can pull it off. I know I couldn't. I'd be on the phone crying my eyes out."

Just then Freddie came running in. Freddie was Annie's golden-of-curl, blue-of-eye firstborn. He was six and the image of his father. His brother, Tom, was four and tawny haired and covered in freckles like Annie.

"Please, may I please have some more raisins?" Annie was hot on ensuring her boys said their pleases and thank-yous. She was hot on good manners in general. Urged on by Greg, who bridled at excessive politeness in small children, calling it bourgeois and twee, I had been less hot with Amy and Ben. The upshot was that my children barged in on adult conversations, wiped their noses on their napkins and gargled with their drinks at mealtimes.

"You may have some more," Annie said, picking up the box and pouring raisins into her son's bowl. "And well done for asking so politely." Annie, who had read all the child care manuals, was also a strong believer in praising good behavior: "Wow, good sharing . . . great listening . . . excellent waiting." I couldn't remember her ever losing her temper with the boys. Instead, when they misbehaved, she stayed calm, took them to one side and quietly explained to them what they'd done wrong.

Just before Greg and I split up, we went to Annie and Rob's for Sunday lunch. At one point, Freddie and Tom, who'd been allowed a glass of fizzy pop each before lunch, started farting. After each—

fairly minor—explosion, they would burst into fits of giggles. Rob tended to be pretty laid-back with the boys and, left to his own devices, would probably have ignored it. Annie, on the other hand, put down her knife and fork and, without raising her voice, said: "Boys, I know it's fun making bottom burps, but you really shouldn't do it at the table."

When the boys carried on farting, Annie threatened them with the naughty corner. Rob told her to lay off, clearly anticipating a scene at the lunch table. But he needn't have worried. At the very mention of the naughty corner, the boys begged to be allowed to stay at the table. They behaved impeccably for the rest of the meal.

That day, seeing Annie in action, I had never felt so inadequate as a parent. When they were small, my kids thought the naughty corner was huge fun and used to go there voluntarily to play imaginary games.

*F*reddie was smiling now, clearly reveling in his mother's approval. "And don't forget to share," Annie said, ruffling his hair. He nodded and disappeared back into the living room, where his brother and my two were watching *Finding Nemo.* Since it was Saturday, Amy and Ben should have been with their dad, but he'd called at eight that morning—sounding not all himself—to say that he'd been throwing up all night. In fact, while we were on the phone he even broke off to puke loudly into a bucket, which proved he had no hidden agenda—not that I really thought he had. In the six months we'd been apart, he'd never once tried to get out of having the children.

He decided he had food poisoning, most likely from some dodgy shrimp he'd had the night before. I offered to come over with fizzy glucose drinks, but he said that all he wanted to do was sleep. I wished him better, and when he said he felt guilty about not seeing the kids, I told him not to worry and suggested he take them out for pizza one evening when he was feeling up to it.

While I put the kettle on for more tea and poured juice for the children, Annie transferred the scones to a Victorian glass cake stand and took them to the table. Pretty, antique tea plates—none of which matched—were already in place. Annie would pick up eye-catching plates and cup and saucer sets at junk shops and flea markets. She owned dozens.

Her kitchen chairs were an idiosyncratic assortment of styles and eras. Then there was the yard sale crystal chandelier that hung over the distressed kitchen table. "Distressed?" my mother had whispered to me the time we popped in to coo over Freddie just after he was born. "It looks suicidal. And can't she afford matching cups?" To my mother, words like "set" and "suite" were sacraments. As far as she was concerned, "shabby chic" was merely shabby.

No sooner had Annie and Rob moved into this house than Annie had started collecting fabric swatches, wallpaper samples, dozens of those tiny tryout tins of paint. Who knew there were so many shades of white? She fussed over tiles and textures, fretted over faucets. She took a course to learn how to reupholster chairs and sofas.

She was also tidy and organized. The upshot was that Annie's house felt like a proper home. Mine was just a place where the kids and I ate and slept.

"Annie, how do you do it?"

"How do I do what?"

"This . . . the baking, the perfectly behaved kids, the stylish, crud-free house. Everything in your life seems to be so calm and well ordered. I feel like I'm always running to catch up with myself."

"You know how I do it," she said, grinning. "I'm a surrendered wife."

I laughed. "Yeah, right. That'll be it."

"You mock, but there's a grain of truth in it."

She was right. There was. Before having the children, Annie had been a radio producer at the BBC. That's where we met. We worked at *The World at One* together. Then I moved to GLB. She stayed on at the Beeb until she had Freddie. She'd always intended to take the year's maternity leave she was entitled to, but a few weeks after their son was born Annie and Rob sat down and had a long talk about the future, now that they were parents. They came to the conclusion that, for them, family life could work only if they assumed traditional roles—Rob as breadwinner and Annie as mother and homemaker.

"You and I are different," Annie went on. "You'd go crazy if you didn't work. I'm not so driven. I enjoy being a full-time mother and making a home. I feel like I'm doing my bit for the next generation. It really pisses me off that stay-at-home mothers are so undervalued. And anyway, Rob could never cope if I weren't here running things."

Rob was a corporate lawyer who was forever tearing about the globe, closing multimillion-pound deals.

"You don't know that."

"Yes, I do. The man gets lost trying to find his way to the kitchen. He hasn't the foggiest where we even keep the Hoover. I truly believe that he thinks the sock and underwear fairy puts all his clean laundry away."

"He'd have to change if you went back to work."

"You mean, like Greg changed."

"Greg's different. He thinks tidiness is petit bourgeois . . . I don't get it, Annie. People had you down as a future *World at One* editor. And you gave it all up to star in *Mad Men*."

"All I can say is that it works for us. It keeps things simple and straightforward. We both know where we are." She took a dish of posh Normandy butter over to the table.

"You think I asked too much of Greg, don't you? And that's why my marriage failed."

"I don't know, Soph. It's not for me to say. Only you can know that."

"But you suspect that if I'd given up work and stayed at home with the kids, Greg and I might still be together."

"Do you think that?" she said.

I shrugged. "Maybe. Who knows?"

Just then all four kids appeared. The movie had finished and they were claiming to be starving. Annie sat them down and began slicing and buttering scones.

Freddie, who was waiting to be served, started spinning his plate. Just as Annie was asking him to stop because there was going to be an accident, the plate crashed to the floor. Dozens of pieces lay scattered around the table.

"Fuck—" Freddie said, slapping his hand to his mouth. "I mean *oops*. Only daddies say 'fuck.'"

It was all I could do not to burst out laughing. When Annie started yelling at Freddie, I couldn't believe it. The rest of the children were stunned into silence. "You naughty, naughty boy. How dare you say that word. It's rude and disgusting. Do you hear me?"

"I'm sorry, I'm sorry—I didn't mean it. Don't shout. Please don't shout." Freddie was clearly distressed. Tears were streaming down his face. I wanted to pick him up and give him a cuddle. Then Annie scooped him up and held him to her, rocking him and kissing him. By now she was close to tears.

"I'm sorry, darling. I'm so, so sorry. I didn't mean to shout. I don't know what came over me."

"Freddie's not a bad boy," his brother, Tom, said.

"No, of course he's not. It was me who was bad."

"Bad Mummy." Freddie was starting to giggle. He gave her a playful smack on the arm and that seemed to be that. He jumped off her lap and Annie carried on handing out scones.

"Now, then, who's for jam?"

I couldn't let the incident go. I knew plenty of mothers who shouted at their kids—myself included—but Annie wasn't one of them. Seeing Annie lose it like that worried me. After tea, when the children had disappeared back into the living room, I asked her if she was OK. "I've never seen you get angry with the boys, that's all."

She avoided my gaze and carried on clearing the table. "It's nothing. Time of the month. I always get low blood sugar."

I could have pointed out that, in all the years I'd known Annie, she'd never mentioned that she suffered from PMS. I could have reminded her that before her outburst she'd wolfed down a couple of scones and jam. I did neither, partly because Rob showed up.

He dumped his gym bag on the kitchen floor—no doubt for Annie to sort out—and declared his manhood with an air-tennis serve before announcing that he had beaten "that smug git Dave Pilkington, seven-five, six-two, six-oh."

"Well done," Annie said, continuing to load the dishwasher.

Rob didn't seem to notice his wife's halfhearted congratulations. He came bounding over to me, wrapped me in one of his bear hugs and asked how I was doing. I told him I was good, much better than I had been. "We wanted to have you and the kids here for Christmas, but my parents invited us there. Come for New Year's Eve. We're having a party."

This caught Annie's attention. "Hang on—that's the first I've heard of it."

"We may as well. We'll never get a babysitter for New Year's Eve. And it'll be fun. You could roast a ham, do a few salads and a couple of your fruit tarts . . ."

"I guess."

"Right, I'd better get a move on," he said, looking at his watch. "I'm due at the airport at seven." He turned to Annie. "Did you pick up my dry cleaning, hon?"

"Yes. And before you ask, I bought you a load of new socks and underpants. They're on the bed. And I've folded your shirts and picked out a couple of ties. And don't forget to pack your cuff links."

"I won't. Did I ever tell you how totally wonderful and amazing you are?"

He planted a kiss on her cheek, downed a remaining scone in a couple of mouthfuls and said he was going to take a shower.

"Fine," Annie said. She picked up Rob's gym bag and started to unzip it.

Chapter 3

"I think you're reading too much into it," Gail said when she called later that evening. "Like she said, Annie was probably just a bit hormonal."

"Maybe, but I've never known her to shout at her kids."

"Oh, come on. We all shout at our kids—especially when we're premenstrual."

"Annie doesn't. At least she didn't used to. And she seemed a bit off with Rob. Not that I blame her. He's not a slob like Greg, but he definitely expects her to run around after him. Until now, I've never seen her get irritable with him. She's always going on about how great her life is, but I think she's finally got fed up with the way he treats her."

"She needs to get a housekeeper. That's what you should have done. It's one of the reasons your marriage fell apart."

"I can't believe you just said that. My marriage ended because I didn't have a *housekeeper*?"

"I said it was *one* of the reasons. What you don't get is that this whole 'new man' thing is a fallacy. Feminism did women no good.

Even now, women are fighting a losing battle. What we have to understand is that men are all lazy, self-absorbed slobs. Football is their religion and the pub is their cathedral."

"That's not true. Plenty of my girlfriends have husbands who are tidy and help around the house."

"Yeah, but they also wear sunblock, Birkenstocks with fawn socks and make chutney. Fine, if that's the type of guy you want, but *real* men are a handful. The only way for a wife to cope with running a home is to get a wife. I'd be lost without Violetta. When you have a full-time live-in housekeeper, there are no arguments about who does what."

I said that I took the point about the lack of arguments. "But Greg and I couldn't have afforded a live-in housekeeper, so it's all pretty moot."

"I bet you anything Frizzy-Haired Feminist has got a housekeeper."

I laughed. "What? Bet she hasn't. Hard-core feminists like her do not employ other women to clean their toilets. They think it's exploitative."

"So by not employing them—in a recession—they're doing them a favor?"

I said it wasn't me she needed to convince.

"So who do you think cleans her house?" Gail said.

"I'm guessing nobody. She probably lives in an even bigger mess than I do, which probably suits Greg down to the ground."

"Anyway, getting back to Annie. You tell her from me to start ringing around domestic agencies."

"Gail, not every problem can be solved by throwing money at it.

And I'm not sure that Annie and Rob could stretch to hire a housekeeper."

"What? Rob's a corporate lawyer. They earn a fortune."

I reminded her that Rob hadn't made partner yet, and while they could afford a twice-weekly cleaner, they weren't quite in the housekeeper bracket.

My sister, the fifty-one-year-old Jewish princess with hair extensions, nail extensions and house extensions so numerous that nobody could find the original four-bed semi, didn't appreciate that not everybody lived like her. Greg always joked that if a beggar approached Gail and told her he hadn't eaten in three days, she would have patted his hand and said: "Darling, you have to force yourself."

Gail had always been the domineering older sister. She denied it, of course, and preferred to think of her bossiness as "mothering." There were nearly twelve years between us—ten between our brother, Phil, and me—and Gail had been "mothering" both of us, but me in particular, ever since I could remember.

I was our parents' "happy accident," and straightaway Gail became Mum's little helper. She learned how to bathe and feed me and change my diapers. When Mum felt like having a nap, she would get Gail to walk me in the pram. I don't think she ever saw me as a sister. I was her "practice" daughter. I certainly always thought of her as my second mum.

For the last few years she'd been trying—and failing—to mother our parents. As they got older, she worried about their health, but they weren't interested in sessions with her personal trainer, consultations with her nutritionist or one of those impossibly expensive health checks, which include a colonoscopy and an MRI scan and which can practically pinpoint the day you're going to depart this world.

The day Mum and Dad left for Florida, Gail and I—plus Gail's husband, Murray, and all four of our kids—saw them off at Heathrow. Between the hugs and tears, Gail didn't stop nagging them about wearing the anti-deep-vein-thrombosis flight socks she'd bought them. "And remember that practically all the food you buy in the U.S. is packed with sugar. They think muffins and granola are health foods. I'm FedEx-ing you a dozen jumbo packs of sugar-free muesli and some eighty-percent-cocoa-solids chocolate bars. Hershey's tastes of vomit."

In the end, Murray had to practically pry Gail and me away from Mum and Dad. We saw them through passport control and they stopped for one final look back. "Go! Go!" I cried, making shooing motions. "And put on the socks," Gail yelled. "Put on the socks." One more wave and they disappeared.

I moaned about Gail's "mothering," but over the last few months she, like Annie, had done her best to lift my spirits. She would phone to announce that she was taking me shopping or that she'd booked us a spa day and would badger me until I agreed to go.

Dr. Phil was on my case, too. He kept calling to ask if I was having suicidal thoughts. He even offered to phone this Harley Street shrink he knew, which managed to make me feel even more depressed.

I felt that the least I could do to return everybody's kindness was to pull myself together, but no matter how hard I tried, I couldn't.

At one point, Annie said she couldn't work out why I was so miserable, particularly when Greg and I had been so unhappy. "You are sure you've done the right thing, aren't you?"

"Of course I'm sure. It's just that being alone after eleven years is a bit of a shock to the system."

A few days after Greg left, Gail made me an appointment with Carl, her West End hairstylist. Apparently, I needed a new look to accompany my new single status. Gail insisted on coming with me to the salon on the grounds that we were having lunch afterwards, so it made sense. Of course, the real reason she came was to project manage the proceedings.

Carl, leather of trouser, permed of lash, greeted us with double kisses and glasses of Tŷ Nant with cucumber slices. He and Gail clucked, tutted and fussed over my lifeless, "thirsty" hair. Every so often Carl, who talked nineteen to the dozen, entirely about himself, would break off from thinning out my "mushroom" head to admire himself in the mirror. "Do you know, girls," he said at one point, finger flicking his hair, "I got up today, took one look at myself and thought, 'Carl, the Lord gave and he just carried on giving.' "

"You just wait until he starts taking away," Gail said. She was standing beside him at the mirror, pulling her skin up over her cheekbones.

Looks weren't simply important to Gail. Gail *was* her looks. Losing them terrified her, but women like Gail didn't go gentle into that particular good night. Every time a new line or wrinkle appeared she was at the Harvey Nichols cosmetic counter buying the latest three-hundred-quid-a-pop potion. I kept trying to assure her that she was still a gorgeous, sexy woman, but she couldn't see past her apparently tote-sized eye bags and marionette mouth.

Just before her forty-fifth birthday, Gail informed Murray that she'd booked herself into a Harley Street clinic for a face-lift. She'd expected him to roll his eyes, tell her she was beautiful and didn't need surgery, and maybe have a brief moan about the ten grand she was about to part with, but Murray—who denied his wife nothing— put both feet down. Nobody was taking a knife to his wife's face. The idea sickened him. He also knew that once Gail started with cosmetic surgery, she would become hooked and that one day he would wake up next to Jackie Stallone. He pulled himself up to his full five foot eight and said that if she had surgery it would be over his dead body.

Gail caved in without a fight. The day after Murray's "over my dead body" speech, she called me. "The man was just so powerful and commanding. There was no way I could defy him. Being forbidden was just so sexy. My legs turned to jelly. The next minute we were tearing off each other's clothes."

From her early teens, Gail's only ambition was to become a model. Mum and Dad begged Gail to study and go to university. "What will you have to fall back on?" became their mantra. Gail wasn't interested. She assumed that with her perfect figure, emerald eyes and olive skin, it was only a matter of time before Mario Testino was on the phone.

For Gail, her beauty represented a passport to a new, glamorous life. For Mum and Dad, it represented a passport to drugs and anorexia.

They tried grounding her, but she took no notice and went out anyway. Meetings were held with her teachers. At one stage Dad even called in Rabbi Finkel. When the rabbi suggested that, painful as it was, Dad might have no option but to stand back and watch Gail make a mistake, Dad called him a putz to his face and changed shuls.

Nothing could be done to "save" Gail. She left school at sixteen, with a few mediocre exam passes. When she was signed by one of the top London modeling agencies, Mum and Dad practically went into mourning.

Gail was never out of work, though—mainly photographic. It turned out that she was too short for the catwalk. Nor was her face quite the stuff of *Vogue* covers. The Bianca Jagger Mediterranean look was so over apparently. But fashion editors on the more down-market magazines loved her look. In the mid-seventies, when her friends were living off student grants in houses fit only for the wrecker's ball, Gail owned a flat in the West End and drove around in a pink Mini Cooper with blacked-out windows.

Once she'd convinced Mum and Dad that she wasn't developing a cocaine habit or starving herself, they started to cheer up. When Gail appeared on the front cover of *Glitz Magazine*, Mum sent copies to the entire family—even the Canadian cousins in Montreal.

I was four when Gail started modeling, so I wasn't old enough to be jealous. If we'd been close in age, it might have been a different story and Mum would have been left to handle the emotional fallout. I can only imagine how grateful she must have felt to be let off that particular hook.

When I was growing up, Mum and Dad always made a point of telling me how pretty I was, but I knew that I took after Dad's side of the family (who had "the nose") and that I would never be in

Gail's league. I decided that my only option was to be smart, so, unlike my sister, I threw myself into my schoolwork and made it to university.

Our brother managed to combine looks and a big brain. What's more, Phil fulfilled every Jewish parent's dream by becoming a doctor. Mum still had the champagne corks from his graduation party. These days "my son the doctor" was professor of orthopedics at the University of Florida College of Medicine.

During her modeling years, men were always coming on to Gail: handsome, charismatic bad boys who played in bands and suffered from severe "conquest" addiction. (And to quote Mum: "God only knows what other addictions.") Of course they ended up hurting her.

She met Murray at one of her girlfriends' weddings. She was one of the bridesmaids. He was the best man.

Even when he was twenty-five, Murray's shirt buttons strained across his paunch. He was also an accountant—albeit one who worked for a top City firm and was earning a six-figure salary.

When Gail announced that they were getting married, Mum and Dad were speechless with delight. They'd been plutzing about her ending up with some drug-ridden rocker who would die of a heroin overdose. Now here she was about to marry a nice Jewish accountant.

Some of her friends assumed that Gail, whose heart had been broken once too often by good-looking creeps, had "settled" for Murray on the grounds that he was hardworking, dependable and would look after her.

Gail might well have been looking for emotional security and there was no doubt that money mattered to her, but there was no getting away from it: Gail was crazy about Murray. When they first started dating, I would hear her on the phone to her best friend, Elaine. She would rave about how funny and kind Murray was and how great he was in bed. Like I said, I'd never been jealous of Gail, but at thirteen I knew enough about sex to know that I was seriously missing out.

These days Murray owned his own accountancy firm. M. Green and Co. had four branches in the South East. Two more were planned for Leeds and Manchester. Gail gave up modeling when she had the children. She described herself as a homemaker and charity worker. "What that actually means," Murray was fond of saying, not without a twinkle in his eye, "is that when my wife isn't barking orders at Violetta or having her ears permed, she manages a little light fund-raising. That is to say, she sells a few raffle tickets to her girlfriends over lunch at the Ivy."

Gail was always quick to point out that the raffle tickets cost fifty quid each and that over the years she must have sold hundreds if not thousands. "That's my contribution to the care of the elderly in this country. What's yours?"

"Anyway," Gail was saying now, "I have a problem far worse than Annie's."

"Don't tell me. Harrods Food Hall has run out of wild Baltic salmon."

"Hey, will you play nice? This is serious."

"OK, sorry. Go on."

"I can't come."

"Where?"

"What?"

"Where can't you come?"

"No. I can't *come*."

"Oh! . . . Right. Gotcha."

"Murray went down on me the other day—God, that man is still such an amazing lover . . ."

It was hard to imagine Murray, with his now even more considerable paunch and nose hair, being an amazing lover, but who was I to argue?

". . . and nothing happened. I couldn't do it."

"Maybe you were tired or feeling a bit tense."

"No, it wasn't that. The thing is—my clitoris has gone numb."

"Stop it. They can't go numb."

First Nancy, now my sister. How many more women were going to regale me with tales of their genitals?

"That's what Murray said. He's like, 'Don't be daft. It'd be like Barcelona suddenly losing the ability to score goals. It's impossible.' " Then he starts mulling and he decides that my clitoris is getting on a bit and that it could be clapped out."

"That must have made you feel *so* much better."

"Absolutely. I said to him, 'What are you suggesting we do? Book it into a retirement home?' "

I laughed. Unlike most of her princess friends, my sister didn't lack a sense of humor.

"Murray is so useless when it comes to this sort of stuff. He thought perimenopause was one of those sixties American crooners." She paused. "Anyway, then—and I kid you not—he gets out his calculator and starts tapping away. Typical accountant. He multiplies the time it takes me to come—roughly twenty minutes—with the number of times we have sex each week—four or five—"

"Hang on—you and Murray have sex four or five times . . . a *week*? That's more than Greg and I managed in a month. And that's when we were vaguely getting along."

"That's because you were both exhausted. I've told you—the two of you needed a housekeeper . . . Anyway, Murray decides that over thirty years I've experienced four thousand five hundred hours of bean twiddling. He seems to think it makes perfect sense that my clitoris has karked it."

"That's ridiculous. They're designed to be twiddled. Four thousand hours or so is nothing more than normal wear and tear."

"Shame it's not under warranty," Gail said with a cackle. "I could have brought a case against the manufacturer . . . So, anyway, I Googled 'numb clitoris' and it turns out it's another menopause symptom. Soph, I feel like I'm falling apart. It's like I'm over the hill and heading down into Crone City."

"Oh, hon . . . I'm sorry this is happening, but how many more times do I have to tell you? You are still a beautiful woman. You are not about to turn into a crone."

"I never thought I'd get old. And now that it's happening I'm starting to panic. I've suddenly realized that beauty isn't a passport like I thought. It's a visa. And mine's run out."

"Gail, you've got to stop this."

"I know. Murray's getting really fed up with me going on. I just wish he'd let me get a bit of Botox."

"You don't need it. He can see how great you look. Fifty-one is not old. And I'm sure the clitoris thing can be helped with hormones. You have to go to your doctor."

"Easy for you to tell me I need hormones, but they can give you breast cancer. I don't want to become a statistic—one of the women for whom the risks outweighed the benefits."

I said I hadn't meant to be flippant. "I still think you need to see your doctor, though."

"I know. Murray said the same."

"It'll be all right. You have to stop fretting. You'll get it sorted. Let me know what the doctor says."

" 'K."

The conversation was winding down when Gail said, "Ooh—I nearly forgot why I called. I wanted to check you're still on for Friday night dinner next week. I've invited this amazing guy. I can't wait for you to meet him."

No. Please. Not another one of my sister's "amazing guys." The second Gail got wind that my depression had lifted, she started trying to fix me up. To give my sister her due, the potential suitors she invited to Friday night dinner—so far there had been three, or maybe four; I was losing track—were all good looking and, more to the point, *comfortable*.

"You think I'd fix you up with a *nebbish*? As if."

What Gail failed to appreciate was that while I wasn't one to turn my nose up at "good looking" and "comfortable," these attributes didn't automatically equal "amazing" in my book.

More to the point, even though I'd cheered up, I wasn't ready to start dating. Gail didn't understand that it took time to get over a marriage breakup, even one that had been fairly amicable. I must have explained this to her a dozen times, but she refused to take it on board. In the end I realized that the only way to stop her nagging was to turn up.

The first chap she tried to set me up with was named Sammy. Or it might have been Lenny. He was in his early forties, divorced and recently installed as chief accountant at the City branch of M. Green and Co.

Sammy/Lenny gave me the impression that he'd been on a How to Make Conversation with the Opposite Sex course. He'd clearly taken on board that it was important to show an interest in the other person. What he failed to appreciate was that showing an interest was different from interrogation.

For an hour or more, Sammy/Lenny ignored everybody else at the table and set about grilling me. What did I do for a living? How long had I been doing it? Did I enjoy my job? How did I manage my work-life balance? How old were my children? What school did they go to? Did I think the state system was stretching them sufficiently? It felt as if he was scoring me points out of ten for each answer. The final question I remember him asking was: "So, Sophie, what's your favorite radio program?"

"It has to be *Coffee Break*, but then I'm biased."

I realized that I had to get this man off my back and start asking him some questions. The problem was I felt so discombobulated that my mind had gone blank. What did you ask an accountant?

"So, Sammy," I said, or it might have been Lenny, "what's your favorite number?"

After Sammy/Lenny there was Clive, Gail's children's orthodontist. While we were having drinks in the living room, waiting for him to arrive, Murray insisted I shouldn't go out with him.

"Why on earth not?" Gail broke in.

"They're rubbish at sex." According to Murray, an orthodontist's idea of foreplay was . . . wait for it . . . "Brace yourself."

Gail rolled her eyes and went to check on the chicken.

No sooner had Clive and I been introduced than he observed that I had a couple of ever so slightly wonky lower teeth—always a good chat-up line. He made up for it by offering me a twenty percent discount on tooth straightening.

After dinner, a slightly tipsy Murray began working through his list of dentist jokes. "OK, why did the Buddhist refuse Novocain? . . . Because he wanted to avoid trans-en-dental medication." Murray hooted. Everybody else groaned. Clive grimaced and started offering around dental floss.

"You know what?" I said to Gail now, re Friday night. "If you don't mind, I think I'll give it a miss. Things are really busy at work, and what with the kids, by the end of the week I'm really exhausted."

"Oh, come on. You're just making excuses. Look, I admit the last few guys have been yutzes and I take full responsibility, but you have to believe me—this one is amazing. Bernice met him at her tai chi class."

Bernice was Murray's sixty-something divorcée sister. "Bernice? Since when did you start taking Bernice's opinion seriously?" Murray's sister had this habit of "tabloiding" everybody she met. They were either a "nightmare" or "amazing." The "amazing" ones tended to be people who were prepared to listen for hours on end while she went on about her successful kids and her failing pelvic floor. The "nightmares" were the people who made their excuses and went to find somebody interesting to talk to.

"Stop it. She means well. You know, she has quite a soft spot for you."

"Only because I let her talk at me. I don't think the woman has ever been known to ask anybody a question about themselves."

"That's not fair." Gail had started laughing. "There was that time in 1987 . . . Anyway, you won't believe what this guy—Mike, his name is—does for a living."

"Go on."

She lowered her voice. "He works for MI5."

"You mean MI5 as in the government security service?"

"The very same."

"So you're saying he's a secret agent."

"I am. How sexy is that?"

"But what's a secret agent doing at Bernice's tai chi class?"

"I don't know. I guess spies are entitled to a private life. Or maybe he was on a mission."

I laughed. "At Bernice's tai chi class in Golders Green. Yeah, that'll be it."

"Well, apparently the instructor is Chinese . . ."

"Oh, well, say no more. That totally clinches it."

"Look, I don't know what he was doing there. All I know is that he and Bernice got chatting. I think for a moment she might have had her eye on him for herself, but she realized he was way too young for her. I don't think he's even forty. So she thought of you. Apparently she spent ages singing your praises and finally she convinced him to come along on Friday night. The woman's gone to so much effort. Please say you'll come."

"Well, I have to admit I'm intrigued."

"So you'll come?"

"How can I refuse?"

"I should tell you he's not Jewish."

"Since when was that a problem?"

"Fine. I thought I should let you know, that's all . . . Just think—I've got a real, live spy coming for Friday night dinner. I hope he likes chopped liver."

As usual, Gail was expecting a houseful of people. Since Friday was Violetta's night off, I arrived early to give her a hand.

She opened the door holding an exquisite table centerpiece made up of calla lilies and artfully arranged greenery.

"You just missed Lola, my florist."

I noted the word "my." The woman was North West London's answer to Marie Antoinette.

We exchanged kisses and I oohed and aahed over the flowers.

"No Amy and Ben?" Gail said.

As I took off my coat, I explained that they were spending the weekend with Greg and the Frizzy-Haired Feminist.

"What's on the agenda?" she said. "An intimate chat with Amy about sexual harassment in the workplace?"

"I wouldn't put it past her."

Gail took my coat and hung it on the hallstand. "God, what does Greg see in this woman?"

Just then the kitchen door opened and Murray appeared. He was in his bathrobe and eating a banana. "Hi, Soph," he said, breaking off from the banana to give me a great big smacker on the cheek. He turned to his wife. "Nice flowers. What did they cost me?"

Gail ignored the question. "Murray, why haven't you got changed yet? More to the point, why are you noshing bananas? You'll ruin your appetite."

"I've barely eaten all day. All I had for lunch was a few dim sum."

"Dim sum. And he wonders why he can't lose the paunch."

"I love it when you scold," Murray said, grabbing his wife around the waist and giving her a speedy but firm kiss on the lips. "It's so sexy. Grrr."

"Get off—I'll drop the centerpiece," Gail said, unable to prevent her face from breaking into a smile. "Uch, you taste of banana."

Murray turned to me. "So, you excited about meeting our man from MI5?"

I had to admit that I was rather.

In Gail's limed oak and granite kitchen, I sprinkled chopped hard-boiled egg on top of patties of chopped liver and asked after her clitoris.

"No change. The doctor's referred me to a hormone specialist. I'm still waiting for an appointment."

In the TV room, Gail's children—Alexa (fifteen) and Spencer (almost thirteen)—had started yelling at each other. "Not again," Gail muttered. She abandoned the fruit platter she was arranging, wiped her hands on her REMEMBER: WINE COUNTS AS ONE OF YOUR FIVE A DAY apron and went back into the hall.

"Spencer! How many more times? Give the remote back to your sister!"

"But she took it from me!"

"Alexa! Give the remote back to your brother!"

"No! I don't want to watch soccer!"

"It's the Sabbath, for Chrissake! You shouldn't be watching anything! Murray, get down here and sort out your children! Tell them to shut up! I've got a chicken in the oven!"

From the upstairs landing: "All of a sudden they're my kids! . . . Alexa! Spencer! Knock it off! Your mother's got a chicken in the oven."

Gail returned to the kitchen and dabbed at her brow with her apron. "Whenever I get agitated the hot flashes start." She fell onto a bar stool. "Teenagers," she said. "You've got it all to come."

Just then her cell beeped the arrival of a text message. She reached across the counter and picked it up. "It's Bernice to say she's in bed with a migraine, but Mike is still coming."

"Doesn't that seem a bit weird to you, him coming on his own? I mean, he's not going to know a soul."

"All I can say is that he must be really eager to meet you."

I could feel myself turning red, so I decided to change the subject. "So, apart from the fighting, how are the kids doing?"

"Well, the latest headline is that Alexa has decided she wants to leave school and go to some performing arts academy."

Alexa had a beautiful singing voice and always took the lead in school musicals. She had singing lessons after school and on the weekends and her teacher was convinced she had a future in musical theater.

"Alexa is very talented," I ventured. "And she loves acting. Maybe she could do with being at stage school."

"Over my dead body. They practically ignore academic subjects at these places. She's a bright kid. I've told her she goes to university and gets her degree. Then, if she's still keen on singing and acting, she can take a performing arts course or apply to drama school. But I won't have her abandoning her studies."

"Like you did."

"Exactly. I was an idiot. I'm not about to have her repeating my mistake. She needs something to fall back on. Alexa is going to university and that's that."

"And what does Murray say?"

"It doesn't matter what Murray says."

By that she meant that Murray was on Alexa's side.

*G*ail's guests—couples they'd known for years, or people they'd become friendly with through Gail's charity work—brought competitive orchid plants and bottles of wine that had just been reviewed in the Sunday magazines. The women, all in their late forties and fifties and all skinny and "extended" like Gail, clucked over each other's outfits: "It's an investment . . ." "You can't go wrong . . ." "They say dry-clean only, but it's only to cover themselves."

I was told that I "looked well," which I knew to be princess code for "you've put on weight." I felt as if they were all looking at me and thinking that I was one family-sized KFC bucket away from throwing the earth off its axis.

One couple, Sharon and Russell Shapiro, had brought their two teenage children with them. Josh and Hannah were close friends with Gail's kids and went to the same school. After everybody had remarked on how tall they were getting and assured Josh, much to his embarrassment, that he wouldn't need the braces for long and they were sure to be off well before his bar mitzvah and the results would be well worth it, the kids disappeared into the TV room, where Spencer and Alexa—having called a truce—were playing on the Xbox.

At one point during predinner drinks and what Murray always referred to as "suburban snacks," Sharon stopped sipping her caffeine-free Diet Coke and turned to Gail. "You know, I really worry about what these computer games do to children's minds. Unless they're educational, they're banned in our house. Gail, please tell me the kids aren't playing war games in there."

"Don't worry. We're really strict about computer games, too." She called out to Murray, who was in the middle of a conversation on the other side of the living room. "Hey, hon, do you know what game Alexa and Spencer are playing?"

"I dunno . . . it might be that new one Spencer just got . . . Something like *Flesh-Eating Zombie Ninjas Take Over the World*."

Sharon was horror-stricken. "Omigod. Murray, are you serious?"

"Of course he's not serious," Gail said, glaring across the room at her husband. "Murray, tell Sharon you're joking."

Murray had just finished placating Sharon when the doorbell

buzzed. "Ooh, that'll be him," Gail whispered, digging me in the ribs. She got up and went to answer the door. "Hello, you must be Mike," she boomed from the hall. "I'm Gail. Welcome to our home . . ."

Mike the secret agent was full of apologies for being late. He'd been stuck in a meeting and couldn't get away.

"Oh, I totally understand," I heard Gail say, each word in italics. I imagined her winking and tapping the side of her nose.

She led Mike into the living room.

"Everybody, this is Mike . . . Mike, this is everybody."

People called out, "Hi, Mike," and waved.

Murray immediately went over to shake hands with Mike and offer him a drink.

Meanwhile, Sharon cornered me and whispered, "So, this is the S-P-Y."

So now Sharon knew. My sister had such a big mouth.

OK, I admit it. I'd been hoping for Daniel Craig. Mike couldn't have looked less like my sexy secret agent fantasy. He was tall and gangly with shoulder-length hair parted down the middle. He was also wearing a suit and tie. The man looked like Jesus going for a job interview.

Murray handed Mike a glass of wine and began introducing him to the other guests. Meanwhile, Gail grabbed my arm and dragged me into the hall. "OK, don't panic about the hair," she whispered. "I'm thinking that maybe he's on some undercover mission that requires long hair. Once it's over, you make an appointment for him with Carl. Aside from that, he's quite nice looking, don't you think? Good teeth. I think there's definitely something to work with."

Gail got busy seating everybody around the table. "And, Soph, I've put you next to Mike." Wink.

Everybody made a start on the chopped liver. As usual, half a dozen conversations were being conducted at full volume around the table: "Kids, don't fill up on bread—there's more to come" . . . "Bastard wanted to charge me five grand over the Blue Book price" . . . "The doctors are carrying out a battery of tests" . . . "Did you keep the warranty?" . . . "I told her, she must have something to fall back on."

"I feel that I ought to apologize," I said to Mike over the din.

"For what?"

"Bernice setting us up like this."

Mike laughed. "Well, I have to admit I don't usually let people matchmake for me, but Bernice is one of those women who don't take no for an answer. Plus she didn't stop telling me how wonderful you are."

"Well, I'm very flattered that you came—especially on your own."

"My pleasure . . . So, Bernice tells me you're a producer on *Coffee Break.* Excellent program. One of the few intelligent radio shows left. I never miss it when I'm at home."

"That's always good to hear—especially from a male listener. Still, I don't suppose you get much time at home. I imagine you're always off on some assignment or other." I stopped myself. "Gosh, I haven't said too much, have I?" By now I'd lowered my voice to a whisper.

Mike looked perplexed. "Actually things are pretty busy at the moment, what with the Christmas rush."

"So even in your line of work things hot up at Christmas? I had no idea."

"I'll say. Shoplifters are a nightmare at this time of year."

"Shoplifters?"

"Yes. In the store."

"Oh, I get it. You tell people you work in a store and that acts as your cover. Very clever."

"My cover? Cover for what?"

I felt the need to lower my voice. "You know."

"Actually, I don't."

"Your cover . . . for your real job . . . the one we can't talk about."

"You think that I have another job? And that I keep it a secret?"

"OK, I get it—this is your way of telling me that you don't want to have this conversation. I totally understand. It's way too sensitive. Let's change the subject."

"Sophie, I'm confused. I honestly don't have another job."

"Of course you don't." Wink. "That's fine. Say no more." Wink.

"So, what is this other job I'm meant to have?"

"You seriously want me to come out and say it?"

"I'd be really happy if you did."

I looked around to check that nobody was listening in on our conversation. "You're a secret government agent."

Mike threw his head back and roared. "What? That's the funniest thing I've ever heard. You think I'm a spook?"

"Yes. Bernice told my sister that you work for MI5."

"Actually, what I am is president of MFI—Mike Flemming Iron-mongery. I own a chain of hardware stores."

"Hardware stores?"

"Yes."

"So you're definitely not a secret agent?"

"Definitely not." He was still laughing.

"Not even secretly?"

"Uh-uh."

"Wow. I've really embarrassed myself."

"Only a bit," he said. "I think it's hilarious. I am going to dine out on this for years. You can blame Bernice. She's a lovely lady, but I'm not sure she's the greatest listener in the world."

"You can say that again."

"So I guess you're not quite so interested in getting to know me now you've discovered that I'm not a secret agent."

"What? No—of course I'm interested." What else could I say?

He looked dubious. It was obvious he could see right through me.

I battled on, nevertheless: "So, how are things in the hardware business?"

I was asking out of politeness and he knew it, but he was kind enough to indulge me.

He was in the middle of explaining that inquiries about house security were up and that sales of catches, latches and bolts had never been higher when I realized that Murray was standing behind us. I hadn't noticed that he'd gotten up and was going around the table topping up people's wineglasses.

"Drop more, you two?"

Murray gave me the first refill. He'd just started pouring wine into Mike's glass when Spencer came by—probably on his way to the fridge to get another can of Coke—and jogged his father's elbow, causing him to lose his balance. One second Murray was filling Mike's glass, and the next vintage burgundy was cascading from the bottle into Mike's lap. By the time Murray had regained control of the bottle the damage had been done.

"Spencer, you klutz! Look what you made me do." Murray was shaking his hands, which were covered in red wine.

"I'm sorry. I didn't mean it." Spencer's voice, which had just started to break, had gone all high-pitched.

"You never *mean* it!" Gail bellowed from the other side of the table. "Why can't you look where you're going?"

"I've said I'm sorry."

Red of face, Spencer disappeared.

Marcia, one of Gail's charity worker friends, who was sitting to my right, began calling for soda water and paper towels.

By now Gail was already halfway to the kitchen. I took one look at Mike's drenched lap. It was clear that paper towels and soda water weren't going to have much impact.

Murray was full of apologies and offered to take Mike upstairs and fix him up with a fresh pair of pants.

"That's really kind of you," Mike said, dabbing at the area with a wad of paper towels, which had appeared courtesy of Gail. "But I think I'd best get home."

"Nonsense," Gail cried. "You can't go. You haven't even finished your chopped liver. Murray, go upstairs and fetch Mike a pair of joggers."

"No. Please. If you don't mind, I think I'd rather go."

"OK," Gail said, "but I'm making you a roast chicken sandwich to take with you, and no arguments." She got up and disappeared into the kitchen.

Mike sat dabbing at his lap, looking as if he didn't know where to put himself.

"It's such a shame you have to leave," I said. "We were just getting to know each other."

He offered me a half smile. Clearly what he wanted to say was: "You know what? I think this is probably for the best."

A couple of minutes later, Gail returned with two foil parcels. "Right, I've made you a sandwich and there's a slice of my home-made cheesecake."

"That's so kind. You really shouldn't have."

"Of course I should. I'm so sorry you have to go."

Mike gave everybody a good-bye, great-to-have-met-you salute, and I walked him to the door. "Give me a call," I said. "Maybe we could go out for coffee or a drink sometime."

"Sure," he said.

But we both knew that was never going to happen.

By the time I got back to the table, the chopped-liver plates had been cleared and replaced with bowls of chicken soup. I'd just picked up my spoon when Spencer appeared in the doorway carrying his laptop.

"Mum . . . Grandma and Granddad are on Skype."

Gail got him to bring the laptop to the table. "And mind the soup. It's boiling hot." She still sounded irritable. It was clear she hadn't forgiven him yet. She made some space on the table and Spencer put the laptop down in front of his mother. Murray got up from his chair so that I could sit next to her.

"Hey, Mum and Dad," Gail said, brightening. "You OK? Soph's here. Can you see her?"

I leaned in and waved. "Hi, parents. It's me."

Mum and Dad's faces froze into a thousand pixels.

By now Murray, Spencer and Alexa had gathered around, along with a few of Gail's friends who knew Mum and Dad.

"Ooh . . . you've got company," Mum said, unfrozen now. "And I can see Murray and the kids." She gave everybody a wave.

"Who's she got there?" Dad said, clearly perplexed. "What time is it?"

Gail explained she had people over for Friday night dinner. "So, where are you?" Gail said. "Looks like you're in a restaurant."

"We're just finishing lunch," Mum said. "Phil had the day off, so he brought us to this wonderful fish place. I just had snapper. It was OK, but you can't compare it to a nice plate of haddock and chips."

Gail asked if they'd got the jar of Marmite she'd sent.

"We did, darling, and thank you. But if you could send out some Yorkshire tea, that would be great, 'cos we're running really low."

Gail said she'd put a couple of boxes in the mail the next day.

"So how are things?" I asked. "We're all missing you."

"We're missing you, too," Dad said. "And the kids."

Mum asked where they were. When I explained that they were with their father and Roz (another piece of news I'd had to break to them a while back), Mum went quiet.

"I still can't get used to this whole situation," she said. "I'm still getting the palpitations."

Dad told her to be quiet and said that nobody wanted to hear about her palpitations. "You know," he said, "there's one thing about living over here that I can't get used to. All Phil and Betsy's friends insist on calling me Chuck. I tell them my name's Charles, but they just slap me on the back and carry on calling me Chuck."

"Yeah, Americans like to shorten names," Gail said. "You'll get used to it."

"I'll tell you one thing I'll never get used to," Mum said. "The portion sizes . . ."

"And your mother refuses to eat hot dogs . . . on the grounds that she always gets the same part of the dog." Dad roared.

"Good one, Dad," Gail said. She turned to me. "You know, sometimes I think that subconsciously I married Murray because his jokes remind me of Dad."

"And the closets are so huge," Mum went on. "The one in our bedroom sleeps four."

"And your mother still hasn't got used to going into shops and having the assistants ask how she is. The other day she spent a full five minutes telling the girl on the supermarket checkout about her hemorrhoids."

"I did not! I was telling her about my neuritis and you know it . . . Listen, I need to powder my nose," Mum said. "I'll be back in a tick."

She disappeared, but we could still hear her. She was asking the waiter for the loo.

"You're looking for Lou?" the waiter's voice said. "I don't think we have anybody of that name working here. What's Lou's last name?"

"No, you misunderstand," Dad said. "My wife isn't looking for a person called Lou. She *needs* the loo."

"She means the restroom," Phil broke in.

"No, I don't," Mum came back. "I don't need to rest. I'm feeling fine. I just need to spend a penny."

"Spend a penny?" It was the waiter again.

"Could you just direct my mother to the toilet?" Phil said.

"And I'll have another Coke," Dad was saying to the waiter. "And don't fill the glass with ice. I'm paying for Coke, not ice."

"Dad, be quiet," Phil said. "People like lots of ice over here."

"But it's a con."

"They don't see it like that."

When Dad got up to go in search of the men's room, Gail and I were able to ask Phil how things were going with Mum and Dad.

"They're a bit of a handful, but we're coping and Betsy's amazing with them. Even the boys like having them around. They're fascinated by Dad's stories about the Blitz."

We were interrupted by the kids at the dinner table, who appeared to be in hysterics.

"It's true," Spencer was saying. "Honest."

"Kids, can you be quiet?" Gail said. "I'm trying to speak to my mum and dad and it's not easy with you lot making a racket."

A few of the other adults shushed the kids, too.

More shrieks.

Gail glared at Spencer, who seemed to be the cause of all the hilarity. "OK, what's going on?" she said. It took Spencer a few seconds to compose himself. "I was just saying that male earwigs have a spare penis, that's all."

"He's just trying to draw attention to himself as usual," Alexa said.

Spencer curled his lip. "Shuddup, Alexa."

"Spencer," Gail said. "I will not have you saying 'penis' at the Sabbath table."

"You just said it."

"It doesn't matter what I say. I'm an adult."

"You know what?" a very pixelated Phil was saying. "Maybe this would be a good time to sign off."

"OK, Phil," Gail said. "I'm sorry about this, but I need to deal with my son."

"Sure. Speak soon. I'll pass on your love to Mum and Dad."

I said good-bye to Phil and told him to say hi to Betsy and the kids.

Gail closed the laptop.

"But why can't I talk about the penis thing at the table if it's true?" Spencer persisted.

"Because we're eating soup!"

"What's that got to do with anything?"

At this point Murray stepped in. "Spencer, I've had enough of you for one night. Now just do as your mother says."

"But it's so cool. If an earwig's penis snaps off during sex, another one pops out of his abdomen."

"You know, Murray," one of the men at the table said, "you have to admit that is pretty clever."

The other chaps laughed their agreement.

"OK, here's another fact," Spencer went on, clearly thinking he had a captive audience now. "A headless cockroach can survive for two weeks."

"Right," Sharon said. "I think it's time we changed the subject."

"Actually, I've got another amazing fact," somebody said. "Did you know that oysters change sex throughout their lives?"

"That's, like, so weird," Alexa said.

"I dunno, sounds like fun," Murray came back.

Spencer screwed up his face. "Dad, what are you, gay or something?"

Sharon seemed to have decided that it was time for her to take charge of the conversation. "So, Gail, how are the bar mitzvah plans going?"

"Well, Spencer still hasn't worked out if he wants the iPhone cake or the bass guitar."

"I've told you," Spencer said with an eye roll. "I don't care."

"But it's your bar mitzvah. You have to care."

"No, Mum—this is *your* bar mitzvah. You're the one who can't stop going on about it."

"Fine . . . so I'll take all your present money, shall I?"

At this point Josh, Sharon's son, broke in: "So, Gail, after what happened have you managed to find Spencer a new bar mitzvah teacher yet?"

"Why would I want to do that?"

I watched the color draining from Spencer's face. He was glaring at Josh as if to say, "One more word and you are dead."

"No. No reason," Josh said.

"Come on, Josh—you started to tell me something."

Josh looked at Spencer. "Spence, you tell her. She's your mother."

"It was meant to be a secret! I hate you, Josh."

Sharon took hold of her son's hand and told him to take no notice.

"Spencer, don't speak to your friends like that," Murray said. "Now apologize."

Spencer mumbled an apology.

"Right," Murray went on. "If you've got something to tell us, just get on with it."

Silence.

Gail said she was waiting. As was the entire table. "Come on, Spencer, why do you need a new bar mitzvah teacher?"

"OK, if you must know . . . I told Mr. Liebowitz that I was a Satanist."

Several people, myself included, burst out laughing.

"A Satanist," Gail repeated, clearly unamused.

"Why on earth would you say something like that?" Murray asked.

"It was a joke."

"Hilarious. I bet old man Liebowitz split his sides." Gail looked at Murray. "You see what you've done? He gets this joke nonsense from you." She turned back to her son. "So what happened?"

"Mr. Liebowitz called me an abomination, kicked me out of the class and told me not to come back."

"Perfect," Gail said. "So why don't I know about this? Why hasn't Mr. Liebowitz phoned me or your father?"

"I told him you'd gone away indefinitely and that Alexa and me were living here alone."

Gail sat shaking her head. "This gets better and better. Is there anything else you want to tell me?"

Spencer shook his head.

"Yes, there is," Josh piped up. "You've missed a bit. What about when you told Mr. Liebowitz that you'd started worshipping owls?"

"Josh, you are such a bastard. I am so paying you back for this."

Sharon turned on Spencer. "How dare you start calling Josh names!"

"Spencer," Gail snapped, "take that back. Right now."

"What? Why?"

"Now! Do it."

"Sorree."

"It'll be all right," I said to Gail. "You'll find another teacher."

"What, when it gets around that Spencer Green's parents left him home alone and as a result he turned into an owl-worshipping Satanist? I think not."

She stood up and said she was going to get the chicken out of the oven.

"Well, you have to admit," Murray said, "so far the evening has been quite a hoot."

Chapter 4

"**S**o," I said, "how was your weekend with Dad and Roz?"

"'K," Amy replied, without taking her eyes off the TV screen.

Ben was even more engrossed and didn't say anything. Greg had dropped the kids off a couple of hours ago and now they were watching *Scooby-Doo* in their pj's and drinking bedtime cocoa.

Amy was sitting cross-legged on the floor, about two feet from the TV. "Hon, please move back from the screen. You'll ruin your eyes." Ever since the kids were old enough to watch TV, those words had been my mantra. I often wondered whether there was any scientific evidence that sitting too close to the TV affected one's eyesight. When I was little, my mother would utter similarly dire warnings: "Sophie, darling, please don't pick your nose. Your nostrils will stretch." I took no notice, but in my teenage years her words came back to haunt me and I started examining my nose in the mirror to check if my childhood booger excavations had caused my nostrils to spread. They hadn't.

Without saying anything, Amy shuffled back a couple of inches.

I sat down on the sofa next to Ben. "So, what did you guys get up to?"

Still nothing from my youngest.

"Dunno. Stuff," Amy said. "Sshh, I love this bit." She and her brother burst out laughing.

"Didn't Dad and Roz take you anywhere?"

"Uh-uh. We just hung out."

"Roz let me take Dworkin for a walk," Ben piped up, deigning to look in my direction. "All on my own."

"She did? I hope you didn't go far."

"No, just around the block." He went back to the TV.

It was clear I wasn't going to get much more out of the kids, so I decided to leave them to *Scooby-Doo* and check my e-mail. I picked up my laptop, which was lying on the coffee table. My in-box contained one new e-mail. It was from Frizzy-Haired Feminist. The subject line was a noncommittal *Hello*, so there was no clue as to what she might want. Then it occurred to me that maybe she'd been feeling bad about the "porn" conversation she'd had with Amy and was writing to apologize and offer me a seasonal olive branch. I clicked on the e-mail and began reading:

> Dear Sophie,
> First, I'd like to say what great children Amy and Ben are and how much I'm enjoying getting to know them.

I could definitely feel an olive branch coming on. Maybe I'd misjudged Roz.

> In fact, we're already starting to feel like family.

Oh-kay . . . that didn't feel quite so olive branch–y.

"Yeah, I saw the Christmas card," I muttered.

"What?" Ben said, turning to look at me.

"Nothing, darling. You just carry on watching TV."

Amy and I are developing a really special relationship and becoming particularly close. She's such an intelligent, thoughtful child and the two of us have wonderful talks.

Like Amy and I didn't? "You arrogant, smug, self-righteous—"

"What do those words mean?" Ben piped up again.

"Oh, I don't know . . . you use them to describe somebody with a big head."

"Mr. Peabody, who teaches year five, has got a big head. It's enormous. And he's really skinny. He looks like this pole with a beach ball on top."

"No, you've got the wrong end of the stick. I mean bigheaded as in boastful."

"Oh. OK. But suppose somebody had a big head and they were also bigheaded? That would get quite confusing, wouldn't it?"

"I suppose it would."

"So what's the difference between the wrong end of the stick and the right end?"

"I really don't know."

"Maybe the right end has fruit and delicious, scrummy berries on it and the wrong end is covered in pythons, poisonous spiders and scorpions."

"If it had berries," I said, "wouldn't that make it more of a branch than a stick?"

"A branch can be a stick. I mean, you can use a branch as a stick."

"OK, if you say so . . . Ben, can we discuss this later? I'm actually trying to read something."

"'K."

I do, however, have some concerns regarding Amy that I feel compelled to raise with you.

"Concerns? She has concerns? Who is she to have concerns?"

I'm not sure that you have given sufficient thought to the way you allow Amy to dress.

"OK, this time she has gone too far."

For example: This weekend, I noticed that she was wearing a short denim skirt and a Hello Kitty T-shirt. I find it hard to believe that you consider this to be an appropriate look for a ten-year-old.

"I don't believe this."

Who was this woman to tell me what was or wasn't an appropriate look for my daughter? I thought back to what Amy had had on when she left the house on Friday. She'd been wearing her short denim skirt, but over thick leggings and the Ugg boots Gail had bought her for her birthday. She hadn't exactly been flaunting herself. And what was supposed to be wrong with the Hello Kitty tee?

As a mother, I'm sure you agree that young girls shouldn't be allowed to wear clothes that sexualize them, which is what Amy's miniskirt did. Meanwhile, the pink top with the girlie cat motif portrayed her as delicate, powerless and insubstantial. For years, feminists like myself have fought to empower girls and women. (Do check out *The Female Eunuch*. Women have come a long way since the seventies, but Greer's work remains hugely relevant.) By allowing Amy to wear this T-shirt, you are undermining the cause and setting it back decades.

What is more, encouraging Amy to follow fashion in such an unthinking, slavish manner is surely the start of the slippery slide. I'm sure you agree that fashion is an active cog in the undeclared war against women. We must encourage our daughters to understand that the buying of clothes is a meaningless, frivolous activity.

On future occasions, I would be grateful if you could ensure that Amy is more suitably dressed when she comes to visit.

Naturally, to protect Amy's feelings, I haven't mentioned my disquiet to her.

With best wishes for Christmas and the new year,

Roz

Heart thumping, ears bursting with steam, I changed the subject of the e-mail to *I want to throttle this bloody woman!!!!!!!* and forwarded it to Gail and Annie. I was about to hit the keyboard again and tell Frizzy-Haired Feminist that she could stick her copy of *The Female Eunuch* where the sun don't shine, when Greg called to say that Ben had left his gloves in the car. I told him not to worry and that he had a spare pair.

"You OK?" Greg said. "You sound a bit stressed."

"Yeah, you could say that. Look, there's something I need to discuss with you. Hang on a tick." I got up, went into the kitchen and closed the door. "OK . . . I just got this really snotty e-mail from Roz about Amy being inappropriately dressed. I'm Amy's mother. Do you mind telling me where she gets off lecturing me about what my daughter should or should not wear?"

"Soph, calm down—"

"No, I won't calm down. Why should I?"

"Because I think Roz has got a point."

Now I wanted to throttle him, too. "What? You're siding with that woman against your child's mother?"

"Actually, I'd prefer it if you didn't refer to Roz as 'that woman,' and I'm siding with her because I think she's talking sense. I'm not sure that Amy should be wearing short skirts at her age. And maybe the Hello Kitty T-shirt is a bit twee."

"Of course it's twee. Girls wear twee at ten. Ten is a twee age. What would you put her in—a Chairman Mao suit?"

"Very funny. But you have to admit that these days Amy's pretty hung up on what she looks like. She paints her nails. She wears eye shadow."

I was fighting not to lose it. "Yes. In her bedroom. She's experimenting. We've been through this. The child is about to hit puberty. Of course she's starting to take an interest in her looks. That's what girls her age do. It's normal."

"But it's so mindless and trivial."

"Yeah, like keeping the house clean and tidy is mindless and trivial. Greg, our daughter is ten. Isn't she entitled to a few more years of fun and frivolity before real life kicks in?"

He didn't say anything.

"Look," I said, changing down a gear, "you're Amy's father and you have a right to object to what she wears—even if I don't happen to agree with you. Roz, on the other hand, does not have that right. She's sticking her nose into affairs that don't concern her, and if you don't tell her to back off, I will."

"Soph, please don't start a fight with Roz. I don't want us all at war in the run-up to the holidays. I agree she's been a bit high-handed and, for the record, although we had a conversation about Amy's clothes, I had no idea she was planning to e-mail you. She shouldn't have done that. Roz is one of those people who acts on impulse and doesn't always think before she speaks. I'll have a word with her. I promise."

"You said that last time, after her porn discussion with Amy."

"I did speak to her. And she promised she'd apologize."

"Well, she hasn't. And anyway, I don't care about an apology. I just want her to back off."

"I will speak to her, I promise. But she's got a lot on right now. Her UK book tour starts tomorrow. Plus it's almost Christmas."

"Poor thing. Must be hectic," I said. "I mean, what with all those cards to write." I'd promised myself that I wouldn't let Greg and Roz see how much their family Christmas card had hurt me, but it wasn't easy.

"Oh, come on. Surely the card didn't upset you. It was just a bit of fun."

"Of course it didn't upset me," I said, aware of how defensive I sounded.

"You know, when couples split up, families morph and change. Ours is no different."

"Greg, please don't patronize me. I do get that. Look, can we drop the subject? Just tell Roz to stop poking her nose into matters that don't concern her and I'll be happy."

He said he would.

I went back to the living room to shut down my laptop and found an e-mail from Annie re FHF's critique of Amy's clothes.

> Whadda bitch!!!!! Assume naked mud wrestling to follow. Please save me front-row seat. Call if you need to vent some more. Annie xxx

I e-mailed back to say that naked mud wrestling might well be in order if the frizzy-haired one didn't get down off her high horse and behave, but for now Greg had persuaded me to let him handle her. Before hitting "send," I added a PS:

> Let's get together soon—without kids. What about lunch one Saturday if Rob's back from his travels and can look after your two?

I was still worried about Annie. I was pretty sure that she wasn't as happy with her domestic lot as she made out and I wanted a chance to have a gentle probe.

The next morning when I checked my e-mail, there was a message from Gail:

Bloody hell!!!!! Who the hell does she think she is? I'm speechless, which has to be a first. This woman is a monster! Take my advice—this situation can only get worse. If you want her out of your life then keep the kids away from her. Insist that Greg see them on his own.

BTW, I couldn't believe it when you told me about Mike and the whole MI5, MFI mix-up. Hysterical. Got Murray's old mum here for a couple of weeks. She's now wearing incontinence pads and refusing to put her teeth in because the dentures hurt. Told Murray to shoot me if I get like that. Speak soon. G X

I wrote back:

Glad you thought MI5 mix-up was hysterical, 'cos I didn't. Re FHF ... has occurred to me to keep the kids away from her, but really don't want to go to war with Greg. Would mean slugging it out in court. Can't put kids through that. Good luck with mother-in-law. Trying to picture you toothless! Is that our destiny—ending up on a Zimmer frame with pee trickling down our legs?

On Friday, there was a farewell drinks do for Liz at the Hog's Hind, around the corner from the office. We presented her with a *Best of Coffee Break* CD and a Clarice Cliff coffee set (she collected art deco china). There were tears and hugs and promises to stay in touch.

"So what are your plans?" I asked her.

Liz said that after years in broadcasting, she suddenly found herself craving the simple life. To that end she had bought an allotment, where she was going to grow vegetables. My first thought was that she'd be bored in five minutes, but I didn't say anything.

Everybody was saying their good-byes when Nancy dragged me to one side. As she usually did at office dos, she'd downed a few too many kir royals. This had resulted in her spending the last hour kissing everybody and telling them how much she loved, valued and appreciated them.

"Sophee," she gushed, letting go of my arm. Her eyes were wide with excitement. "I have the most amazing news. Brian has finally agreed to go into sex therapy. Isn't that wonderful? I've already phoned Virginia Pruitt thingy and we've got our first session this week. I just hope that finally we can make some progress with my vulva. I can't thank you enough for the recommendation and I promise faithfully to keep you up to speed."

I was in no doubt that she would.

Then she threw her arms around me. "I love you, Sophee. I really love you. And I value and appreciate you, too. I really should tell you more often."

On Monday, I got to the office two hours late. I knew that the media change consultant (whose identity still hadn't been revealed by the bosses at GLB) was due to start work that morning and that a meet and greet had been arranged for nine. I left home at my usual time and should have been in by eight.

Putney to Vauxhall went without a hitch. For once I even managed to get a seat. Then, as I was standing on the escalator heading for the Victoria line, the announcement came: owing to "a person on the tracks" at Stockwell, passengers could expect serious delays.

I went up to the street and tried hailing a cab, but by now it was raining and there were none to be had. Eventually I headed back into the tube and along with all the other wet, frustrated commuters waited over an hour for a train. When it finally arrived, the crowd surged on board. The train crawled along, stopping for minutes at a time at each station, I with my rear end pressed firmly against some chap's groin.

Of course, it hadn't been raining when I left home and I'd come out without an umbrella. By the time I'd walked from Oxford Circus to the GLB building behind Carnaby Street, my hair, which for once I'd not only blow-dried but ironed because this morning of all mornings I wanted to create a good impression, was soaking and plastered to my skull.

I got out of the lift and headed straight for the office kitchen. There was always a pile of clean tea towels in the cupboard under the sink. I would use a couple to dry my hair. Except today, there weren't any. I guessed they'd all been used and the cleaner had sent them to the laundry.

I was attempting to dry my hair with a couple of squares of paper towel when Nancy appeared. "God, what happened to you?" she said, accusing rather than concerned. Nancy was so much more agreeable when she was drunk.

"Forgot my umbrella and there was a person under a train at Stockwell."

"Typical. You know, sometimes people can be so inconsiderate. I've got nothing against suicide per se, but throwing oneself under a train makes such a mess. And do they really have to do it on a Monday morning when everybody's so frantic?"

"Yeah, Wednesday would be better," I said, "when we've all got into our stride. Or Friday—it's the end of the week. Nobody gives a toss about Fridays."

"Very funny, but you know full well what I mean." Nancy took a Diet Coke from the fridge. "Anyway, for your information, the media change consultant arrived over an hour ago, along with a couple of GLB bigwigs. You missed the meet and greet. It goes without saying that as senior producer, your absence was noted."

I carried on rubbing at my hair. "I'm sorry, but there was nothing I could do."

"Well, you'd better go and introduce yourself and offer your apologies."

"Thank you, Nancy. I hadn't thought of that . . . So, what are we dealing with, some big shot who's announced he's here to kick ass, not kiss it?"

"Actually, he's a she," Nancy said.

"Oh God." I was imagining some haughty, chisel-faced despot.

"I have to say that at first glance she seemed quite pleasant. But I suspect it's only an act—you know, the charm before the storm."

By now we'd been joined by Des. He was one of only three male producers who worked on the show. Des was in his fifties and a really talented producer. Even though he'd worked on *Coffee Break* for twenty years, his gifts had never been properly rewarded. This was on account of his being an activist in the National Union of Journalists and something of a left-wing agitator. Somebody only had to be served an undercooked chicken burger in the staff canteen and Des was practically calling for strike action. A few months earlier, when all the loos in the building ran out of toilet paper—some manager had forgotten to place the order—Des decided it was a capitalist plot. The way he saw it, the lack of toilet paper was a message from management to the workers to let them know that it wasn't there to wipe their arses.

"Too right," he was saying now, re Nancy's charm-before-the-storm remark. He flicked the switch on the kettle. "Take it from me that, underneath the smiles and superficial civility, the woman is a regular Nazi in nylons."

"Oh, and FYI," Nancy said to me, "she's Australian. And get this—the woman is called . . . Shirley Tucker Dill. I mean, who was her father? The Jolly Swagman?"

"I just Googled her," Des said. "She's some hard-hitting corporate firefighter who goes around the world nursing ailing companies back to health. The media is her specialty. Oh, and apparently Shirley Tucker Dill is known in the business as STD."

"Wow, people must truly adore her," I said.

Nancy tugged at the ring pull on her Coke can and went hunting for a glass. "This is not looking good. She hasn't said what her plans are for the program, but if this woman takes *Coffee Break* down-market and turns it into some trashy tabloid chat show, she's not going to want me presenting it. I'm far too highbrow."

It was true. Nancy was too highbrow, but did she have to be quite so snotty?

"Right," I said, after Des had left with his mug of tea. "Guess I'd better go and say hi to Shirley Tucker thingy."

"Dill," Nancy obliged. "And maybe it's best you don't go in looking like you've just been rescued from the *Titanic*." She put her hand into her jacket pocket. "Here." She handed me an elastic hair band.

"Brilliant. Thanks." I could never work Nancy out. Her self-centeredness drove everybody round the bend. Then she would perform some small act of kindness, which would leave people thinking she wasn't so bad after all. Ditto when she got drunk and started kissing everybody.

"By the way," Nancy said, halfway out the door with her glass of Coke, "you'll find Shirley Tucker Dill in Liz's old office."

I put a brush through my still damp hair and pulled it back into a ponytail. I felt like a fourteen-year-old about to be hauled up in front of the school principal.

Shirley Tucker Dill's door was open. I gave a polite tap.

"Hello, I'm Sophie Lawson," I said, hovering in the doorway.

Shirley Tucker Dill looked up from the papers on her desk and pushed her reading glasses onto her head. She couldn't have looked less haughty or chisel faced. Sitting in front of me was a plump, smiley woman—sixtyish at a guess—with big cotton-candy hair, her crepey bosom spilling out of a very mauve, very low-cut, cheap Lycra top. If she was the devil, she certainly wasn't wearing Prada.

"G'day, Soph," she said. "Come in, come in. We missed you at the meet and greet." Her face still on full beam, she bustled around to the front of her desk and took my hand in both of hers.

"I'm so sorry about that." I explained about the person under a train at Stockwell.

"No worries. Better late than never. Now, then, sit your body down and I'll sort us out a cuppa. Dunno about you, but I'm as dry as a dead dingo's donga." I took that to mean that Shirley Tucker Dill was very thirsty indeed. I said that I would love a cup of coffee. She motioned me to the leather sofa. Meanwhile she went to the door that connected her office to the one belonging to her PA. "Wend—two coffees, please. Quick as you like. And where are those financial reports I asked you for?"

So she'd kept Wendy on. Wendy had been Liz's PA.

"I put them on your desk," Wendy's voice came back.

"Oh, right." Shirley Tucker Dill went to her desk and started leafing through the stack of papers.

"What's going on? There's nothing for 2008 or 2009. Wend, could you get in here?"

Wendy appeared and shot me the briefest of eye rolls. She was a young graduate, her heart set on a career in media management. Everybody liked Wendy. Liz had thought the world of her. She was obliging and easygoing, not to mention great at her job. Nothing got under Wendy's skin. Until now, it seemed. After only a few hours in Shirley Tucker Dill's employ, the poor girl was clearly feeling the strain.

"I'm sorry, Shirley. I must have forgotten to print it off." This was a first, seeing Wendy flustered.

"Wend, I need you to get your act together. I've got a meeting with the finance director later. We're meant to be going over the new budget proposals and you're sending me in unprepared. I need that printout right away."

"I'll do it as soon as I've got the coffee."

"No, Wend. You'll do it now."

"Fine."

Shooting me another glance, Wendy left the room.

Since this was Shirley Tucker Dill's first day in a new job, I felt that I should give her the benefit of the doubt and put her behavior down to anxiety. But deep down I suspected that Nancy and Des had got her pegged. Despite her superficial charm, Shirley Tucker Dill clearly had despotic tendencies.

She came over and lowered herself into the armchair opposite me. "You know, Soph," she said, crossing her legs and revealing rather too much fat, dimpled thigh. "I've heard a lot of good things about you."

"Really?"

"Yes. From Liz. I called her last night to get the lowdown on everybody who works on the program. She sang the praises of the entire team, but she singled you out. Said you do a terrific job and that you're very popular in the office."

I felt my cheeks burning. I wasn't good with compliments. "That's very kind of her."

Just then Wendy appeared carrying a folder. Shirley Tucker Dill didn't say anything. She merely motioned her hand towards the desk.

"Kindness has nothing to do with it," Shirley Tucker Dill continued. "Liz was telling it the way she saw it. Look—as you'll discover, I'm not one to beat about the bush, so I'll get straight to the point. Liz suggested that you should take over as editor."

It had occurred to me that as senior producer I might be considered for Liz's job, but I'd rejected the notion on the grounds that GLB had appointed a media *change* consultant, not a media keep-things-pretty-much-as-they-are-with-a-few-tweaks-here-and-there consultant.

"I'd assumed you'd be bringing in somebody new," I said. "You know—fresh blood and all that."

"Why on earth would I want somebody new? By all accounts, you're great at your job and I'm a firm believer in rewarding talent." Could this mean she wasn't planning drastic changes to the program after all?

"Thank you. I appreciate that," I said.

"Now, as far as money is concerned, they won't be able to offer you a pay raise right away. You'll appreciate that these days the budget's pretty tight, but if things work out there might be a small salary increase sometime next year. So, what do you say?"

"Shirley, I'm very flattered—"

"So, can I take that a yes?"

Not exactly. I couldn't accept the job until I knew for certain that she wasn't planning to turn *Coffee Break* into some trashy tabloid show. If she was, then I would have to turn it down. I wasn't about to become Shirley Tucker Dill's puppet and implement changes that would destroy the program.

"Shirley, there's something I need to ask you. We all know that James Harding is insisting on a complete face-lift for the program, so I'm assuming that you'll be making quite a few changes—"

With exquisitely bad timing, Wendy reappeared. She was carrying two cups of coffee on a tray, which she set down on the low table in front of us.

"By the way," she whispered to Shirley Tucker Dill, "the chairman is waiting outside. Apparently you had a meeting arranged."

"Good God! Of course we did. Well, don't leave the poor man hanging around outside. Show him in, show him in."

Shirley Tucker Dill and James Harding fell into each other's arms.

"Jimmy, you old bastard!"

These two clearly went way back.

"Less of the *old*, if you please." "Jimmy" grinned.

"So, why weren't you here to meet me when I arrived?"

"Apologies. I was driving down from Manchester. The M1 was chockablock coming into London." He took both her hands in his and stepped back. "You're looking good, Shirley."

"Flatterer. Truth is, we've both packed on a few pounds over the years. But thank Christ I still have more hair than you." Shirley Tucker Dill turned to me. "Jimmy and I met when we were both interns at Radio Mersey in Liverpool. I'd come to the UK for a year as part of my university journalism course. Of course Jimmy was follicly challenged even then, bless him . . . So, I take it you know Sophie Lawson."

James Harding, who appeared a good deal less at ease with this talk of his lack of follicles than Shirley Tucker Dill, turned to me and looked blank. "Yes . . . of course."

"We've met a couple of times," I said, stepping in to save the chairman from embarrassment. "At various GLB functions, but I'm sure you probably don't remember me. I'm one of the producers on *Coffee Break*."

"Actually," Shirley Tucker Dill said, "Soph is the senior producer, but not for much longer. I've just offered her the job of program editor and she's said yes."

Before I could say anything, James Harding was shaking my hand and offering me his congratulations.

"Yeah, good on ya, Soph," Shirley Tucker Dill said. "I've got this feeling in my waters that you and I are going to make a great team."

"The thing is," I said, "now that I've got you both here, there are a few questions—"

Shirley Tucker Dill was looking at her watch. "Soph, to be honest I really don't have time to chat now. Maybe we could hook up again later. Right now Jimmy and I need to talk business."

"Oh . . . of course. No problem," I heard myself say. "I'll leave you to it."

I headed back to my office, furious with myself for not standing my ground. Shirley Tucker Dill and James Harding might have had urgent business to discuss, but, without being rude, I could have insisted they hear me out. Instead, I'd allowed this woman to dismiss me as if I were the office junior. I wasn't easily intimidated, but despite her homey charm Shirley Tucker Dill oozed autocratic brusqueness, the certainty and self-belief that said, "Nobody messes with me."

Intimidating as she was, there was no way that I could allow her to bulldoze me into accepting the editor's job—at least not until I knew her plans for the program. She had suggested that we meet again "later," whenever that might be. I wasn't prepared to wait. I pulled myself up to my full five foot, four and a half inches and decided to call Wendy to see if I could get back in to see Shirley as soon as her meeting with James Harding was over.

Back at my desk, I dialed Wendy's extension, but there was no answer. I decided to give it a few minutes and try again. Meanwhile,

I started listening to a feature that one of our freelancers had just handed in. It was a cheery piece on the social consequences of the Black Death with particular reference to the persecution of ethnic minorities such as the Jews. I couldn't concentrate. I could imagine a time when I might be able to turn my mind to pus-oozing boils, but this wasn't one of them.

I was in the middle of dealing with e-mails when Greg called. He wanted to know if I'd received a letter from my lawyer outlining his maintenance offer for the children.

"I know it should be more," he said. "And I'm working on it. The thing is, now that I'm living with Roz, I'm contributing towards her overheads, so at the moment it's the best I can do. But if you think about it, things would be even tougher if I was still paying rent on that flat."

I agreed that this was some consolation. The problem remained that once all the household bills were taken care of, there was no money left for emergencies. If the roof started to leak or the car needed work, our only option was to pay for the repairs by credit card.

Raiding the kids' school fees fund was an option, but not one either of us could entertain. The idea of our children paying for our divorce and their education suffering as a result was unthinkable.

"What a bloody mess we've made," I said.

"I know, but there's nothing to be achieved by beating ourselves up. We have to move on."

"I guess . . . But what about the lawyers' fees? Have you thought about that?"

"Selling the tank should raise a few grand," Greg said.

"How's that going? Any progress?"

"A few people have shown an interest."

"But still no actual takers," I said.

"Soph, you don't seem to understand that I'm doing my best here."

"And for your information, so am I."

I told him that I was planning to let Klaudia go. Not that it was going to be easy. We all thought the world of her and she'd worked so hard to keep the kids' spirits up after Greg left.

I explained that Debbie-from-down-the-road had offered to do the school run and watch the kids each evening until I got home. She said she owed me big-time, since Klaudia had spent months ferrying Ella and Jack to and from school after she'd slipped a disc. "Of course, I said she didn't owe me a thing, but she insisted. It seems like too good an offer to turn down."

I also mentioned that I was dispensing with Mrs. Fredericks's twice-weekly cleaning services. She was always going on about how impossible it was to reach the dirt in my house because the place was so untidy and full of crap. There really didn't seem much point in keeping her on. I'd just have to make time to clean the bathroom and kitchen, vacuum, dust, change the bed linen, do the laundry . . .

Greg seemed pathetically grateful, but I couldn't conceal my bitterness.

"Though why the children and I should suffer so that you can shack up with your new girlfriend beats me."

"Soph, stop it. It's not like that. I'm not doing this to spite you, and like I just said, living with Roz works out much cheaper than paying rent on a flat. And I honestly don't think she's being unreasonable asking me to contribute towards the bills. We have to accept that splitting up costs money. It's as simple as that."

"Yeah, you're right, I guess. I'm sorry."

I glanced at my watch and realized that *Coffee Break* was about to air. Missing the show was practically a capital offense. "Greg, I gotta go. I need to listen to the program. Don't worry about the maintenance stuff. I'll e-mail my lawyer and tell him to accept your offer."

As soon as I put the phone down, I tried Wendy's extension again. Still no reply. Nancy had told me that Shirley Tucker Dill was planning to watch the program go out. Maybe she'd taken Wendy with her.

I needed to get hold of Shirley before the daily postmort. I couldn't risk her announcing my promotion in the meeting. I decided to try and collar her before it started.

The moment the program was over, I headed for the elevator, hoping to catch her. People came and went, but there was no sign of Shirley Tucker Dill. Then Tess emerged. Tess was our most junior producer and today, for only the second time, she had been put in charge of the show.

Despite being not long out of university, Tess was showing great promise and I knew that she would be eager to impress Shirley Tucker Dill. I hadn't had the heart to warn her that her star feature on a women's puppet theater collective was unlikely to find favor with our media change consultant. Judging by the taut expression on the poor girl's face, Shirley Tucker Dill had already had words with her about it.

"So, what did she think of the program?" I said, knowing perfectly well what the answer would be.

"She pretty much hated everything—even the serial."

Tess looked close to tears. Shirley Tucker Dill would be coming out of the lift at any moment and I didn't want her to see Tess crying. I suggested we duck into the ladies' for a minute.

"She called the show 'boring' and 'worthy,'" Tess said, leaning against a sink. "And she gave me a right roasting over the puppet theater piece." Tears started to roll down her cheeks.

I put my arm around her. "Tess, this isn't your fault. You're a talented producer and we all know how hard you work. This is about our new media change consultant having issues with the whole character and makeup of the show. As we suspected, she isn't a fan. God only knows what changes she's got in mind."

By the time Tess and I got to the conference room, Shirley Tucker Dill was already there, seated at the head of the long table and chatting to a couple of other producers. I would get no chance to speak to her now. I decided that my only option was to let her announce her plans for the program. If they were as radical as we all expected, I would have no option but to tell her—in front of everybody else—that I couldn't take the job after all.

It was a couple of minutes before we were all assembled. The tension was palpable. I suspected that today's studio managers had already let it be known that Shirley Tucker Dill had been less than impressed by the program.

"Good morning again," Shirley Tucker Dill said, with that same disarming smile. "This is of course my first postmortem, so I'd be grateful if you'd be gentle with me."

There were a few nervous titters.

"To kick off, though, I'd like to make a few comments about today's show." She offered another smile before steepling her fingers and regarding us over her reading glasses. "To put it mildly, it left me seriously underwhelmed."

People shuffled in their seats. Looks were exchanged. Tess looked ready to blub again.

"OK, I'm not going to sugarcoat the pill. As I've already told Tess, the feature on women's puppet theater collectives was about as boring as a wet weekend in Wooroloo. The piece on Chinese women being forced to have abortions if they disobey the government's one-child edict was just plain depressing. Ditto the feature on people sleeping on the streets in London. If there's one thing you should know about me, it's that I don't *do* depressing."

"So," I ventured in an attempt to lighten the atmosphere, "I suppose a piece on the Black Death would be out of the question."

STD burst out laughing. "Good one, Soph. You really know how to wind a woman up."

Tess started to speak. "Shirley, for the record, I'd like to say that I worked really hard putting today's program together and—"

"I'm sure you did. Don't get me wrong. I'm not accusing anybody of laziness. I'm accusing the lot of you of being excruciatingly dull and boring."

That was telling us.

"You should know that I have spent the last few weeks listening to recordings of *Coffee Break*. It's polished and slick, I grant you, but at the same time it's unbearably worthy and middle class. If I have to listen to another piece on tampons made of bark or Inuit women setting up seal cooperatives, I think I might be forced to eat my own face. It ends now. Do I make myself clear?"

"Crystal," Nancy muttered.

"I'm assuming," I said, "that from now on you see the program moving in a different direction."

"You betcha." Shirley Tucker Dill, hard-arsed corporate fire-fighter, leaned forward in her seat and prodded the air with a purple-frosted talon.

"I want the show sexed up," she went on. "I want younger, hipper guests, more human-interest stories and media gossip. I want *X Factor* contestants talking about their personal struggles. I want transsexuals, rape and incest survivors."

Eyes rolled. More looks were exchanged. Pens were flung onto notepads. If Shirley Tucker Dill noticed our nonverbal dissent, she chose to ignore it.

More than anything, she wanted stars, stars, stars. What she didn't mention was that the budget was so tight that the program was hardly likely to attract A-listers. That meant we'd be forced to broadcast in-depth interviews with the likes of David Hasselhoff's pool guy.

Shirley Tucker Dill's plans for the program were far more draconian than anybody had expected. We were all too shocked to speak—even Des, which was a first.

Rather than pause to gauge opinion or permit discussion, she continued to set out her demands. Finally, just as it was looking like the end would never come, she started to wind things down by saying how much she was looking forward to working with everybody. I realized that any moment now she was going to announce my appointment as program editor. I had to set the record straight before anybody had the chance to think I'd betrayed them. I opened my mouth to speak, but Nancy beat me to it.

"The thing is, Shirley," she said, "although we're all agreed that the program needs a bit of fine-tuning—we know it can be a bit worthy—none of us is entirely sure about the wisdom of taking it down-market."

Shirley Tucker Dill's heavily penciled, overplucked eyebrows formed arches. This was a woman unused to being challenged.

"Our listeners are educated, middle-class women," Nancy plowed on, "who aren't really interested in tawdry human interest stories or Paris Hilton's views on the world."

There were several "hear, hears." Once again I tried to speak, but this time it was STD who got in first.

"The listeners you have at the moment may not be interested," STD came back at Nancy. "That's why we have to find new ones. The point you're missing is that *Coffee Break* is hemorrhaging listeners. The old codgers are all dying and nobody's replacing them. If the show is to be saved—if your jobs are to be saved—there is only one way forward. We have to broaden the show's appeal. And I should tell you that James Harding and the rest of the GLB board are in agreement."

"But *Coffee Break* is an institution," somebody piped up.

"So was the Third Reich, but we got rid of that." STD laughed. "Look, I know that this has all come as one hell of a shock, but I assure you that this strategy is the only one that makes sense."

"I disagree," Nancy said.

"Disagree all you like, but let me be clear. I fully intend to see these changes implemented. As your former leader the late, great and glorious Iron Lady once said: 'The lady is not for turning' . . . Now, if there's nothing else, there's one more announcement I would like to make."

This was it. She was about to tell everybody that I'd accepted the editor's job.

"Shirley, I'm sorry, but if I could just break in—"

"Ah, our new editor is already exercising her powers, I see . . . Oops—I seem to have let the cat out of the bag."

"Excuse me?" Nancy said. "Sophie has taken the job of editor?" She turned to glare at me.

"Reckon she has!" Shirley Tucker Dill said before I had the chance to open my mouth. "I'm sure you'll agree that as senior producer she was the obvious choice and I know that you'll be offering her your full support as the program changes kick in."

Shirley Tucker Dill glanced at her watch and grimaced. "Stroll on a boat! Sorry, people, 'fraid I'll have to love you and leave you. I've got a meeting with the finance director."

She pushed back her chair. "Remember, I'm counting on you, Soph," she said. With that she picked up her briefcase and headed for the door.

Nancy was glaring at me again, arms folded. "And she's counting on you for what, might I ask? To convince us to do as we're damn well told?"

"No. Absolutely not. Please let me explain."

"I really don't think any explanation is needed. She must have told you her plans in the meeting you had with her this morning. Suffice it to say that the words 'turn' and 'coat' spring to mind. So how much did she offer you? It was clearly enough to make it worth your while?"

"Oh God," Tess said. "Sophie, please say you haven't become STD's bitch."

"I most certainly have not. Look, will you both take it easy. This isn't what it looks like."

"So you haven't taken the job?" Des said.

"No . . . yes . . . well, sort of."

"Sort of?" he persisted. "Come on. Have you or haven't you?"

I explained what had happened in the meeting. "The upshot is that STD thinks I've taken it, but I haven't actually said yes."

"And you really expect us to believe that?" Nancy said. "I mean, what abandoned wife with two children is going to turn down a promotion and a hefty pay raise?"

"Nancy, I'll thank you not to refer to me as an abandoned wife. I've told you before, there was no third party involved."

Several people accused her of being out of order. At least she had the good grace to blush.

"And there is no pay raise. At least not for the time being. And even if I do get one, it won't be until next year and STD has made it clear that it'll be minimal." I took a deep breath and tried to calm down. "But now that I know what STD's plans are, I have no intention of taking the job. As soon as she's out of her meeting with the FD, I'll go and explain."

"If you ask me," Des said, "that would be a seriously bad move."

I looked at him. "How do you work that out?"

"It's obvious," Des said, tweaking a couple of beard hairs. "If you turn down the job, then STD will be forced to advertise for a new editor. That means we end up with somebody who knows nothing about the program and has no loyalty to it. This person isn't going to give a stuff about taking the program down-market. They're simply going to roll over and, as Tess so eloquently put it, 'become STD's bitch.' That means we end up doing battle with two people rather than one. With you as editor, we have a spokesperson. It means we can at least try to fight STD's changes."

It occurred to me that he might have a point. Judging by the noises of approval coming from around the table, it had occurred to other people as well.

There was one thing holding me back.

"Just to clarify," I said, "when you say I would be your spokesperson, are you suggesting that I would be doing battle with STD on my own?"

"You wouldn't be *alone* exactly," Des said. "We'd all be behind you, supporting you all the way."

There was a chorus of agreement.

"Yes, but why do I get the sense that this would be from another building?"

"Come on, Sophie," Des said. "Since when have you been scared of confrontation?"

"Since I met Shirley Tucker Dill. The woman's a tyrant." I looked at Des. "Why can't you be our spokesperson? After all, you're our NUJ rep and you've been rabble-rousing for years."

"Usually I would seize the opportunity with both hands, but in this instance I see my role more as coordinating action from the shop floor."

"Meaning she scares the pants off you, too."

"Not at all. I just think that as editor you will have her ear more than the rest of us. Plus I can be pretty aggressive when I want to be, and I think I might rub her up the wrong way."

"Des, you are so full of crap. Just admit you're scared."

"OK, hands up. I'm terrified."

"Well, I'm not," Nancy said. "The woman's as common as muck. She doesn't scare me one iota."

"So you be our spokesperson," I said.

"Believe me, I'd be more than happy to oblige, but I suspect that my days on *Coffee Break* are numbered. Now that STD is planning to tabloid the program, she's going to want some ditzy airhead presenter who eats M&M's in alphabetical order."

Des agreed that was a possibility. "But you'll get a damn good payoff."

"I don't want a payoff. I want a job. And with all the media cutbacks, the likelihood is I'll never work again. Have you any idea how many applicants there are for every presenting job? I may be damned good at what I do, but the truth is, I'll never see twenty-five again."

"Come on, Nancy," I said. "We're all in this together. Let's just take it one day at a time, eh?"

She gave a shrug. "I guess I have no choice."

I turned to Des. "So what's the possibility that I could be sacked if I become too much of a thorn in Shirley Tucker Dill's side?"

"She can't sack you for disagreeing with her and trying to change her opinion. As editor you have a right to express your views. It's probably a long shot, but she might just respond to some gentle persuasion. Come on, Sophie, what do you say?"

Nancy had just admitted she didn't have a choice and now I was aware that I didn't have one, either. Yes, I was scared of taking on Shirley Tucker Dill. Despite Des's reassurances, I was even more scared of losing my job, but people were relying on me. I couldn't walk away.

"OK," I said. "If everybody's happy, I'll leave things as they are with Shirley and take the job."

Des, ever the shop steward, called for a show of hands. It was unanimous. I was the new editor and the "workers'" official spokesperson.

Before we drifted out of the conference room, Des made a short, rallying, "Remember, everybody—as Marx said—we've got nothing to lose but our chains."

"Speak for yourself," I muttered.

Chapter 5

*B*ack in my office, I carried on listening to the interviews and features I'd commissioned over the last few weeks and which had been due to go out in the New Year. I wondered how on earth I was going to get them past STD. The piece on the Black Death was clearly for the scrap heap, but there were several items I was determined to fight for, particularly one on postpartum depression and another on parenting autistic children. The secret to placating her might be to balance them with some humorous offbeat items.

By midafternoon my head was starting to ache. I guessed it wasn't surprising, bearing in mind all that had happened in the last few hours. I took a couple of Tylenol, which had almost no effect, and struggled on until five o'clock. By then my desk was pretty much clear, so I decided to call it a day.

An hour later—after a journey that couldn't have been more different from the one I'd had that morning—I was heading out of Putney Station. I walked home slowly, hoping the air would ease my headache. I mulled as I walked. Was I really up to taking on Shirley Tucker Dill? What if the worst happened and she managed to fire me?

How would the kids and I survive without my salary? I'd taken the editor's job because I didn't want to let down my colleagues, but if I lost it, I'd be letting down Amy and Ben—again. That was unthinkable.

As I slid my front-door key in the lock I was aware that, despite the mulling and worrying, the tension in my head had eased. The walk and the air had done their job. I stepped into the hall and was met by shrieks and laughter coming from upstairs. I remembered that Amy and Ben each had a friend over for tea. They were all making such a racket that they didn't hear me come in. I took off my coat and headed to the kitchen. Klaudia was at the stove, spatula in hand, frying sausages.

"Everything OK?" I said by way of greeting.

Klaudia turned around. "Fine." It was then that I saw her red eyes and cheeks streaked with tears.

"Sweetie," I said, going over to her, "what on earth's the matter?"

"I am not knowing how to tell you." She was starting to sob.

I took the spatula from her, laid it on the counter and turned out the light under the frying pan. Taking her gently by the arm, I led her to the kitchen table. We both sat down.

"Come on, what is it? Have you had a fight with Marek?"

Marek was her boyfriend back in Warsaw. She shook her head.

"What is it, then?"

"I hef baby."

"You hef baby? Where? Here? You mean somebody's asked you to look after it?"

"No. I yam expecting baby."

"Omigod . . . You're pregnant?"

"Yes. It happen when I go home. Marek and me, we have relations with naked penis."

"Ah, that would explain it. Having relations with naked penis probably wasn't the best idea. So I'm guessing you're not very happy about this."

"No. We very happy. Even though we not plan baby."

"That's brilliant. So why the tears?"

"I hef to leave you and the children. Marek wants me to go home and for him and my mother to look after me. I yam so sorry I let you down."

I leaned forward and gave Klaudia a hug. I'd been dreading having to tell her that I couldn't afford to keep her on and here she was letting me off the hook. I couldn't believe it.

"Oh, Klaudia, you aren't letting us down. You're having a baby—you have to focus on that now. You mustn't worry about us."

"But I do worry. Amy and Ben are still much missing their father and I should be here to ease their pains."

"They'll be fine. It's been six months now. I honestly think they're over the worst. And you have been so wonderful with them—particularly since Greg left. I don't know what I would have done without you. I'll never be able to thank you enough."

"Eet has been my pleasure."

I got up, put my arms around her and gave her a hug.

"You know, Klaudia, we're really going to miss you, but we'll manage . . . somehow."

"You sure? You really mean that?"

"Absolutely. Now dry those tears."

Once Klaudia had calmed down, I went upstairs to say hi to the kids. Amy and Georgia, her best friend (for this week at least), were practicing their lines for the school nativity play. Except it wasn't called a nativity play anymore. There had been a letter from the school telling parents that this year ("in accordance with our approved diversity procedure") the children would be performing a multicultural generic holiday play. Georgia was playing the Hindu god Vishnu and Amy was an Eskimo. Topping the bill was a boy in year four who would be doing an impersonation of Elvis singing "Winter Wonderland."

"Hey, Georgia. Hey, Amy. How was school?"

"Good, thank you," Georgia said in that singsong voice of hers. Everybody said what a sunny child she was. Her mother put it down to having breast-fed her until she was five.

"And how was your day, Amy?"

" 'K."

"What did you get up to?"

"Dunno. Stuff. Look, Mum, please can you go away? We're practicing."

Amy was reaching that age where her parents were becoming an embarrassment, but I supposed I should be grateful. At least she'd said please when she asked me to beat it.

Next door, Ben and Arthur were sitting on the floor, surrounded by pillows and cushions. Propped up against these were the TV remote, the CD player remote, the long-defunct video player remote, the Apple TV remote and an old computer keyboard. "Hi, boys. You OK?"

"Sshh . . . we're trying to work out the code."

"The code?"

"For our time machine," Arthur said. "We need the right code so that we can get to Bef-lehem to see the baby Jesus."

Clearly the school's efforts to suppress their pupils' interest in the nativity story hadn't worked.

"Mrs. O'Reilly," Arthur went on, "brought a model of the nativity scene into school."

"That must have gone down well," I muttered.

Mrs. O'Reilly was Arthur's teacher. She'd been at the school for over thirty years. She was one of those devoted, strict-but-kind teachers who managed to bring out the best in even her dullest pupils. The children loved her. Ditto the parents, who would far rather have had Mrs. O'Reilly running the school than the drippy—in accordance with our approved diversity procedure—Mrs. McKay.

"She took the whole of year three into the hall," Ben went on, "and said that this was a Christian country and Christmas was a Christian festival and that it was wrong that we weren't being taught the story of baby Jesus."

"Mrs. O'Reilly said that?" Even as an agnostic Jew, I couldn't help thinking good on her. But there could be no doubt that once the principal and the school governors got wind of her politically incorrect challenge, her days at Parkhall Primary School would be numbered. I could only assume that she'd done it because she wasn't far off retirement and didn't give a damn what the head and the governors thought.

"Yeah," Ben said, "and then she told us the nativity story, but I remembered it from playgroup."

"Me, too," Arthur piped up, clearly not wishing to appear uninformed.

"Mrs. O'Reilly," Ben continued, "said that the three wise men brought presents for the baby Jesus and one of them got him aftershave."

"Really? I didn't know that."

"Yeah, it's called Franky's Scents."

Just then Klaudia called up to the kids to tell them tea was ready. The boys sprang to their feet. Clearly, paying homage to the Christ child couldn't compete with the unholy delights of a plate of sausages and oven chips. They thundered hippopotamus-like down the stairs. I heard Ben begging Klaudia to let them eat in front of the TV. Knowing that I usually gave in to this demand, Klaudia didn't put up a fight.

Still giggling to myself about Franky's Scents, I went into my room, got changed out of my work clothes and put on a pair of joggers and a sweater. As I headed back downstairs I could hear Amy and Georgia talking at the kitchen table about getting tattoos when they were older. Georgia wanted Winnie the Pooh above her ankle, and seeing as her mother had two dolphin tattoos (one on each breast, no doubt), she didn't think this would be a problem.

"If I asked to get a tattoo," Amy was saying, "my dad would go mental, but Mum wouldn't mind. She's pretty cool."

How about that? I wasn't such an embarrassment to my daughter after all. In fact, I was one of the "cool" mums. For a few moments, I basked in the warm glow of self-congratulation.

"Mum," Amy said as I came into the kitchen, "you wouldn't mind me getting a tattoo when I'm sixteen, would you?"

"I guess not. So long as it was done safely and it wasn't huge."

"So a tiny butterfly at the top of my arm would be OK?"

"I think that could be cute."

Amy looked at Georgia. "I told you she was cool."

I was busy basking again, but Amy interrupted. "Mum, there's no ketchup and we're out of Coco Pops. Plus I had to have whole wheat toast for breakfast this morning."

A quick check of the fridge and cupboards revealed that these weren't the only things we were out of. I decided that since the kids were occupied with their friends and not clamoring for my attention, I would nip out and do a supermarket run.

I pushed my cart up and down the aisles and thought about Klaudia leaving and how she would be the fourth person to have "deserted" Amy and Ben in the last few months. My children were about to develop abandonment issues—I just knew it. They would grow up believing there was no point getting into relationships, because in the end people always walked away. They would need therapy. Who was going to pay for that? Unless our finances improved, it wasn't going to be Greg and me. In a few years we could have two disturbed young adults on our hands and no way of providing them with the help they needed: one more thing to beat myself up about.

I reached the aisle with jams, pickles and preserves. So far, the only thing in my cart was a giant box of Tampax Super. I picked up a jar of sauerkraut and put it back. It was only Greg who liked the stuff.

I was heading towards the deli counter, wondering yet again if there was anything more Greg and I could have done to save our marriage, when I had a head-on trolley collision with another shopper. Barely looking up, I offered an "Oops-sorry-my-fault." After a speedy disengagement, I carried on down the aisle.

"Soph?" the male voice said. "Is that you?"

I stopped and looked over my shoulder. I saw a guy about my own age in jeans and a reefer jacket. The floppy nineties hair had gone and been replaced by a short, trendy cut, but the face that smiled out from the dark stubble was unmistakable. It had aged a bit, but in a good, Brad Pitt kind of a way. There was no doubt, the man still had it goin' on.

"Omigod! Huckleberry!"

As he came towards me, I did an about-turn with my cart. We pulled up alongside the posh Bonne Maman jams and threw our arms around each other.

"Huckleberry—I don't believe it."

Huckleberry. The Southern states of the U.S. probably contained a smattering of Huckleberries, but over here it was the kind of twee name a child gave his hamster. A wife in search of an affectionate pet name for her husband's penis might happen upon Huckleberry. No parent would consider it a suitable name for their son.

Unless, of course, those parents happen to be the Taylors. In the seventies, Huckleberry's father, Byron, had been a lecturer in American literature at the University of Norwich. His wife, Mimi, was a performance poet. They were both huge Twain fans and had apparently always planned to name their firstborn son Huckleberry.

"So, how long has it been?" I said, taking in the smoky gray eyes that had always been his trademark.

"I don't know. How many years since we left university?"

"Too many. So how are you? What are you up to? The last I heard, you were teaching in Somalia."

A passing old lady tutted because we were blocking the aisle. We apologized and moved ourselves and our carts closer to the shelves. I clocked that his cart contained several frozen pizzas and ready meals for one. Then I noticed my box of Tampax Super. I grabbed a jar of pickled onions and stood it in front of the box.

"Yes, I was working at a village school not far from Mogadishu."

"So you really followed your dream."

He looked ever so slightly awkward. Maybe these days it embarrassed him to be reminded of his former idealist self. "I guess I did," he said.

I'd known Huckleberry since high school. Nobody dared make fun of his name. Huck was over six feet, well built and seriously good looking. Girls practically fell at his feet and he did nothing to fend them off. Huck became known as Huck the Fuck. I fancied him something rotten, but he was way out of my league. I was too scared even to speak to him.

By coincidence, we ended up at the same university: Manchester. I studied English. He did modern history. Both in the arts faculty, we found ourselves hanging out with the same crowd and going to the same parties. By then I'd had a couple of boyfriends and my confidence had improved. I wasn't quite so scared of him anymore. That wasn't to say I could have gone up to him and asked him out on a date. And anyway, Huck always had a gorgeous blond drama student on the go.

Despite his Huck the Fuck handle and the eat-as-much-as-you-like buffet that was his sex life, Huck was a highly intelligent, thoughtful chap. Like me, he was a member of the university Unite Against Fascism society. Occasionally, after the Thursday night meetings, the two of us would go for a drink in the student union bar and exchange views on the struggle.

Huck would tell me that he was determined to do something meaningful with his life. "I'm not interested in money. I want to be of use." Behind his back, people said it was all a romantic, idealistic pose and took the piss. Some even did it to his face, but Huck's determination never faltered. Straight after university he did Voluntary Service Overseas and spent several years teaching in India. Even after Greg and I were married, Huck was still sending me postcards telling me what he was up to. (Despite my denials, Greg was convinced he was an old flame who couldn't quite let go.) When he went to Africa in the late nineties the postcards petered out.

"So, what on earth are you doing in these parts?" I asked.

"Well, after Somalia I went back to India for a few years. I was teaching slum kids in Mumbai. In the end I decided that after all these years in Africa and India, I was missing home, so about six months ago—much to my parents' delight—I decided to come back. I applied for a job working for a charity that runs youth clubs for underprivileged kids. Long story short, I got the job." He paused. "So, what about you? The last I heard, you were at the BBC."

I brought him up to speed.

"*Coffee Break* is a great program," he said. "I always listened to it when I came home on visits."

"Well, the way things are going, it may not be much longer for this world." I explained about the plans to take it down-market.

"That's sacrilege. You guys should think about going on strike."

I told him that the thought had occurred. "So you're working at a youth club around here?" I asked.

"Yes. My official title is senior manager. In other words, I'm in charge. It's at the Princess Margaret houses."

"Blimey. You must have your work cut out there."

He gave a half smile. "You could say that."

The Princess Margaret public housing projects had been built in the sixties as part of London's slum clearance scheme. Bleak didn't begin to describe it. Not long ago, one of the newspapers had called it "an emblem of urban decrepitude." It consisted of acre upon windswept acre of drab impregnable concrete blocks—apparently inspired by Le Corbusier—connected by dank passageways and tight stairwells that provided refuge for addicts and muggers. There were filthy curtains behind rotten window frames, showing little sign of life.

"During the day we feed the homeless. In the evening we attempt to keep the kids living there occupied. Not that we get many turning up. Playing table tennis on a crappy old table with no net doesn't exactly get their adrenaline pumping. It wasn't long before I discovered that nearly every teenager there is a member of a gang. Hardly a week goes by when some kid doesn't get knifed."

"I know. It always makes the headlines in the local paper. What sort of a society lets children grow up in these places? You drive past and you see these beautiful, innocent babies in their buggies and wonder how they'll end up."

"I have that thought every day," he said.

I was so enjoying catching up that I suggested we each finish our shopping and meet in the supermarket café for a quick cuppa. I said

I couldn't stay long because I wanted to get back to the kids and spend some time with them before bedtime.

Half an hour later we were sitting at a table looking out over the car park and drinking weak cappuccinos.

Huck asked about Amy and Ben. I took out my phone and showed him pictures. He seemed genuinely interested. "They look like great kids."

"They are, and they've been through so much recently."

"In what way?"

"Their father and I split up six months ago."

"I'm so sorry. That must have been hard."

"Yeah," I said, spooning my cappuccino froth. "It wasn't great."

These days, I made a point of not going on about my marriage breakup. Apart from Annie and Gail and my other close friends, people weren't interested in hearing the ins and outs of what was, after all, just another divorce saga. Huck didn't say anything—he clearly wasn't about to pry—but there was something about his expression that seemed to be inviting me to talk. I found myself telling him about the separation.

"I am so sorry," he said when I'd come to the end of my tale. "What a shitty time you've had."

I managed a smile. "It hasn't been easy, but it feels like the worst is over." By now I felt that I'd burdened him long enough with my woes. I decided to change the subject.

"So," I said, "is there a Mrs. Huck?" Bearing in mind the frozen pizzas and ready meals for one, I sensed that there wasn't.

He shook his head.

"Ah, same old Huck, still playing the field," I said, grinning.

"Hardly. I've spent the last two decades living in huts and tents, miles from anywhere. Believe me, the field was pretty limited. I've had a few flings on trips back home, but that's all they were. Plus, as you get older, you realize that casual affairs aren't really very satisfying."

"So there's been nobody serious?"

"Uh-uh."

I took a sip of coffee. "So tell me more about Africa. Why did you stop sending the postcards? I used to look forward to hearing from you."

"I apologize," Huck said. "It was nothing personal—honest. The thing is, when you're working in the middle of nowhere and there's no phone or Internet, you become very inward looking. I found myself focusing entirely on the people I was trying to help. The rest of the world didn't seem very important. I carried on writing to my family, but that was about it. All my friends got pissed off with me. In fact a few even stopped being my friends."

I offered him a smile. "Well, I forgive you. I totally get how you would cut off from the world."

We carried on chatting, but I was aware that it was getting late. By now Arthur and Georgia would have been picked up. I wanted to get back to the kids for sofa and TV time. "Huck, this has been great, but I really do need to get going. My babysitter never minds working late, but I don't like taking advantage of her good nature."

"Of course. I shouldn't have kept you."

"You haven't, honestly. I've really enjoyed catching up."

"Me, too. Look, why don't we do it again? Maybe we could meet up for a drink?"

I almost looked around to check he wasn't asking some hot blond who had just walked in. "OK. Yes," I said. "I'd like that."

"Great. I'll call you."

I wrote my number down on a napkin and we hugged good-bye.

"A bit of me thought I'd heard wrong," I said, chopsticks hovering over a bowl of kung pao shrimp. "I mean, you should have seen the girls he dated at university. They were stunning. They all looked like fashion models. And here he was asking me out. *Me.* Sophie Lawson with the nose."

"Oh, behave," Annie said. "The way you go on, anyone would think you were the spawn of Cyrano de Bergerac. Your nose is beautiful."

"OK, fine. Whatever." I moved in on a particularly plump shrimp and pincered it.

"No. Enough with the 'whatever.' I've seen the way men look at you."

"OK," I said, my mouth full of delicious shrimp. "I admit that I scrub up reasonably well."

"Finally!"

"So now can I get on with telling you about Huck?"

"Tell away."

"OK. So last night the phone goes and it's him to say he's working flat out until after the new year, tending to the homeless and kids from the projects, and how am I fixed for the beginning of January?"

"And you consulted your diary," Annie said, helping herself to more Singapore noodles, "and told him you'd need to move a few things around, but you'd do your best to fit him in."

I laughed. "Yeah, something like that. Of course, by the time I put the phone down reality had set in. There was no way he was asking me out on a *date* date."

"Naturally . . . what with your hideous nose and all."

"Correct. Plus it's not like we have history or anything. We were only ever friends at school. I think now that he's back in the UK, he's feeling lonely. Apparently he lost touch with quite a few of his friends. He's probably looking for people to hang out with."

"OK, have it your own way, but if you ask me, there's no way he's asked you out simply because he wants to hang out and chat about old times. The man is coming on to you. A fiver says I'm right." She spooned up some crispy beef and added it to her bowl of noodles.

"OK, you're on," I said, laughing.

It was the Saturday before Christmas. Rob was back from a ten-day stint in Sydney and had taken the boys to see Chelsea play Arsenal while Annie and I had lunch in Chinatown.

"So," Annie said, "you all set for Christmas?"

I said I'd bought the kids' presents and that the tree—always re-ferred to in our house as the Chanukah bush—was up. "But you know me—I'll probably buy a turkey that's too big for the oven, run out of Scotch tape on Christmas Eve and end up wrapping presents with the aid of a stapler. Plus the house is going to be in even more of a mess than usual." I explained that I'd had to let Mrs. Fredericks go.

"How did she take it?"

"Not well. Money's really tight for her and she relies on her cleaning jobs. I paid her up to January, but I felt absolutely dreadful. If there had been any other way . . ."

"I know. Please don't beat yourself up. You did your best. Come on, let's change the subject. So, are you getting Greg anything for Christmas?"

I said probably not. "Doesn't feel right, somehow. Plus, if the kids see us exchanging gifts, it might send the wrong message and make them think we're getting back together."

Annie said she hadn't thought of that.

"So," I said, "you on top of everything holiday-wise?" It was a daft question. This was the woman who had a Christmas Clock Countdown app for her phone and had started buying presents in September. Two years ago we'd gone to Annie's for Christmas lunch. She'd made her own cheese straws, mulled her own wine, decorated the house with spicy scented candles and fresh greenery. Her goose was roasted to perfection. Ditto her spuds, honey carrots and red cabbage.

"Yeah, I think it's pretty much under control," she said. "The boys and I stirred the pudding last night. We're taking it to Rob's parents. It'll be my contribution to lunch. All I've got left to do is ice the cake. And I thought I might have a go at stollen bread this year."

"What, no mince pies?"

"Oh, I did them days ago. They're in the freezer."

I burst out laughing. "Of course they are. God, just listening to you makes me feel exhausted."

"I enjoy doing Christmas. It's about being together as a family and I want the kids to have something to remember." She stopped herself. "Oh God. I shouldn't have said that—what with you and Greg . . . I wasn't thinking."

I patted her hand and reminded her that for Jews—even lapsed, correction, *collapsed* ones like Greg and me—Christmas wasn't that big a deal.

I topped up our wineglasses. "Annie, can I ask you something?"

"Sure."

"Look, you can tell me to mind my own business, but I've been worried about you."

"About me? Why on earth would you be worried about me?"

"It's just that the other day when I was over at your place with Amy and Ben, you got really angry with Freddie. It's so unlike you to lose it with your kids. I've been wondering what it was about and if you're OK."

She shuffled in her chair. "It wasn't about anything. I told you. It was just the time of the month. I was feeling ratty."

"Really? You sure there's nothing else going on?"

"Soph, I'm fine. Honest. I was having a bad day. Don't you have bad days with your kids?"

"Of course I do. All the time."

"Right, so there you go."

Just then her phone beeped from inside her bag. She took it out and read the text. "Jesus. Why can't he bloody do it for once?" she muttered. "Why does it always have to be me?"

"What's up?"

She forced a smile. "Nothing. Just Rob being a prat."

"You know, in all these years I don't think I've ever heard you call your husband a prat. Come on, Annie, speak to me. What's going on?"

She picked up her glass and downed a large glug of wine. "I'm just a bit fed up, that's all."

"Are things all right with you two?"

"We're great. Rob just annoys me sometimes."

"Like when he just assumed you would put on a New Year's Eve party."

"Yes." She drained her wineglass.

"You seemed fairly pissed off with him."

"Not much gets past you, does it?"

"Oh, come on, Annie. It was pretty hard to miss."

She poured herself some more wine. "I just wish that once in a while Rob would stop treating me like the hired help."

"You sound like me before Greg and I split up."

"He's not untidy like Greg. It's just that he believes that as a stay-at-home wife and mother, I should be responsible for all the domestic duties and that includes seeing to his dry cleaning, ironing his shirts and making sure he never runs out of clean socks and underwear. That text just now was him asking me to stop off on the way home to pick up the pants he left at the dry cleaners to be shortened. Here I am having lunch with you for the first time in ages. Plus he knows that I've been slogging away for weeks doing Christmas stuff, and he can't bloody leave me alone for five minutes." She looked like she might burst into tears. "So you're right. I'm not OK. In fact, I'm very un-OK. And FYI, the New Year's Eve party isn't happening. I managed to find a babysitter and told Rob that he was taking me out to dinner instead."

"Good for you . . . But why didn't you tell me about all this? I'm your best friend. How long have you been bottling this up?"

"A year. Maybe more."

"Now I feel guilty because I didn't pick up that you were unhappy."

"Don't. I've worked very hard at hiding my feelings."

"You can say that again. I thought you were deliriously happy. You were always going on about how you enjoyed staying home to raise the boys and how you felt you were doing your bit for the next generation. Talk about an Oscar-winning performance. You totally had me fooled."

"I wasn't lying—at least not in the beginning. Then, gradually, my feelings started to change, but there was no way I could tell you. I knew that the moment I admitted to another person that I was unhappy, it would become real. I wouldn't have been able to live in denial anymore." She was having trouble controlling the tears now. "This isn't what I signed up for, Soph. It just isn't. I didn't realize that by staying at home to raise our kids and run the home, I would feel so lost."

"How do you mean?"

"I don't know who I am anymore. I'm either Freddie and Tom's mum or Rob's wife. I'm never Annie. I'm not a person; I'm an appendage." She wiped her eyes with the heel of her hand.

"That's nonsense. Of course you're not an appendage. You're still you."

"No, I'm not. Do you remember how I was when I worked at the BBC? I thrived on the pressure. I was confident, articulate, never afraid to speak my mind in meetings. It's you who keeps reminding me that people had me down as the next editor of *The World at One*. Now I'm this pathetic, insecure person who lives through her children."

"Annie, I won't have that. You are anything but pathetic."

"OK, get this. Last night I couldn't sleep because I was lying awake fretting about how many playdates the boys have had this term and plotting a mental graph of their popularity rating. I've got nothing else to think about apart from them and running around after Rob. My brain feels like it's turning to mush—like something abandoned at the back of the fridge."

I took both her hands in mine. "Come on, we all worry about our kids. You worry if they're as smart as other kids. You worry about how many friends they've got. It's normal. Has it occurred to you that you're exhausted because it's Christmas and you need a break?"

Annie shook her head. "It's not Christmas. I've been feeling like this for ages. Maybe I'd be able to cope if it was just the kids making demands, but Rob's just as bad. Marriage needs to be a partnership of equals, but ours isn't. Because he earns the money, Rob is the self-appointed senior partner. He has absolutely no respect for what I contribute to our family."

"I'm sure that's not true. He just takes you for granted, that's all. The only person who's lost respect for you is you."

She wiped her eyes again. "Soph, do you think I should go back to work? You went back when your kids were still babies."

"Yes, because it was the right thing for me. That's not to say I haven't had to live with the guilt. You even think that my working helped destroy my marriage."

"I never said that."

"No, not in so many words. Annie, you've always believed that while the boys are young, your place is with them."

"I know, and deep down I still believe it, but the thing is, being at home with kids is so bloody boring. I know Tom's at school and Freddie's at playgroup, so in many ways I'm over the worst, but it still feels like I spend my entire life responding to their wants and needs. Do you know what I did yesterday? I counted how many times they called out 'Mummee,' and do you know how many it was?"

"I don't know. Twenty?"

"Fifty-seven."

I admitted that did sound like a lot.

"Rob says I've made a rod for my own back. He says I'm too available and that I should tell them to bugger off occasionally. I suspect he's got a point. Anyway, now they're hyper because it's almost Christmas and I'm constantly refereeing fights. I'm worried that Tom's developing violent tendencies. When I asked him a few weeks ago what he wanted for Christmas, he said, 'Stuff that explodes.' This from the child who was raised on *The Very Hungry Caterpillar* and *The Gruffalo*. I make sure they're not exposed to violence on TV. And when I think back to all the hours I used to spend with him making green eggs and ham out of Play-Doh . . ."

"Hon, listen to me. Everything you are feeling is normal. Being at home with young children is boring. The point is that so few women admit it. It's one of the last taboos. If we admit that motherhood bores us, what sort of mothers are we?"

"I wanted to be such a great mother."

"You are a great mother. You are an amazing mother. You've given so much of yourself to your kids, and by doing that, you've created wonderful memories for them."

"But I've failed."

"How on earth have you failed?"

"I've failed because I'm not happy. Staying at home to raise children is supposed to be this fulfilling, joyous experience. And I'm so miserable."

"That's because you're finally admitting that you can't go on being this human vending machine, constantly dispensing care and attention. You have needs, too, and they have to be met."

"So do you think I should go back to work?"

"That's not for me to say. Only you know that. What I do think is that you need a proper rest and a break from the boys."

"But I only just had a break. Rob and I were in China for two weeks."

"That was back in the summer. You're allowed another one. It's not a crime."

I'd managed to make her laugh. "I think about going back to work all the time," she said. "But what's the point of even trying to get a job in broadcasting? There's nothing out there, and even if there were, I've been out of action for so long I'm not sure anybody would take me on."

"Might still be worth putting out some feelers at the BBC. You must have loads of contacts."

"OK, let's imagine for the sake of argument that I got a job. What then? What about the boys? What about Rob?"

"I guess with two salaries coming in, you'd get a housekeeper. Talk to Gail. She thinks housekeepers save marriages."

"Actually, that's not so daft," Annie said, smiling. "She may have a point, but even then it would feel like I'd be letting the boys down."

"If it turns out that working makes you feel better about yourself, then you won't be letting them down. Kids need parents who are happy and fulfilled, not miserable and resentful. But like I said, it has to be your decision."

"I know."

I could see the panic on her face.

Chapter 6

Six thirty a.m., Christmas morning

"Jingle bells, Batman smells, Robin's run away. It's no fun when his smelly bum keeps farting every day. . . ."

I pulled the duvet over my head and tried to ignore my children, who were bouncing on my bed and—in between belting out scatological versions of Christmas songs—demanding to open their presents.

"But can't we just open one small present each?" Amy whined.

"No," I said. "You have to wait until your dad gets here. That was the deal." Greg wasn't due until nine. A bit of me wished I'd asked him to sleep over last night in the spare room. I'd thought about it, but in the end I'd decided I wasn't ready. Every time Greg and I spent time together—like at the kids' multicultural generic holiday play—my emotions began churning and for the next couple of days I felt a bit discombobulated and down. I knew that having their father here on Christmas Day was right for the children. I also knew that I needed to protect my own emotional equilibrium. That meant keeping the time I spent around Greg—

particularly in what had been the marital home—to a minimum.

For the umpteenth time I suggested the kids go downstairs and
put on *The Muppet Christmas Carol* DVD, which they'd never seen and
which I'd bought for the sole purpose of entertaining them until
Greg arrived. "I'll take a shower and then I'll come down and make
pancakes. How's that?"

"I bet you've got us a puppy," Ben said, landing hard next to my
right ear. "To make up for you and Dad splitting up. Dillon in my
class said his parents got him a dalmatian when his parents got divorced."

"They haven't got us a dog, dummy," Amy said, climbing into
bed with me. "We would have heard it barking."

"Not if they gave it to the neighbors to look after, double dummy.
So when can we get a dog?" My son yanked the duvet off my head.
"When can we?"

Finally realizing I had no choice but to embrace the day, I hauled
myself into a sitting position. "I've told you, it's just not fair having a
dog when we're out all day—especially now that Klaudia's gone.
Now can we please change the subject?"

"So," Ben persisted, "you and Dad definitely haven't got us a
puppy, then?"

"Correct. And please will you stop jumping? You're going to
damage the mattress."

"I'm getting up," Amy said, sliding out of bed. "I want to put on
my glitter nail polish."

Amy disappeared. Ben carried on bouncing. "But you've got me
the go-kart I wanted, haven't you?"

"What? Ben, this is the first time I've heard you mention a go-kart. And anyway, have you any idea how much they cost? They're hundreds of pounds."

"God, this is going to be such a rubbish Christmas." He came down hard on his bottom. "I mean, now that you and Dad have split up, you're meant to spoil us. Dillon's getting a go-kart for Christmas. And his dad's taking him and his sister to Disneyland Paris."

"Good for Dillon. Now will you please go and watch TV and let me get up?"

I sat on the edge of the apricot plastic bath with its cracked side panel and began brushing my teeth. The eighties bathroom—cheap frosted glass shower cubicle, his and hers sinks (apricot) set into beige marble-effect laminate—had always depressed me. But right now it wasn't the apricotness, or the mildewed, clogged grot that was making me sad. It was the "his" and "hers" sinks. In particular: the "his."

The glass shelf above Greg's sink used to be full of his stuff: toothbrush, electric razor, blades and shaving foam dating back to when he didn't own an electric razor, nose hair trimmer, dental floss, mouthwash, half-used tubes of Tums, antiperspirant guaranteed to keep his man-pits fresh for forty-eight hours. Now the shelf was empty. Below it, the sink—which on the days that Mrs. F didn't come to clean had always been caked in soap scum, beard and nose hairs—was spotless. I switched off the electric toothbrush, ran my hand over the apricot porcelain and felt my eyes welling up.

The doorbell rang bang on nine. Greg still had his key, but had stopped using it. He said that since this wasn't his home anymore, he felt awkward letting himself in.

"It's Dad! Yay." The kids—dressed now and full of blueberry pancakes—abandoned *The Muppet Christmas Carol* and rushed to the front door. I got up from the sofa and paused the DVD.

The next thing I heard was cries of delight from the hall. "Dworkin! You've brought Dworkin!"

"Mum," Ben yelled. "Dad's brought Dworkin."

"So I gather," I said.

A moment later the Irish setter—chestnut of coat, floppy of ear, a touch of gray about her whiskers—lolloped into the living room.

Amy and Ben were all over Dworkin, patting and stroking her and demanding to know if they could take her for a walk. Then Greg appeared, his head obscured by a giant poinsettia.

"Roz's mother's allergic to dogs," he said, still taking refuge behind the poinsettia. "She'd booked her into a kennel—the dog, that is, not her mother—but then it occurred to her that it might be fun for the kids if I brought her here."

Apparently unfazed by her new surroundings, Dworkin helped herself to an armchair. Ben and Amy knelt down and carried on petting her.

"I brought her food and water bowls," Greg said, handing them to me.

"How thoughtful . . . Look, I don't mind about Dworkin; I just wish you'd asked, that's all."

In fact I did mind. Not about Dworkin per se, who was giving every impression of being a gentle, affable creature, but about what she represented as far as the children were concerned. Judging by their reactions—Ben's in particular—the dog and therefore Roz had made their Christmas.

"You're right," Greg said, finally emerging from behind his protective shrubbery. "I should have called."

"Don't worry," I said, getting down off my high horse. "She looks like a real softy. I can see why the kids adore her."

"I wasn't sure what to bring," he said. "So I got you this." He handed me the poinsettia. "And I've got a couple of bottles of bubbly in the car." He went to fetch the champagne. Meanwhile Ben started jumping up and down, demanding that he and Amy be allowed to take Dworkin for a walk.

"Can we? Can we?"

"But you've been nagging me for hours about opening your presents."

By now Dworkin was asleep on the armchair, drool seeping from her mouth. I said it was probably best not to wake her. "Tell you what—why don't we do presents first? And afterwards you can take her for a walk."

I went into the kitchen to make coffee. When I got back, Greg had dug out our cheesy *I Heart Christmas* CD.

"Oh, by the way," he said. "Roz sent you this—as a sort of peace offering."

"Really? Goodness—how thoughtful. I honestly wasn't expecting a gift."

Even though I disliked the woman, I couldn't help feeling guilty that I hadn't gotten her anything.

Greg handed me a parcel wrapped in coarse brown fabric. I ran my hand over it. "Unusual," I said.

"Yes, it's jute. Roz refuses to use wrapping paper for environmental reasons. You can recycle this stuff." I wondered how I might recycle a square of jute. I supposed I could always unravel it and fashion it into an inch of rope.

The gift tag was made from brown card. It read, "Sorry we got off on the wrong foot. Happy Holidays and warmest regards, Roz."

"That's really lovely," I said. "I'll open it later. Let's do the kids' presents now."

A few minutes later, champagne cooling in the fridge, we were all sitting around the tree, listening to Kylie singing "Santa Baby," the kids ripping into their presents, barely noticing that my unenvironmental wrapping paper was held together with staples.

It was just like old times. Only it wasn't.

In the end, I'd gotten Greg a bottle of Scotch. I'd decided it was mean not to get him anything and booze seemed suitably unintimate. I'd also given the kids money to buy presents for their dad. Ben got him a wireless computer mouse in the shape of a mouse and Amy got him a *World's Greatest Goals* DVD. With money Greg had given them, the kids bought me my favorite Space NK jasmine-scented candle.

Since we weren't a "real" family anymore, I suspected that the present giving and receiving would be particularly sad and poignant. I wasn't wrong. As I gave the kids thank-you kisses and hugs, I could feel tears at the back of my eyes. I knew Greg was feeling emotional, too, because he held the children so tight that they couldn't breathe and begged to be released.

The good news was that Greg and I hadn't been short money to pay for Christmas. He'd cashed in a pension plan he'd forgotten about. It didn't amount to much, but it was enough to cover Christmas.

Since Ben had decided that, present-wise, this was going to be the worst Christmas ever, I imagined him going into a strop when he saw what his father and I had bought him. But his GX Racers Tightrope Terror—essentially, performing stunt cars—and night-vision goggles seemed to hit the spot. Ditto the very generous Amazon gift certificates from Betsy and Phil.

Having never been allowed weapons, the Nerf Vortex Nitron Blaster ("with an electronic scope and pulsing lights to assist with accurate aiming") that my parents sent him went down a storm. Mum and Dad sent Amy a Home Pedicure Set for Girls. She loved it, which pissed Greg off no end. Greg and I got Amy everything she'd asked for: a pink iPod Nano, the Hannah Montana microphone alarm clock and a necklace with a silver jelly bean pendant.

"Oh, and Roz got you both a present," Greg said.

"Non-gender-specific, naturally," I muttered, so that only Greg could hear. I imagined ancient Japanese wind instruments or hand-carved yo-yos.

"OK . . . wait for it," Greg said. "You are going up in a hot air balloon."

"Wicked!"

"When?"

"Later in the year. As soon as the weather turns a bit warmer. And you won't be on your own—Roz and I are coming, too."

"Mum, isn't that amazing?" Amy said.

"Er . . . yes . . . absolutely . . . Greg, can I see you in the kitchen for a moment?"

"What now?" He followed me out of the living room.

I stood, arms folded, my back against the kitchen counter. "How could you have let Roz organize something like this without checking with me?"

"What are you on about?"

"I'm on about you allowing her to put our children's lives at risk and me not being allowed a say in the matter."

"Oh, come on. People don't die in hot air balloons."

"How do you know?"

"Because—anticipating that you'd blow a fuse—I Googled hot air ballooning accidents and it turns out that on average there is one injury for every thousand journeys. Have you any idea how that compares with car accidents?"

"So what?"

"What do you mean, so what? It proves that going up in a hot air balloon is pretty damn safe."

"But you or Roz should have asked my permission."

"Will you just listen to yourself? Who do you think you are? I refuse to come running to you every time Roz and I want to do something with the kids. You let our ten-year-old daughter wear nail polish and I have to lump it. Now she tells me that you've said she can have a tattoo when she's sixteen. Fabulous. Will I get a say in that? The heck I will. Roz asked me if it was OK to take the kids hot air ballooning and I said yes. Get over it."

"So for you this is about scoring points, and sod our children's safety."

"I can't believe you just said that. Do you really think that's the kind of father I am?"

"Why can't you two ever stop fighting?" Amy yelled. She was standing in the doorway, looking as if she might burst into tears. "It's Christmas. I can't believe you're doing this."

I went over and put my arms around her. "Sweetie, I'm so sorry. We didn't mean to upset you. But Dad and I weren't actually fighting. We were just having a disagreement, that's all."

"No, you were fighting. I heard you. So do Ben and I get to go up in the hot air balloon or not?"

"Of course you do," I said.

"Promise?"

"Promise."

"OK." Sniff.

I gave her a final hug before letting Greg scoop her up.

By now Ben had appeared. He gave no indication he'd heard the commotion. I said that now might be a good time for him and Amy to take Dworkin for a walk. "But I want you back in twenty minutes. And make sure you stick together. And don't go near the main road."

A moment later they had their coats on. Even though it was broad daylight, Ben insisted on wearing his night-vision goggles. Amy said he looked like a dork, but that didn't put him off. He grabbed Dworkin's lead and Greg and I watched as Ben and the dog set off down the garden path. Amy followed, three or four paces behind, as if to say, "I am *so* not with them."

I went back into the kitchen. Greg had put the kettle on for more coffee.

"So are we cool about the balloon trip?"

"I guess," I harrumphed. "Look, I'm sorry for being a control freak, but I would have appreciated a phone call, that's all. Taking the kids hot air ballooning isn't like taking them to the zoo. It's risky."

"Relax. They'll be fine. Now can we please let it drop and change the subject?"

I wasn't inclined to, but I felt I'd made my point. "Fine . . . So, any takers for the tank?"

"Uh-uh. I guess it's only to be expected at Christmas, when people are spending so much money. I'm sure things will improve come the new year."

I could have gone into my usual accusatory gripe about Tanky, but in the spirit of goodwill and because I'd promised Amy there would be no more fights, I decided not to.

"Let's hope so," I said.

"Turkey looks pretty impressive," Greg said, nodding towards the twelve-pounder waiting to go into the oven.

"I've put an entire pack of butter under the skin like you're supposed to and shoved a couple of oranges up its backside along with the stuffing. So I'm hoping it won't be as dry as usual."

"I don't ever remember your turkey being dry."

"You're just being polite."

"No, I'm not."

"God, how awkward is this?" I said. "You being a guest on Christmas Day, bringing me a poinsettia, being polite about my turkey?"

He managed a smile. "People in the same boat tell me it gets easier as time goes on."

By now the kettle had boiled. I made more coffee and we talked about the kids, which seemed a safe enough topic.

"By the way," I said, "Ben seems to think we should be spoiling him more, to make up for separating. He was pissed off we didn't get him a go-kart for Christmas."

"Mercenary little so-and-so. Suddenly our separating has become a retail opportunity. I'll talk to him."

I suggested that, since it was Christmas, we should let it go.

We took our coffee into the living room. I sat on the sofa. Greg took an armchair. It felt so odd, the two of us keeping our distance like this. The conversation turned to work. I gave him the latest on STD.

"It's all a bit weird at the moment. Because the relaunch of the show isn't happening until the new year, nothing's changed yet. Right now, there's this phony peace going on." I explained how STD had even turned up to the Christmas party, got pretty merry and ended up singing the Aussie version of "The Twelve Days of Christmas," which was all about possums playing, dingoes dancing and emus laying.

He asked me how the kids were managing without Klaudia. I said they were really missing her. We'd taken her out for a good-bye pizza and given her a framed photograph of her with Amy and Ben. "It was that one of them splashing in the sea at Brighton. Of course, we all cried buckets, but she's spoken to the kids on the phone and she sent them a Christmas parcel full of the most disgusting Polish sweets. Of course, the kids can't get enough of them. She's promised to call the moment the baby's born."

It was past three before we sat down to eat. Ben came to the table still wearing his night vision goggles. I'm pretty sure he'd kept them on only to wind his sister up. Dworkin passed on the starter—my homemade parsnip and apple soup—but decided to join us for the main course. She sat on the floor between Amy and Ben, her bowl full of particularly moist turkey, roast potatoes, green beans and sweet-and-sour red cabbage. She wolfed the lot, including the cranberry sauce.

It seemed easier to let the children lead the conversation. Amy was full of the summer-term school trip to an Outward Bound center in Devon. "We get to go rappelling and canoeing. And there's horse riding. It's going to be amazing."

"I didn't know you were into that kind of stuff," Greg said.

"What, because she wears nail polish?"

He ignored the comment, which was probably for the best.

Amy carried on chatting about the trip and all the gear she would need—rucksack, walking boots, Windbreaker, fleece, sun hat.

"Mum," Ben piped up, clearly determined to draw the parental attention back to him. "For my birthday can I invite the Six Dwarves?"

"Your birthday isn't for months," Greg said, "and anyway, don't you mean the Seven Dwarves?"

"Nah. I'm not inviting Grumpy. You know what he's like."

Greg and I burst out laughing. Meanwhile, Amy turned on her brother.

"You can't invite the Seven Dwarves. They don't exist. Snow White is just a story, dummy."

"Shuddup, schlemiel. I meant people dressed up as dwarves."

I put down my knife and fork. "Will you two stop calling each other names? And, Ben, I've told you about using that word."

"Well, she is one."

Amy opened her mouth to retaliate, but Greg got in first. "Hang on—has anybody noticed we've forgotten to pull our Christmas crackers?"

For Ben, this was always the best bit of Christmas lunch. He loved reading the daft jokes and riddles.

"Dad, pull mine with me!"

I pulled Amy's with her. A few moments later, having discarded the plastic key rings and miniature screwdriver gift sets, we were exchanging jokes.

"OK," Ben said, already giggling, "what's Santa's favorite pizza? . . . Wait for it . . . One that's deep pan crisp and even."

We all groaned. Then the kids got Greg to play "Rudolph the Red-Nosed Reindeer" on his head. The festive atmosphere was restored.

Nobody had room for Christmas pudding, so we decided to save it for later. I suggested that before we got stuck into *Home Alone*, *The Wizard of Oz*, *The Great Escape* or whichever annually repeated "Christmas favorite" was showing on TV, we Skype Grandma and Granddad to say merry Christmas.

As usual, this meant Skyping Phil. We caught him, Betsy and their boys, Adam and Luke, in the kitchen. They were having breakfast with Mum and Dad.

Phil panned the laptop camera around the room so that we could see everybody. They were all in their pj's and wearing party hats. The grown-ups were drinking mimosas. Betsy said hi from the stove, where she was frying bacon while simultaneously putting cinnamon rolls in the oven and yelling at one of my teenage nephews to find the maple syrup.

"Nope, we're fresh out," a voice said.

"Shoot. I cannot believe I have run out of maple syrup, today of all days. Don't worry, we can use honey."

"Honey on bacon? Euuch. Dad, you have to go to the store."

"What, on Christmas morning?" Phil said to his son. "No way."

"Then nobody's going to eat the bacon."

"No, you mean you're not going to eat it, which means there will be more for everybody else."

"Will you two stop bickering?" Betsy chimed in. "Honey will be fine. Phil, are you watching the toaster? It's been acting up and I'm worried the bagels are going to burn."

"We don't need bagels," my mother was saying. "The cinnamon rolls will be fine."

"I could manage a bagel," Dad came back. "I can't eat pastries for breakfast. The fat aggravates my reflux."

"Don't worry," Phil said. "There are bagels coming."

"I don't think so," Betsy came back. "Phil, get over here. There's smoke coming out of the toaster. I ask you to do the simplest thing . . ."

I had a great deal of affection for my sister-in-law—probably because her house was even more messy and chaotic than mine. Unlike me, though, Betsy didn't let it bother her. Phil said that at the hospital she was all organization and efficiency. At home she was Roseanne.

The other difference between Betsy and me was that she had a husband who tidied up after himself and actually did more housework than she did. Granted, Phil's contribution didn't amount to a whole hill of beans, but the point was he was willing. "And that means the world," Betsy had said to me, more than once.

By now Amy and Ben were more than a tad bored watching pixelated images of their Florida family bickering over breakfast. "Just say thank you for your presents," I whispered. "And then you can go and watch TV."

They did their duty, as did Adam and Luke, who apparently loved the iTunes gift cards we'd sent them. On the grounds that Christmas was all about kids, we adults had long since imposed a no-buy zone. So every year we sent gift certificates to Luke and Adam and every year Phil and Betsy reciprocated with gift certificates of identical value for our two. Greg called it farcical. I called it Christmas.

Greg said hi and merry Christmas to Mum, Dad and the rest of the family. Then he took the kids to the other end of the room to watch *Home Alone 4*.

My mother's face filled the screen now. "Greg looks well," she said. Assuming that the pictures she was getting of us were just as pixelated as the ones we were getting of her, I had no idea how she could tell. "You know, it's so lovely to see you being a family again."

"Mum," I said, lowering my voice, "please don't start getting ideas. This is for one day. We're doing it for the kids, that's all."

"And I bet they're happy to see you together. You know, maybe you should think about going back into counseling."

"Esther, don't start." It was my dad. I could see the edge of his unshaven chin. "You promised you wouldn't start . . ."

"I'm not starting. I'm just pointing out that children are happier and do better in life when they have parents living under the same roof. It said so in this magazine article I read the other day at the hairdresser's."

At this point, Adam asked Mum and Dad if they had any maple syrup at their place. Dad said he thought they might. "I'll go take a look," he said, getting up from the table.

For a few minutes, the rest of us carried on chatting and exchanging news. Then Betsy suggested that Mum take me on a tour of her new bathroom.

Mum and Dad had just finished refurbishing the granny annex. I'd seen the new kitchen, but Mum and Dad still hadn't shown me the bathroom. I'd heard all about it, though—from Gail. She'd had the tour a few days earlier, just before she, Murray and the kids left for their customary Christmas break in the Canaries. "I can't help thinking," Gail had said, "that mint tiles with an eggplant bath mat and toilet seat cover is all a bit *meh*. Why is it that when it comes to decorating, our mother can only think in edible colors?" I suggested to Gail that maybe she should ease up on our eighty-year-old mother, but I couldn't help laughing. Mum had always been the same. I remembered the last time she decorated the living room at the old house and how she'd adored showing off her salmon drapes and guacamole broadloom.

"Oh, you should see it," Mum was saying to me now about the bathroom. "I keep all my guest hand towels in this pretty wicker basket."

"Yeah," Phil butted in, "except she won't let anybody use them because she says they're for guests. So I have to go into the kitchen and wipe my hands on a dishcloth."

Betsy said that if Mum was going to take me on the grand bathroom tour, she should be quick because breakfast was almost ready. Mum said she needed to go to the little girls' room, so she suggested that Phil should head off with the laptop and that she would catch us up.

Phil picked up the laptop and led me out of the kitchen and onto the patio. We crossed the lawn and went on past the pool and Betsy's vegetable patch, which had long gone to seed. At the bottom of the garden was a small white rendered bungalow. This had been built by the couple who'd previously owned Phil and Betsy's house. They ran a hot tub business and the bungalow had been used as an office and showroom. When Mum and Dad agreed to come to Florida, Phil and Betsy had set about converting it.

"So how are you and Betsy coping with Mum and Dad?"

"Actually, it's working out a lot better than we thought. Betsy drives Mum to the supermarket a couple of times a week, but they manage to get out and about on the bus. They seem to be taking life much more in their stride. They've even started going to the seniors' day center in town and by the sound of it they're making friends. They seem to be very anxious about not invading our privacy, though. In fact, we have to nag them to come over."

I said I was glad things were going well. I also said I felt guilty about him and Betsy having to take full responsibility for Mum and Dad as they approached advanced old age. "It's a huge ask. It feels like Gail and I palmed them off onto you."

"Come on—you did not palm them off and you know it. Betsy and I asked them to come and live with us. It was our decision. And you know how laid-back Betsy is. She just rolls with the punches."

By now we were outside the bungalow. I could see Mum's new

mushroom drapes. Phil was about to knock on the door. Then he stopped.

"I can hear Dad on the phone," he said. "Maybe we should give him a minute."

" 'K."

For a while, neither of us spoke.

"Soph," Phil said eventually, "are you getting that?"

"What?"

"Listen."

I listened.

Dad must have moved to the open window because I could hear every word.

"No, it's probably safer if I come to you," he was saying. "Where do I find you? OK, I know where that is. Top bell. Anita. That's a pretty name. You know, Anita, I have to admit that I'm a bit nervous about this. The only woman who's ever seen me naked is my wife. So I guess we should talk about payment . . . Fifty dollars. That seems very reasonable. Oh, and would it be OK if I brought a couple of buddies with me?"

I heard myself yelp. "Omigod! What the——? Phil, correct me if I'm wrong, but it would appear that our octogenarian father is planning to have group sex with a hooker."

"Yeah, that was pretty much my take on it. Although, in fairness, they could be planning to bang her one after the other."

"Wow. That's put my mind at rest no end."

Just then Mum appeared. "Phil, what are you doing waiting outside? Let's go in and show Sophie the bathroom."

"Shit, Phil," I hissed. "We can't go in. Dad's still on the phone. Mum will hear everything. You have to think of something."

He did. "Mum . . . actually Sophie's got to go," he blurted. "Ben's just been sick. Too many sweets. Why don't you and I get back to the house?"

The picture on my screen was all over the place now, but I saw Phil take Mum's arm and start leading her away from the granny annex.

"But Ben was fine a few minutes ago," Mum protested. "And where's your dad with the maple syrup?"

"He's coming. He's coming."

The screen went black.

Chapter 7

"I can't believe it," Gail said, all winter white fun fur and Canary Islands tan. "Dad sees hookers?"

"Well, so far it's hooker, singular."

"Whatever. And he takes his buddies. Words fail me. It's sick, perverted, obscene. Our father involved in this kind of debauchery? And at his age. How could he do this to Mum? Has he gone stark staring mad?" She paused. "I've got it. It's Alzheimer's. He's losing his mind. It's the only explanation."

I had to admit that the possibility had occurred to me and Phil. "On the other hand, when you speak to him he seems no different than usual. He's not confused. His memory's fine."

"Alzheimer's can strike in odd ways," Annie said. "Risk taking can be a symptom. One night my granddad wandered out of his care home and the police caught him playing chicken on the motorway."

It was New Year's Day and Gail, Annie and I were at Gino's on Hampstead Heath, about to order brunch.

Gail and I had a New Year's Day tradition going back years, of taking a long walk on the heath and then going for brunch at Gino's. We had a strict no-husbands-or-kids rule, but a girlfriend at loose ends was always welcome. Today Annie had come along. She'd called yesterday to wish me a happy new year. During our brief conversation—I was getting dolled up for Debbie-from-down-the-road's New Year's Eve bash and running late—it emerged that she was still feeling pretty troubled and hadn't been sleeping. She said that as much as she wanted to go back to work—and there had been a development in that area, which she would tell me about when we had more time to talk—the idea of leaving the boys was tearing her apart. The upshot was that she felt in dire need of a shoulder for crying on and hoped that mine might be available. Since Annie and Gail had always gotten along and two shoulders had to be better than one, I suggested she join us on the heath.

This New Year's Day, though, the rain was falling like bullets, so we'd been forced to abandon our walk. Instead we'd headed straight to Gino's.

Annie looked tired and I was eager to move the conversation onto her troubles, but Gail—whose sensitivity to people's emotional needs rarely extended beyond her own—was preoccupied with Dad, his buddies and Anita the hooker, and she refused to let the subject drop. She seemed to find it gruesome, but unputdownable.

She managed to break off when the waitress came to take our order—three full English breakfasts, OJ and cappuccino—but the moment the waitress was gone, she was off again.

"What about Mum? It would kill her if she found out."

"And suppose he gave her some kind of disease," I said. "Greg reminded me that the statistics among the elderly have skyrocketed in the last few years."

Gail shook her head. "Christ, it doesn't bear thinking about." She paused. "So you discussed this with Greg?"

"I couldn't not. He saw the look on my face after I came off Skype. He knew something was up."

"Phil has to talk to Dad," Gail said. "He's a doctor. He'll be able to work out whether it's Alzheimer's. Assuming it's not, then he needs to read him the riot act."

We decided that the only way forward was to have a conference Skype with Phil and Betsy.

By now the waitress had arrived with our plates of bacon, eggs, sausages, tomato and fried bread. As we downed our OJ, squirted brown sauce over our fry-ups and acknowledged that we could already feel our thighs thickening and our ventricles slamming shut, we asked the waitress if, when she brought us our coffee, she could also furnish us with white toast, butter and jam.

"So," Annie said, doing her best to sound chirpy. "How was everybody's New Year's Eve?" She dipped some sausage into creamy fried egg yolk. "Rob dragged me up to town to this new French place, which I have to admit was sensational, but the West End was mobbed. We couldn't get parked and had to walk for miles. And when we came out, it was pouring, just like it is now. There were no cabs, so we were soaked by the time we got back to the car."

"Well, at least you got out," Gail said. "Murray and I were in bed by nine." It seemed that Murray had come back from the Canaries with a "chest." "I suppose I could have left him, but you know what men are like. He managed to do such a good impression of a Victorian miner expiring from silicosis that I didn't have the heart."

"Well, Debbie's party was great," I said, explaining that I'd been able to accept the invitation only because the kids were spending New Year's with Greg and his mother at her place. "Debbie and her husband had managed to off-load her kids, too, so we all got pretty wasted. I think I must have rolled home some time after two. I remember not being able to get my key in the door and that I was singing 'Girls Just Wanna Have Fun.'"

It suddenly struck me how insensitive and Gail-like I was being. The night before, Annie had phoned me almost in tears and I hadn't even asked her how she was. I was about to tell her how worried I was about her and ask how she was doing when Gail broke in.

"So, Soph, how was Christmas Day with Greg?"

"Oh God—yes, how did it go?" Annie said, clearly eager to find out and giving no impression she felt I was neglecting her.

"As usual, seeing him has left me feeling a bit discombobulated. It just felt so odd having him there as a guest in his own home. Oh, and we also managed to have a fight."

I explained that FHF wanted to take the kids up in a hot air balloon. The consensus was that I should have been consulted and had every right to feel put out that I hadn't been.

"Oh," I said. "And FHF got me a Christmas present."

"No! You're kidding," Gail said.

"According to Greg, she meant it as a peace offering."

"So what did she give you?" Annie asked.

I bent down and reached into my bag. I wasn't sure why I'd

brought it with me—to give Gail and Annie a laugh, I suppose. "OK, you have to promise not to make me put it on."

"Don't tell me," Annie said. "It's one of those Christmas sweaters covered in reindeer and holly."

"Far worse," I said as I unpacked FHF's Christmas peace offering and laid it on the table.

"What on earth is that?" Gail said, peering at the thing as if it were some newly discovered animal species.

"It's a hand-knitted Peruvian earflap hat," Annie obliged.

Gail looked none the wiser.

Then, before I could stop her, Annie shoved the earflap hat on my head. "Ooh, very vegan women's cooperative, I'm sure." She burst out laughing.

"Gorgeous, isn't it?" I said to Gail, turning my head to the left and then to the right so that she could get the full effect.

My sister leaned forward, her fingers making tentative contact with the long-plaited tassel. "I say again. What is it?"

Just then the waitress arrived with the toast and jam. "Oh—and, miss," Annie said, "my friend would like a side order of mung beans with that, please."

I snatched off the hat, slapped Annie playfully on the arm and explained to the bewildered-looking waitress that my friend was joking.

"Hang on," Gail said. "There's something I'm not getting. Does FHF genuinely think this thing is attractive or has she sent it to you because she knows it's horrible and she's just being a bitch?"

I said that I couldn't be certain, but judging by the pictures I'd seen of FHF, I suspected it was the kind of thing she wore herself.

Annie agreed that earflap hats were the epitome of earthy feminist chic and said I had no choice but to give FHF the benefit of the doubt and send her a polite thank-you note. She picked up a piece of fried bread and wrapped it around some streaky bacon.

"I can't believe I'm eating this," Annie said, bringing the bread to her mouth. "Usually when I'm stressed, I go right off food."

"Lucky you," Gail said, making a start on the toast and jam. "I'm the complete opposite."

"She's not wrong," I said, watching my sister's knife quarrying into thick Normandy butter. "When Carl, her hairdresser, threatened to move to New York, she gained thirty pounds."

"I did not," Gail said, laughing. "It was only five and you know it. So come on, Annie—why are you so stressed? Soph has only put me partly in the picture. Why don't you tell your Aunty Gail all about it."

Suddenly my sister had morphed into Dr. Ruth.

Annie didn't hold back. She told Gail how she'd finally admitted to herself that being a full-time mum was depressing the hell out of her. "Don't get me wrong. I love the boys to bits, but I'm getting almost phobic about being around them. Before I had children, I had all these romantic notions about motherhood."

Gail burst out laughing. "Of course you did. We all did. Then reality sets in and you realize that kids are essentially noise covered in poo and puke and that they stretch your patience—not to mention your vagina—to unimaginable dimensions. Like you, I'd give my children my kidneys and both lungs if they needed them, but there are times—like when they use your Chanel lipsticks as face paint—that you wish you'd stayed a virgin."

I said that, for me, it was when Amy refused to sleep for months on end and I had to get up and go to work each morning. But I took her point.

"It wouldn't be so bad," Annie said, "if Rob helped around the house. I know he works long hours and he's permanently exhausted and I do try to make allowances, but so far this Christmas there hasn't been a single occasion when he's done something without being asked. And even then he wouldn't get up off his behind until he'd finished reading the paper or messing about on his laptop."

"Where have I heard that before?" I said.

Gail said that Murray was the same. "I think he genuinely believes that if he loads the dishwasher, his penis will drop off."

"I've tried explaining to Rob that I'm tired of being at everybody's beck and call and that I feel like a glorified maid, but he just thinks that I'm run down and need a tonic."

Gail made the point that if Annie carried on like this, she'd need Prozac, not a bloody tonic. "Take my advice. Go back to work and get yourself a nanny-slash-housekeeper. That way, everybody's needs are taken care of and you get to start exercising your brain again."

"Gail's right," I said. "There may not be any jobs at the BBC, but why don't you at least put out some feelers?"

"I have," Annie said. "That's the problem."

I asked what she meant.

"One of my old contacts suggested I give the *Today* program a call. Long story short, one of the producers is going on maternity leave for six months and they can't find a suitable replacement. So I went in and saw the editor and he offered me the job on the spot. It starts at the end of January."

"Annie, that's amazing," I said. "The way things are right now, have you any idea what a stroke of luck that is? So what did you say?"

"I said I needed some time to think, which didn't go down too well, bearing in mind I'd made the first approach. I think he thought I was a bit bonkers."

"I'm not surprised," Gail said. "For your sanity's sake, you must take it. What does Rob say?"

Annie sat spooning cappuccino foam.

"You haven't told him, have you?" I said.

"Uh-uh."

"Why on earth not?"

"Because I know what he'll say. He'll tell me that we had an agreement and that if I go back to work, I'll be letting down the boys."

"He's bound to say that," Gail said, waving a jammy knife to emphasize her point. "Emotional blackmail is the first weapon men reach for. What he's actually worried about is who's going to pick up his dirty underpants and book his haircuts. Here's what you do: refuse to engage with those arguments. You can't let Rob get even the faintest sniff that your mind isn't made up. At the first sign of weakness he will launch an entire arsenal of guilt-seeking missiles and the battle will be lost."

"But I hate the idea of this becoming a battle. Surely I need to be reasonable and listen to what he has to say?"

"Honey, reason will get you nowhere. It's reason that's kept you where you are for so long. Hit him with a fait accompli. But of course there can be no treaty unless you offer him something in return."

"The housekeeper," Annie said.

"The housekeeper. Trust me. Find the right one and she will save your marriage, your family, but most of all . . . your sanity."

"OK. I'll do it. If I'm honest, I'm not sure I have much choice."

"Good girl," Gail said. "You won't regret this. I promise."

Just then my cell went off inside my bag. I reached down and began rummaging.

"What's the betting it's Huck the Fuck?" Gail said. By now she was fully up to speed with my supermarket encounter with Huckleberry. Like Annie, she was convinced that he fancied me. "You know, I vaguely remember him," Gail was saying to Annie. "I think Soph brought him home once or twice. He was gorgeous. You could see why all the girls called him Huck the Fuck." She laughed. "Huck the Fuck. What a great name."

Finally I found my cell. Gail was right. It was Huck. I pressed "answer."

"Hey, Fuck. How are you?"

Chapter 8

"Hello? Sophie, is that you?" Huck's voice was barely audible through the static. It didn't help that Annie and Gail were roaring with laughter at my "Hey, Fuck" remark. Never had I been so grateful for a bad connection. Huck tried calling back a couple of times, but the line was still impossible. In the end I said I would phone him from my landline when I got home.

Gail and I hugged Annie good-bye in the car park. She was still anxious about telling Rob that she was planning to go back to work, but promised she wouldn't put it off any longer. "I'll let you know how it goes," she said, then turned to leave.

After Annie had driven off, Gail and I went first to her car and then to mine and exchanged belated Chanu-mas gifts for our kids. As usual, I had gotten Spencer and Alexa iTunes gift cards—the same as I'd gotten for Phil's kids. Judging by the feel of the exquisitely gift-wrapped parcels my sister handed me, she had, as usual, gone to one of those exclusive kids' boutiques in North West London and bought my two kids dry-clean-only Italian knitwear.

"By the way," I said, slipping the parcels into my bag, "have you found a new bar mitzvah teacher for Spencer?"

"What? You must be joking. Nobody's prepared to take on my little Prince of Darkness. They all say the same thing—that he's not mature enough to be bar mitzvahed. They think we should postpone it."

"How on earth are you supposed to do that?"

"That's what I said. Everything's booked for April—the tent, the caterers, the band. I've ordered the flowers, the disposable cameras, not to mention two hundred mini iridescent favor bags and the SPENCER'S BAR MITZVAH key rings to go in them."

It turned out that it wasn't just Spencer who was giving my sister sleepless nights. Alexa was still insisting on giving up mainstream school and going to a performing arts academy to learn how to be Beyoncé.

"Anyway, the good news is, my clitoris is pretty much back to normal, thanks to the hormone patch the doctor gave me. Apparently it contains testosterone, so I'm playing this joke on Murray. I've started watching TV shows like *What's My Car Worth?* and *Ultimate Factories.* You should see his face."

I gave my sister a hug. "You're so funny, do you know that? It's one of the reasons I love you."

"You know one of the reasons I love you?" Gail said. "You're strong. Stronger than I could ever be. I don't know how you've coped on your own these last months."

"I couldn't have done it without you. You know, I'm not sure I've ever said thank you for everything you've done."

"I won't say it was a pleasure, but you're welcome."

"Happy new year, Gail."

"You too, hon. And may this year bring you only good stuff."

I laughed. "Even *some* good stuff would be nice."

We exchanged final farewell kisses and thanked each other again for the kids' gifts.

"Oh, and let me know what happens with Huck," Gail said.

"How many more times? Nothing is going to happen. He's just looking for somebody to hang out with."

"Oh, behave. Annie's right. He is so into you. Now go and have some fun. It's time."

I knew that if I put off writing a thank-you note to FHF, I would forget to do it. So the moment I got home I grabbed some writing paper and a pen. I thanked her for the "fabulous" hat, adding that I was sure it would come in really useful once the serious winter weather set in. I signed off by wishing her all the best for the new year. As I sealed the envelope and added a stamp, I allowed myself to think that her peace offering and my profuse thanks might signal a fresh start between us.

The note out of the way, I called Huck. He seemed really glad to hear from me and asked if I was free on Saturday night. I told him that Saturday was great. The kids would still be with Greg—they were off school until the following Monday—which meant I didn't even have to find a babysitter.

"Fantastic," he said, sounding almost surprised, as if he'd pulled off a bit of a coup. I found myself thinking that maybe he was into me after all and that he was asking me out on a proper date.

"How do you feel about meeting early?" he continued.

"Sure," I said, flattered by his fervor.

"I thought maybe you'd like to see the youth club. I'd really like to show you around and you can get some idea of the work we do."

"The youth club? Oh—I mean, fine. Yep, that sounds good." Suddenly, this wasn't sounding so much like a date as a field trip.

"Might be best if you don't bring your car," Huck said. "Wheels have a habit of going walkabout over at Princess Margaret, particularly after dark."

It occurred to me to call Greg and ask if I could borrow Tanky for the evening.

"If you take the bus, you can text me when you're almost there and I'll meet you at the stop."

Since we were meeting after dark, I wasn't about to protest at his gallantry.

"That'd be great. Thanks."

I wished that Annie and Gail were here listening to our conversation. I wanted to say: "OK, wise guys, I've just been invited to take the bus to the youth club at the Princess Margaret projects, one of the most violent and notorious housing projects in London. Does that sound to you like he's asking me on a date?"

"The thing is," Huck went on, "and I know this is a bit of a cheek, but I'd like to pick your brains. You see, the charity that runs the club—it actually runs dozens nationwide—is monumentally strapped for cash. We get some lottery money and a small amount of government funding, but it goes nowhere. What we need is media coverage. That way, we can really raise awareness. It's important people know how bad things are for the kids growing up in hellholes like Princess Margaret. I was hoping you might have some advice on how to go about it."

"Absolutely. You give me the tour and afterwards we can have a bit of a brainstorm."

"Afterwards," he said, "I thought we could go for dinner at Chez Max."

"Chez Max? As in Chez Max on Putney High Street?"

"Yes. Why? Is that not a good idea?"

"No. I mean yes. Chez Max is a great idea."

Chez Max was a small, intimate bistro where couples cozied up by candlelight, giggled over the pinot grig and licked each other's dessert spoons. In short, dining à deux at Chez Max was a semivertical expression of a horizontal desire. So Huck was asking me out on a *date* date after all.

"Actually, I've never been there," he said.

Ah. "You haven't?"

"No, but people tell me the food's great. And it's really quiet apparently, so we'll be able to have a proper talk without being disturbed."

So there would be no mutual spoon licking. My only consolation was that I had won my bet with Annie about whether or not Huck was into me and she now owed me a fiver.

Two days later I was back at work, along with the rest of the *Coffee Break* staff. The program had been pretty much off the air over Christmas and New Year's. The couple of shows that were broadcast had been prerecorded before the holidays and were still in the old format. As usual, they were a bit ponderous and dry, but I was still convinced that the only thing the program needed by way of improvement was a few creative tweaks here and there. Even though STD had made it clear she wasn't about to make a U-turn, I couldn't give up. It was almost two months to the program relaunch. There was still time to change her mind.

To that end, I'd spent a fair amount of time over the break working on a new look for *Coffee Break,* which I hoped—naively perhaps—would satisfy STD's need to make the program more popular and populist, without turning it into tabloid trash. I e-mailed my ideas to the other producers, who added some of their own, but at the same time they echoed my thoughts about being naive. The general view seemed to be that I was whistling in the wind.

I'd been at my desk a couple of minutes when Nancy popped her head around the door to wish me a happy new year.

"Not that anybody here has got much to look forward to," she added. "Your proposals are excellent—I take my hat off to you, Sophie—but we all know STD won't go for them in a million years. It's just a matter of time before I'm out of a job."

I begged her not to give up.

"I'm doing my best, but everything feels so damned awful right now."

"What about the sex therapy? How's that going?"

"Not great. I had such high hopes when we started, but Brian still finds it embarrassing to talk about my vulva, which in turn isn't improving my genital self-image. Virginia suggested I have a clay replica made of it, which I could hang in the bedroom and Brian and I could take a few minutes to admire it each day. But to be quite honest, I'm not sure I fancy letting some potter fill my vagina with plaster of paris. Anyway, Brian's homework for last week was to find a non-anxiety-inducing name for it, which Virginia thought might make things a bit easier. And do you know what he came up with?"

"What?"

"Becks, because it reminds him of beer."

Before my face had a chance to break into a smile, the phone rang. It was STD summoning me to her office for a "quick chin-wag."

"Sorry, Nancy," I said. "Gotta go." I picked up the folder containing my program proposals. "I know STD's going to be a difficult nut to crack, but I've got some really good ideas here. With a bit of luck, I might just pull it off."

"If you ask me," Nancy said, "you're going to need a damn sight more than a *bit*."

I could hear STD well before I reached her office.

"OK, now I am madder than a Baptist in a brothel. Where the hell are those quarterly expenses figures? Wendy, will you get in here?"

I tapped on STD's door. "If it's a bad time, I can come back."

"No, come in, Soph. Come in. I need to talk to you. Happy new year, by the way." STD was standing in the doorway that linked her office with Wendy's. "Where is she? Here I am, busier than a one-armed cabdriver with crabs, and she's done a runner."

"And a happy new year to you, too. Look, I'm sure Wendy's only popped to the loo."

"Well, I wish she wouldn't do it on my time . . . Right, sit your body down." I took a seat on the other side of STD's paper-strewn desk.

"So," she said, lowering herself into her leather swivel chair. "Where are we at? I'm assuming that programming-wise everything's in a go situation for the big day?"

"I'd like to think so." I handed her the folder. "This is an outline of ways I think we can revamp the show. As you can see, I've proposed that we ax the serial. I've acknowledged that the program badly needs more humorous, offbeat items. More important, we need to be catering to a younger audience and less caught up with stodgy items on gardening and natural history. But at the same time I want to see us continue to discuss important social and political issues. I want us to carry on campaigning. Over the years, we've affected government policy, which has in turn changed people's lives. We can't give up on that."

STD looked less than pleased. "But I've told you precisely what needs to done. I thought I'd made myself very clear."

"You did, but if you could just take a look . . . You'll see that at the back I've designed a sample program, which I think just about hits the right balance."

She moved her specs from her head to her nose and began sifting through the pages. "Right. So what do we have here? . . . Women talking about postpartum depression? A feature on raising autistic children? A studio discussion on women's pay? What's going on here, Soph? This isn't the brief I gave you and you know it."

"But if you'll look you'll see it's got much more popular appeal. I've suggested we find a couple of producers who used to work on *Britain's Got Talent* to give candid interviews about what goes on behind the scenes. We could invite Alia Hashim onto the show—she's this Muslim stand-up who performs in the hijab. She's the hottest new thing on the comedy circuit, and caused a sensation at the Edinburgh Fringe. She does all these gags about how her parents are panicking because she's twenty-two and not married and how she feels like an out-of-date milk carton."

STD looked like she was going to bust her girdle.

I decided to press on. "I've also suggested an interview with Leonard Cohen, who's going to be in town in the spring. He's doing a tour and promoting a new album. Once we've talked about his music, I thought we could try to get him talking about how it feels to still be a sex symbol at almost eighty."

"I can't believe I'm hearing this." STD removed her specs. "I told you what I wanted and you have purposely defied me. Where are the human interest stories? 'I stole my sister's husband' . . . 'He tried to kill me on my first date' . . . 'I spend thirty grand a year on my nine-year-old's clothes, but she's not spoiled' . . . Where are the soap stars talking about how they came back from the brink?"

"We can't do it."

"What do you mean, you can't do it?"

"I mean that nobody who works on the show has the heart to see it destroyed and turned into tabloid trash."

STD leaned forward. "Sophie, read my lips. *Coffee Break* is hemorrhaging listeners. This is the only way forward."

I wasn't about to be intimidated. "No, it's not."

"You're questioning my judgment?"

"Yes, I am. Look, we all know that the show needs a revamp. All I'm asking is that you put your faith in me, along with my producers and reporters, and let us make the changes we know will work and bring in more listeners. If we fail, we'll think again about your proposals."

"A few months?"

"Six, tops."

"You want me to risk God knows how much money . . . on a punt?"

"It's more than a punt. I'm pretty sure it's going to work."

"I don't make decisions based on 'pretty sure.' My plans for this program have been tried and tested all over the world. They are a dead cert."

"So you won't even discuss some kind of a compromise that works for all of us and most importantly the listeners."

"There will be no compromise."

"Come on, Shirley. I beg you not to dig in your heels like this."

STD leaned back in her chair. "I've said my piece."

"And that's your final word."

"It is. And from now on, I expect everybody on the team to fall in and start toeing the line. Do I make myself clear?"

I stood up. "Crystal."

"Don't let me down, Soph, or you may have to reassess your position here at GLB."

I was upset and angry—not to mention scared to death of losing my job—but I wasn't surprised by STD's reaction. I headed straight to Des's office.

"Don't panic," he said when I'd told him what had happened at the meeting. "She's just sounding off and trying to intimidate you."

"Well, she certainly succeeded."

"She knows you're good at your job and that the staff respects you. That's why she promoted you. She needs you."

"I'm not so sure. The way I see it, there is no way STD is going to change her mind. I was mad to think she would. She didn't say as much, but if you ask me she's gunning for a confrontation."

"And if she is, we'll be ready for her."

"Meaning?"

"Meaning that the workers control the means of production."

"You're suggesting we go on strike?"

"Possibly, if it comes to that."

"And you really think people are going to support a walkout? Des, nobody's had a pay raise in two years. People have got kids and mortgages. There isn't a single person who could afford to go on strike."

The bus pulled up at the stop. Huck was waiting for me, looking seriously hot in his beanie hat and stubble, his coat collar turned up against the wind.

We greeted each other with double kisses. He smelled of the cold.

"I really do appreciate you coming," he said. "I realize it's a hell of an ask dragging you out here, particularly after dark."

I smiled. "Should I have brought Mace?"

"You'll be fine," he said. "Most people here know me." I was aware of him looking at me. "You OK? You seem—I dunno—a bit anxious. Nothing is going to happen to you. Honest."

I was anxious, but not about walking through the Princess Margaret projects. "Sorry, it's not fear you see—it's worry. I had no idea it was so obvious. It's work. There's a possibility we could be going on strike."

"From what you told me the other day when we met, it sounds like it could be your only option if you want to save the show."

"That's what our union rep thinks. The thing is, if we walk out, I've got no idea how I'll make ends meet."

"Talk to the mothers who live here. They'll tell you all you need to know about making ends meet." He stopped. "Sorry. That was insensitive. I didn't mean to make you feel guilty."

"No, you're right. I don't know the first thing about being hard up. And the truth is that if we do go on strike and it gets to the point where I can't manage, I have family who will rally around. My ex has family. I'll always be able to put food on the table."

"Well, if you need it," he said, "I've got this great cookbook that I bought when I was a student. It's called *A Hundred Ways with Mince.* I'd be more than happy to lend it to you."

I said I would bear it in mind.

We started walking. I took in the smashed paving stones, the graffiti, the bits of litter and tinfoil stained with crack being carried in the wind like autumn leaves.

"Welcome to your local neighborhood ghetto," Huck said. "First I would like you to note, if you will, the concrete landscape raw with suffering and social deprivation."

"Believe me, I'm noting."

"To our right you will see the general store with its barricaded windows. To our left, the church surrounded by razor wire."

In the distance a child's voice was crying out from one of the apartment block landings: "Mum, Dad . . . it's cold out here. Let me in . . . Come on, you smackheads. I know what you're doing in there."

"The secret is to keep looking up," Huck said.

I frowned a question.

"You always have to be on the lookout for kids throwing supermarket trollies off the roof. Then there are the ones who blow up cars with firecrackers or slash tires with knives right in front of the neighbors, in broad daylight. People are too scared to call the police for fear of retribution, so the kids don't even bother to run away anymore."

"Do you mind telling me how people manage to stay sane in all this?" I said.

"A great many don't."

I noticed a group of boys—fat trainers, hoods, jeans slung so low that the crotches practically came level with their knees. They were hanging around one of the stairwells. Two of them noticed us, broke away from their mates and came loping across.

"You know these boys?"

Huck nodded.

"Safe, man," one of them said, knuckle-pounding Huck. "So what's happenin', blud?"

"I'm good. So you two coming to the youth center? It's Saturday night." He paused for dramatic effect. "We've got hot dogs."

The boys started laughing. "Hot dogs? Nah. We gonna get pot."

"OK, well, maybe I'll see you later."

"For real."

The pair ambled off.

"I guess hot dogs can't compete with weed," Huck said.

Just then the smaller of the two stopped and looked back. "She chug, man."

"Thanks," Huck called out. "I'll tell her."

"What?" I said.

"He said you're very attractive."

I colored up. "Really? Aw, that's sweet."

"They're not all bad kids," Huck said. "The problem is that no-body's offering them a future. Instead they're caught up in a tide of drugs and hopelessness."

"Meet the underclass," I said.

"You got it. Some of them are third-generation drug addicts. They've had nobody to parent them. They don't know what it's like to live in a home where people go out to work. All they've ever known is violence and squalor. Is it any wonder they're practically feral?"

I guessed not.

The youth club was a graffiti-covered concrete box with a flat as-phalt roof that was riding up, and presumably letting in the wind and rain. The window frames were rotten and peeling. The windows themselves were covered in a lattice security screen. This was badly bent—evidence that attempts had been made to break in.

"Well, this is it," Huck said, standing aside to let me in.

The first thing I noticed was the temperature. The place was freezing.

"Heating's on the blink again," Huck said, reading my mind. "The furnace needs replacing, but of course there's no money."

I stood looking around. The walls were bare. Seating came in the form of plastic public-institution-style stacking chairs. Most of these were covered in gum and cigarette burns. There were two Ping-Pong tables, both without nets, a giant TV blaring in one corner.

There were maybe twenty kids in tonight. The mood was lackadaisical. They were mostly watching TV. A couple of lads were shooting hoops. Two white girls, each with half a head of cornrows, were attempting to play Ping-Pong on one of the netless tables, but nobody knew how to keep score and they were starting to argue. Suddenly everything kicked off and one of the young youth workers had to intervene and restore order.

"You get the picture," Huck said. "Tempers are constantly on a knife edge. It takes nothing to get these kids raising their fists or pulling a blade."

Off the main hall were half a dozen smaller rooms, all of them empty. "I've got these rooms earmarked for activities like dance, drama, music, art, filmmaking," Huck explained. "But right now we've got no money for equipment or instructors."

We went back out into the hall. The kitchen was at the far end, behind a long counter. "Volunteers come in each day to cook lunch for the homeless, but we can't afford to feed the local kids on a regular basis. I'm desperate to get a breakfast and supper club going. If it weren't for their free school lunches, some of these kids would actually go hungry. And during the holidays some of them do."

He introduced me to some of his coworkers. The young men and women—black, white, Asian, mixed race—radiated energy and enthusiasm, which, bearing in mind the lack of funding and the myriad other obstacles, seemed remarkable. I discovered that one or two had been raised there in the projects. By some miracle they had managed to stay on at school, take their exams and get to university. Now they were back, determined to do their bit for the next generation of Princess Margaret kids.

"Oh, and this is Araminta," Huck said as a girl came jogging over to join the group. "She's the newest member of the team."

"You must be Sophie." Araminta beamed, shaking my hand, which none of the others had done. "We're all so glad you could make it. Has Huck given you the tour yet?"

I said that I thought he was about to.

"Excellent. There's just so much that needs to be done, but what with all the government cuts and the new welfare reforms, we're really up against it. It's so frustrating because we're all just raring to get going with new projects."

Araminta was a slender, blond-haired beauty. She was dressed just like the others—jeans, baggy jumper—but unlike the others she had an accent that made Catherine, Duchess of Cambridge sound like the hired help. How she fit in here with her upper-class grace and charm, I had no idea.

"What I don't understand," I said, turning to the whole group now, "is how you all manage to stay so positive, considering you have almost no money."

The general view was that there was no choice. One particularly earnest girl with blond dreadlocks insisted that things would change.

The way forward was to keep trying to raise money and putting pressure on the government. "But to give up hope would be to betray these kids."

"Hear, hear to that," Araminta said.

I took the point. We were still standing around chatting, a few of the workers having to break off from time to time to settle disputes among the kids, when I noticed a chap coming towards us pushing a mop. He was sixty maybe, but tall and straight of back.

"Out of the way, if you please, ladies and gents. This floor will not clean itself." I clocked the lumpy red nose that said alcoholic, the grubby woolen cardigan, the frayed checked shirt and military tie. I wondered what his story was.

"But you've already done it twice today," Huck said.

"I know, but these young people bring in so much mud. It's their trainers. The soles are so badly designed. Dirt collects in the crevices. Somebody should complain to the manufacturers. I might even do it myself."

"Sophie, I would like you to meet Pemberton."

Pemberton offered me his hand. "And that's not Mister Pemberton," he said. "Just Pemberton. It's the way I like it."

"Pemberton used to be a butler," Huck said.

"Indeed I did. I buttled for the best, you know . . . everywhere from Blenheim Palace to Belgravia."

"And now he helps us out at the center, don't you, Pemberton?"

"Indeed I do. When I can get on, that is. Now, then, I would be most grateful if you would kindly move to one side."

We duly moved.

Once the tour was over, we headed to Huck's car.

"Sorry it's such a crap heap," he said, opening the door to an ancient Ford Fiesta that couldn't have been worth more than a hundred quid. "No point in having a decent car around here. This is easily replaced if the kids decide to firebomb it."

Fifteen minutes later we were being shown to our table at Chez Max. I was glad to be in the warm and even gladder when Huck suggested we order a bottle of merlot.

"Whenever I go to nice places, I feel so bloody guilty," he said. "But I've learned that unless you have the occasional treat, you end up with nothing left to give."

"I get that. Nobody could do the job you do with an emotional fuel tank constantly running on empty."

He noticed my hands. "God, they're white with cold. Sorry the heater wasn't working in the car." He took one of my hands in both of his and began rubbing. It felt good being touched. Correction: it felt good being touched by Huck.

"Ooh, that feels better," I said after he'd been rubbing for a minute or so. "I can feel the life coming back."

He started on the other hand, stopping only when the wine arrived.

"So, what happened to poor old Pemberton?" I asked.

"Booze." Huck explained that Pemberton had been a drinker all his life. "For years he managed to hide it, but eventually he started drinking on the job. People from the best houses have little time for drunken servants and he got the sack. He'd drunk his savings, his wife had left him and he had no family to speak of. So he ended up sleeping on the streets. He lives in a hostel and we let him help out at the center."

"Poor man."

"I know. I think about these people and realize how easy it is to find yourself homeless. Talk about 'There but for the grace of God'—" He stopped himself. "I'm sorry. Time to change the record. Work tends to get to me and I end up getting maudlin."

We ordered comfort food: lamb shanks braised in wine with mustard mash. Chez Max didn't disappoint. It was sublime.

He asked me how my Christmas had been. I found myself telling him about Christmas morning and how I had stood in front of the his and hers sinks in the bathroom feeling sad. "For a few moments, the aloneness was just so overwhelming."

"I know it's an old cliché, but you have to give it time."

"You're right. People keep telling me the same thing, but I miss us being a family." Now I was the one getting maudlin. "So, come on, how was your Christmas?"

Huck said that the youth club had been open to the homeless as well as to kids whose drugged-up parents were too out of it to feed them. "It was pretty full-on, but I managed to get home for a couple of days."

He explained that, until he could find somewhere to live, he was staying with his parents. "Mum can't believe her luck. Not only am I back from Africa, but I'm living at home and sleeping in my old bedroom. She hasn't stopped clucking. Don't get me wrong—I love her to bits and I do appreciate her ironing my pants and socks, but she can be a bit smothering."

We talked about parents and I told him how much I was missing mine. "And of course my old dad has started having group sex with hookers." The words were out before I could stop them. I had this tendency to lose my brain-to-mouth coordination when I drank. Huck burst out laughing.

"I'm not kidding. My dad is seeing this hooker named Anita. In a weird way we're all hoping it's an aberration brought on by Alzheimer's. I'm not sure we could forgive him otherwise."

Huck said he took the point. "So he can still . . . you know . . . perform at his age? That's something, I suppose. I mean, there isn't a man alive who doesn't live in fear of ascension deficit disorder."

"Well, I'm sure you don't have anything to worry about on that score." Once again my inner thoughts had made it onto the outside.

"Huck?"

"Yes."

"Could we pretend I never said that?"

"Sure."

"So how's about we order dessert?"

I chose lemon tart. He went for the crème brûlée. We didn't have to wait long.

"How's yours?" I said.

"Fabulous."

I watched the guy at the next table load his dessert spoon with chocolate brownie and bring it to the lips of his female companion. A moment or two later, she reciprocated with some creamy meringue.

"The other youth workers seem like a great bunch," I said. "I can't get over how enthusiastic they all are. I guess they're too young for the cynicism to have set in."

Huck smiled. "Cynicism is something you really have to fight in this job—particularly as you get older. Once it gets the better of you, you might as well give up."

"Araminta's not quite what you'd expect," I said.

"I know. She's an odd one. If it had been left to me, I'm not sure I would have hired her. Don't get me wrong—she's a great girl. She's super smart, her heart's in the right place and, believe it or not, the kids there have really taken to her. I think it's because they've never come across anybody like her before. They treat her like some kind of weird specimen. But if you ask me, she's just biding her time until some banker whisks her off her feet and she can return to the country to sprog. She's actually Lady Araminta Elphinstone—suffice it to say that she and Pemberton get on like a house on fire. Her dad owns this huge manor house and her mother's something on a horse."

"Umm, I can see that an unreconstructed Marxist socialist such as yourself might have issues with that."

"You know me so well," he said, smiling.

I sat there feeling oddly relieved.

"So," I said, "I've been having some thoughts about how you could get some media coverage for the youth club."

First I suggested he have a chat with Greg, who I thought might be able to sell the story to the *Vanguard*. "I'll make sure he knows to expect your call." I also thought it would be a good idea for him to make contact with Judy, an old friend of mine who specialized in charity PR.

"But won't she expect some huge fee?"

"Yes, but only after she's raised stacks of money on your behalf. She takes her commission from the proceeds."

Finally I suggested that life at the Princess Margaret housing projects might make an item for one of the late-night news programs. I gave him the names and numbers of a couple of contacts I had at BBC 2 and Channel 4.

"Sophie, I don't know what to say. I can't thank you enough."

"Don't thank me yet. Wait until you get a result. Then I'll let you bring me back here for dinner."

"You're on."

I offered to pay half the bill, but he wouldn't hear of it. Even though it was barely a five-minute walk to my house, he also insisted on driving me home.

"I've had a great evening," I said as he pulled up outside. "And it was a real eye-opener seeing around the youth club."

"I hope it hasn't depressed you too much. And thanks again for the contacts. I'll let you know how things turn out."

"Make sure you do."

We double kissed good-bye. A moment later I was standing in the freezing night air watching him drive off.

Chapter 9

Greg dropped Amy and Ben home first thing on Sunday morning.

"So did you have a good time with Grandma Val?"

Amy shrugged. "It was OK."

"No, it wasn't," Ben came back, dropping his rucksack at my feet. "She never stopped kvetching. She didn't let us watch TV and she made me wear two sweaters to go out and Dad didn't even say anything. She's such a nudnik."

"Your grandmother is not a nudnik," Greg said. "She's getting old. I didn't say anything because I didn't want to upset her. And anyway, you managed to get one of the sweaters off without her noticing."

The kids never really enjoyed themselves when they went to stay with their paternal grandmother. For the last couple of years, Greg and I had done our best to keep visits to a minimum, but it was hard because Val adored Amy and Ben and loved having them come to stay. The children objected to going on two grounds. First, she fussed over them in exactly the same way as she had fussed over their father. She worried about them being too cold, too warm, too thin. She was forever pressing food on them. "And I'll cut the crusts off your bread, darling, shall I?"

Then there was the TV issue. Although Val owned an ancient portable, she disapproved of "all the intellectually bankrupt drivel" that was shown and watched very little apart from the news and the occasional wildlife documentary. When she came to stay with us, she was forever pointing out that Greg and I allowed the kids to watch too much TV. This, she opined, would serve only to dull their brains. Despite our protestations and theirs, when Amy and Ben went to stay with her, she refused to let them watch more than twenty minutes each day. Instead, they were expected to avail themselves of her extensive book collection. C. S. Lewis was encouraged. Cartoon Network was not.

"They were so miserable," Greg said. "I cut the visit short."

"Dad took us back to Roz's," Ben announced. "And I've been teaching Dworkin to high-five. She can almost do it."

"Good for you," I said, tousling my son's hair.

"You got time for a cuppa?" I said to Greg.

"I would, but I have to get back."

"Yeah, Dad's got to help Roz," Ben piped up. "She says the house needs a good spring clean. But I don't understand. It's still winter."

Amy rolled her eyes. "It's just a phrase. You can spring clean any time of year."

I was flabbergasted—not that Roz, the militant feminist whom I'd assumed until now lived in politically correct squalor, was spring cleaning, and in January to boot, but that Greg was helping her.

"Mum," Amy said. "Please close your mouth. You look like a fish."

I turned to Greg. "Run that by me again. You are helping Roz to spring clean?"

"Yes. What's wrong with that?"

"Well, for a start, it involves *cleaning*. You know . . . scrubbing sinks, loos, ovens—that sort of thing."

"People change," he said.

"Clearly. So what brought it on?"

"Easy," Amy piped up. "She told Dad that in her house a conventional gender-based allocation of chores wasn't an option."

My flabber having been gasted for the second time in as many minutes, I stood blinking at my daughter. "Excuse me? How on earth did you remember all that?"

"Roz explained what it meant and it just stuck in my brain. And I think she's right. Men should share the chores."

"She also told Dad," Ben said, "that he needed to get his sorry arse into gear. That bit stuck in my brain."

My jealousy had turned to amusement. I found myself grinning at Greg. "I'm trying to imagine you in a frilly pinny with a feather duster in your hand. I bet you look really cute."

"Whatever," Greg said, refusing to engage with my teasing—or even look me in the eye. Was it possible he was actually ashamed of how he'd behaved when we were together?

He said he had to go.

"OK, but remember to wear rubber gloves at all times. You don't want to become a martyr to dry, chapped hands. They can be murder, particularly in winter."

"Very funny." With that, he kissed the kids good-bye and turned to go.

Unable to resist one final tease, I started singing. "Gonna shake and vac, put all that freshness back . . ."

Since Amy and Ben were glued to the TV, getting their first cartoon hit in days, I decided to call Annie. I was bursting to tell her about Greg having turned into the Pine Sol Lady.

"She has so got him under her thumb," Annie said, laughing.

"I think she probably has. And I have to say I take my hat off to her."

"Oh, stop it. The woman's a tyrant. Would you honestly want to be like her—bullying your man into submission?"

"Well, it seems to have worked. Pleading and yelling got me nowhere."

"And bullying won't get her anywhere in the end. Greg's no wuss. Right now he's still in love, but he won't put up with it for long. One day soon he is going to snap. Mark my words."

"You reckon?"

"I'd put money on it."

"Don't do that," I said, laughing. "You've already lost one bet."

"What do you mean?"

"I mean my so-called date with Huck. You had it so wrong and I had it so right." I gave her a rundown of the evening.

"So there was no mention of meeting up again?"

I explained that we'd vaguely mentioned him taking me out for a thank-you dinner if he managed to get some publicity for the drop-in center.

"So do you think he was just using you and that all he wanted was to pick your brains about this publicity thing?"

"Not intentionally. The impression I get is that he's so focused on raising awareness about the Princess Margaret projects he'll do whatever it takes to achieve it."

"Well, if you ask me, the man's a fool and doesn't know what he's missing. Don't let him get to you."

I told her that Huck was the least of my worries. "It seems like there's a real possibility we might be going on strike. God knows how I'll manage for money."

"Hey, come on. Don't panic. You know Rob and I can always help you out."

"I know, and that's so sweet of you, but I can't start borrowing money from you guys. Please don't think I'm being ungrateful. It's just that I'd be scared it would get in the way of our friendship. I'd hate that."

"OK, but the offer stands."

"Thanks, hon. I appreciate it . . . So, have you spoken to Rob about going back to work?"

"I have."

"And?"

"And it was nothing as bad as I thought it would be. He wasn't exactly jumping for joy and he kept going on about how this wasn't the deal we'd made, but in the end he said that so long as I took charge of finding somebody to take care of the kids and the house, it was my call. I couldn't believe it. I think he was just glad to find out why I'd been so down. He'd been scared that I was ill."

"So there were no recriminations?"

"None. He's been a real grown-up. So I called the editor at *Today* to say I'd take the job. Then I started contacting domestic agencies. I've got three potential housekeepers coming for interviews."

"Annie, you've done brilliantly. I'm so proud of you. So how do you feel?"

"Like this could be a new beginning for me, but at the same time I'm scared to death. I mean, work-wise, I've been out of action for so long. Plus I'm worried about how the boys are going to cope."

"Look, they might kick up at the beginning, but they're going to be fine."

"That's what I keep telling myself."

M onday was the start of the new school term. The day began with Amy and Ben whining about having to be left at Debbie-from-down-the-road's.

"But you both said how much you were looking forward to it. You get the chance to play with Ella and Jack."

"Yeah, but Ella was horrible to me the whole of last term," Amy said. "She's been playing with Megan."

"Oh, I'm sure they'll let you join in if you ask."

"No, they won't, because I like Georgia and Isobel."

"And they don't like Georgia and Isobel?"

"No, they do, but Megan hates Isobel because Isobel kicked her brother, who's in year four. And Lola hates Megan because she went off with Tanya."

"Hang on, where does Tanya fit in?"

"God, you haven't listened to a word, have you?"

"No, I have. I have, honestly. It's just a bit complicated, that's all."

"Admit it. You don't care about my life. All you're concerned about is your bloody job."

"Oh, Amy, that's not true and you know it."

"And we miss Klaudia," Ben piped up. "She used to cook us pancakes for breakfast."

"Well, I'm sure Debbie's got toast and cereal. And if you want pancakes I can make some tonight for a treat."

Apparently that wouldn't be the same.

By the time I waved them off on their twenty-second walk to Debbie-from-down-the-road's, I was feeling so guilt-ridden and wrung out that all I wanted to do was climb back into bed. Instead I put on my coat, picked up my briefcase and headed to the station. There, I picked up a double-shot espresso and a copy of the *Independent*.

I sat on the train sipping my coffee and pretending to read the newspaper. I couldn't concentrate, though. All I could think about was the situation at work and the potential crisis that lay in store.

When I switched on my computer, I found that STD had sent a companywide e-mail to say how "disappointed" she was by our response to her proposals. She made it clear that these were non-negotiable and she wasn't about to backtrack. The ball was in our court.

Days went by and STD kept her office door open, as if to say, "If you want to come crawling, losers, I'm listening."

Nobody took her up on her offer. The consensus was that we should call her bluff. Meanwhile Des called a staff meeting and said that, assuming STD refused to budge, we needed to think carefully about what our next move should be. It was then that he raised the possibility of taking strike action. The idea didn't go down well. Several people admitted that their overdrafts were so big that losing even a month's pay could bankrupt them. Des kept begging everybody to stay calm. "I've been in touch with the union and there will be strike pay." He claimed not to know how much, but the rest of us were in no doubt that it would be a pittance.

L ate on Friday, just as I was getting ready to leave for the day, my phone rang. It was Huck.

"I have news," he said, sounding very excited indeed.

"Go on."

"Your friend Judy has come through big-time. I tell you, she doesn't hang about. She didn't even wait for me to call her. The moment she got your e-mail, she was straight on the phone to say the project sounded right up her street and to ask if she could visit the youth club. She came the next day, met the staff and some of the kids, and the bottom line is, she's going to start work on a PR campaign."

"Oh, Huck, that's amazing. I'm so pleased."

"And it's all down to you. I can't begin to tell you how grateful I am. So how's about I take you out to dinner to say thank you? What about tomorrow?"

I said that would work. It was the weekend, so Greg was due to have the kids again.

"Great. So where do you fancy going to eat?"

"Indian would be good. I know this great place in Tooting."

He said he would pick me up at eight.

No sooner had I put down the office phone than my cell started ringing.

"Sophie. You have to help me. I don't know what to do."

It was my mother, sounding utterly terrified.

"What's happened? Is it Dad? Is he ill?"

"No. Nothing like that. There's a man."

"A man? What man? Where?"

"Outside. He's been peering in at the living room window. Sophie, I'm really, really scared."

"Where's Dad?"

"He's gone for a walk. Phil and Betsy are at the supermarket and the boys are at soccer practice. I'm completely alone. Please help me."

"Mum, try to calm down. You have to call the police. Can you see his face? Can you describe him?"

"No. I think he must be crouching down. All I can see is the top of his baseball cap. But I just get this sense that he's evil."

"OK, dial nine-one-one. Now."

"Nine-one-one?"

"Yes, it's the American emergency services number."

"Oh, I didn't realize it was different from the one back home. I've been dialing nine-nine-nine. I couldn't work out why the phone wasn't ringing."

"Mum, the number to dial is nine-one-one. Hasn't anybody told you that?"

"No, and please don't shout. I'm scared enough as it is."

"OK, I'm sorry. You have to dial nine-one-one. Have you got that?"

"Yes."

"Good. Right, I'm going to put the phone down now. You call the police and I'll call Phil."

"I've already tried, but it keeps going to voice mail."

"He's probably on another call. Leave it with me. Now just hang in there and try not to panic."

"OK. Bye."

I spooled through my contacts list and hit Phil's number. He picked up on the first ring.

"Hello?" Phil's voice was barely a whisper.

"Phil, it's me. Why are you whispering?"

"I'm on a mission."

"What? What sort of a mission? I thought you were at the super-market. Listen, Mum's been trying to get you."

"I had my phone on vibrate. What's going on? Why did she call you?"

"She's in trouble. Drop whatever you're doing. She's seen a Peep-ing Tom hanging around outside the house."

"What? Oh God. She's seen me."

"You? How can she possibly have seen you? You're at the super-market."

"No, I'm not. I'm outside her window."

"What? It's you? You're the Peeping Tom?"

"No, of course I'm not the Peeping Tom. I thought I'd let myself into the house and take a look around, but I wanted to be certain nobody was home. That's why I've been hovering."

"But why on earth didn't you just knock on the door?"

"I didn't think of that. I got a bit carried away, I guess."

"And why do you want to search the house?"

"I thought I might find some evidence that Dad's got Alzheimer's. You know, piles of unpaid bills, his keys in the fridge. It would be so much easier to confront him if I thought there was something wrong with him."

"I get that, but if he found out you'd been snooping, have you any idea the ruckus it would cause?"

"I know. It was a stupid thing to even think of doing."

"You're not wrong, 'cos now you're in deep shit. Mum saw you and she's called nine-one-one."

"Fuck. What do I do?"

"OK, get in there and tell her you were checking the brickwork. Pretend the pointing needs redoing or something. But for Chrissake do it quick. The police are on their way."

A burst of static did little to block out the sound of approaching sirens.

Chapter 10

Dear Sophie, thank you for your thank-you. So glad you liked the hat. Yes, those earflaps can be really useful when the wind starts to bite.

I'm e-mailing because a thought occurs. As you know Amy is about to enter puberty. This is not only a period of rapid growth and development, but it is often the time when young people start to reflect on their sexuality. I am sure you agree that it is important for Amy to know that, straight or gay, bisexual or pansexual, she will be loved, accepted and respected by all of us. It struck me that you might find it difficult to have such an intimate conversation with her—in which case I am more than prepared to step into the breach. Do let me know your thoughts.

All best,

Roz

PS: Maybe we could get together for coffee sometime?

I couldn't believe it. The woman was incorrigible. Was there no way to get through to her? I was tempted to reply as follows: *You ar-*

rogant, patronizing, condescending bitch. Butt the fuck out of my life or I will be forced to run you over.

It was Saturday morning and Greg had just picked up the kids. As usual, he was taking them back to FHF's place. Then they were all going out to lunch. I thought about calling and asking him to turn back. He needed to see this e-mail. But I knew what he'd say—that I shouldn't confront FHF because it was important to keep the peace for the sake of Amy and Ben. Then he would promise me, as he always did, that he would deal with her. Sod that. A lot of good "dealing" with her had done. I decided not to call him. Instead my fingers began flying over the keyboard.

> Roz,
> Once again you have crossed a boundary and interfered in matters that don't concern you. As Amy's parents, Greg and I will decide when and how to confront issues concerning our daughter's personal development. If I find out that you have broached the subject of Amy's sexuality—or indeed discussed any other private intimate matters with her—I will prevent you from having any further contact with her.
> Sophie

"Stick that up your matriarchal society and smoke it," I muttered. Then I pressed "send."

In the end I decided to forward FHF's e-mail along with my reply to Greg. I realized he would accuse me of declaring war on her—and he'd be right. But I didn't give a damn. If there was going to be a war, then bring it on.

I was driving to Annie's, ostensibly to have coffee, but really to meet her newly hired housekeeper, Kathleen, and give her "the once-over" (Annie's phrase, not mine), when I got a text from Phil: *Disaster averted. Managed to convince Mum and police there was no pervert and that it was just me checking brickwork.*

I pulled up outside Annie's and texted back: *Thank God. Now Betsy doesn't have to visit you in Big House. Meanwhile stop being such an arse. Hugs and kisses, S XX.*

Annie's front door was opened by a busty, bustling woman I took to be Kathleen.

"You must be Sophie," she said, all smiles and top o' the mornin' Irish accent. "Oime Kath-leen. Come in. Come in. I've heard so much about you. Terrible thing with your husband. Terrible thing. But the good Lord never sends us more pain than we can cope with and that's a fact."

"You think?"

"I do. I do. Having said that, my knees are giving me terrible gip just now. I'm a martyr to the pain. To tell you the truth, I could really do with the Good Lord easing up a bit, but at my age I suppose you have to expect it."

Kathleen led me into the kitchen. Freddie and Tom were painting at the table. Annie was spooning coffee into the French press. I gave her a hello hug and said hi to the boys.

"OK, you two," Annie said. "What do you say to Sophie for the wonderful LEGO sets she sent you for Christmas?"

"Fank you," Tom mumbled, engrossed in his painting.

His big brother was more forthcoming. "Yeah, it was great. Dad helped me build this massive monster. Then Mum trod on it."

"Oh, come on, Freddie," his mother said, pushing the plunger down in the coffeemaker. "It was an accident. You left it in the hall for me to trip over."

"Yeah, but you still destroyed it."

"Now, now," Kathleen broke in. "Your mammy's already said it was an accident. Let that be an end to it." She turned to me. "Don't you think Annie has the most beautiful house? And she did it all herself."

"I know. She's amazingly talented."

"You should see my room. It's like something from one of those TV home makeover shows."

"Oh, stop it, you two," Annie said, coloring up.

Just then Freddie knocked his plastic beaker of paint water onto the floor.

"Oops."

"Not to worry, darlin'," Kathleen soothed. "These things happen." She picked up a roll of paper towels off the table, tore off a wad and got down on her knees, cursing the Good Lord as she went. A few seconds later the puddle of gray water was gone. Kathleen struggled to her feet and let out a loud *oomph*. "There you go. All done. Now, then, Annie, what do you think these two would like for their lunch? How's about I make you some of my special homemade burgers. Big-man food, that's what growing lads like these need."

"With chips?" Freddie said.

"Absolutely. And I make them from scratch, too. None of your frozen rubbish."

"Actually," Annie said, "I'm out of spuds."

Kathleen said it was no problem and suggested she and the boys take a walk to the supermarket. "And maybe we'll stop off at the park afterwards. They can sail Tom's new boat on the pond."

"Yay."

Tom went to find his boat.

"Can I bring my ladybug?" Freddie asked.

"Yes, but only if you promise to let it out of that matchbox when we get to the park. Surely the poor thing will die of suffocation, and you don't want to be killing ladybugs."

"I wouldn't kill it. Plus you don't usually see ladybugs in winter, so it's really special. I've put airholes in the box and it's got leaves to eat."

"That's good, because killing them is a sin. Ladybugs are the spirit of the Virgin Mary."

"So ladybugs have the ghost of Jesus's mother inside them?" Freddie was looking none too happy.

"Something like that," Kathleen said.

I was waiting for Annie to say something to her about not frightening the boys with talk of ghosts, but she didn't.

After they'd gone, Annie and I sat drinking coffee at the kitchen table.

"So what do you think of Kathleen?" Annie said. "Freddie and Tom adore her. She's so maternal."

"She's definitely that."

"I just know that when I start work, the boys are going to be fine with her. I've already let her do the school run a couple of times. And Rob loves her because she irons his pants and socks and feeds him second and third helpings of Irish stew. He says it reminds him of visits to his gran in Dublin when he was a kid. I have to admit the stew she cooked the other night was magnificent. You should taste her dumplings."

"She seems perfect," I said. "Exactly what you're looking for. But I have to say that remark she made about ladybugs being the spirit of the Virgin Mary bothered me slightly."

"You're kidding. And I thought I was the worrier. All Rob's Irish family go on like that—particularly the old ones. Kids learn to take it with a pinch of salt."

"Really? OK, if you say so."

Annie told me to stop fretting and topped up my coffee mug.

"I've got something to show you," I said, unfastening my bag and handing her a printout of my latest e-mail from FHF.

Annie took a sip of coffee and started reading. "I don't believe this. Right. That's it. There's nothing else for it. The woman has to die."

"Don't think it hasn't occurred to me."

"I mean, where does she get off on being such a bitch? Have you spoken to Greg?"

I said that I'd forwarded the e-mail to him and was waiting for him to get back to me.

"Well, if you ask me, it's about bloody time he put her in her place."

"I know, but he clearly has a problem confronting her."

"You need to have another talk with him. He has no right to let her treat you like this."

"Well, if he doesn't stand up to her, I will. If it comes to it, I'll talk to my lawyer. It might be possible to keep her away from the kids."

"Good for you."

I swallowed some coffee. "Oh, FYI, I'm meeting Huck again tonight." I explained about Greg wanting him to write a piece for the *Vanguard* and Judy agreeing to work on a PR campaign.

"Oh-kay . . . and this isn't a date, just like last time wasn't a date?"

"Correct. He just wants to thank me for helping him."

Annie raised an eyebrow and said that, on second thought, she would wait a few days before letting me have the fiver she owed me.

A s usual, the Taste of the Raj—Formica-topped tables, bring your own booze—was packed with young medics from the local hospital down the road. While we queued for a table, Huck said—what must have been for the third or fourth time since he'd picked me up—how grateful he was for everything I'd done.

"Huck, you have to stop thanking me," I said, laughing. "All I did was e-mail a few people."

It turned out that Judy wasn't the only one who had come through. The night before Greg had called him and suggested he write a first-person opinion piece about the Princess Margaret houses and how successive governments had failed the families living there.

It went without saying that I was delighted for Huck that Greg had called, but at the same time I felt oddly sad. Years before, when Huck sent me postcards from India, Greg used to get jealous. My husband's behavior irritated me, but at the same time I knew it was a sign of how much he loved me. Back then it would have taken one hell of a lot of persuasion on my part to get Greg to lift a finger to help Huck. Now that had all changed. Greg had moved on. He had no feelings left for me and didn't give a damn that Huck and I were back in touch.

The BBC and Channel 4 hadn't made contact—at least not yet—

but as Huck said, bearing in mind he hadn't expected anybody to take an interest, two hits out of four was pretty amazing.

After fifteen minutes, a waiter finally showed us to a table. "It's so good speaking to people like Greg and Judy—and you, of course," Huck said. "Most people are so hard on the kids we try to help. They think the poor should be able to pull themselves up, but hardly anybody understands that poverty isn't simply about bad housing and going without stuff. It's about going without love. It's about going without respect. It's about not being valued. It's about being raised surrounded by violence and abuse."

I was enjoying listening to him. He spoke with a passion that drew you in. There was something enormously sexy about that.

"So, changing the subject," he said, "how are things at work? Do you think this strike is going to happen?"

"Pretty much," I said, picking up a menu. "Unless Shirley Tucker Dill does a U-turn, which seems highly unlikely. What with everything else, it's a pressure I just don't need right now."

"Meaning that you're still struggling with the breakup with Greg?"

"Actually, it's something—or rather someone—connected to the breakup rather than the breakup itself." I hadn't meant to tell him about FHF, but despite having off-loaded to Annie, and later on to Gail, I was still fuming.

We ordered some samosas and chana chat to start, followed by chicken ginger and lamb keema. The waiter brought us some glasses and a bottle opener and Huck and I started on the Cobra beers we'd bought on the way over. For the next fifteen minutes I knocked back the beer and let rip about FHF while he listened, his expression alternating between amazement and concern.

"How do you get through to somebody like that?" I said finally.

"I'm not sure you do. She's a controlling, spiteful woman with a bee in her bonnet about her superior mothering skills. Wouldn't surprise me to discover that she was actually a pretty crap mother."

"You reckon? Funny, the thought never occurred to me."

"A great intellect doesn't necessarily equal a great mother. I wonder what she's hiding."

I decided that I had monopolized the conversation for long enough. "So, how's it going living back with your mum and dad?"

"To tell you the truth, it's getting pretty unbearable. They're both retired, so I'm all they've got to focus on. I've started flat hunting, but on my salary there's not much I can afford."

A thought immediately occurred to me. "Don't suppose you fancy renting my attic room. If we vote to go on strike, I'll be desperate for some extra money. It's pretty big and it's got an en suite—admittedly, it was installed in the mid-eighties and I accept you might be put off by brown porcelain and imitation gold taps . . ."

"Say no more. It sounds perfect."

"But you haven't even seen it. You might hate it."

"OK, so when can I come around?"

"Well, right now it's full of junk. Why don't we say Monday night? That'll give me time to have a clear out."

"OK, you've got a deal."

I spent all of Sunday dejunking the attic room and doing my best to make it look presentable. I managed to disassemble the baby cot that Amy and Ben had both used, ditto the high chair. It was a struggle and I strained muscles I didn't know I owned doing it, but I just about managed to find space for them, plus the baby bath and the playpen, in one of the eaves' cupboards. That done, I bagged up the rest of the stuff that was lying around the room. This included piles of old clothes, books, board games and a foot spa (unopened) that Val had bought me five or six birthdays ago.

I cleaned the en suite—the imitation gold taps cleaned up rather well, actually—and vacuumed and dusted. Because we'd only ever used the room to store junk, it contained no furniture—not even a bed. I decided that if Huck wanted to take it, the simplest thing would be to order everything online from Ikea. It would be here the next day.

I'd just put the last bag of rubbish out for the bin men when Greg called. He wanted to know if it would be OK to bring the kids home a bit later than usual. He and FHF had taken them to the science museum and they'd only just gotten back. "Roz and I are about to start dinner. I should get the kids back to you by nine." So they not only spring cleaned together, they cooked together. Greg really had changed. When we were together, he'd gone through a phase of cooking (and causing chaos in the kitchen) if I was going to be home late, but it had never been an activity we shared. As I imagined them chopping and slicing and sharing a bottle of wine, I couldn't help feeling jealous.

Any other time, I would have told Greg not to worry about feeding the kids and would have suggested he drop them back so I could cook them dinner. Tonight, though, I was so knackered that I was grateful for some extra time to myself. All I wanted was to soak in a hot bath.

"By the way," he said, "re Roz's last e-mail to you . . ."

"Greg, if you're going to start making excuses for her, I don't want to hear them. Roz has attempted to undermine me for the last time. I meant everything I said to her. If I get the slightest hint that she is pressing Amy for information about her sexuality or trying to advise or influence her, I will stop her and Ben coming to stay. Is that clear?"

"You won't have to do that," he said. "I've dealt with it."

"Meaning?"

"That's my business, but suffice it to say the situation has been resolved."

They'd clearly had a massive fight. Finally he was standing up to her.

"Whatever," I said. "But I'm telling you—one more incident like this and I will be speaking to my lawyer."

"Like I said, it won't be necessary. And I'm sorry."

I was suddenly aware of how miserable he sounded. I almost asked him if he was OK, but I decided against it. I wasn't about to interfere in his relationship with FHF. Like he said, that was his business.

*F*irst thing on Monday morning, Des popped his head around my office door. I was in the middle of reading a letter from James Harding. This confirmed that the management's backing for Shirley Tucker Dill was unequivocal and unanimous. "We have every confidence in her ability to take *Coffee Break* forward and would urge you to offer her your full support. I don't need to remind you that failure to do so will jeopardize the future of the program and put jobs at risk . . ."

"I take it you've seen this," I said, directing him to a chair.

"Yep, and here's where I'm at. I think that you should have one more go at taming the shrew. Assuming that fails, we take a vote on whether to go on strike."

"Bloody hell. You mean today?"

"I mean now. I think her time is up."

"But do you really think people will come out in favor of strike action? Granted, we're all furious and frustrated with STD, but I don't think anybody's got the stomach for a walkout. Maybe I should go and talk to James Harding?"

"Uh-uh. He's totally under her thumb. I've had dealings with Harding. He's essentially a decent bloke, but he's the type who enjoys being told what to think. The man's letting STD walk all over him. You'll get nowhere with him. Here's the thing: if we walk, they're left with dead air to fill. STD can offer as much money as she likes, but no freelancer who values his or her career will dare to cross the picket line."

"But what if James Harding decides to cut his losses and pull the show?"

"In that case, we admit defeat, get down on our knees and beg him not to. Then we go back to our jobs, toe the party line and get very, very miserable."

"That's assuming Harding doesn't ax the show anyway, just to be vindictive."

"You're right, it does," Des said. "Striking is a risk. But the way I see it, we can't just sit back and let *Coffee Break* be killed off without a fight. We need to have a go at saving it. At least then we can look back and say we did our best. I know people are hard up, but I'm pretty sure that going on strike for a few weeks isn't going to ruin anybody."

I said I wasn't so sure.

"And there will be strike pay. It won't be a lot, but nobody's going to starve." He paused. "But before we decide on anything, you need to have one more go at STD. Will you speak to her?"

I said that I would. There was nothing to lose.

As I walked into her office, STD leaned back in her chair, her face one great big sphere of smug.

"Good to see ya, Soph," she said, pushing her specs onto her head. "So, you and your cronies have finally seen sense. No need to grovel. I'm prepared to go easy on you. And there are no hard feelings, at least not on my part. I guess the best woman won." She offered me a seat, but I said that I would rather stand.

"Shirley, I'm not here to tell you we've backed down. I'm here to try to persuade you to start negotiating with us."

"Sophie, we've had this conversation. Are you deaf? I've told you, it isn't going to happen."

"Then you leave us no alternative."

She let out a laugh. "What? I don't believe it. You lot are going on strike? You don't have the balls."

"Actually, we do have the balls. The point is we would rather not take strike action if it can be avoided. Shirley, please will you rethink your position?"

"At the risk of repeating myself . . . there will be no negotiation."

"And that's your final word?"

"It is."

"OK, I guess there's nothing more to be said."

"Let me tell you, Soph, you are making a big mistake taking me on—a big, big mistake."

I made my exit through the open door that connected with Wendy's office.

"I got all that," she whispered, unable to conceal her glee. "Bloody woman's a monster. I've had enough. If there's a strike call, count me in."

Half an hour later we were holding a staff meeting in the canteen. I spoke first to say that I'd just had a conversation with STD and that she was adamant there would be no negotiation. The mood was angry and frustrated, not least of all because nobody could afford to strike.

Then Des got up to rally the troops. *Coffee Break* was an award-winning national institution, the jewel in GLB's crown. He urged us to think about the good it had done, the campaigns the program had launched, the opinions and lives that had been changed. We couldn't go down without a fight. It was unthinkable. The vote was carried—but only just. Those of us who voted in favor hadn't stopped feeling petrified about striking; we'd simply allowed ourselves to be "rallied" and voted with our hearts.

I decided to call Greg right away. I was dreading having to break the news to him, but he needed to know that for the foreseeable future we would be down to one income. He reacted just as I expected.

"It's actually going ahead? Oh, for fuck's sake. This is all I need."

"What? Like I do need it?"

"That's not what I'm saying."

"Greg, I know you're angry, but this isn't my fault."

"Of course it isn't your fault. Did I say it was?"

"No, but you sound like you're blaming me."

"I'm sorry. I don't mean to. But I've got all this other shit going on."

"What shit? What are you talking about?"

"It's nothing. It doesn't matter."

I was pretty sure that he was talking about him and FHF. My guess was that their fight had been pretty major. He must have read her the riot act about her e-mail. Then she hit the roof.

"But what are we going to do for money?" Greg said. "We're on the edge as it is. We can't go begging to our parents—it's so bloody undignified at our age. And there's no way I'm touching the kids' school fees fund."

"I agree, but for the time being let's just try not to panic. Des is convinced that management will cave in after a couple of days."

"Well, he'd better be right. That's all I can say."

I decided there was no point saying anything about renting the attic room until Huck had agreed to take it.

The last thing I wanted was for Amy and Ben to start worrying about money—so far Greg and I had been careful not to share our financial concerns with them—but since I wouldn't be going to work tomorrow or the next day or probably for many days after that, I felt I had to tell them what was going on. Amy asked if she would still be able to go on her school field trip. Ben wanted to know if he could still have a birthday party. Despite not having the foggiest idea where Greg and I were going to find the money, I reassured them on both counts. Satisfied that their needs would be taken care of, they asked no more questions and carried on as normal.

When I raised the possibility of taking in a lodger and that I'd met somebody who might be interested in taking the attic bedroom, the kids seemed delighted. Ben liked the idea of having a man in the house again because it meant there would be somebody to protect us from burglars. Amy asked if he was any good at math. "I could really do with some extra help. You're hopeless and Dad's so bad at explaining things over the phone."

Huck took about three seconds to decide that the room was perfect. We sealed the deal with a glass of wine at the kitchen table and I introduced him to Amy and Ben.

"Huckleberry's a weird name."

"Ben, please. That's rude."

Huck smiled. "Yes, it is a bit unusual. My mum and dad named me after Huckleberry Finn."

"So you're named after part of a fish?"

"Huck Finn is not a fish, stupid," Amy broke in. "He's a character from *Tom Sawyer*. I watched it at Georgia's."

I glanced at Huck and shrugged. "Why read the book when you can watch the movie? . . . Amy, you should read *Tom Sawyer*. It's a very famous book. It's a classic."

"No point now that I've seen the movie. So, Huck, what job do you do?"

Huck explained that he helped homeless people and children from poor homes.

"What, you mean like Jesus or Bono?" Ben said. "Bono helps poor people. I know 'cos there's this boy in my class who's related to him."

"Not exactly like Bono, no. I run a youth club for poor kids."

"Do they take drugs?" Ben asked.

"Some of them do."

"Cool."

I stared openmouthed at my son. "Ben! I cannot believe you said that. Taking drugs is never, ever cool."

"Dante in my class—his dad says drugs are cool because they expand your brain. Maybe if I took some drugs I could build a flux capacitor."

"You don't even know what that is," Amy said.

"Yes, I do. It's in *Back to the Future*. It's the thing that Doc builds into the DeLorean. It's what makes time travel possible. But I don't understand enough about it yet."

"Well, I can assure you," Huck said, "that taking drugs wouldn't help. Drugs mess with your brain. They don't improve it."

"But Dante's dad says—"

"Ben, I don't care what Dante's dad says. Huck works with kids who take drugs. He knows the terrible harm they can do."

"The other night," Amy piped up, "when we were coming home with Dad, he had the car radio on and this man called in and he said that poor people are lazy scroungers who sit on their backsides all day watching flat-screen TVs, eating KFC and drinking our taxes. And then this government person came on and sort of agreed. If somebody from the government says it, then I think it must be true."

I didn't know where to put myself. "Amy, Dad and I are always telling you how important it is to question what people tell you—even adults and especially adults who are right-wing politicians."

"What's right-wing?"

"Maybe your mum can explain that later," Huck said. "But let me tell you a bit about being poor. The thing is that when you're brought up in poverty and you've never seen your mum or dad go out to work, you start to believe that there is no future for you and that there's no point in working hard at school or trying to get a job."

"So people take drugs to try to make themselves feel better," Amy said.

Huck nodded. "Pretty much."

I glanced at the kitchen clock. It was getting late. "OK, you two, time to get ready for bed. Say good-bye to Huck."

They protested about being shooed upstairs, but eventually they disappeared.

"They're great kids," Huck said.

"I like to think so, although I have to admit that their views on drugs and social welfare need some urgent honing."

Huck laughed. "They're so young. You should be pleased they even have views about that kind of stuff."

I said I guessed he was right and topped up our glasses.

After Huck had gone, I went to check that the kids were in bed. Ben was fast asleep, but Amy was awake with the bedside light on.

"You OK, sweetie?" I sat down on the bed and kissed her forehead.

"Dad and Roz are being weird with each other. You know,

snapping and being moody—a bit like the way you and Dad used to get. I think maybe they had a fight."

"They did, but I spoke to your dad and they've sorted it out now, so I'm sure they'll start cheering up soon."

"I wish Dad could come back here to live. I really miss him."

"I know, darling. I know."

"Can I have a cuddle?"

"Of course you can."

I climbed into Amy's narrow bed and we made spoons, me with my arms around her waist. "Better?"

"Better."

"Ames, can I talk to you about something?"

" 'K."

"You know what it means to be gay, don't you?"

"Mum, I'm ten. Of course I know about being gay and anyway you told me when I was five. We saw those men kissing at the bus stop. Remember?"

As if I could forget. "Why are vose mens kissing?" she'd said, her small, inquisitive face looking up at me. "Only mummies and daddies kiss?"

I'd done my best to explain same-sex relationships to my little girl who was barely out of nappies. She nodded, apparently having taken it all in, and then asked if we could go and feed the ducks.

"I just want to let you know," I was saying now, "that if it turns out that you're gay, Dad and I would be totally OK with that. I mean, being gay isn't freaky or weird or abnormal. It's just that some people are gay the same way some people have ginger hair. And whatever you are is fine."

"Good, because I'm definitely a lesbian."

"You are?"

"Yeah. And so are Georgia and Isobel."

"Really?"

"We decided to be lesbians because the boys in our class are so horrible. They chase us and call us names. And some of them don't wash. Toby, who sits at my table for science—his hair smells and he swears."

"But I thought you liked Justin Bieber. And what about Zac Efron?"

"They're just part of my straight phase. I've grown out of that now."

"OK."

"Georgia, Isobel and I have decided we're going to share a house and be lesbians. Boys suck."

I held my daughter a bit tighter. "Some do, hon. There's no doubt about that."

Chapter 11

We formed a picket on the pavement outside the GLB offices. Des had arrived with a giant HANDS OFF COFFEE BREAK banner made out of an old bedsheet. The wobbly uppercase lettering had been written in green emulsion. Apparently he'd had some left over from last summer, when he'd given his front door a fresh lick of paint. I was given one end to hold; Nancy agreed to take the other, but not before she'd whined about how holding up a banner for any length of time was going to give her pins and needles in her arm.

Des had also managed to locate a brazier, for which—since the temperature had dropped to below freezing—we were all supremely grateful. A picket wasn't a picket without a brazier. It was the essential strike action accessory. Whenever you saw people picketing on the TV news, they were always huddled around one. Nothing said "We Shall Overcome" like a brazier glowing militant red.

Today the entire *Coffee Break* team was in attendance, all bundled up in hats and scarves. Nearly everybody had come with garden chairs and rugs. Wendy even brought one of those sleeping bags with arms and legs. Nancy muttered something about how being on strike in the bitter cold was no reason to lower one's sartorial standards and said that Wendy looked like a blimp.

People poured instant coffee from flasks brought from home. Nancy was the only one who insisted on getting a latte from Starbucks. While we sipped our coffee, Des announced that he wasn't expecting everybody to show up every day in the cold. He'd worked out a rotation. "Thank God for that," Nancy said. "Because standing outside in this wind is going to play absolute havoc with my skin."

Nancy's mood didn't seem to have improved since the last time we'd spoken. I asked her how things were between her and Brian.

"Oh, I don't know," she said, ostentatiously rubbing the top of her arm. "We don't seem to be making much headway. I was so upset about him deciding to call my vulva Becks that I called Virginia and asked if we could have an extra session. It was dreadful. Brian got angry and really let rip. He accused me of being too bossy and domineering in bed. He said I lie there barking orders at him and that I shout if he gets it wrong. The result of all this is that he doesn't feel like complimenting my vulva. He said that I've undermined him and that all his confidence is gone. He says that's the real reason he needs Viagra and that it has nothing to do with his age. The upshot is he doesn't feel like complimenting my vulva—or any other part of me, come to that. He said I'm difficult and domineering outside the bedroom, too. He called me a diva. Tell me honestly, do you think I'm a diva?"

"Well . . ."

"I know I can be demanding—especially at work—but I honestly don't mean it. The thing is, I just get so uptight because I want everything to be perfect. I know I shouldn't take it out on other people, but I can't help it."

"I get that. On the other hand, you can be pretty scary."

"That's what Brian said. I'm starting to realize that this problem we've been having in bed isn't his. It's mine. Virginia thinks I should start having therapy on my own to get to the bottom of my anxiety and temper. Do you think I should?"

"Going into therapy's never easy. It forces you to come face-to-face with yourself and that can be really uncomfortable. In the end, though, I think it can be worth it."

"You're right. I should take the risk. Brian is the best thing that's ever happened to me and I don't want to push him away. I have to do it."

"Good for you. I think you're making the right decision."

"I hope so. Now can we put this banner down for five minutes? My arm's gone completely numb."

Just then a taxi pulled up. STD got out, paid the driver and, making a show of ignoring the picket, marched towards the office. Over the next few minutes, the rest of the GLB management arrived, James Harding among them. It was then that it struck me—the point we'd all been missing and the reason STD didn't give a damn if we went on strike. I went over to Des. "I've just realized something. Are you aware that most of the GLB management started their careers in broadcasting?"

"So?"

"So . . . don't you see? STD's got a ready-made team that's fully equipped to produce the new-style *Coffee Break*—at least for the time being."

"Shit."

"I'll second that."

The next day, the latest issue of *Radio World* appeared on the news-stands. *Coffee Break*'s planned relaunch was the cover story. This was hardly a surprise, since STD was big buddies with the editor. The piece was more like one of those brownnosing puffs that appear in *Hello!* than journalism. There was a heavily airbrushed half-page photograph of STD, who was quoted as saying: "I am proud to be part of a new, innovative radio show that will honestly reflect the concerns and interests of ordinary people."

On Wednesday, the new-style *Coffee Break* hit the airwaves. Those of us manning the picket listened on Nancy's iPad:

"Good morning, folks, and welcome to your newly revamped, new-style *Coffee Break*, presented by me, Shirley Tucker Dill. For the next hour I'll be bringing you all the hot showbiz gossip. Find out if Kim Kardashian is set to join the *X Factor* panel and . . . is it possible that Sharon Stone is about to become U.S. secretary of state? Coming up later, we'll be talking to the man whose porridge exploded and left him lying in a pile of rubble. Also in the studio, the middle-aged mum who has just spent a hundred thousand pounds on a total body lift, and the woman who lost half her body weight on the Cap'n Crunch diet. But first, here to talk about her debut novel, *A Dark and Horny Night*, is Paris Hilton look-alike Nokia Moet . . . Nokia, welcome to the show, and I have to say you're looking very lovely. Maybe you could talk us through the outfit you're wearing . . ."

We shook our heads in disbelief. Nancy looked as if she might burst into tears. "What has this woman done? What has she done? I would just like to say on behalf of everybody here today that I feel violated—utterly violated."

"She's made a laughingstock of herself—that's what she's done," Des said.

I looked at him. "I wouldn't be quite so sure. She's bound to get a rave review in *Radio World* and after that she might start pulling in a whole new audience."

That night, Gail and Annie rang to say they'd heard the program. Annie described it as "beyond dross." Gail said it was so appalling that she was going to write a letter of complaint to the British Broadcasting Authority. Even Greg called to say how horrified he was.

"We all are," I said. "But what if it catches on? There's such a market for this sort of trash."

Greg said I was just feeling tired and stressed and that I shouldn't lose faith in the taste and integrity of the public. I promised to try, but I wasn't holding out much hope.

"By the way," I said. "I have one small piece of good news. I've rented the attic bedroom."

"You've got a lodger? Bloody hell—that's brilliant. Why didn't I think of that? So who have you got—a student?"

"Actually, it's Huck. He was living with his parents and they were driving him round the bend, so I suggested he move in here. Seemed to make perfect sense."

"Of course. Why not?" I picked up something tentative and hesitant in his voice.

"Greg, are you sure you're OK with this? You don't have a problem, do you?"

"Don't be daft. Why should I? We need all the money we can get right now."

Huck arrived on Saturday morning carrying a large rucksack and a holdall.

"Goodness, is that all you've got?"

"That's it," he said, smiling. "When you're always on the move like I am, you learn to travel light."

"But what about books and DVDs?" I said. He bent down and pulled an iPad out of the holdall.

"All I need's on here," he said, waving it at me.

The Ikea van had arrived earlier and now there were umpteen flat packs lying upstairs, their contents waiting to be assembled into a bed, dresser and wardrobe. I'd offered to get somebody in to build the furniture, but Huck said that since I'd paid for it, the least he could do was put it together.

"Have you had breakfast?" I said.

"Um . . . not as such."

"Coffee and a bacon sandwich suit you?"

"You bet."

Huck was scheduled to work that afternoon, and since it was already past ten, he was pretty eager to get cracking on the furniture. I suggested that I bring breakfast upstairs.

Ten minutes later I was climbing the steep attic stairs. One hand was holding a plate of bacon sarnies. The other was gripping the handles of two mugs of steaming coffee. Why I hadn't thought to use a tray, I had no idea.

By now Huck had made a start on the wardrobe. He was sitting on the floor screwing a hinge into one of the white melamine doors.

The moment he saw me, he got to his feet, relieved me of the plate and mugs and put them down on one of the large pieces of melamine. As I was thanking him, I noticed the sheet of instructions spread out on the floor.

"Ah, how refreshing—a man who actually reads instructions. Greg would never look at them as a matter of principle. It was the same when he got lost. He thought asking for directions was a challenge to his masculinity."

"Well, I'm hopeless without instructions," Huck said.

"Oh, so was Greg," I said, handing him a mug of coffee. "Most of our furniture ended up looking like weird sculptures that had escaped from the Tate Modern."

We sat on the floor drinking coffee and working our way through the stack of bacon sandwiches.

"So Greg doesn't mind me moving in?"

"Greg? God, no. He's only too grateful."

"So how are things between you two?"

"I guess it's all quite civilized really. So many divorcing couples end up at war, but we've managed to stay on pretty good terms."

"But you're still struggling with the breakup?"

"A bit, but it gets easier with time." It didn't occur to me that his interest was anything more than friendly concern.

He picked up the second hinge, along with some screws.

"Do you remember when we were at university?" he said. "And

we used to go to those Unite Against Fascism meetings on Thursday nights?"

"Of course. How could I forget all the heated discussions about whether we, as militant antifascists, could mobilize more people than the anarchists."

"Then you and I would go to the pub for a pint and discuss the part played by the class war in the formation of the British Union of Fascists in 1932 . . . except I don't remember what conclusion we came to."

"I'm not sure we came to any."

The second hinge secured, he was looking at the instructions to figure out what to do next. "I had such a crush on you in those days," he said without looking up.

I started laughing. "What? You had a crush on me? But you dated all those gorgeous girls. Why on earth would you have had a crush on me?"

"You were just as gorgeous."

"Yeah, right."

"You were. And anyway, all those girls were airheads. Most of them ended up as posh party organizers and marrying hedge fund managers called Tobias."

"As opposed to Marxists called Huckleberry."

He roared.

"So why didn't you ask me out?" I said.

"I was too scared."

"Scared? Why?"

"Because you were clever, and back then I felt threatened by clever women."

"Hence the airheads."

"Yep."

"Well, I have a confession, too. I had a massive crush on you."

"Get away."

"Come on. Don't act so surprised. You were really cute." I stopped myself from saying "and you still are." "Every girl I knew had the hots for you."

"Yeah, but like I said it was only the bimbos. Most of the intelligent girls thought I was this pretentious, lefty pseudointellectual."

"I didn't."

I decided I would stay and help with the furniture construction. I'd just unpacked the parts to a dresser named Trondheim when I heard the landline ringing downstairs. "I'd better get that. It might be Greg. He's got the kids this weekend."

I dashed into my bedroom and picked up. It wasn't Greg. It was Phil.

"Phil, it's the middle of the night over there. What's wrong? Are Mum and Dad OK?"

"I can't sleep. And nor can Betsy. We've been lying awake for hours."

"Why?"

"OK, well, Mum and Dad went out yesterday and I kinda let myself into their bungalow."

"You kinda let yourself in. Phil, either you did or you didn't. Which is it?"

"I did."

"You idiot. I can't believe you did this. Not after what happened last time."

"You just don't get it, do you? I'm the one who's been landed with the job of confronting our father about this hooker. Finding some evidence that he isn't well wouldn't necessarily make it easier—it's going to be a difficult conversation anyway—but if I had an explanation for his behavior, I could play the concerned doctor instead of the furious, moralizing son. I'd just feel more comfortable in that role."

"Phil, of course I get it. I know this is going to be a horrible conversation, but I can't believe you went snooping after the trouble you almost got into last time. Didn't Betsy try to stop you?"

"She didn't know."

"OK, so I take it—since you're calling me in the small hours—that you discovered something."

"Yes, but nothing that indicates Dad has Alzheimer's. Unless the symptoms include developing a porn habit."

"Excuse me? Our father is into porn?"

"I found a pile of DVDs in the bedroom."

"Oh, stop it."

"It's true. Among many, many others, there was *Lawrence of Her Labia*, *Forrest Hump* and *Saturday Night Beaver* . . . And they were all in Dad's dresser, where Mum could easily find them."

I tried to make sense of what I'd just heard. "OK, let's look at this rationally. Some men are into porn. Dad would appear to be one of them—even at his age. Under normal circumstances I'd say it's none of our business. But if looked at alongside the fact that he's seeing a hooker and that Mum would be destroyed if she found out about either of these things, let alone both, I think it is our business. You have to speak to Dad and soon."

"I know. And I will. I promise."

When I told Gail about the porn DVDs, she hit the roof. "Why has Phil been arsing around all this time? Get back to him and tell him from me that he has to speak to Dad right now." Even though she was angry and upset, there was an unusual sharpness in her voice.

"Gail, you OK? You sound incredibly het up. Is there anything else going on?"

"Ask your niece."

"Alexa? What's she done?"

"Applied to this performing arts academy without telling me or her dad. She filled in all the forms on her own and forged our signatures."

"You're kidding."

"Uh-uh. And guess what? She did an audition—again all on her own—and she got in. They love her."

"Gail, that's amazing. You have to hand it to her—she's got balls . . . just like her mother."

"I knew you'd say that. But having balls isn't enough to make it in this world. I want her to have a proper education. What happens when the showbiz career doesn't work out? What will she have to fall back on?"

"What does Murray say?"

"That we should let her go to stage school. He says that if we fight her, she'll turn against us and we'll lose her."

"You know what, hon? Hard as it is to hear, I think Murray's right. You could lose her and that's unthinkable."

"I know, I know. It's just that she's so young. She thinks she knows her own mind, but she doesn't realize that a few years down the line when she's got no work, she could come to seriously regret her decision."

"OK, so maybe then she'll go back into education. It's not the end of the world."

Gail gave a bitter laugh. "You know, I never realized until now what I put Mum and Dad through when I left school to start modeling."

I went back up to the attic. "Family ructions," I said to Huck. "My brother has uncovered my dad's porn stash and you'll never guess what my niece has done . . ."

In the time it took me to build the dresser, Huck managed to finish the wardrobe and the pine double bed. We moved the furniture into place—rearranging it a couple of times—and then I started unpacking the new bedding I'd ordered. Ten minutes later the bed was made up and we stood back to admire our work. Huck said he could probably do with a desk, but I wasn't to worry; he'd buy that, along with a nightstand and a couple of bedside lights.

Before leaving for work, he brought down all the cardboard packaging and left it outside with the recycling. Greg wouldn't have done that unless I'd nagged.

After Huck had gone, I retired to the sofa and started channel surfing. As it was Saturday afternoon, the viewing choices were limited to soccer, rugby and snooker—or, for the women, a Danielle Steel miniseries from the eighties and back-to-back editions of *How Clean Is Your House?*

I switched off the TV and began looking around the living room. It was even more of a mess than usual. In fact the whole house was more of a mess than usual. Since letting Mrs. Fredericks go, I was managing to keep the place sanitary—that is to say, I was cleaning the bathroom and loo, swabbing down the kitchen surfaces, mopping the floor and doing laundry, but the ironing had pretty much gone to pot, and it had been ages since I'd dusted or given the place a thorough tidy. What with work and seeing to the kids, plus the shopping and cooking, I was just too tired. The worse the mess got, the more intimidating it became.

In the spirit of feeling the fear and doing it anyway, and because I didn't want Huck to think I was a slattern—not that he seemed to have noticed the state of the house, or if he had he'd been too polite to say anything—I found myself standing up and heaving the heavy cushions off the sofa. This revealed a rich seam of fluff, dirt and fossilized potato chips. Among the larger items were two pizza crusts, several slices of pepperoni—brittle with age—a couple of pound coins and one of Amy's barrettes. There was also a T-shirt that belonged to Greg, the one with the DUNDER MIFFLIN logo. I had no idea what it was doing there. Maybe the kids had borrowed it for some reason. Perched on the edge of the sofa so as to avoid the springs, I picked up the shirt and began smoothing and folding it. I would give it to Greg tomorrow when he brought the kids back.

When I'd finished vacuuming the sofa and living room, I gathered up a load of Amy and Ben's junk and took it upstairs to their rooms. Once I'd off-loaded it, I realized I was holding the T-shirt. Instead of taking it back downstairs and putting it on the hall table or in the kitchen, I went into my bedroom and placed it in one of the empty drawers of what had once been Greg's dresser.

Afterwards, I went back downstairs and started cleaning the oven.

Chapter 12

Huck got back from work around seven, just as I was opening a bottle of wine. I'd assumed that as it was Saturday, he'd be working at the youth club until late, but it turned out that he'd only popped in to catch up with some paperwork. His colleagues were staying on to take charge of the night's hot dogs and entertainment.

"Join me?" I said, reaching for another glass.

"I'd love to, but I really don't want to intrude on your privacy."

"You're not. Believe me, I'd be glad for the company."

"OK, if you're sure."

We took our wine into the living room. I sat on the newly spruced-up sofa. He took one of the armchairs. We sipped our drinks and made slightly awkward small talk.

I said again how great the attic was looking and tried to persuade him to let me pay for any extra furniture he needed. He wouldn't hear of it. I said, well, OK . . . if he was sure. There was a few seconds' silence. Then he started telling me about a fire at the Princess Margaret houses. It had happened a few hours earlier and one of "his" kids—a fifteen-year-old named Troy—had been arrested on suspicion of arson. "That boy is a tragedy waiting to happen. Five people were in that house. It's a miracle nobody was killed."

We were discussing Troy's prospects for the future and agreeing that they looked pretty grim when Huck stopped. "Sophie, you know what we were talking about this morning?"

"Which bit?"

He looked down at his wineglass. "The bit where I told you I used to have a crush on you . . ."

"Huck, if you're embarrassed about that, please don't be. It was years ago. We were kids."

"I know, but the thing is . . . God, I'm not sure I know how to put this . . . the thing is, I think I still have a crush on you. When we bumped into each other in the supermarket, all the old feelings I had for you came flooding back. It was like no time had passed. Of course I realize you probably don't feel the same way. I mean, why would you? It's been years, plus you've just been through a marriage breakup and you're still struggling with that. I really have no right to burden you with my feelings." He stood up and put his wineglass down on the coffee table. "I think I'll head up to my room. I've said too much."

By now I was on my feet. I went over to him. "Huck, you are not burdening me. Honestly."

"Really?"

"Absolutely."

"If I'm honest," he said, "the real reason I asked you out was because I wanted to get to know you again—that's not to say I didn't value your help and advice as well. I'm incredibly grateful—"

"Huck."

"Yes?"

"Would you please stop talking and kiss me?"

"You want me to kiss you?"

"I think it's customary under these circumstances, don't you?" He was so nervous, so hesitant. I couldn't believe that this was the man they used to call Huck the Fuck.

"Yes, but I need to be sure you're OK with it. I know you're still feeling vulnerable—"

"Will you just come here . . . ?"

I put my arms around him and kissed him gently on the lips. He didn't protest. Instead he kissed me back. A moment later we were making out like a couple whose plane was going down.

I took him by the hand and we climbed the stairs to the attic.

That night, as Huck touched, caressed, probed and entered me, made me come again and again, it was like discovering sex for the first time—only heaps better because we were both experienced.

The next morning, when we woke we made love again. Twice. At my instigation. Huck laughed and called me insatiable. He was right. I'd lived through a famine and I was ravenous, starved. I couldn't get enough of him.

"Huck, you have to tell me if I'm too much, too needy. Greg and I— Well, let's just say it's been a long time . . ."

"Soph, please don't apologize. Last night and this morning have been amazing. Truly amazing."

"So what happens now?" I said as we lay cuddling. "I mean, it's all a bit awkward. You live here, so you can hardly pull on your pants and go home, leaving me sitting by the phone hoping you're going to call and ask me out again."

He began stroking my hair. "OK . . . Ring, ring . . ."

I started laughing. "Hello?"

"Hey, it's Huck. Listen, I just wanted to say that I had a great time last night. Any chance you'd like to get together again?"

"I think you know the answer to that question. But there's one proviso. We never sleep together when Amy and Ben are in the house. And for the time being, I don't want them to know there's anything going on between us. Let's just see how things develop and wait until we've got something to say."

"Absolutely. Point taken."

*H*uck spent the rest of the day working on his article for the *Vanguard*. Once he'd finished, he asked me if I'd mind taking a look at it. I was about to when the phone rang. It was Phil.

"So," I said, "how did the conversation with Dad go?"

"Actually, I haven't had it yet. I've been building up to it. But I think I've finally plucked up the courage. I'm walking over to the bungalow as we speak. The thing is, I haven't got a clue what to say. I mean, how on earth do you begin that kind of conversation?"

"OK . . . Well, I think you need to come straight to the point. Don't pussyfoot. It'll make it much harder for both of you."

"So what do I say? 'Hey, Dad, how's it hanging? Oh, and by the way, I hear you and your buddies have been having group sex with some cheap hooker called Anita.' "

"No, what you do is you sit him down and tell him that the two of you need to have a serious talk. Then you tell him you know about Anita."

"God, can you imagine the man's embarrassment? Not to mention mine."

"Can you imagine Mum finding out?"

"Point taken. OK, I'm hanging up now. I'm at the house."

"Good luck and let me know how it goes."

"Will do . . . Soph, wait."

"What?"

"The living room curtains are open." Phil was whispering now.

"So?"

"So I can see right in."

"What's wrong with that?"

"I'll tell you what's wrong— Oh . . . my . . . God. They're naked."

"Who's naked?"

"Mum and Dad. And a load of other old people. There must be a dozen men and women in the room. And they're all naked. Nobody's wearing any clothes."

"It's OK, Phil—I may not be a doctor, but I know what naked means. So who are these people?"

"I dunno. Friends from the old folks center maybe. And there's this woman with a camera. Shit, Soph. I think there's some kind of orgy going on and the woman's photographing it. This is sick. Truly sick."

"And Mum's there, too? I don't believe it. What the hell is going on?"

"That's what I intend to find out. OK . . . I'm going in."

"No, Phil, don't! If Mum and Dad are into weird, pervy sex, it's none of our business. Get out of there—"

But I was too late. Phil had hung up.

Ten minutes later he was back on the phone.

"Jeez, Phil, what on earth happened in there?"

"I made a total arse of myself, that's what happened. I barged in, guns blazing, demanding to know what the hell was going on. It turns out that this Anita woman is actually Anita Delgado—I'd never heard of her, but she's some famous portrait photographer. Has had exhibitions all over the world, apparently."

I said the name rang a vague bell. "What, and she's into photographing old people having sex? Very nice."

"No. It's nothing like that. Her latest project is a study of old age. It's due to be shown at the Museum of Modern Art this summer."

"OK, but why photograph the old people naked?"

"She says it's all about empowering the elderly. It's about them showing the world that they're not ashamed of their wrinkles and saggy bits and that they're proud of who they are. She wants the world to start noticing old people and stop treating them as if they're almost invisible. She's calling the exhibition Gray Pride."

"Huh. I like that."

"Anyway, Mum and Dad got involved after she advertised for sitters. Turns out Dad was intrigued because the idea of becoming invisible really resonated with him. Plus Anita had a budget for the project and was paying fifty dollars a session. So he went along to see her and took a couple of his buddies for moral support. The men went home and talked to their wives. Various meetings were held and in the end everybody decided that the idea had political as well as artistic merit and they agreed to sit for a series of photographs. Today Anita was shooting a group portrait."

"Huh. Mum and Dad allowing themselves to be captured in all

their naked glory. Who'd have thought? But why didn't they say anything to us?"

"They were scared we'd disapprove."

"Gail might have, but once I was certain it was all aboveboard, I'd
have been all for it."

"Me, too," Phil said. "In fact, I'm really proud of them, aren't you?
I mean, it takes some guts to do something like that."

I agreed that it did. "But there's something I don't understand.
Where does Dad's porn stash fit into all this?"

"It doesn't. God, he was furious with me when I admitted I'd
been snooping and found it. Anyway, the bottom line is, our parents
have, shall we say, a rather creative sex life."

"Oh, stop it. Mum and Dad are into porn? I don't believe it."

"Well, you'd better believe it, because they both admitted to it."

"Really? . . . I don't know what to say. For the first time in my life,
I'm starting to think that we don't know our parents. I mean, what
else are they going to hit us with? Have you checked the backyard for
cannabis plants?"

My brother laughed. "You know what, though? Regarding their
porn habit, I have to confess I'm a bit jealous. I mean, Betsy and I,
we've never—"

"No, Greg and me, neither."

As soon as I got off the phone from Phil, I called Gail. I might have
misjudged her, because once she'd gotten over the shock, it became
obvious that she was rather taken with the idea of our parents' being
"hung" in the Museum of Modern Art. "Omigod, can you imagine?
I can see it now: walls of Picassos, Mirós, Warhols and then you've got
Mum and Dad. This magnificent photographic portrait. And who

cares if they're naked? The way I see it, this is a glorious celebration of old age. People will be so impressed. I can't wait to see Sharon Shapiro's face when I tell her."

On the other hand, when I told Gail about our parents' porn stash, she claimed to be disgusted.

"As you know, Murray and I have a very rich and creative sex life, but we've never watched porn. It's so tacky and lower middle class, a bit like clip-on bow ties."

But I could tell she was just as jealous as Phil and me.

"What was all that about?" Huck said when I finally got off the phone.

I explained.

He roared with laughter. "Brilliant. Go, geezers!"

I put the kettle on and started reading Huck's *Vanguard* piece.

"Feel free to be as hard as you like," he said. "I'm no wordsmith."

But he was. Not only that, but he'd painted a picture of life at the Princess Margaret houses and outlined what he thought needed to be done to improve the lot of the families living there—namely improvements to the benefits system—without being mawkish or strident.

"It's brilliant," I said. "They're going to love it . . . once I've sorted out all your split infinitives, that is."

"Show me! Where have I split an infinitive? Where?"

I started laughing and assured him I was only teasing.

"Oh, by the way, Greg will be dropping the kids off soon. I think maybe I should introduce you."

Huck was less than keen. "But I've just had sex with his wife. This is going to feel awkward, to say the least."

"Soon-to-be ex-wife," I pointed out. "And why should it be awkward? It's not like we're going to tell him we're sleeping together."

"I know and I'm probably being paranoid, but I just have this feeling he'll put two and two together."

I told him he was being ridiculous. "And even if he did put two and two together, it's none of his beeswax who I sleep with."

After Huck and Greg had shaken hands, they seemed to feel obliged to engage in a few minutes' small talk.

"So, you're settling in OK?" Greg said.

"Absolutely fine. Sophie's been a great help, sorting me out with new furniture." I noticed Huck playing with the loose change in his pocket. "Oh, and I've finished the piece on the Princess Margaret houses. I'll e-mail it to you tomorrow."

"Great. I'll look forward to reading it."

"It's excellent," I chipped in. "Right up the *Vanguard*'s street."

By now Greg had retreated virtually to the front door. It was obvious that he couldn't get away fast enough.

Contrary to Des's predictions, the strike was showing no sign of coming to an end. Like everybody else on the picket line, I was worried sick about how long I could last money-wise. The rent on the attic room would help, but it wasn't a complete rescue plan. It was Huck—or rather the wild jungle sex I was having with Huck—that managed to keep my spirits up.

The days I wasn't helping man the picket often coincided with Huck's working a late shift. That meant he was home until midafternoon. As soon as I got back from the school run—a consequence of the strike that the kids were really enjoying—Huck and I would head for the attic. We spent hours making love. I was still ravenous and greedy. I wanted to devour him, be devoured. And he obliged, with bells on. Afterwards we would lie in bed cuddling, eating and making crumbs and talking about his plans for the youth club if only he could raise the money.

So long as we weren't actually doing it when *Coffee Break* aired, I usually made a point of listening. Huck said he didn't know how I could bear to have it on, but like everybody else who'd worked on the program, I had this gruesome need to find out how bad the program had become. Pretty bad was the answer.

When STD wasn't discussing vajazzle dos and don'ts or the hottest celebrity fringes, she was interviewing women whose nipples were bigger than their boobs or who were sleeping with their daughters' boyfriends.

If Huck had an entire day off, we might take a drive into the country and have a pub lunch. Sometimes we'd take in an early afternoon movie—along with small groups of seniors who got in half price and spent the ninety minutes asking each other what was going on and who was who. In between they rustled candy wrappers.

Once or twice—when the temperature went above freezing—we took a stroll along the South Bank. Huck enjoyed checking out the secondhand-book stalls. I preferred looking at the stalls full of arty handmade jewelry.

Once, as I was admiring a hot pink papier-mâché brooch, he came over to me full of excitement. He'd found a 1940 edition of Trotsky's *History of the Russian Revolution* and managed to buy it for a song. "And I got this for you," he said.

He handed me a copy of Albert Camus's *The Stranger.* "Wow. Thank you."

"It's one of his best. You haven't read it, have you?"

"Uh-uh."

"It's about the absurdity of man's position when faced with a universe of indifference. Really gets you thinking. Trust me. You'll love it."

"I'm sure I will," I said, kissing him on the cheek. We moved on and I took one final backwards glance at the hot pink brooch. I suddenly remembered that Greg had bought me something similar, but in green. It was for our second or third wedding anniversary.

"So, apart from reading Trotsky and making love to me," I said later, as we lay entwined like mangrove roots in our postcoital glow, "what do you do to relax?"

He admitted that relaxing wasn't something he was very good at.

"What about sports?"

"I played a bit of soccer when I was young, but to be honest, sports bore me."

"Greg and I used to love going to comedy clubs. You'd get loads of acts that were embarrassing and useless, but I remember seeing Ricky Gervais before he was famous and thinking that he was destined for the big time."

"Oh, right. He's the *Office* guy, isn't he? I've watched a few episodes, but I'm not quite sure what people see in him."

"That's because you haven't given yourself a chance to get into it. I've got all the episodes on DVD. How's about we watch them together?"

"Sure. I'd like that." His mind seemed to be wandering.

"What?" I said.

"Oh, I dunno. We just received the latest crime figures involving kids at Princess Margaret. They make pretty depressing reading. Have you any idea how much theft there is these days in multistory car parks?"

"God, that is wrong on so many different levels."

"How do you mean?"

"It was a joke. Multistory car parks have different levels, get it?"

"Oh. Yeah. Right. Most amusing."

Huck wasn't keen on our relationship going public and neither was I. But Annie and Gail had known me long enough to sense that I was keeping something from them. It wasn't long before I admitted that I'd been sleeping with Huck and that we were in a sort of relationship. Gail, who was far more up-front about these things than Annie, was already asking when she was going to meet him.

"The thing is," I said to Huck, "I know that Gail will just keep on nagging until she's worn me down. It occurred to me that the simplest thing to do would be to invite her and Annie over for a cuppa on Sunday afternoon. You'll just *happen* to be around. That way we keep it casual, and Amy and Ben won't suspect anything."

That coming weekend, Greg couldn't have the children because he and FHF were off on a city break to Prague. (Things had clearly settled down between them.) Since Amy and Ben would be with me, I suggested that Annie and Gail bring their kids when they came around on Sunday. I thought it might make the atmosphere more relaxed and that Huck might feel less like he was on some kind of inspection parade.

I made Gail—who was more likely than Annie to say something out of turn or put her foot in it where Amy and Ben were concerned—to promise that she would think twice before she spoke.

"What do you take me for?" Gail said. "I'm not completely clueless, you know."

This from the woman who'd once found herself in the lift at Virgin Atlantic HQ and suggested to the blond, bearded man standing next to her, who was wearing chinos and a polo shirt, that dressing down for the office might not be entirely appropriate. He'd smiled at her, apparently not in the least bit offended, and said that it was the one advantage of owning the company.

It hadn't occurred to me that Alexa and Spencer would actually come. As it was the weekend, I assumed they'd be busy hanging out with their friends. But when I opened the door, there they were. I asked Gail later if they were here under duress, but she insisted she hadn't put any pressure on them. Apparently they both felt they hadn't seen their cousins in a while and wanted to say hi.

"So how are things, Spence?" I said as I took everybody's coats. "You found a bar mitzvah teacher yet?"

"Nah. Dad's helping me a bit, but he's useless."

"So I'm assuming you've abandoned the dark arts."

"What?"

"She means the black magic," Gail said.

"That was only ever a joke. I'm actually into real magic now."

"Really? You know Amy and Ben love magic tricks. Don't suppose you feel like showing them a few? They're in the living room."

"Sure."

"By the way," Alexa said, "Mum's letting me go to stage school. She says I have you to thank for persuading her."

"She's letting you go? Oh, Lexie, I'm so pleased. But to be honest, I think her mind was made up before she asked my opinion."

"Well, thanks anyway."

"My pleasure, hon." I gave my niece a hug. "It's going to be a hard slog, you know—combining academic work with performing."

"That doesn't worry me. It's what I want to do. You wait and see how hard I work."

Gail looked at me and shrugged. "What can I do? She's a chip off the old block."

Spencer and Alexa disappeared into the living room and we made our way into the kitchen. "You've done the right thing," I said to Gail.

"God, I hope so."

A few minutes later Annie arrived with Freddie and Tom. The boys could hear the screeches and laughter coming from the living room and ran off to see what was going on. "Spencer's showing them his magic tricks," I explained to Annie.

I left Annie and Gail to chat while I took drinks and potato chips to the kids. Huck had offered to go to the baker's to buy cakes for tea, but wasn't back yet.

I could hear Ben from way down the hall. He was begging his cousin to tell him how one particular trick was done and getting pretty pissed off that Spencer was refusing.

"It's magic," Spencer kept saying.

"Yeah, right," Ben said. "How old do you think I am?"

Alexa was yelling at her brother, telling him he was being mean and snotty.

Spencer told her to shut up and said that if David Copperfield went around telling everybody how his tricks were done, there would be no magicians left.

"It's not magic. You're lying," Freddie said to Spencer. "I'm only six and I know there's no such thing as magic. It's a trick. You shouldn't lie. Kathleen who looks after us says lying is a mortal sin and liars go to hell."

"Freddie's right," Tom piped up.

"Yeah, and they get given internal dalmatians . . . and . . . and torments. And this fire-and-brimstone stuff comes down all over you and it's so hot that your skin boils off and your eyes pop . . ."

I heard Tom burst into tears.

"Oh, Tom, it's all right," I said, charging into the living room with my tray and depositing it on the coffee table. "Don't let Freddie frighten you." But Tom's tears had already turned to giggles. Spencer had produced a mini Mars bar from behind the little boy's ear and he was busy unwrapping it.

I was back in the kitchen, about to tell Annie how Freddie had scared his brother half to death with Kathleen's grisly vision of hell, when Huck appeared, looking particularly cute in his stubble and gray cashmere sweater. He put down the carrier he was holding and greeted Gail and Annie with handshakes. Then, without being asked, he proceeded to slice four tea cakes in half and pop them and some crumpets under the grill. Afterwards, he went in search of butter, Marmite, jam and plates. I could see that all this wasn't lost on Annie and Gail. I made us all mugs of tea and Gail yelled at the kids, telling them there were hot tea cakes and crumpets for those who wanted them.

Annie seemed fascinated to hear about Huck's work and kept asking him questions. I noticed that while Huck was speaking—which admittedly he did at some length—Gail seemed to glaze over. I couldn't work out if that was because she was bored or because she disliked not being the one holding court. She perked up once she was able to bring the conversation around to her charity "work," so I decided it was probably the latter. "Far be it from me to toot my own horn," she said to Huck, "but within half an hour of an international disaster being announced on the news, I'm organizing a ball. Tell you what—why don't I organize one to raise money for the kids at Princess Margaret? Or better yet, why don't we get people to live on junk food for a week and they could get sponsored for every pizza and Big Mac they eat?"

Huck shot me a WTF look. Then he explained to Gail that my friend Judy was already organizing a PR campaign and he didn't want to step on her toes.

"So how's your work going?" Huck said to Annie. "Sophie tells me you've just started back at the BBC."

She let out a theatrical groan. "Exhausting. I had no idea I'd be this tired."

Looking at Annie more closely, I could see she looked a bit heavy eyed. "The program airs at six each morning, but I was promised I wouldn't have to do any early shifts. Of course, the moment I start, the editor announces that things have changed. Turns out another producer just left. They're advertising the post, but until they've filled it, I'm in at four thirty, three days a week. Of course, by the evening I'm ready to drop and I pretty much go to bed at the same time as the boys. This means I'm spending almost no time with Rob. I can't tell you how pissed off he is. I said that at least now he knows what it's like for me when he's away, but it didn't cut much ice. He said that if I have any interest in preserving our marriage, I should hand in my notice."

"But you've only just started."

"That's what I told him. We've agreed that I should give it a few weeks and see if they manage to find another producer."

"But Kathleen's working out OK?" Gail said.

"The woman's an angel, an absolute angel. If it weren't for Kathleen, I wouldn't be able to cope at all."

"Well, far be it from me to toot my own horn," Gail repeated, "but I did tell you that a housekeeper is the only way forward."

I'd been planning to pull Annie aside and raise the issue of Kathleen's view of hell and how it was affecting the boys—poor Tom in particular—but now that I knew how much she was struggling at work and that her sanity depended on Kathleen, I didn't have the heart to say anything.

The kids took their crumpets and tea cakes into the living room. The initial quiet, brought about by their sitting stuffing their faces, was followed by sounds of squabbling. Huck said he'd go and calm them down and help them choose a DVD.

"So," I whispered after he'd disappeared, "what do you think?"

"He's gorgeous, he's domesticated," Annie said, "and judging by the silence coming from the living room he's obviously great with kids."

"Yeah, I get the impression that the kids where he works pretty much hero-worship him."

I watched Gail pick up Albert Camus's *The Stranger*, which was sitting on the kitchen counter. "Whose is this?"

"Mine. Huck bought it for me at a secondhand-book shop."

She was reading the dust jacket. "'. . . an intimate study of alienation . . . Camus assumes that the universe has no meaning. For him the only question that matters in life is why we shouldn't commit suicide.' Sounds like a right laugh. You actually going to read this?"

"Of course," I said.

The next morning Debbie-from-down-the-road took the kids to school so that I could get to the picket line by eight. The temperature had dropped below freezing again and the sky was heavy with snow. Wendy appeared with a tray of bacon rolls and coffee. We wolfed them down like half-starved refugees.

"Well, the good news is," Des said, "our regular listeners are posting like mad on the strike Web site and on our Facebook page. They're furious about the new program. They're all saying the same thing—that they feel betrayed. Somebody's started a 'bring back the old-style *Coffee Break*' campaign. They're also setting up a petition to submit to James Harding. What's more, there have been complaints to the Broadcasting Complaints Commission about the poor quality of STD's show. Several people have written to the prime minister. They've even written to the Queen. It's unbelievable. I had no idea we'd get this sort of support."

"It's all great stuff," I said, "but I'm not sure where it's going to get us."

Just then a minibus pulled up. Nobody paid it any attention until a group of about a dozen banner-carrying middle-aged women climbed out and came striding over. "Middle Wallop Women's Institute come to lend our support," one of them declared, looking as if she was about to salute us.

Our stunned silence turned into cheers and applause.

"I can't tell you how utterly disgusted and appalled we all are by what's happened. *Coffee Break* is part of what puts the *Great* into Britain. How dare some Australian upstart come along and destroy it. It simply won't do."

There were cries of "Hear, hear" from the rest of the Middle Wallop Women's Institute.

A few moments later, a second bus pulled up and another group of women emerged. It turned out that they were from the Upper Wallop and Lower Wallop branches of the WI. They presented us with food hampers, bottles of whisky and blankets.

But that wasn't the end of it. The "bring back the old-style *Coffee Break*" campaign had clearly been gathering momentum. By the end of the morning, a hundred of middle England's best and most dowdy were standing shoulder to shoulder waving their DON'T BREAK COFFEE BREAK banners and singing "We Shall Not Be Moved."

By midafternoon the reporters and TV crews had arrived.

A few hours later, when I went to collect the kids from Debbie-from-down-the-road's, they came rushing to the door. "Mum! Mum! We just saw you on the news."

Chapter 13

*O*ver the next few days, thanks to the newspaper and TV coverage of the strike, more and more people joined the picket line. They came from as far away as Scotland and Cornwall. Most arrived in groups, in hired buses, like the ladies from the Women's Institute. Some came by tube. Others drove. One woman hitched from Penzance. Groups tended to stay for a couple of days. They booked themselves into bed-and-breakfasts, which didn't come cheap in central London.

Surrounded by her fans, Nancy was in her element and went around signing autographs and being starry and patronizing. "Thank you so much for coming, my dear," she'd say. "You have no idea what this means to us, having ordinary civilians join us in our plight."

Sometimes there were as many as three hundred people on the picket line. That didn't stop STD and the rest of the management team crossing it each day, apparently unperturbed by all the hissing and booing. Whenever James Harding appeared, he was met by cries of "traitor" and "turncoat." When two women pelted him with eggs and flour, the police decided it was time to have a presence on the picket and sent a couple of good-natured constables—both *Coffee Break* fans, as it turned out—to keep the peace.

By now the reviews of the program had started to appear. Apart from the expected rave in *Radio World*, it was universally panned. The *Times* called it "mucky" and "prurient" and "fodder for the brain-dead." The *Independent* asked if tabloid broadcasting had finally reached its nadir and called for James Harding to resign. "How could the man who once championed such an intelligent, thought-provoking program as *Coffee Break* dismantle it in favor of this twaddle and tripe? James Harding should hang his head in shame." The *Daily Mail* printed an editorial lamenting the loss of a great British institution: "For four decades *Coffee Break* was a beacon of British broadcasting. These days it panders to an ignorant, uncouth underclass made up of people whose interests rarely extend beyond their next KFC Bargain Bucket or new Adidas jogging pants."

Eventually the viewing figures were in. Des managed to get hold of them through a mate who worked on the listings pages of one of the newspapers. The numbers were disastrous. *Coffee Break* was managing to attract a few thousand listeners at best. Des was euphoric and declared that victory was ours.

"But Harding and STD are still crossing the picket," I said. "There's no sign of the program being pulled."

It didn't help that, in an interview with one of the papers, James Harding had made the point that new programs often took a while to catch on and that all *Coffee Break* needed was time to find its feet.

Des called him deluded. "Take it from me. This strike will be over in a week."

———

A week later, we were still manning the picket line. James Harding and Co. clearly weren't budging. Des kept sending around e-mails, appealing to us to keep the faith. It would all be over soon, he promised, but nobody had the stomach or, more to the point, the savings to take it much further.

Worried as I was about money and whether I would have a job to go back to when the strike was over, part of me was feeling pretty upbeat. I was enjoying being in a new relationship. It was early days, but I wasn't ruling out the possibility of it getting serious. I was especially enjoying the sex. Huck was so brilliant at it and I still couldn't get enough of him.

When his piece appeared in the *Vanguard*, I couldn't have felt more proud. I insisted we go out to celebrate. "There's a new Italian around the corner I've been meaning to try. My treat."

Natalie, the new sitter—who was Debbie-from-down-the-road's university student niece—came to mind the kids. It hadn't occurred to me that they would read anything into Huck and me going out—after all, they knew that we were friends from way back. Plus I'd made it clear that we were celebrating Huck's newspaper debut. Ben didn't seem at all bothered, but a look came over Amy's face, which wasn't entirely happy.

After an excellent dinner with a bottle of vintage Soave that Huck insisted on paying for, we walked home arm in arm. We agreed that it seemed ridiculous to be saying good night at the end of the street. Huck begged me to sleep in his bed. I needed all my willpower to say no. Instead we snogged in the shadows like a couple of teenagers. When he opened my coat and his hand began stroking my inner thigh above my stocking tops, I did nothing to stop him. My tongue simply went deeper into his mouth. When he pulled the crotch of my panties to one side, I felt myself let out a whimper of delight.

"Come to bed with me," he whispered, pushing his fingers hard up inside me. There was a second thrust. Then a third. "You're so wet. You know you want to."

"Of course I want to. But we can't. We agreed. Remember?"

"But the kids won't know. You can go back to your room afterwards."

"Oh, cheers. That makes me feel so wanted. And what if one of them wakes up and needs me while we're at it?"

Huck was sliding moisture over my clitoris. My head was on his shoulder. It was as much as I could do to keep upright. "Come on. Let's finish this at home."

I pulled his hand away. "No. We have to stop this. We're adults, for Chrissake. We can wait until the morning."

"I'm at work in the morning."

"OK, the afternoon, then. The next morning. Whatever."

Annoyed with him for putting pressure on me, I walked on ahead, rearranging myself and doing up my coat.

He caught up with me. "I'm sorry," he said. "I don't know what came over me. I just fancy you so much, that's all."

"Ditto, but I don't want the kids knowing what's going on until we've worked out where this relationship's heading. And that's going to take time. I thought you understood that."

"I do. I just let my urges get the better of me, that's all. Am I forgiven?"

"I guess, but when Amy and Ben are around, keep your urges in check. OK?"

He bowed his head and pulled a little-boy-being-scolded face.

"I promise. God's honor." He took my hand. "Oh, by the way. Could I ask you a favor?"

I smiled. "Sure."

It turned out that he was due to hold his weekly staff meeting the following night, after the club closed at around nine. But the furnace at the center was playing up again and he wondered if I wouldn't mind if he held the meeting at my place. "All we need is use of your kitchen table for an hour or so."

"No problem," I said. "You're more than welcome any time."

When we got back, I paid Natalie, checked that the kids hadn't given her too much trouble (they hadn't) and showed her out. Then I said good night to Huck—who, after everything I'd said, still gave me a lingering, pleading look. I bashed him over the head with a magazine and went upstairs to check on the children.

As usual, Ben had kicked off his duvet. I pulled it back over him and kissed him on the forehead. "Night-night, sweetie."

The moment I went into Amy's room, she sat up in bed. "Sorry, hon. Did I wake you?"

"I haven't been to sleep."

"Why? What's wrong?"

"Mum?"

"What, darling?" I sat down on the side of her bed.

"Are you going to marry Huck?"

I hadn't been expecting this, which was pretty stupid considering the look on her face when I'd told her that Huck and I were going out. "Marry him? Where on earth did that come from? Amy, just because two people who've known each other for years go out to dinner, it doesn't mean they're going to get married. And besides, I'm not even divorced from your dad yet."

"I wasn't talking about you going out to dinner."

"What, then?"

"I dunno. It's more the way you are with him. You talk to him like you used to talk to Dad when you were getting along."

Not a lot got past my daughter. She'd sensed the intimacy between Huck and me.

"Amy, tell me something. Are you worried about me getting married again one day?"

She burst into tears.

I took her in my arms. "Oh, sweetie, what is it? What's going on?"

She couldn't speak for a few moments. Eventually, she wiped her eyes.

"It's Dad," she said.

"What about him?"

"Well, you know that he and Roz haven't been getting along and I thought that if they split up . . ."

". . . Dad and I might get back together."

She nodded. "And now you've ruined it 'cos you're going to marry Huck."

"Darling, your dad and I are getting a divorce. There's no way we're going to get back together. Don't you remember how miserable we all were those last few months before we split up?"

"I guess."

"Huck and I are friends and that's all." Seeing how upset she was, I wasn't about to say any more than that. "If that changes, you and Ben will be the first to know. Nothing is going to happen suddenly. Now please try to stop worrying."

"'K."

I gave her a squeeze.

"Now come on, you need to get some sleep."

"Mum?"

"Yes?"

"Will you sing me a song?"

*T*he staff meeting had been arranged for nine thirty. Araminta arrived first. Huck brought her through to the kitchen, where I was loading the dishwasher. While Huck went to find extra chairs, she and I stood chatting and I put the kettle on. This was the second time I'd met her and once again I found myself thinking how beautiful she was—and so different from the rest of the youth workers, with her posh accent and impeccable manners.

"This is such a lovely house," Araminta said. "I couldn't help noticing you've kept all the original cornicing, and I got a glimpse of the fabulous fireplace in the living room."

"The house could be lovely," I said. "But it needs so much work. Starting with a massive chuck out and tidy up. The thing is that, with a full-time job and two kids, I never seem to get around to it."

"I know how you feel. Mummy and Daddy are the same. They've got this massive place in Oxfordshire. It's a complete mess, but Mummy's far too busy with the horses and her charity work to sit down and sort out what needs doing."

Araminta was such an enigma—rich aristo working in the slums. How did that work? "So what took you to Princess Margaret?"

"Rebellion," she declared. "I find my parents' life so stifling. People like them have no connection with the real world. I couldn't face ending up like them. So I've been annoying them ever since—"

"You can say that again," Huck said, coming in with two dining room chairs. "I've just discovered that this woman almost took holy orders."

Araminta rolled her eyes and turned to me. "Huck hasn't stopped teasing me since I told him. I did not nearly take holy orders. I studied theology at Oxford, that's all. I was going through a religious phase at the time and I knew it would piss Mummy and Daddy off. They're staunch atheists. Then during one summer vacation I went to do volunteer work in Africa, and seeing starving babies die in their mothers' arms, I turned into a nonbeliever, too."

I said that I could see how that might happen. "So, you studied theology. Don't suppose you could help my nephew learn his bar mitzvah portion." I said it as a joke—a throwaway comment to lighten the atmosphere.

"Absolutely," she said with a flick of her long blond hair. "I'm fluent in Hebrew and Aramaic." Of course she was.

"Are you serious? You'd really take him on?"

"Yes, if he's up for it. But why can't he go to regular classes?"

I explained about him telling his elderly teacher that he was a Satanist and getting kicked out.

Araminta roared. "I rather like the sound of young Master Spencer. Why don't you get his mother to give me a call?"

Just then the doorbell rang. The rest of the youth workers had arrived en masse.

I stood chatting with them while I finished making tea. I could see Huck wanted to get started, so after finding a packet of chocolate biscuits, which I emptied onto a plate and left on the kitchen table, I took myself off to the living room and called Gail to tell her about Araminta's offer.

"But she's not Jewish? Is that allowed?"

I laughed. "What? You think God's going to send down the bar mitzvah police?"

"I suppose not. OK, I'll call her. Huh, so Spencer could have an Oxbridge theologian teaching him his bar mitzvah. Finally I've got one up on Sharon Shapiro. Soph, I don't know how to thank you. You are a star."

I must have dozed off on the sofa. The next thing I knew it was almost midnight. I couldn't hear any voices coming from the kitchen, so I decided it was safe to go in and make some hot milk. I opened the door to find Huck and Araminta deep in conversation. "That's brilliant," Huck was saying. "I wish I'd thought of that."

"OK, so let's bounce it off Judy."

When he saw me, Huck looked up. "I've got a meeting with Judy in the morning. Araminta's offered to come with me. She's got this amazing fund-raising idea involving Twitter. People bid to get retweeted or followed by a celebrity. Isn't that totally brilliant?"

I had to agree that it was.

Chapter 14

On the morning of Ben's birthday party—as opposed to his actual birthday, which had been a few days before—Greg turned up smelling powerfully of dung.

Ben, who had answered the door, came charging into the kitchen holding his nose. "Mum! Mum! Dad stinks of poo! It's really bad. I think I'm going to be sick."

"Ben, stop it. I'm sure your dad doesn't stink of poo."

"He does. He probably couldn't get to the loo in time and had an accident."

"I think that's highly unlikely. Your father is many things, but I'm pretty sure that incontinent isn't one of them."

Just then Huck appeared in the doorway, grinning. "I'm not even going to ask what this is about."

"Probably for the best," I said, waving him good-bye. He was spending the day with his mum and dad. He'd decided to make himself scarce because it was Ben's party and he didn't want to intrude on a family day. I felt guilty he felt he had to leave, but I hadn't put up a fight.

Ben said bye to Huck and then turned back to me.

"But Dad is in a continent. Europe."

"I don't mean that kind of continent."

"What other types of continent are there? There's Europe, Africa, America, Asia, Scandinavia . . ."

The kid certainly knew his continents.

"Ben, that's enough. I'll explain later."

"You always say that. Just to shut me up."

Just then Greg appeared in his socks.

"I just met Huck on his way out."

"Yeah, he's spending the day with his parents."

Greg look relieved.

"So what's going on? Ben seems to think you've pooed your pants."

"Cheers, Ben . . . Actually, I've trodden in some manure. I've left my shoes outside on the step." He explained FHF had dispatched him to a farm in Surrey to pick up some sacks of manure. "We're landscaping the garden and Roz wanted some decent organic muck for her roses."

I glanced out the kitchen window. The grass needed cutting. The bindweed needed attacking. The old toys and rusty garden furniture needed clearing. "Roz certainly keeps you on your toes," I said. "You only just finished helping with the decorating. How did that go, by the way?"

"Very well. Turns out I'm pretty good with a paint roller. And I've learned how to hang wallpaper."

"Huh. Who'd have thought?"

"I'd better clean my shoes," he said.

What? He wasn't leaving them for me?

"I'll take them outside to the garden tap. I might need some disinfectant, though." He went over to the cupboard under the sink. Huh. I used to doubt he knew where the kitchen was kept, let alone the disinfectant. Turned out he knew all the time.

Nobody saw Amy come in. "I think you ought to know that there are two dogs on the step, sniffing Dad's shoes."

B en's entire class had been invited to his birthday party, plus Freddie and Tom. In the end he gave up on the idea of inviting the six dwarves and decided on a time travel theme instead.

Everybody was to come dressed in a costume from the past: Egyptians, medieval knights, cowboys. No pressure there, then. The mums were going to hate me. This year, even though money was tight, I'd decided to placate the mothers by spending a bit extra on party favors.

It was Greg who suggested that Ben should make a time capsule. He'd intended it as a party activity, but Ben, who loved the idea in principle, was less than keen on involving his friends. He wanted us to make a family time capsule.

Greg ordered the specially designed airtight container on the Internet. Each of us put in things that were relevant to Ben. I chose the BabyGro he wore when we brought him home from the hospital after he was born. I also included some of his first paintings and drawings, along with a copy of the *Times* from the day of his birth, which Mum had given me as a keepsake. Greg put in photographs he'd taken a few moments after Ben's birth. Amy didn't own anything that was particularly Ben-related, so she added stuff that was her-related: a Justin Bieber CD and copies of *Mizz* and *Teen Now*. Ben put in a completed sticker album along with some Blu Tack ("'cos that's how we stuck things"), his copy of *Harry Potter and the Philosopher's Stone* and several dead insects in a jar ("'cos insects might become extinct and scientists of the future could bring these back to life").

After Greg had cleaned his shoes we all trooped into the garden. It was agreed that we should bury the capsule under the apple tree. Greg found a rusty spade in the shed and we all took turns at digging. When it was done, Ben picked up the capsule.

"One day," he said, in the manner of a priest presiding at a graveside, "I will open this time capsule and remember when we were still a family."

Greg and I tried making the point that we hadn't stopped being a family. But Ben wasn't having it. In proper families the parents lived together. It was hard to argue with that. Amy agreed with her brother and said that she was fed up with her friends—who surprisingly all came from families in which the parents were still together—feeling sorry for her.

After lunch, Ben went to get changed into his Marty McFly outfit. This had been easy to put together since it consisted of a red sleeveless padded jacket, a checked shirt and jeans (which he'd already owned). Amy had agreed to come to the party, but, being nearly eleven, she insisted that this was purely in a supervisory capacity. "There's no way I'm dressing up in some goofy costume."

Greg sat at the kitchen table blowing up balloons while I made a start on the party sandwiches.

"Wow, fantastic cake," he said, eyeing the beautifully crafted De-

Lorean covered in edible silver paint, which had pride of place on the counter. "The kids are going to love it. So what did that set us back?"

I explained that one of the mums at school had made it and charged only for the ingredients. "She's taking a specialty cake baking course and did the DeLorean as one of her assignments. Yesterday, when she took it to be it marked, her tutor gave her an A."

Greg said he wasn't surprised.

"So," I said, licking peanut butter off my thumb, "how are things with you?"

"Work's OK," he said. "But things are a bit tricky between Roz and me." It didn't occur to me that he would open up about him and Roz. Until now he'd been pretty cagey.

"I thought the Prague trip might help sort things out," he continued. "But to be honest, we're struggling."

"Greg, I realize that some of what's going on between you two has to do with me falling out with Roz. I just want to say that I had no intention of coming between you, but her behavior has been intolerable."

"You don't have to tell me." He threw a balloon into the air and bashed it with his fist.

"Thank you for supporting me on this. I'm really grateful."

"That's OK . . . You know, what Ben said before about us not being a proper family anymore really upset me."

"Me, too. But we're doing our best. Given time, the kids will adjust."

"I guess. Maybe it's just the mood I'm in. The other thing that got to me was seeing those photographs of Ben as a newborn. They brought back so many memories."

"For me, too. Do you remember how I was in labor for seventeen hours? It was agony. They say the second baby's easier, but it was much worse than with Amy."

"The thing I remember most is you hitting me and telling me in no uncertain terms that you would never let me near you again. I had that bruise on my arm for two weeks."

I couldn't help laughing. "Yes, but I did say sorry afterwards."

"You did. And I accepted your apology rather gracefully, if I remember."

"I can still see the midwife handing him to you and you bursting into tears."

"I did not burst into tears," he said. "I welled up a bit, that's all."

"Yeah, right. If you say so."

"What about when we brought him home and Amy took one look at him and said we should 'send him back to his own garden.'"

"She must have thought we'd harvested him from some local vegetable patch."

Greg started on another balloon and I finished sawing a pile of sandwiches into triangles.

"Look," I said eventually. "There's something you should know. It's about Huck. The thing is . . . well . . . we're sort of together."

He didn't seem surprised. "I'd kind of worked out there was something going on."

"You had? How?"

"It was seeing you together the other day. You just seemed very comfortable."

"I had no idea we'd let our guard slip. Amy noticed, too."

"Oh, great. So the kids know? I don't get you, Soph. When I

started seeing Roz, it was ages before I introduced her to the kids—partly at your insistence. And it was several months after that before I moved in with her. You bump into an old flame and a few weeks later the two of you are shacked up."

"OK, first of all, Huck was never an old flame."

"Whatever."

"He was looking for somewhere to live and I had a spare room. At the time—as you well know—I was going out of my mind worrying about money. It seemed like the perfect solution. You said so yourself. I certainly don't recall you raising any objections."

"You're right, I didn't. I don't know why, because even then I had my suspicions about the two of you. You know, Soph, after all the kids have been through, I can't believe you're doing this to them."

"OK, let's get a few things straight. Huck and I are not 'shacked up.' We never, ever sleep together when the kids are in the house. We never touch in front of them. We don't even sit on the sofa together."

"And yet Amy still picked up that there was something going on between you."

"I guess that's girls for you. Anyway, I've told her we're friends and she seems perfectly cool with that. With hindsight, maybe the situation isn't ideal. And OK—if I'm being totally, searingly honest, I think I was starting to have feelings for Huck before he moved in. I'm sorry if I've fucked up, but I swear that we're being careful around the kids."

He seemed to calm down. "Maybe I'm being too hard on you. I think I'm just pissed off because you seem to be getting your life together and I'm struggling."

"I am still on strike, you know."

"OK, work aside, you seem to be getting things sorted."

"Hey, come on. You will, too. You just need to keep working at it. I'm not going to pretend I like Roz, but you've told me how much you love her, so I'm assuming she has qualities that I've never seen."

He didn't say anything.

"Soph, do you ever think we did the wrong thing by splitting up?"

"In the beginning, sure, but I know that if you and I had stayed together we would have ended up killing each other. You're only having doubts because you and Roz have hit a rough patch."

"Yeah, I guess you're right."

On Monday morning, I was driving home after dropping the kids off at school when my mobile rang. It was Des.

"It's over."

"What?"

"It's over. Management caved."

"You're kidding."

"I'm not. What did I tell you about keeping the faith? I just got a call from one of the senior board members. Apparently they spent the whole of Sunday discussing the audience figures. James Harding pleaded for more time to improve them, but instead they held a vote of no confidence and he ended up being sacked as chairman and resigning from the board."

"I'm stunned. I never thought they'd get rid of Harding. So what happens now?"

"Well, STD's been asked to clear her desk and a new chairman has already been appointed."

"Blimey. They didn't waste much time."

"And I've just been informed that the new chairman would like to see you ASAP."

It was over. I practically skipped to the station. Outside the GLB building, the picket was nowhere to be seen. The only evidence that there had ever been a strike was a rain-soaked banner poking out of one of the trash cans.

By now I was starting to feel nervous. *Please, God, don't let the new chairman be some fire-breathing despot.* I knocked on the door.

"Come in."

I knew that voice. Sitting at the large mahogany desk, looking every inch the company chairwoman, was Liz. The same Liz who had retired as editor of *Coffee Break* to tend her garden.

"Liz? No! You're the new chairman?"

"I am, but I'm not sure if I should be referred to as chairman, chairwoman, chairperson or chair. What do you think?"

"It's bloody fantastic—that's what I think." A moment later we were throwing our arms around each other. "So how . . . when . . . ?"

"I got a call last night from one of the board members—right in the middle of *Downton*, if you please. I almost didn't pick up. Anyway, he told me that James Harding had stepped down and that they wanted to appoint a new chair. He hinted heavily that if I were to put myself forward, the vote would go in my favor. I agreed on the spot and they voted late last night."

"But I thought you were busy tending your parsnips and cabbages."

"I was climbing the walls after a week. Nobody told me how boring retirement is. I was desperate to get back to work." She went over to the drinks cupboard. "One of the perks of the job." She smiled. "Come on, it's after eleven. What do you fancy?"

"Oh, go on, then. I'll have a small G and T."

"Coming up."

We clinked glasses. "Congratulations, Liz. I can't believe I've got my old boss back."

She led me over to the leather sofa. "OK," she said as we sat down. "Here's the deal. It goes without saying that we want you as permanent editor. And I've managed to negotiate you a pretty decent pay raise, which will come into effect immediately."

"Thank you. I really appreciate that."

"Believe me, it's my pleasure. Now, then, the plan is to take the program off the air for a couple of weeks to give you and the rest of the team some time to come up with a format that's fun but without compromising the program's more heavyweight content."

"Actually, we came up with some ideas and proposals ages ago. I showed them to Shirley Tucker Dill, but of course she trashed them."

"Why don't you let me take a look?"

I said I'd head off to my office and e-mail them to her right away.

The mood in the office was euphoric. Des had been out and bought several bottles of sparkling wine. People were hugging and kissing and punching the air. Wendy and several of the other PAs were even doing a conga through the office. By now everybody knew that Liz was the new chairman of GLB. Des had told them.

"But you didn't tell me, you mean sod!" I said as he handed me a plastic cup of sparkling.

"I thought you'd enjoy the surprise."

I had to admit that seeing Liz sitting behind the chairman's desk had been one of the best bombshells ever.

I called everybody together and gave them a rundown of my meeting with Liz. "The moment she's signed off on the program proposals, we get going on the new show. I'm sure she'll get back to me by this evening, so I suggest everybody take the rest of the day off and we'll reconvene tomorrow . . . And by the way—well done, everybody, for hanging in there. I think we owe Des a big thank-you for all his hard work and for keeping our spirits up."

A huge cheer went up.

By now it was getting on for midday. It occurred to me that Annie would be finishing her shift at the BBC, which was only a few minutes' walk away. I thought she might fancy lunch. She whooped and cheered when I told her the news about the strike. "I'd love to do lunch, but you'll have to come back to my place. Kathleen's off to the dentist and the boys have got a half day off school, so I need to be around."

I said I'd meet her outside Broadcasting House in twenty minutes.

Meanwhile, I went to my office and e-mailed all my ideas and proposals to Liz. Afterwards, as I headed back down the corridor, I noticed that the door to STD's office was open. I stopped and popped my head around the door. Despite everything that had gone on, I couldn't let her leave without saying good-bye. She was loading her stuff into a cardboard box.

"Hi, Shirley."

STD looked up. I could tell she'd been crying because her mascara had run, giving her panda eyes.

"Soph. G'day." She wiped her eyes, making the panda effect worse.

"Look, I just wanted to say that I'm sorry things ended the way they did."

She raised her palm in front of her. "Nothing for you to be sorry about. I rarely eat humble pie, but I'm prepared to admit the best woman won. You were right and I was wrong. I misjudged the audience. It's as simple as that."

"Thank you for that. I appreciate it."

"I admire you, Soph. You've got spunk. You know what you want and you go all out to get it. In many ways, you're a bit like me. I'm glad they've made you permanent editor. You've got a great future ahead of you. In a few years you're going to be awesome."

I felt my face redden. "I don't know about that."

"Take it from me."

"So what will you do now?" I asked. It occurred to me that even a career as illustrious as STD's might not survive such a high-profile failure and that she could be cast into the wilderness.

"I'm heading back to Sydney for a few weeks of R and R and then I'll consider my options. I've got a few irons in the fire."

I said I was glad and I meant it. She'd been a demon to work for, but in the end she was a gallant loser. I couldn't help admiring that.

"Right, well, I'd best be off," I said. "Good luck."

"You, too, Soph. Knock 'em dead."

"I'll do my best."

We shook hands and STD went back to her packing.

I'm so glad it's all over," Annie said, putting her arm through mine as we walked to the car park. "I've been so worried about you and how you were going to make ends meet if it went on much longer."

"Well, you can stop now. I've been made permanent editor and I've got a pay raise."

"Oh, hon, that's amazing. I'm sorry we're going to have to celebrate with a cuppa and beans on toast back at mine, rather than going out."

"No problem," I said.

"So how are you?" I asked as we climbed into her car. It was a daft question. She looked exhausted.

"I'm so tired that I've stopped sleeping—if that makes any sense. The doctor says it's stress. He's given me some sleeping pills. But I don't want to become reliant on them."

"But you can't go on like this." I made her promise to take them for a couple of nights, just so she could catch up on her sleep.

"So what's new with you and Huck?" she said.

"Well, I ended up telling Greg about him and he's pretty pissed off. He's worried how it's going to affect Amy and Ben. Amy's already worked out there's something going on. I did my best to convince her that we're only friends, but I'm seriously worried that Greg's right and that by letting Huck move in I may have fucked up big-time."

"Soph, you have to stop beating yourself up. You know how worried about money you were. Renting your spare room to Huck made perfect sense—and if I remember, Greg thought it was a great idea."

"I know. I keep having to remind myself."

"If you ask me, Greg isn't worried about the kids. This is about Huck. He's jealous."

"I had the same thought. He asked me if I thought we'd made a mistake splitting up."

"I rest my case. He's unhappy with Roz and wants you back."

"Well, if he thinks he can come running back to me the moment he hits a few bumps in the road, he can think again."

"I agree. On the other hand, he does seem to have changed. He decorates, gardens, cleans his own shitty shoes."

"I don't care. I can't forgive him for treating me the way he did. I just can't."

Annie let us into the house, hung up our coats and went to find Kathleen and the boys. "You know, they had such fun at Ben's birthday party. I think they both enjoyed being with older kids. Made them feel really grown up."

I said I was glad they'd enjoyed it.

Freddie and Tom were sitting on the living room floor building LEGOs. "Hi, guys," Annie said. "Where's Kathleen?"

Freddie said she was in the kitchen. It was then that we both noticed the boys were wearing their backpacks. We could see they were heavy from the way they were leaning forward. "Boys, those things look like they're really weighing you down," Annie said. "You can't be comfortable. I'm assuming it's part of your game, but what on earth have you got in them?"

"Supplies," Freddie said. "We're on an adventure."

"That's a lie," Tom shot back at his brother. "You know what Kathleen says about lying."

"OK," Annie said, looking puzzled. "So what's really in the backpacks?"

"Reminders of our sins," Tom declared.

"What?"

"Reminders of our sins," Tom repeated. "Kathleen put them there."

"Sshh, you numpty. We weren't supposed to say anything."

"Your sins?" Annie shot me a WTF look. "Kids, stand up. I need to see inside."

The backpacks were so heavy that the boys struggled to get up.

Freddie turned around and let his mother unzip the top pouch. "Oh my God. Soph, take a look at this."

I looked. I couldn't believe what I was seeing. The pouch was full of rocks. "The woman's off her head," I muttered.

"Kathleen says," Freddie continued, "that carrying rocks is good for our souls because it reminds us that we are sinners."

I watched Annie's eyes fill with tears. "Soph, get these things off the kids, will you?" With that she disappeared into the kitchen. She made no attempt to keep her voice down. She was a lioness defending her young. "Kathleen, do you mind telling me what the hell you're doing, forcing Freddie and Tom to go around weighed down by a ton of rocks?"

"Annie, calm down or you'll be having a stroke."

"Don't you dare tell me to calm down. Answer my question."

"Children need to know that they are born sinners and they need to atone for their wickedness."

"What? Where do you get this tripe?"

"The Good Book says—"

"I don't give a flying fuck about the Good Book. You're insane. Do you know that? Totally, utterly insane. Pack your bags and get out of my house. Now."

Half an hour later, Kathleen was gone, I was making tea and Annie was sitting cross-legged on the floor with the boys doing her best to convince them that babies do not come into this world programmed for evil.

I got back to Putney around six and went straight to pick up Amy and Ben from Debbie-from-down-the-road's. I told them that the strike was over and announced we were going out for pizza to celebrate. I thought they'd be pleased. Instead they looked miserable. "I'm going to miss you taking us to school," Ben said. "And being around when we get home." I assumed he was speaking for both of them.

"Oh, guys, I'm sorry. I know you've enjoyed us being together more and so have I, but I have to get back to work."

"OK," Amy said. "How about you increase our pocket money to make up for it?"

"So you're saying that cash will wipe away your tears?"

"Pretty much."

"OK, so what sort of a raise are you looking for?"

"Fifty percent."

"No way. Thirty."

"Forty."

"Thirty-five."

"Done."

Ben, who hadn't done percentages in school yet, looked at his sister. "Is that a good deal?"

"I think I've hammered out a reasonable settlement," she said. Then she turned back to me: "Mum, why are you looking at me like that? You're the one who's been on strike. I've picked up my negotiating skills from you."

When we got home, Huck was in the kitchen with Araminta. They were sharing a bottle of wine.

"You're just in time to help us celebrate," Huck said. "Guess what—the BBC and Channel Four both want me on their late-night news programs. Plus we just had a really productive meeting with Judy, who thinks that Minty's Twitter idea definitely has legs."

"Oh, Huck, that's brilliant. I'm really pleased things are going so well."

"Mum's got news, too," Amy said, clearly not wanting me to be outdone.

"The strike's over," I said. "We won. James Harding got booted off the board and STD's been sacked."

"And Mum's got a pay raise," Ben piped up.

"Good for Mum," Huck said. He turned to me. "Well done, Soph. I knew it would work out. So come on, how's about a celebratory glass of wine?"

I said I would join them in a few minutes. First, I needed to make sure that Ben got in the bath. Then I had to wash Amy's hair. She still liked me to do it sometimes as a treat.

By the time I rejoined Huck and Araminta, they had a load of papers spread out in front of them and were deeply engrossed in a discussion about fund-raising. I poured myself a glass of wine. "Maybe I'll take myself off to the living room," I said.

"No, stay," Huck said. "We'll be done talking in a couple of minutes."

But I knew they wouldn't be. "Actually, I'm really tired. I think I'd rather put my feet up and watch TV."

I headed into the living room and checked my e-mail to see if Liz had gotten back to me with her thoughts on the proposal. She had:

> All fab. Go for it. I just know we're going to have a major success on our hands.
>
> Liz x

I closed my laptop. "Please, please don't let me fuck up."

Gail rang in the middle of the news. She said she'd spoken to Araminta on the phone and that she sounded lovely. "She's agreed to tutor Spencer on a Sunday morning. Thanks again for finding her, Soph. I can't tell you how grateful I am." I could hear Murray in the background. "Tell her I'm grateful, too!"

It was eleven before Araminta left—which didn't surprise me. She popped her head around the door to say bye and to apologize for ousting me from my kitchen.

After he'd shown her out, Huck joined me on the sofa. "Don't you think Minty's amazing? Not only is she great with the kids at work, but she's so creative—so full of ideas to promote the cause. Judy was really impressed."

"You're rather smitten with young Araminta, aren't you?"

Huck burst out laughing. "Oh my God, you're jealous."

"No, I'm not."

"You are."

"OK, a bit maybe. It's just that she's really beautiful and clever and you spend so much time together."

"Yes, discussing the PR campaign. I don't think you appreciate how much there is to do."

"I do understand," I said. "I'm sorry. I'm just feeling a bit tired and insecure, that's all."

"Well, stop it. You have nothing to worry about. Minty is not my type. The woman plays croquet, for crying out loud."

With that, he kissed me very thoroughly indeed.

Chapter 15

After much debate it was decided that *Coffee Break*'s makeover should include a new name. We knew that renaming it was risky because it could alienate our older listeners. On the other hand, the *Coffee Break* handle seemed twee and old-fashioned and wasn't going to help the show broaden its appeal. Several names were suggested. When we put them to the vote, one clear winner emerged: *Women's Lip*. It was a tad last millennium, but we were on familiar enough terms with the women of middle England—even the younger ones—to know that they wouldn't respond well to a name that was too out there.

We also decided to lose the serial, on the grounds that it was dated. Ditto the dull and long-winded items on nature and crafts.

The two weeks allotted to us by Liz were spent brainstorming, planning and redesigning. Meetings tended to go on well into the evening. (Suffice it to say that Amy and Ben registered their dismay in the most voluble terms.) By the end we were all pretty wrung out—not to say apprehensive. There was a general gut feeling that the new format would work, but nobody was sure. It was Liz who kept everybody's spirits up by telling us that we were doing a great job and that *Women's Lip* represented the dawn of an exciting new era in women's broadcasting.

During those two weeks, Huck and I didn't see much of each other. The publication of the *Vanguard* piece coincided with more rioting in London, Leeds and Manchester. The plight of the underclass was big news and pretty much overnight Huck had become the media's social-deprivation commentator of choice. When he wasn't appearing on TV or radio, he was giving talks and lectures all over the country. On top of that, Judy's PR initiatives were beginning to bear fruit. Donations were coming in not just from individuals, but businesses as well.

I'd watched him on TV several times, and he was impressive. He wasn't merely intelligent and articulate, but he was expressing original ideas, which were driving a new debate about how to combat poverty. He was calling for the leaders of all three parties to sign on to a hundred-year plan to fight deprivation and raise up the underclass.

He argued that governments were by nature shortsighted—they could never see further than the next election. Huck insisted that in order to lift people out of the poverty trap it was important to think long term and recognize that results couldn't be achieved between one election and the next. Change would take decades. Most politicians and commentators thought he was a daft idealist. He responded by saying that he wasn't ashamed to be called an idealist and that idealism was precisely what modern Western politics lacked.

After his last TV appearance I texted him: *Great stuff. Idealism gets me really horny.*

His bosses at the charity, aware of what an inspirational ambassador for the poor they had, made sure he had the time off he needed to pursue his extramural activities. He also managed to negotiate leave for Araminta—albeit unpaid—on the grounds that she was an invaluable aide and adviser.

I still couldn't help thinking that her role went beyond that of adviser, but on the nights they were away together, Huck would call me before bed and was always full of how much he missed me and couldn't wait to ravish me.

*F*inally, the first edition of *Women's Lip* was about to go live to the nation.

I stepped into the lift with Nancy. Des, today's producer—who had been put in charge of the maiden show in return for all his hard work during the strike—was already down in the studio setting up. Liz was there, too. The editor didn't usually watch the program go out. The chairman of GLB certainly didn't. But she and I had so much emotion, not to mention our professional futures, invested in the new program, that we had to be there to see it out of the starting gate.

Nancy was nervous, but had been behaving impeccably. Everybody had noticed the change in her. She wasn't making quite so many demands and had started making polite requests rather than barking orders. I hardly dared say it, but the therapy seemed to be working.

The doors closed and the lift headed towards the basement.

"There are moments," Nancy said, "when I still can't believe we beat STD."

"Me, neither."

"And I think it's totally brilliant that you've been made permanent editor. I hear you got a hefty pay raise."

"It certainly wasn't hefty, but I'm not denying it's going to make life a bit easier."

"I bet you can't wait to start spending money on clothes. Just think. You can ditch all your old work outfits and get into some decent tailoring. I'm pretty sure Joseph goes up to your size and I'm always here if you need any advice."

"I'll remember that," I said. The woman might have been making progress in therapy, but she was a long way of being cured.

Today's program lineup was impressive. Samantha Cameron had agreed to come on and talk about the ups and downs of raising small children at No. 10 Downing Street. We had Whoopi Goldberg talking about her new movie, followed by a discussion on women's rights in Afghanistan. Finally, in place of the serial, Nancy was hosting a phone-in on tattoos—did women love them or loathe them?

We were just about to go into the studio when my mobile rang. Nancy went on ahead while I stopped to answer it.

It was Mrs. McKay, the head teacher at the kids' school. I could feel my heart beating against my chest. Mrs. McKay called parents only when there was bad stuff to report. Something had happened.

I wasn't wrong. It seemed that there had been a serious "incident" in the playground. Ben and Arthur had gotten into a fight during which Ben had thrown an almighty punch. This had caused Arthur to fall to the ground and cut his head. He was now in the ER with his mum.

"Ben punched Arthur? But they're best friends. Is he seriously hurt? Is he going to be OK?"

"I'm sure he'll be fayne," the head soothed in that Miss Jean Brodie accent of hers that Greg so loved to impersonate. "He has a cut on his head. He may need a stitch or two and they'll probably want to X-ray him to check there's no further damage."

"Oh God. I have to phone his mum. But how did the fight start?"

Mrs. McKay said she didn't know. Ben was nursing a bruised hand in the medical room and wasn't saying much. "I think he's in shock. The wee laddie didn't realize his own strength."

"But Ben tends to shy away from fights. I don't understand it."

"Nor does his class teacher. She says it's totally out of character. I think it would be best if you came and collected him. Then, when you get home, see if you can get him to open up about what went on."

"OK, I'll be there in an hour."

"Oh, and when you get here, perhaps you could pop into my office first so that we can have a wee bit more of a chat about what might have caused Ben's outburst."

"Of course." I pressed "end." Greg and I were going to get the blame for this. I just knew it. Mrs. McKay was going to say Ben's behavior was a result of stress caused by the separation.

I pushed open the heavy studio door. By now it was seven minutes to airtime. "Sorry, everybody, but I've got a domestic emergency. I've been called in to see the head at Ben's school." I explained what had happened.

"Go," Liz said. "Everything's fine here. Des has got everything under control, haven't you, Des?"

"Absolutely."

"And don't worry about Ben. He's not turning into a delinquent. I've had three boys. Girls bitch, boys fight. It's the natural order of things."

I managed a smile.

"I'm not sure that's entirely true," Nancy said. "In my experience children—like mine—who've been exposed to Montessori teaching tend to be far less aggressive."

I didn't have the time or the energy to argue. I told everybody to break a leg and headed back to the lift.

Ten minutes later I was on my way to the tube and sobbing on the phone to Greg.

"Soph, take a deep breath . . . What's happened?"

I told him. "Greg, this is our fault. The separation has been too much for Ben. He'll be shoplifting next—you wait."

"Don't be daft. You're upset and you're overreacting. We have no idea why Ben hit Arthur. Right, I'm leaving the office now. I'll meet you at the school."

"You don't have to come. Honest. I can handle it. There's no point in us both taking time off work."

"I think we should both be there. It gives a better impression if separated parents present a united front."

I didn't argue.

Just as I'd predicted, Mrs. McKay—earth tones, ethnic earrings—kicked off by probing me about the separation. Her theory was that Ben might be suffering from some kind of posttraumatic stress.

Before I had a chance to say anything, Greg walked in. "With respect, Mrs. McKay," he snapped, "I think that's nonsense."

"Ah, Mr. Lawson. Do come in and sit down." They shook hands and he sat. "Now, then, I understand that you might be feeling a bit defensive about what happened. Parents often do. It's not pleasant to discover that your son has carried out a violent attack on another child."

"Ben is *not* violent," Greg came back. "He must have been goaded."

Just then—to my complete and utter horror—the door opened and in walked Frizzy-Haired Feminist, her frizzy hair partially covered by a Peruvian hat with earflaps. It was identical to the one she'd sent me.

"What the hell is she doing here?"

"Sophie, please calm down," FHF said, offering me a condescending smile.

Her face was more elfin and waiflike than in her photographs. She was actually very pretty in the flesh. I hated her even more.

I looked at Greg. "I repeat . . . what is she doing here?"

"I called Roz to cancel our lunch date, but when I explained what was going on with Ben, she thought she ought to come with me to the school." He looked uncomfortable. I could tell that he wasn't happy about her being here.

"Indeed I did. I think I can explain Ben's behavior."

"And you would be . . . ?" Mrs. McKay said to FHF.

"Roz Duffy."

"Not *the* Roz Duffy—the wraiter?"

"For my sins." FHF smirked.

Ugh.

"I have to say I'm a huge fan. I've read *A Feminist Guide to Global Warming* three times."

Of course she had.

"I'm also Mr. Lawson's new partner," FHF continued. "And I spend a lot of time with Ben—and Amy."

"Yes . . . mainly discussing pornography," I said.

FHF swung around. "Amy raised the subject. What was I supposed to say?" She turned back to Mrs. McKay. "Since I'm with the children so much, I think I might have some useful insights into Ben's behavior."

"Excellent," Mrs. McKay chirruped. She found a chair for FHF and invited her to sit down. "Now, then, why don't we all take a deep breath and discuss this calmly?"

"OK, Roz," I said. "Tell me. Precisely what are these insights you have into my son's behavior?"

"It doesn't take a therapist to see that he's a very angry little boy."

"Rubbish," Greg and I shot back in unison.

FHF wasn't deterred. "Parental separation is never easy for children. I know. I've been there."

I wanted to throttle the woman, but I couldn't help thinking back to the little speech Ben had given before we buried the time capsule. Maybe he was angry and until now he'd been keeping it bottled up.

"I have been trying to get Ben to open up about his feelings for a while now," FHF continued.

"And has he?" Mrs. McKay inquired, her head at an earnest tilt.

"Not yet. But I'm sure he will."

Mrs. McKay nodded.

"He's clearly not used to expressing his emotions," FHF said. "I get the impression that Sophie doesn't allow her children to express unpleasant feelings such as rage. Her inability to allow this means that those feelings burst out inappropriately."

I lunged forward. If Greg hadn't stopped me, I think I would have yanked off the woman's stupid hat and started pulling her frizzy hair out by the roots.

"Let me deal with this," he said. He glared at FHF. "You really are a piece of work."

"Mr. Lawson, please try to calm down."

He told Mrs. McKay to be quiet and turned back to FHF.

"Sophie and I may have our differences, but she is a wonderful mother and always has been. If anybody needs to address her short-comings as a mother, you do. Maybe you should look at why you've got two druggy sons who've dropped out and sleep for a living."

What do you know? Huck's instinct about FHF had been right.

"I don't need this," she said. "I was just trying to help, that's all." She looked at Greg. "I'll wait for you outside."

"Don't bother. I'm going to spend some time with Sophie. We need to speak to our son."

Mrs. McKay clearly didn't know where to put herself. "I think that might be for the best," she said.

FHF couldn't get away fast enough. On her way out, she and Greg exchanged glares. After bidding Mrs. McKay an embarrassed farewell, Greg and I headed towards the medical room to collect Ben.

"Thank you for standing up for me in there," I said.

"It didn't take much effort. I meant every word of it. You are a great mum and the kids adore you."

Ben was in tears all the way home. He kept saying how he hadn't meant to hit Arthur that hard, that he was sorry and was Arthur going to be all right?

As soon as we got in, he made a beeline for the TV remote. He clearly wanted to block out what had been going on. "Maybe later," Greg said, taking the remote from him. "First we need to talk about what happened between you and Arthur." He led him over to the sofa and sat him on his lap. I went and sat beside them.

"I know it's been hard for you with Dad and me splitting up," I said, tousling his hair. "And we realize you've probably got a lot of angry feelings towards us, but you can't take them out on other people."

"I didn't," Ben said.

"Are you sure? You need to be honest. Dad and I will understand."

"This isn't to do with you and Dad. I swear."

"What did I tell you?" Greg said. "OK, what is it to do with?"

Ben started to sob again. "I didn't mean to hit him that hard. I didn't. Honest."

I wanted to cuddle him, but Greg held up his palm.

"So you keep saying," he said to Ben. "But you did mean to hit him?"

"Yes."

"But why?" I said. "Arthur's your best friend."

"He's not my best friend. He hates me."

"Hates you?" Greg said. "I'm sure he doesn't hate you."

"He does. At my party, I told my friend Olly the real reason I didn't want to go back to the Stone Age in my time machine."

My mind flew back to the conversation that Ben and I had had on this subject. But that was ages ago. I couldn't believe it was still on his mind. "Because you're scared of mammoths?"

"Yeah. Anyway, I made Olly promise not to tell anybody, but the next day at school he told Arthur and Arthur started calling me a wimp and a scaredy-cat. Then everybody else joined in. It went on for days and days. They were all chasing me around the playground calling me names. And in the end I couldn't take it anymore."

"So you lashed out at Arthur."

He nodded.

"And not one of the teachers saw what was happening?" Greg said.

"I told my teacher, Miss Clark, that Arthur was calling me names and she just said to keep away from him."

Greg got to his feet. "Right. Where's the phone? I need to have another word with Mrs. McKay."

While Greg was telling Mrs. McKay a few home truths at full volume, I tried to explain to Ben why punching people wasn't the best way to settle disputes.

"I know, but it happened before I'd even thought about it. I was just so angry."

"I get that, but you have to apologize to Arthur."

"All right, but he's got to promise to stop teasing me."

"I wouldn't worry about that. I think you've made your point."

"Arthur's going to be all right, isn't he? He's not going to die?"

"Of course he's not going to die, but he is going to have a very sore head."

I dug my mobile out of my bag. Before Ben did any apologizing, I had some of my own to do. I went through my contacts list until I found Arthur's mum's number.

"Abby, it's Sophie Lawson. I can't tell you how sorry I am about what happened. I don't know what to say. I feel terrible. Is Arthur OK?"

"He's fine. They taped up his cut and we're back home. Look, I've been talking to Arthur about what happened and he's admitted that he and some other kids had been chasing Ben and calling him a wimp. I'm furious with him. Somehow I've managed to raise a nasty little bully. I'm so sorry."

"Don't be. Ben's teacher wasn't quick enough off the mark. If she had been, this whole thing might never have happened."

Abby and I agreed that both boys needed to take their share of the blame. We also decided that rather than risk another fight breaking out at school the next day, it would be best if they got together straightaway to say their sorrys. I said that Ben and I would be over in ten minutes.

As we left, Greg was still on the phone, bawling out Mrs. McKay and accusing her and Miss Clark of negligence. I called to him that we were off to see Arthur. He gave me the thumbs-up.

*B*en and Arthur didn't exactly fall into each other's arms. That was for girls.

They eyed each other warily for a few moments. In the end it was Ben who broke the silence.

"Hi."

"Hi."

"How's your head?"

"Still hurts. They thought it might need stitches, but they taped it instead."

"Sorry I hit you."

"Sorry I chased you and called you names."

"The tape looks cool."

"Yeah, but I really wanted stitches."

"So d'you want to play something on the Wii?"

"If you want."

Abby and I took this to mean that they were best friends again.

Before I left, I got a text from Greg: *Leaving now. McKay deeply apologetic. Has promised to call you. Speak soon. G.*

Saturday was the start of half term. The children's old nanny, Joyce, who had looked after them when they were little, had invited them to spend the week with her at her bungalow in Brighton. The children hadn't taken any persuading. Amy and Ben loved Joyce. They also loved Brighton. Joyce took them to the amusement arcades and let them eat hot dogs and cotton candy. Sometimes the three of them played bingo at one of the parlors on the promenade. Ben knew most of the calls, but what they loved most was the possibility of winning money.

Greg said he would drive the kids to Brighton. "I need to go down to the farm to see how the tank's holding up in the wind and rain, and Brighton's only a few miles farther on." I didn't ask if there were any buyers in the offing because it was obvious there weren't.

Greg arrived just after nine. I handed him a box of Belgian chocolates and an orchid plant. They were a thank-you to Joyce for having the kids.

After I'd waved the three of them off, I had a shower. Then, wearing only a bath towel, I made my way upstairs to the attic.

Huck and I spent the rest of the morning catching up on all the sex we'd been missing lately because we'd both been working so hard. I was still putting in long hours on *Women's Lip*, which had received some excellent reviews. The *Independent* called it "gutsy" and "punchy." The *Times* singled out the item on tattoos, describing it as "fun, without being trite." There were also hundreds of congratulatory e-mails. It was all great stuff, but none of it meant anything until the audience figures were in.

Huck was working far harder than I was. When he wasn't giving talks and interviews, he was hosting charity auctions to which A-list celebrities had donated personal memorabilia and/or a "fan experience." Huck informed me that the latter meant you got to talk to them for three minutes. But the money was coming in. There was already enough to refurbish the youth center and buy some sports equipment and a decent sound system. On top of that, a couple of Premier League soccer players had offered to coach the kids in the local park, and the choreographer who'd designed the dance routines for the West End production of *Me and My Gal* had offered to give a weekly dance class.

A few hours later, Huck and I lay half dozing in each other's arms. "I'm hungry," I said. "You hungry?"

"I could eat."

"I could heat up some soup. And there's some garlic bread in the freezer."

"Sounds good."

"And then afterwards how's about we make a start on my boxed set of *The Office*?"

"Nah, I've got work to do. Besides, I caught a couple of episodes while I was away last week. Can't say I enjoyed it. Overrated, if you ask me. Minty said the same."

"Oh, well, if Minty says . . ."

He laughed. "Behave. Go make soup."

I got out of bed and reached for Huck's bathrobe. "So you really hated it?"

"Pretty much."

I plodded downstairs. I'd just put the garlic bread in the oven when the phone rang. It was Greg to say the kids had been safely delivered and he was leaving Brighton now.

"Oh, and Joyce says thank you for the chocolates and the orchid."

I thought he sounded a bit down. "Greg, you OK?"

"Not really. I was going to tell you earlier, but I didn't want the kids to hear. I've left Roz. We haven't stopped yelling and fighting since the school episode."

"Wow . . . I'm so sorry, but I can't say I didn't see it coming."

"I know. It's been on the cards for ages. In the end, I couldn't see any point carrying on."

"How do you feel?"

"Pretty crappy, but relieved. The woman's a piece of work. She's the most arrogant, self-centered, self-serving, controlling, domineering person I've ever come across. I know love is blind, but is it deaf as well? God only knows what attracted me to her."

"Maybe you like powerful women. I was never much cop at being domineering."

"You were pretty good at yelling." I could hear the smile in his voice.

"So what now?"

"I'm looking for a flat, but meanwhile I'm staying with Ken Wallis, the *Vanguard* news editor."

Greg asked me not to tell the kids about his having left FHF. He said that since it was his cock-up, he'd rather break the news to them himself.

"So, how are you?" he said.

"Fine. Just hanging out."

"With Huck?"

"Yeah, kinda."

"Right . . . well, I'd best hit the road."

"OK, see ya. Look after yourself and stay in touch."

"Sure."

When I got back upstairs with soup and garlic bread, Huck was on the phone with Minty. "Mint, that sounds amazing. You are a genius. OK, I'll be with you in half an hour and we'll flesh it out a bit more."

Huck stood up and started pulling on his jeans.

"Mint's totally reworked my speech for tonight. She's added a new opening and conclusion. It's so much stronger. I don't know how she does it."

"Huh, so she's *Mint* now . . ."

He pulled on his T-shirt. "Soph, stop it. I don't have time for this."

Chapter 16

Liz called me into her office. The audience figures were in. They were up sixty percent. Twenty would have been OK. Thirty would have been great. But sixty was staggering. Of course, we realized that the rise was partly due to people wanting to check out the new show. The numbers would no doubt fall off a bit.

"Well done, Soph. You did it. This is brilliant news." She poured us drinks and we toasted the future of *Women's Lip*.

Later on, she invited the rest of the producers and reporters to join us. She made a short speech thanking everybody for their dedication and hard work. "And to show you precisely how grateful we all are at GLB, a celebratory drinks party has been arranged at Soho House."

We were allowed to bring plus-ones, but Huck said he couldn't make it. He and "Mint" would be driving back from Leeds. How, with all this gallivanting, Araminta was finding time to tutor Spencer I had no idea, but somehow she was managing to fit it in and, according to Gail, she was working wonders.

"He's almost word perfect. She seems to really connect with him. To be quite honest, I think he's a teensy bit in love with her."

"He's not the only one."

"How d'you mean?"

"I'm pretty sure there's something going on between her and Huck. She goes with him on all his speaking gigs. They're often away overnight and she's pretty much all he talks about."

"So have you asked him what's going on?"

"Yeah, but he insists their relationship is strictly professional."

"Maybe it is."

"Oh, come on. You know as well as I do what sort of reputation Huck had when we were young. It was impossible to keep up with all his girlfriends."

"I know all that, but people grow up. They change. He told you he'd changed."

"Yes, and I made the mistake of believing him."

She let out a long breath. "OK . . . I wasn't going to say anything, but I could tell he wasn't right for you."

"How?"

"Way too earnest."

"Greg could be earnest."

"True, but he could also sit and talk to Murray about soccer and cricket. I can't imagine Huck doing that."

She wasn't wrong.

"And what sort of a bloke buys his girlfriend books by existentialist philosophers? Big mistake. If you ask me, there's only one way to a woman's heart and that's through the Harrods jewelry department."

I couldn't help laughing.

"Soph, it might be my imagination, but you don't seem too bothered that Huck might be cheating on you."

She was right. I wasn't *that* bothered. Granted, no woman enjoys being traded in for a younger, prettier model, and I couldn't deny being angry and jealous, but if he had decided to move on, it wasn't going to reduce me to a weeping, shaking heap. That was because I didn't love him.

I'd fallen in love once before—waltzing down Charing Cross Road—and the feelings I had for Huck didn't come close to what I'd felt that night.

I think I just wanted him for the sex," I said to Annie. We were standing at the bar at Soho House. Since Huck hadn't been able to make the drinks do, I'd invited her along as my plus-one.

"Well, I guess it's hardly surprising, bearing in mind how bad things were between you and Greg in the bedroom department."

"So I used him."

"Oh, come on. He used you, too. When you met he'd only just got back from Africa. You said yourself that he seemed pretty lonely."

"Did I tell you," I said, "that he doesn't like *The Office?*"

"Oh, then you *have* to dump him."

"You're being sarcastic, aren't you?"

"Of course I am. I mean, are you seriously suggesting giving the man his marching orders because he doesn't share the same taste in comedy as you?"

"No—I'm merely taking it into account."

Annie laughed. "You are bonkers. You know that, don't you?"

"I'm not bonkers. Comedy connects people. You have to share a sense of humor—laugh at the same stuff. If you don't, you're done for." Thinking about it, I wasn't sure that Huck laughed very much at all. I thought I loved his earnest, intense manner, but I missed laughing. Greg and I had laughed all the time. In the beginning at least. Our favorite pastimes had been sex, eating and watching comedy. In that order. Huck and I shared a love of food and sex, but we didn't share a sense of humor. Instead we shared discussion and debate, views on existentialist novelists. (Or we would have, had I gotten around to reading *The Stranger*.)

"Actually," Annie said. "You might be right. Rob and I adore *Mr. Bean*."

"You're not serious. You like slapstick? I never knew that about you."

"What's wrong with slapstick?"

"No . . . nothing. The point is, you both like it."

"OK," Annie said. "Suppose he's not sleeping with Araminta. Will you still dump him?"

"Probably."

Finally we spotted a table. We picked up our drinks and battled our way through the thicket of people. Liz seemed to have invited every journalist in London. I'd spoken to her a few minutes earlier and she'd said how delighted she was by the turnout. I didn't rain on her parade by reminding her that the majority of hacks would go anywhere for a free drink and a honey-glazed sausage on a stick.

"So," I said to Annie as we sat down, "how's your mum coping with the boys?"

"Oh, you know Mum. She's always bursting with energy, but I can see that looking after them five days a week is getting too much." She looked down at her drink. "Actually . . . I've decided to hand in my notice."

"I'm not going to say I'm surprised, but are you absolutely sure?"

She nodded. "I can't go on working these hours. The powers that be have decided they can't afford to hire another producer, so my shifts won't change. It's too much. I'm still not sleeping. I'm seeing almost nothing of Rob and I'm ratty with the boys . . . who are still traumatized by what Kathleen did to them. I reported her to the nanny agency, by the way. Mine was the third complaint they'd had, so they've dropped her from their books."

"I should think so . . . So as far as work goes, what will you do?"

"Well, I've realized that being a stay-at-home mum isn't an option. I've talked it over with Rob and I think I might do an interior design course, get a proper qualification and set myself up in business. What do you reckon?"

"I reckon that sounds brilliant."

"I can set my own hours. Be around for the kids and Rob."

"So you're still going to run around after him?"

"I'll get an au pair maybe, but I know that Rob's not going to change. And I do love him. I'm not like you. I don't have the energy to try to change him. I don't want us to spend our lives yelling and fighting."

"You mean, like Greg and me."

She didn't say anything. "I have a good life, Soph. Rob loves me to bits. We have a lovely home. He spoils me with fancy holidays. He just has this Achilles' heel."

"And you're able to live with it?"

"Marriage is all about compromise."

"Maybe I didn't compromise enough."

"It was different with you and Greg. The man was a complete slob. Rob's just your average male chauvinist pig."

I couldn't help laughing. "Come on, why don't I get us a couple more mojitos?"

I fought my way back to the bar.

"Soph!"

"Greg—what are you doing here?"

"I was invited. Liz must have money to burn. Half of Fleet Street is here—even the political editors. Anyway, I thought I'd stop by and offer my congratulations. You've done a wonderful job, Soph. You should be really proud of yourself."

"Thanks. I just hope we can keep it up."

"You will. I don't have any doubts about that . . . So Huck's not with you?"

"He couldn't make it. I came with Annie."

Greg asked what we were drinking.

"So, you heard from the kids?" he said after he'd ordered two mojitos and a beer for himself.

I said they'd been texting several times a day. "They seem to be having a great time . . . So, how are things with you?"

"Camping out isn't great."

"No luck with finding a flat, then?"

"Nope. Not as yet." He paused. "Soph . . . I actually had another reason for coming this evening. There's something on my mind that I need to discuss with you. Could we go and talk somewhere private? The roof terrace maybe?"

"But I can't leave Annie on her own."

"It'll only take a couple of minutes. I'm sure she won't mind."

As it turned out, when we got back to the table, Annie was busy talking to Nancy. They knew each other slightly. Brian was one of

Rob's clients and the two women had met once at some company dinner.

I could tell that Nancy was drunk because she was asking Annie if she thought Rob paid sufficient attention to her vulva when they made love. "I mean, does he tell you how beautiful it is?"

"I don't know . . . I guess he does . . ."

"What on earth is she on about?" Greg muttered to me.

"I'll explain later."

He said he wasn't sure he wanted to know.

"These days, Brian has got so much better at complimenting mine. He's even given it a name. First he wanted to call it Becks—after the beer—but I wasn't having that, so I decided on Agape, which is Greek for 'divine love.' "

"That's nice."

Annie caught sight of Greg and me. She gave me a look as if to say, "Thank the Lord the cavalry's here."

"Greg," Nancy cried. "How wonderful to see you. Now, then, I demand to know how you could possibly leave the wonderful Sophie for that dreadful Duffy woman? I met her once. Talk about full of herself. Of course, I put her in her place. 'Duffy,' I said, 'just shut up and bloody well shave.' That stopped her in her tracks."

Greg was trying to stifle a laugh. "I wish I could have been there to see that," he said.

I whispered to Annie that Greg wanted a private word on the roof terrace. She said not to worry. She would take Nancy to find Brian.

"Oh, and have you heard about STD?" Nancy said. "She's working for Simon Cowell in LA."

"Really? I'm amazed she found another job."

"According to my spies, she recently pitched a new show to Cow-ell. It's called . . . wait for it . . . *America's Got Canine Talent*. Apparently he went crazy for the idea and asked her to be the exec producer."

We all agreed that *America's Got Canine Talent* was right up STD's street and that she'd probably do a great job.

Greg and I climbed the narrow staircase to the roof terrace. It was full of groups of raucous journos who'd come up for a smoke. Greg waved to a chap from the *Vanguard*, who seemed particularly wasted. We found a table next to one of the outdoor heaters.

"So . . ." I said. "What did you want to talk about?"

Greg put his beer down on the table. "I've been rehearsing this all day. Now I don't know where to start." I'd never seen him so nervous. "The thing is . . . do you think there might be any possibility . . . ? I mean, would you consider . . . ? Shit, Soph, I want you back. Would you at least think about it?"

"Greg, you've just come out of a relationship. You're feeling low. You're sleeping on a mate's floor. You're not thinking straight. You and I getting back together would be a huge mistake."

"But I've changed. It's taken me until now to realize what an arse I've been and that I cocked up big-time. I was a slob. I took you for granted. I tried to make it look like you were a madwoman for want-ing a clean, tidy house. I'm so ashamed, you've no idea."

"You know what really gets me?"

"What?"

"That you were able to change for Roz, but not for me. Why wasn't I worth changing for?"

"It wasn't that you weren't worth it. I just didn't get it. It was only when I began living with Roz that I realized what an arrogant arse I'd been. It was Roz who pointed that out and, cow that she is, I'll always be grateful to her for that. The moment I moved in with her, she made it clear that I was expected to pull my weight around the house. There was no room for protest or debate. I either respected her rules or I was out. And you know what was odd?"

"Go on."

"I started to enjoy it."

"Oh, please. Next you'll be telling me you found it *healing*. You didn't enjoy it. You got in with it because you were scared to death of Roz and she beat you into submission."

"Look, Roz can be hard going, but she did not beat me into submission. And, OK, maybe it wasn't the actual housework I enjoyed so much as seeing the results. I realize now that a home needs to be more than somewhere you go to eat and sleep. It needs to be clean and comfortable, a place where you can relax. I fucked up, Soph. I will spend the rest of my life being sorry for that. You were the love of my life and I pushed you away. I destroyed so much."

"You did and that's why it's too late. I'm not sure I'll ever stop being angry with you for how you treated me."

He nodded. There were tears in his eyes. "I can understand that. So, you and Huck . . . Do you think you'll make a go of it?"

"Actually, I think I'm about to end it. Things haven't worked out."

His eyes lit up. "So that means we could—?"

"Greg, haven't you been listening to a word I've said? Do you honestly think that after everything that happened between us, you can simply apologize, tell me that you'll load the dishwasher and empty the trash now without being asked, and I'll let you waltz back into my life?"

"I waltzed into your life once. Remember?"

"Of course I remember. But like you say, you destroyed all that."

"You're right. I guess I made my bed . . ."

"I guess you did."

That night Huck didn't come home. I'd texted him just after midnight, but he didn't reply.

When I got back from work the next day, he was in the kitchen unwrapping a frozen pizza.

"Sorry about last night," he said by way of greeting. "I crashed at Mint's. I was too tired to drive any farther."

"Oh, cut the crap, Huck. We're a five-minute drive from Araminta's. Look, I've had a long day and I'm knackered. I'd appreciate you being straight with me. Are you and Araminta having an affair?"

He gave me this little-boy-lost look. Then he came over and tried to put his arms around me. "Don't be angry," he whispered. "Why don't we go upstairs." I pushed him off.

"You know what I've realized?" I said. "One of the reasons I didn't make a play for you at university was because I knew you'd let me down and that there was no point. I was wiser at nineteen than I am at nearly forty. Can you believe that?"

"I haven't let you down."

"Huck, stop this. I'm getting really angry now. For the last time—"

"OK . . . I admit it. Mint and I have been having a thing."

"*A thing.* You mean you've been sleeping together."

"Yes. Look . . . you and me . . . we had our fun. We kept each other company for a while and you have to admit the sex was amazing. But maybe it's time we both moved on."

I let out a bitter laugh. "I can't believe I fell for your line about how you'd changed and didn't play the field anymore."

"That was true. In the wilds of Africa there was no field."

"But now you're home, and one has opened up again."

"Something like that."

"You know, it beats me how somebody like you, with such a highly developed social conscience, could treat women the way you do."

"I'm flawed. What can I say?"

"You could say that you're nearly forty and that maybe it's time you got unflawed."

"Actually, I think Mint and I could make a go of it. We think so much alike. She's a great girl."

"And suddenly you don't care that she's a toff."

"I was being shamefully narrow-minded. She's made me realize that I am as prejudiced about the upper classes as they can be about the poor. She's not responsible for the class she was born into. None of us are."

"How easy it is to change your tune, once you've got your leg over."

"It's not like that."

"Whatever. Like I said, it's been a long day and I can't be bothered to argue. Just do me a favor and go."

He said he would go upstairs, pack a bag and come back for the rest of his things.

While he was packing, I opened a bottle of wine and sat at the kitchen table trying to read the paper.

Twenty minutes later he was back. He put the door keys I had given him on the table. "So, no hard feelings, then?"

"What? Of course there are hard feelings. But don't flatter yourself. I will get over you."

As he turned to go, he noticed the copy of *The Stranger* lying on the counter. "If you're not going to read this, would you mind if I gave it to Mint? It's right up her street."

"But you gave it to me. It was a present."

"Yeah, but it's not really your thing, is it?"

"Probably not . . . Oh, for God's sake. Take it."

"Cheers."

With that he was gone. I picked up his frozen pizza and put it in the oven.

Chapter 17

Since Greg had taken the kids to Brighton, it seemed only fair that I should pick them up, but Greg said that he would prefer to go as he felt that Ken and his wife could do with some space. "Plus I need to tell the kids about Roz and me splitting up."

They arrived home about two. Greg didn't stay. We both knew that it would feel awkward if he hung around. I followed him to his car and told him that Huck and I were over and that he'd moved out.

"He was seeing somebody else."

"Miserable sod," he said. "Some people never change. You OK?"

"I'll be fine. I'm not sure it was ever that serious."

He told me to take care and kissed me on the cheek.

Ben took off his coat without speaking to me or even making eye contact and then ran up the stairs. I called after him: "Ben, you OK?"

"No . . . Dad and Roz have split up, which means I won't see Dworkin ever again. I can't believe they did that. And Amy and I won't get to go up in a hot air balloon like they promised us at Christmas." I heard his bedroom door slam.

I turned to Amy, who was kicking off her boots. "So, how do you feel about Dad and Roz splitting up?"

"Roz was OK, but in the beginning—before all the fights started—they were always smooching and kissing. I hated that. At least now I don't have to share him."

I gave her a hug. "I get that."

"Suppose I'll have to get used to sharing you with Huck, though."

"Actually, you won't." I raked my hair with my fingers. "God, this has all happened at once rather. Dad and I really didn't plan it like this. Huck moved out. He found a bigger place. He realized that he needed more room."

"What you're saying is, he dumped you."

"It was sort of mutual."

"So now that you're both on your own again, couldn't you and Dad at least think about getting back together? He's really changed, you know. He even irons."

"You're kidding. Your dad irons?"

"Yeah. He does all his own shirts. Sometimes he even ironed Roz's stuff. He's not like he used to be. Honest."

"I'm glad to hear he's changed, but the thing is that before we split up, your dad and I were making each other very unhappy. If we got back together, the fighting would probably start all over again and that wouldn't be fair to any of us."

"But at least you could try. What's the harm in trying?"

"The harm is if it all breaks down again, you and Ben would go through a second trauma."

"Well, I'm prepared to risk it. Roz says if you don't take risks in life you live to regret it."

"Good for her." I suggested Amy get herself a snack while I went upstairs to try and calm Ben down.

I was halfway up the stairs when Amy called up to me: "Oh, and by the way, I never really liked Huck. He hated SpongeBob. Who hates SpongeBob? It's, like, the most hilarious thing on TV."

Greg e-mailed me the next day. He said he would do whatever it took to win me back and could we at least discuss it some more? I e-mailed back to say that I couldn't see the point.

No sooner had I told Gail about Greg wanting me back than my mum was on the phone. "Oh, darling, think of the children. They need a father. And deep down Greg's a good chap. Couldn't you find it in yourself to forgive him? And it would make me feel so much better, knowing you were back together. The palpitations haven't got any better, you know."

I told her that, as concerned as I was about her palpitations, I really didn't think I could forgive Greg.

Gail, Annie, Phil and Betsy all said the same—that of course my relationship with Greg was none of their business and of course I had to make my own decision about whether or not to give our marriage another go, but that people did change and that surely it could do no harm to keep the lines of communication open.

Amy and Ben hadn't the slightest idea that their father wanted to come home.

Having been so certain, I eventually got to the stage where I didn't know what to think. It didn't help that work was taking it out of me. I was still putting in long hours at the office. *Women's Lip* was doing far better than anybody had expected, but I didn't dare take my eye off the ball and I was beginning to feel the strain. Amy and Ben picked up on my stress and reacted by getting irritable and telling me that I was neglecting them.

When I should have been asleep, I lay awake grappling with the Greg question. How did I know that he wasn't making overtures simply because he was unhappy and on the rebound from Roz? On top of that, I'd just split up from Huck. I was miserable and vulnerable. I was equally capable of falling into the rebound trap. I kept on reminding myself how unhappy Greg and I had been and how angry I still was with him.

Spencer's bar mitzvah was the first Saturday in April. My sister arrived at the synagogue, all froufrou feather hat and double air kisses and eyeing up the other women's outfits.

Mine didn't present her with much competition. Over my dress I was wearing a black PVC trench coat. Amy insisted it was really cool, but I was beginning to wish I'd taken it back to the store on the grounds that it, along with the red beret I'd bought to go with it, made me look like a Parisian hooker.

Greg took one look at me and burst into "Bonnie and Clyde," but I could tell from his expression that he approved. That cheered me up.

Murray wore a fuchsia tie and a weary, resigned look that seemed to be saying, "Do you know how much this event has cost me?"

Spencer looked splendid in his bar mitzvah suit, which of course had been tailor-made.

Mum and Dad, who had been persuaded to make the trip because Phil and Betsy and the boys were coming, wore heavy coats and complained about the cold and the damp and the lack of parking. "They should have valet parking," Dad insisted. "In Florida, it's all valet parking. On the High Holy Days, even the synagogue has valet parking."

His elderly cousin Arnold overheard the valet parking remark. "What do you mean, the synagogue has valet parking? It's against Jewish law to drive on the Sabbath and on the High Holy Days. What kind of a Nazi synagogue to you belong to anyway?"

"Ach, the Americans don't take all that not-driving nonsense seriously."

Spencer read his portion without a single slipup. Araminta had sent Gail a note saying how distraught she was that she couldn't be there. It seemed she was busy helping Huck prepare a presentation on ending child poverty, which he had been invited to deliver on Monday morning to David Cameron and his cabinet at No. 10. The hope was that the government would at least lend an ear to Huck's thoughts on ending child poverty, but most of all he wanted them to increase their grants to children's charities like the one that ran the youth club at the Princess Margaret Houses.

After the service, everybody gathered around a very relieved Spencer to slap him on the back and wish him mazel tov. Whiskery old aunts that the poor child hadn't seen since his circumcision pinched his cheek and drew him to their bosoms. Gail went around saying, "My son's a man now. Can you believe it?" Even Murray had cheered up and was back in form, making jokes about the bar mitzvah boy whose parents wanted to do something a bit different and insisted on holding the ceremony in space. "So they schlepped everybody to the Mir space station. And when they got back the boy's bubbe said she hadn't really enjoyed it because there was *no atmosphere!*"

Immediate family and friends—a hundred of us, at a guess—went back to Gail's for a buffet lunch.

We were met by waitresses with trays of champagne. (Of course, the whiskery aunts wanted cherry brandy and their husbands demanded Scotch, so Murray was dispatched to find some.)

The canapés included sushi and sashimi, all presented on Asian-style soup spoons. These, too, didn't go down well with the elders.

"What's this? Raw fish? Who invites a person into their home to eat fish they haven't bothered to cook . . . Sidney, go see if you can find some mushroom vol-au-vents. And if there's no cherry brandy, ask one of the waitresses to put the kettle on."

Even some of Gail and Murray's friends looked down their noses. But that was only to be expected.

"Of course, we had tuna niçoise skewers at Josh's bar mitzvah," Sharon Shapiro said, looking down her not-inconsiderable nose.

Lunch was Cajun-style salmon. "Burnt-style, if you ask me," was my aunty Minnie's verdict. This was followed by a few hours' break, during which most people went home. After a change of clothes, they would return in the evening for the main event: the dinner and dancing. This was being held in a tent that had been erected in Gail's garden.

By now the florist had arrived with the centerpieces, the tables were being laid and the band was setting up.

Greg and I—and a few of the elders—stayed. I was going to get changed in Gail's bedroom. While Gail plutzed about the table plan—"Thinking about it, I'm not sure if I should have put the Levys next to the Golds"—Murray went to get some Pepto-Bismol and the football score, Mum and Dad went upstairs for a nap and the kids went to watch TV.

"Don't suppose you fancy stretching your legs," Greg said to me.

Since I'd had too much wine and was at risk of dropping off in the armchair, I said, "Why not?"

We put on our coats and headed for the park, which was just around the corner.

"Greg, can we not talk about getting back together? There really is no point."

"But surely there's something I can say to change your mind. I mean, think of all the good times we had."

"I do. Often. But they're in the past."

"I know, but if we worked at things, there could be more good times. Soph, I love you. I've never stopped loving you."

"What about Roz? You said you loved her."

"I was infatuated. I was on the rebound. The feelings I had for her never came close to what I felt and still feel for you."

"I think you're on the rebound now. I've told you—you're panicking, that's all. You don't really want me back."

"I do. You and I are meant to be together. I know that."

"How?"

"I dunno. I just do. We're the right fit."

"Meaning?"

"Meaning we get each other. We make each other laugh."

"We used to. Not recently."

"I know, but we're still the same people. I bet I can still make you laugh."

"Go on, then."

"What? I can't be funny to order."

"You just said you could."

With that he started doing a perfect impersonation of Sharon Shapiro. I burst out laughing. "Idiot."

"See, I've still got it. I think you do still love me."

"What, because you made me laugh with your Sharon Shapiro impersonation?"

"I think it means something." He grabbed my arm. We stopped walking and he stood looking straight at me. "Tell me you don't love me."

"Greg, you were my first real love. You're the father of our children. Of course I love you. I'll always love you. But alongside that is all the hurt and anger I still feel. I don't think I can get past that."

He looked so sad and lost, I thought he might cry. "Is that your final word?"

"Yes."

"OK, I don't think there's much more to be said. I don't fancy going to the park anymore. Let's head back."

—

Of course, Gail sat Greg and me next to each other at dinner. He told me I looked lovely in my off-the-shoulder emerald dress. I thanked him and then struck up a conversation with a pharmacist named Benny who was sitting to my left. For most of the evening he lectured me on the dangers of long-term antibiotic use. At least I think that's what he was talking about. The Abba medley coming from the band was so loud that I struggled to hear him.

I danced with the bar mitzvah boy, my dad and Phil, but not Greg.

"Why don't you and Greg have a dance?" my mum nagged. "Go on. Do it for me and your dad. He looks so handsome."

There was no getting away from it. Greg did look handsome. He was wearing the Armani suit we'd bought him with some of the money his grandmother had left him. At one point, Gail threatened to drag the pair of us onto the dance floor. I had to beg her not to.

Greg dropped us home just after midnight. Ben had fallen asleep in the car, so he carried him inside and up to bed.

"Right, I guess I should be getting back," he said after the kids were tucked up.

"Sure. I'm sorry," I said.

"For what?"

"The way it's all turned out."

"Yeah. Me, too."

I headed up to bed. I'd just gotten into my pj's when I found myself standing next to Greg's dresser. I opened the drawer. Inside was his Dunder Mifflin T-shirt that I'd found down the back of the sofa and hadn't been able to part with. I sat on the bed and smelled it, but it didn't smell of Greg. It still smelled of pepperoni pizza.

Couples' Therapy—Session 3

"**B**efore we start," Virginia says, turning to me, "I'd just like to check that you have no pubic hairs about your person."

My face turns scarlet. "Absolutely—I mean, apart from the ones that are actually attached to my person."

"Good, because even now I'm still finding the odd one in the rug."

"I'm very sorry about that. My behavior was disgraceful and, under the circumstances, I'm very grateful that you've agreed to see us again."

Virginia smiles. She actually seems glad to see us back. My guess is she wants to have another crack at "saving" us.

She straightens her skirt and crosses her legs. Our cue to begin. "So . . ."

"Well, it's like I explained on the phone," I say. "Greg wants us to get back together. At first I was adamant that it would be the wrong thing and now I'm not sure. I'm really confused."

Virginia gives me one of her nods and asks us to fill her in on what's been going on since she last saw us.

"So," she says when we've finished. "Both of you had affairs that didn't work out and now you seem to be saying that you've rediscov-ered feelings for each other."

"Definitely," Greg says.

"No, not *definitely*. OK, yes, I do have feelings for Greg, but I'm also still angry with him about the way he behaved. He keeps telling me he's changed, but I don't trust him. I can't let go of the past."

Greg explains how, in matters domestic, Roz helped show him the light. "I'm not the same person now." He outlines his new do-mestic skills and explains that he has learned to exercise them without being asked. "And I've got all these plans for the house. I thought we could put in a new kitchen and bathroom. Redecorate throughout. Chuck out all our old furniture. Have the garden land-scaped."

"But I've been begging you to do these things for years!"

"I know. And I didn't listen. I'm sorry."

"I accept that with my pay raise we could afford to do everything now, but what worries me is that you're all talk and you won't follow through. I can't bear the thought of us ending back at square one."

He opens his shoulder bag and pulls out a wad of glossy kitchen and bathroom brochures. "I've got loads more at home. I've done masses of research on masticating toilets."

Just hearing Greg say the words "masticating toilet" makes me laugh.

"Please give me a chance. I'm begging you."

I can feel Virginia looking at me. "What is it, Sophie?"

"OK . . . this isn't easy. When I was with Huck, the sex was amazing."

Greg winces.

"Now that I've experienced that, I don't want to go back to what Greg and I had—a sexless marriage."

"You know, you and Greg were never truly sexually dysfunctional. What got in the way was all the anger and resentment you felt towards each other. But you said yourselves that it wasn't always like that. Do you remember telling me how when you first got together you would make love for the entire weekend? Then there was the time you made love in the sand dunes in Spain. I'm sure you remember that."

Our blushes tell her we did.

"You had such a wonderful beginning. You can take strength from that and move forward."

I look at Virginia Pruitt. "You're telling me I should give him a chance, aren't you?"

"That has to be your decision. All I will say is that sometimes it's necessary to take a leap of faith."

"But I'm still so angry."

"Fair enough and nobody is suggesting that Greg moves back home immediately. Take it slowly. Go on dates—exactly as I suggested when you first came to see me. Get to know each other again."

"What do we tell the children?"

"Tell them the truth. They'll understand. Children only get anxious when they sense that the truth is being kept from them."

"And if it doesn't work out?"

"They'll understand that, too."

"But they've been through so much."

"You're right. They have, but like I said, this involves a leap of faith."

Greg reaches out and takes my hand. "Soph, please will you take that leap with me?"

Greg drives me home. We don't say too much during the journey. My head's too full. I still can't decide what to do.

As we pull up outside the house, I notice two empty Dumpsters.

"God, next door must be doing building work again. More noise."

"They're not for next door."

"How do you know?"

"I ordered them this morning."

"What? Why on earth would you do that?"

"I thought that maybe I could come over next weekend and you, me and the kids could have a massive chuck out."

I sit looking at him. "You mean that? We'd do it together?"

"Absolutely. It'll be fun."

"When I used to say that, you ignored me."

"I know. I was an idiot. But I'm trying to make up for it. Turn around and take a look at the backseat." I look. There are mixer taps, showerheads, door handles and samples of carpet and hardwood flooring.

"Good God."

"Now come and take a look in the trunk. I've got something amazing to show you."

We get out. I notice that whatever is in the trunk is so large that the lid won't close. It's secured with rope. Greg unties it and the lid springs up. I find myself staring at a toilet. A white porcelain toilet.

"Greg. You got me a toilet. And it's not even our wedding anniversary."

"Yes, but this is no ordinary toilet." He hauls it out of the trunk and stands it on the pavement. "It has the most advanced flushing system in the world. It can flush two pounds of carrots, eighteen large hot dogs, twenty golf balls and three pounds of large gummy bears."

"What? All at once?"

"No, of course not all at once."

"Even so, I'm impressed."

"You know how you were always nagging me about blocking the loo? Well, this toilet means that I'll never block it again. Don't say I never buy you presents."

I stand there shaking my head. "You really have changed, haven't you?"

"Absolutely." Before I know it, he's pulling me towards him and kissing me. I feel myself kissing back.

"Say you'll do it," he says. "Take that leap with me?"

"OK."

He hugs me so tight that I can't breathe. "I will make this work. I promise."

"You'd better."

"And the first thing I'm going to do is have another go at finding a buyer for the tank."

"I dunno . . . Maybe we should reconsider. I mean, a man is entitled to some fun."

"Are you serious?"

"Yes, but doing up the house has to be your first commitment. Agreed?"

"Agreed."

"I don't know what to say."

"Just don't let me down."

"I won't. I promise."

"OK," I say. "That's not the only promise I need from you."

"OK, what else?"

"First we adopt a dog for the kids. Ben was devastated when he realized he wasn't going to see Dworkin again."

"OK, but who's going to walk it and look after it during the day?"

"We'll get a dog sitter and you and I will have to share the evening walks."

"Deal."

"And can we also make sure the kids get that hot air balloon trip you promised at Christmas?"

"Absolutely."

"Great. And soon as we've finished renovating the house, I want us to rehire Mrs. Fredericks."

"Agreed."

"Really?"

"Really. I'm not having us spend out all this money on doing up the house just to have the place turn into a dump again."

I'm taken aback.

He says he'd best be going. "OK, see you Saturday bright and early."

I tell him the kids and I will be waiting.

He gets into the car and drives off, leaving me standing on the pavement, staring at the toilet.

Photo © Jonathan Margolis

Sue Margolis was a radio reporter for fifteen years before turning to novel writing. She lives in England with her husband.